SPITFIRE

"Don't be gettin' the idea I came here because I like you, Matt Worthington. This visit is strictly business."

"Business means dealing, doesn't it?" he teased. "I might be persuaded to trade a bit of gossip for a kiss."

He brought his lips within inches of hers; the look in his eyes shook her heart. "Matt?" she murmured.

"Yes, love?"

"I want you to know I ain't enjoyin' this or nothin'."

He lifted a brow. "For someone who's not enjoying herself, you're sure giving a good performance."

"Why you scoundrel, I ought to—"

"You know what your whole trouble is, Carrie O'Leary?" he cut in. "You talk too damn much!" He fiercely covered her lips with his . . .

SPITFIRE

SONYA BIRMINGHAM

AVON BOOKS ◆ NEW YORK

AVON BOOKS
A division of
The Hearst Corporation
105 Madison Avenue
New York, New York 10016

First Avon Books Printing: January 1991

AVON TRADEMARK REG. U.S. PAT. OFF. AND IN OTHER COUNTRIES, MARCA REGISTRADA, HECHO EN U.S.A.

Printed in the U.S.A.

RA 10 9 8 7 6 5 4 3 2 1

Spitfire is dedicated to my parents, Colonel and Mrs. H. T. Tucker. My mother sparked my imagination and set my mind dreaming—and my father taught me to love history and the written word. Through all the moves and all the miles, they were always there and they always cared.

Chapter 1

Colorado's Western Slope—Winter, 1883

The Denver and Rio Grande's whistle shrieked as it
chugged into Crested Butte and grated to a halt. Moments later a door slammed and Carrie O'Leary nimbly
exited the train. She stooped and released a small mongrel
from her jacket, then tossed a shawl over her auburn hair.
A blustery, spruce-scented wind moaning past her, she
trudged up the deserted depot ramp, her footsteps crunch-
ing in the grainy snow. She fingered the pistol in her jacket
pocket as her heart thumped in time with the panting engine. Sweet Mother of God, can I *do* it? she wondered as
she navigated the station's slippery planks. Do I have the
nerve to actually kidnap that rascally newspaper editor?

She scanned the town's long main street, noting the row
of streetlamps that glowed through a snowy veil, to illu-
minate the dreary afternoon. Eyes fixed on the *Crested
Butte Courier*'s softly lit window, she marched away from
the depot. Mother Mary, 'tis a wild, desperate thing I'm
doin', she thought guiltily. Nothing she had learned at the
Denver boarding school would help her now. What she
needed today was a good dose of the raw courage that had
brought her da from Ireland, chasing his dreams. But,
sweet heaven, her father would skin her if he knew!

At the corner of Elk and Maple, she paused near a
hitching post to knock ice from her father's oversized
boots. She blinked the snowflakes from her long lashes

1

and glanced back at the slow-moving mongrel. "Come on, Bandit. Don't be so slow!" she ordered.

When the shaggy mutt reached her side, he raised one paw and stared up with puzzled eyes. She sighed, patted his head, then turned and slogged ahead while he followed, keeping up as best he could. Her long skirt flapping, she slipped to the *Courier*'s window. There she squeaked a small circle on the cloudy pane. Her heart sank at the sight of an empty room, dominated by a printing press and a cluttered desk. "On the outside lookin' in again," she muttered, rubbing her stiff hands. "Seems that's always the lot of a miner's brat. But I'm going to change that fact, Bandit—starting today!"

A sharp gust whined through the surrounding spruce and drew her attention up toward the snowflakes swirling around the corner lamplight. The rumble of the northbound train reminded her that in less than twenty minutes the last run of the day would head south—full or empty. What was she to do? She lowered her gaze from the misty lamplight and smacked her hand against the pane. Damn him . . . damn the rogue for not being there, she thought. Tears misted her eyes as she put her arm on the window and enlarged her small, clear circle.

Perhaps she was too late . . . perhaps, Mr. Important-Newspaper-Editor Matt Worthington had already swaggered to the Elk Mountain House Hotel, so plush even the halls were heated. No doubt he was bellied up to the walnut bar relishing jolly company, while her father coughed out his lungs in their shack down the line.

A horse's nervous whinny made her whirl about. The hotel's stableboy stared at her while he brought out a customer's mount. Lord, she had to hurry and find the man. The street would be crowded at suppertime and she didn't need an audience for *this* operation. Ignoring the heavy feeling of hopelessness that settled around her heart, she scooped Bandit up and tucked him inside her jacket.

The sudden sound of a door slamming inside the office riveted her eyes on the *Courier*'s window. Clenching a

cheroot between his white teeth, a tall man strode in from
another room and slid a suit coat from a rocking chair.
Then he stuffed his pockets with more cheroots from an
open box on the desk. She could see him plainly, and the
imposing figure looked just like her father had described.
So *this* was the handsome devil who was driving all the
ladies crazy. She had expected him to be a fine figure of
a man, but she hadn't expected the fire in his eyes, or that
determined, square jaw. Faith, she hadn't expected the man
to be so wantonly good-looking.

She pressed her reddened hand against the window and
watched him shrug into the finely tailored coat. Next, he
slapped a Stetson atop his glossy black hair and flung on
a muffler. Snug-fitting, gray-striped trousers outlined his
long legs and tight buttocks. The man didn't spend all day
sittin' at a desk—that was certain. His stomach was as flat
as the back of an iron skillet! When he turned to pull an
overcoat from a garment tree, his eyes locked with hers.
She leaped back as if she had been burned, but not before
those startling eyes had raked her form with . . .

What had she glimpsed? Contempt, amusement—or
something more disturbing? A prickly blush heated her
bosom when she realized the man had appraised her as if
she were a doxy. "Blood and thunder! Look at that," she
told Bandit, whose head peeked from her jacket. "The
man thinks he's so almighty powerful he can go around
strippin' the clothes off any woman he pleases with those
eyes!"

Had the scoundrel heard her through the window? She
watched his sensual features for a reaction while Bandit
squirmed against her side. Evidently he had not, for he
flung her a careless smile which lit his eyes with such
mirth, she had to fight an answering smile. To her displeasure, her anger dissipated like snow sliding from a
high-pitched roof. But using every ounce of self-discipline,
she held her face marble smooth, even when he moved to
the window to get a better look at her.

The good-looking scamp was as slippery as a trout's

belly, she thought while she glared back. Did the rogue think he could laze about, warm and important with his expensive cigar, and ooze his charm all over her, just like that? And her with her hair all stuck to her forehead and the icy wind whipping her skirt around her legs indecently. To make matters worse, when he slipped into his overcoat, an embarrassing warmth rippled through parts of her body that decent young ladies didn't even talk about. And what a perky, cheeky thing the feelin' was! Mary, Jesus, and Joseph, she hadn't planned on this.

She realized she needed to dredge up some quick courage. But how could she when her knees were already quivering like jelly and fear coated her mouth with a dry, bitter taste? Like a helping hand, her father's words whirled through her mind, and lifted her heart. "Carrie, me darlin', if you have a hard job, 'tis best to get on with it . . . no dream comes true till you go to work." Exhilaration gradually perked through her trembling body.

She straightened, and placed Bandit on the street. After all, this was America, not Ireland, wasn't it? And *someone* had to stop the Worthingtons. Why, the situation was downright illegal! "My God, I've come to accost the rascal, and *accost* him I shall," she muttered, and sharply motioned him outside. She wouldn't let the attractive devil trap her in the warm office and fob her off with a few platitudes.

After adjusting the damper on a potbellied stove, he tossed her a questioning look, which rushed shivers down her spine. A second later he blew out the kerosene lamp, plunging the office into shadows. The door creaked open, and the scrape of a key in the lock made her stomach lurch. The moment had arrived. If she wanted to see her dream come true, she had to act *now*. She stepped forward. Her shaky hand clenched the pistol butt as she shoved the muzzle between his wide shoulders. "Mr. Worthington, I'll be askin' you to come with me. There's someone I want you to meet."

Startled, Matt Worthington pivoted on a high boot heel and scanned her upturned face. God Almighty, what was the girl doing with that pistol? He had thought she was a young trollop from shantytown plying her trade, but at close range he could see her eyes were too frightened, too innocent. Surely there was no cause for alarm here. He relaxed and eyed her silky, baby skin that looked as white as a fresh pail of jersey cream. Her lop-eared dog's fierce stance and bared teeth made him grin.

"Mr. Worthington, don't be lookin' at that dog. I'm talkin' to you!" She lowered her voice a notch and raised the pistol with a menacing air. "If you ain't acquainted with pistols, this ain't no peashooter you're lookin' at. It's a .45, and I'm told it's capable of blowin' a sizable hole in your middle!"

He studied her hot, smoky green eyes, fighting an urge to brush back the curls plastered to her smooth brow. "Yes, I'm quite aware of what you're holding," he rumbled.

Her eyes glittered as she sized him up again. "Look, mister . . . if you ain't figured it out yet—you're bein' abducted!"

Matt drew on the cheroot and flipped through his mind, wondering if she might be related to one of his cast-off lovers. He had heard of outraged men committing such desperate acts. But a woman? It had been his observation that a woman usually retaliated with her tongue instead of a weapon. He watched the self-confidence fade from her eyes while he held his ground. Soon angry disappointment stamped her white face.

"I'll be askin' you just once more to step along, Mr. Worthington. There's a train waitin', and I'll be catchin' my death of cold while we stand here jabberin'."

Recognition sparked in his mind at her low, husky, Irish lilt. *"Wait a minute . . .* I've seen you before. You're old Shamus O'Leary's daughter, aren't you?"

"Yes, Carrie O'Leary is my name, and 'tis my father I'm takin' you to see."

He tossed his cheroot aside and squinted at a snow-lashed schoolhouse at the end of Elk Street. "Why, I haven't seen you since you were a scrawny girl walking to that school. Where the hell have you been?"

She looked uncomfortable with his familiarity. "This ain't no tea party, you know. I'm tryin' to carry on a businesslike abduction here! If you must know, after Mam died, Da scraped up all he had and sent me to Denver. Said this was no fit place for a girl to be growin' up without a mam to watch over her." Determination crept back into her eyes and she rubbed her thumb over the pistol butt. As if sensing her mood, her mutt growled and raised his hackles. "We've got more important things to talk about now," she continued. "I want you to discuss the situation at the Silver Queen with my father."

"The Silver Queen? What makes that topic newsworthy?" he asked smoothly.

"There's been a whole string of accidents there lately. Men have died in the Silver Queen."

"Do you think I don't know that? They died because of their own carelessness."

"That's what you Worthingtons would like everyone to believe, ain't it?" she blurted out. "No, they died because John Worthington is too stingy-hearted to upgrade his shoddy equipment or give the men proper rest periods." She glared at him.

He shoved balled hands on his hips. "Is that right? Well, how the devil did you get to be such an expert on the subject, missy?"

"Da knows the real truth—he works in those pits every day. As soon as I read about the last accident where his best friend was killed, I slammed my suitcase on the Denver and Rio Grande and came home. I don't want him dead, too." Her outstretched arm trembled with the weight of the heavy pistol. "Saints above, I told you all this in my letters. Don't you ever read your mail?"

"I had no idea you'd written me."

She tossed a glance at the depot, where the train sat

building steam, then darted her gaze back to him. *"Good Lord*, how did you get to be an editor anyway? I came back two weeks ago, and since then I've sent four articles to the Letters to the Editor column and requested interviews *three* times. You've ignored them all. I had to take control and make somethin' happen!"

He narrowed his eyes, then traced her slight form and said, "Well, Jenny screens my mail . . . she probably tossed them out."

"Jenny?"

She looked as if she might burst with frustration. Amusement tugged up one side of his mouth. "My assistant. She's been with me for years."

"You're cooler than the underside of a pillow, ain't you?" she flared. "It's plain to see you're just protectin' your family name. Besides . . . this situation is gettin' a mite ridiculous, don't you think? Me holdin' this gun out like a fool, and you standin' there like some great booby, while we make small talk. I don't care if John Worthington is your uncle and the richest man on the Western Slope . . . you're goin' to publish the truth for everyone to read. Let's catch that train!"

He considered twisting the gun away from her and reopening his office. She looked frozen, and cozy warmth still lingered in the tight room. The bottle of whiskey nestled in his jumbled desk drawer would make her feel better, too. Yet he hesitated. She was dead wrong about the mine, but he admired her audacity. And something else about her tugged at his heart. Those fiery eyes were so proud, he thought, remembering the schoolgirl who had worn her rags like a queen's cloak. She would be crushed.

Besides, this unusual situation interested him. Later he would be busy with his ranch, but he was presently office-bound and bored. To top everything else off, he smelled a good story. True, Jenny expected him for a late supper at the hotel—but Jenny could wait.

Carrie tightened her hand around the pistol butt and

squinted. "Mr. Worthington . . . I'd feel real bad about
blastin' a hot piece of lead into your heart."

He flashed her a quick grin. "I don't think I'd feel too
good about it myself."

She snapped back the pistol and shot him a blistering
glare. "Mr. Worthington! Let's catch that consarned train.
You may be rich and powerful, but you ain't bulletproof!"

He waved his hand and graced her with a wide smile—
a tender smile. "All right, all right. You can put that hog-
leg away. It won't be necessary."

"Nevertheless," she replied, shoving the pistol into his
pocket and jamming it into his ribs, "I'll just be puttin'
my hand in your pocket—to keep it warm—till we get on
the train. That is, if you don't mind?"

Its bell clanging, the single-gauge engine chugged past
the depot and steamed to the edge of town. Gathering
speed, the locomotive clickety-clacked over a switch
crossing and stormed into the mountain valley. Inside the
deserted, musty-smelling car, light from the bobbing lan-
terns flickered across the two passengers.

Carrie eyed Matt warily for a moment; then, sighing,
she moved her gaze from him and, absently fingering the
pistol, glanced out the window. Her face thoughtful, she
settled back into the plush seat as the outskirts of Crested
Butte slid away. Soon the shabby mining town was no
more than a smudgy blotch. He watched her mongrel—
Bandit, she had called him—snuggle next to her legs while
she scanned the snowy foothills, warm with sunset color.

After several minutes, she whipped her head around and
glared at him. "Just what are you starin' at, Mr. Worthington? You seem altogether too unconcerned for a man
in your condition!"

He grinned and tugged down his Stetson. "Well, this is
the first time I've ever been kidnapped by a pretty lady. I
thought I'd just lie back and enjoy it."

She huffed and narrowed her eyes.

He shoved back his hat to meet her challenging stare

and imagined wheels clicking in her head. Silly chit, did she think he would try to escape from such a lovely captor? Smiling, he fished out a cheroot and watched her scowl as the jiggling train rumbled into the twilight. Obviously, by the set of her jaw, he would have to make the first move. "Didn't know the old gal could move so fast," he offered at last.

She put away the pistol and wedged herself into the corner like a wet, ill-tempered kitten. "Yeah," she grunted, "Tim is really poundin' it. The fireman must be breakin' his back."

"Tim?"

"The engineer. I ride the train so much I know them all."

He lit the cheroot and filled the car with its brandy-scented sweetness. Through the thin smoke, he studied her clothes. Her jacket was simply cut and threadbare; her skirt was ragged; her cast-off boots were clumsy. What a shame she had to wear such attire. Earlier, when she had removed her shawl, he had observed her trim figure with interest. And her damp hair . . . it looked soft as silk, and the color was the loveliest auburn he had ever seen.

Wrinkling her nose, she made a face. "How many of those stinky cigars have you got?"

"Quite a few. I was preparing for a long evening with Jenny."

"Oh, yeah, that's the old lady who's been workin' for you for years—the one who threw out my letters. What were you two doin' . . . workin' on a story?"

Amusement coursed through him, making him grin. "Yeah, something like that."

She smiled slightly and looked over the dim car. "Well, it seems like we're the only passengers, Mr. Worthington," she observed in a dry tone. "I didn't see anyone else get on. It bein' so late and cold and all . . . anybody with a grain of sense has to be huggin' their fire today."

Making the most of the unguarded moment, he eyed her

fine features. "Then why did *you* pick today for your adventure, Miss O'Leary?"

"Got my courage up, that's why. Been thinkin' about it ever since I got back from Denver days ago, and I couldn't wait any longer." She pushed back the window drapes and stared again at the rapidly passing scenery.

The little heller has always been a fighter, he decided while he watched the last light glint in her shiny hair. He let his memory slide back to a day he had stood at his office window observing a pack of grubby miners' brats straggle up Elk Street. Four years ago she was only beginning to blossom, but she had stood out like a diamond in a coal bucket. Her eyes bold and defiant, she had challenged the bullies who tried to pick on the little ones clinging to her skirts. Steering his mind back to the present, he puffed smoke into the chilly air and flicked his gaze over her. "Does your father know about your little escapade?" he asked suspiciously.

She looked at him as if he had just grown a set of horns. "Lord, no! He'd kill me. But I think he'll see the advantages your stayin' the night will present. He's a clever man. Besides, I'd rather get forgiveness than permission any day."

He laughed and rubbed the side of his stubbled jaw. "Staying the night, you say?"

"Of course. This is the last run, you know. You'll need the time anyway. Da has a lot to tell you . . . and I have a lot for you to read."

Matt rumbled out another laugh and stretched his legs. "God Almighty, girl, you take the rag off the bush! Do you really think you can force me to read something at gunpoint?"

She glared at him. "I was hopin' it wouldn't be necessary to put a gun to your head, but I *have* noticed the device is a fine attention-getter."

He chuckled, eyeing her appreciatively. God, what a proud beauty she was. With that soft, glossy hair drying around her cheeks, making her complexion all pink and smooth, she looked like a Rubens angel. And he knew no man alive could look into those black-lashed eyes and not ache to crush her satiny lips against his. She was even more beautiful than the famous Dovie Benningfield he had met in London last fall.

Warmth hummed through his loins as he remembered the raven-haired music-hall singer, who had promised to visit him in the summer. After an opening-night party, she had lured him into a brief affair with an intensity that belied her relaxed, East End origins. He compared the two women. Both were lovely, but Dovie's beauty was as artificial as her upper-crust accent; Carrie's allure was as genuine as the morning dew.

She shifted uncomfortably under his admiring gaze. "There you go again, lookin' me over like I was a slab of meat some waiter had just brought out for your inspection."

He chortled as he eased the cheroot between two fingers and lowered his hand. "Lord, you *do* have a way with words, don't you?"

"You bet! You see, when your brain is all you have, you've got to use it." Anger flickered in her eyes. "No wonder you look so sleek and smug. You've never had your dreams smashed, and had to figure out how to keep goin' time and time again, like Da." She tore a packet of papers from her bosom and slammed them into his hand. "Seems like you need somethin' to do with your eyes anyway, Mr. Worthington. Try readin' this!"

He glanced at the bulky packet and arched one brow. "What's 'this'?"

"Somethin' I was workin' on durin' the ride into town."

After a sharp glare from Carrie, he placed the cheroot between his teeth and opened the folded papers. Seconds later he squinted and looked up in afterthought. "How did you get interested in writing anyway? And how the *devil* did you come up with this wild abduction plan?"

"I've been studying English and Writing in Denver, Mr. Worthington," she explained as her dog snuggled closer.

He grinned and shifted his weight. "You've been studying *English?*"

Anger clouded her face. "Oh, I know I ain't supposed to use *ain't*—and I ain't goin' to when I write everything up the last time. *Ain't* just feels good and comfortable, like an old pair of shoes." She jabbed her finger at the papers. "Writin' these articles was the only way I could think of to help the miners. Now, go on—take a look!"

He blinked and studied her earnest face, at a loss for words. "Oh, *hell,*" he finally muttered. "I might as well, because this conversation isn't going anywhere." Snapping out the papers, he settled back and scanned her work. She had listed the harsh working conditions the men endured, and in a final section, she proposed passionately worded remedies for each situation.

Carrie tossed her hair aside and watched him flip the pages back and forth with a bored air, puffing away while he analyzed her work. "My God, man, how long is it goin' to take you to finish?" she asked.

He met her remark with lofty silence.

The train careened around a curve, sliding several pages to the floor. *"Well?"* she prompted, picking up the papers and handing them back to him.

He slipped the gnawed cheroot from his mouth and frowned, disappointed. This wasn't possible story material, as he had hoped; it was an assassination attempt. "Do you *really* think I'd print an article that slandered my own name?" he asked acidly. "I haven't been in the Silver Queen for almost a year, but this is outrageous. I doubt you have all your facts straight."

"How about four dead men for facts!"

"I talked to the superintendent and several of the miners who saw the accidents. They all told me the same thing—the men just got careless. What do you say to that?"

"I say they were scared to death of old John's paid thugs."

Outrage flamed through him. *"Thugs?* That's ridiculous! John has raised me since I was five years old, and I know he would never stoop to such tactics. He is an honorable man.''

Color blotched her face. "How would you know what's going on in Crested Butte? I heard you went off to London before the accidents happened and let someone else run your paper.''

"John assured me!'' he rumbled, sitting forward.

She pursed her lips and shook her head thoughtfully. "Oh, he did, did he? Well, every bell you hear ain't the dinner bell, Mr. Editor. What a grand world this would be if everyone told the truth, even John Worthington.''

He clenched his jaw and stared at her.

Her expression turned apologetic. "Don't take it so *hard*, man," she said lightly. "I know blood's thicker than water, and all that. But, faith, everybody has sorry kinfolk. Yours just happens to be the tush hog of the Western Slope!''

"Carrie, every time you open your mouth you're losing ground,'' he warned as he leaned back again. Lord, he was furious, but he hadn't felt so alive and involved in ages. For the first time in years, a woman had managed to stir his brain as well as his glands.

She looked away and huffed. "Well, if you don't believe the truth when you read it, what about the rest of it, then? What about the writin' . . . the style?''

"It's . . . interesting,'' he finally observed in a begrudging tone, "but it's biased and you've gone off on tangents and grammatically it's a mess. Are you sure you've been studying English?''

"Is there somethin' wrong with your ears? I *said* I was studyin' it, didn't I? I'm—I'm just a little behind in my grades, that's all.''

With a great sigh, he shook his head. "There are many mistakes. You have some dangling participles, several misspelled words—''

"Misspelled words? God in heaven, man, did you understand what it said?'' She snatched up the papers and shoved them in her jacket pocket. "Men have died already

and you're ramblin' on about misspelled words and danglin' participles.'' She watched him settle into the seat and
silently dismiss the subject. ''No doubt your heart beats
faster every time you crack open a bottle of red ink!'' she
added, blinking away tears.

She swallowed and blankly eyed the mountain wall that
whizzed past, inches from the window. But seconds later,
she smiled. Her smile growing, she looked at him and,
exaggerating her Irish lilt, proclaimed, ''Faith, I suppose
you're right. And how lucky I am . . . a poor ignorant
girl the likes o' me to have you to correct me, Mr. Worthington. Of course, 'tis a good thing you weren't there when
they were writin' the Constitution,'' she said merrily.

He raised his brows. ''Why is that, Carrie?''

''Because, if *you'd* been there, the poor sufferin' bastards would still be workin' on the grammar!''

He leaned into the high-backed seat and closed his eyelids. *Damn*, what a tongue she had! He held his face rock
still to keep from laughing. At last he opened his eyes and
saw her smug smile, then met her twinkling eyes for what
seemed an age.

Carrie jumped when the back door slammed. She turned
and eyed the conductor who lumbered in, bundled in several railroad jackets and a floppy-eared cap. He beamed
and ambled toward her, while Bandit stood and wagged
his tail in greeting. ''Here you go, Joe,'' she said, pushing
a worn pass toward the man. ''Punch it twice.''

Matt studied the old man, whose lined face looked
vaguely familiar. ''Hold on,'' he ordered, fumbling in his
pocket. ''I'll pay my own way.''

The conductor punched the pass once, then scratched
his head and looked at Matt. ''Who's your friend, Carrie?''

''This is Matt Worthington, Joe. He's the editor of the
Crested Butte Courier.''

At the mention of the Worthington name, the man
cocked his head attentively. ''Oh, yes, Mr. Worthington!

I remember seein' you, now. Make quite a few trips into Denver, don't you?''

Matt nodded and tossed his cheroot into a nearby spitoon. ''The snow has really piled up this week. How are the tracks?'' he questioned while he paid the man.

Joe gripped a seat back, bracing against the curve. ''Oh, there's no real trouble. The tracks are clear, Mr. Worthington, that they are. But you're right—the stuff is piled up to the edge in some places. In fact, Gunnison is sendin' out a load of section hands to dig out the tight curves tomorrow. With all the snow sheds in such bad repair, it keeps them busy most of the winter, and—oh, where to?'' he interrupted himself while he took the money. Matt shot a glance at Carrie, who scratched Bandit's ears as the animal stretched out beside her again.

''Let us off at Three Arrows, Joe,'' she requested. Matt knew that Three Arrows, which had once been a thriving gold camp, was now a whistle-stop servicing a string of shacks.

''Really, it's those damn snow cornices that give us trouble,'' Joe continued, warming to the story. ''The wind just eats away at their bases and you never know when one of them is goin' to fall and cover the tracks, or worse yet, start an avalanche. We've been lucky this year . . . so far they haven't had to bring the big snowplow out from Denver.'' The conductor handed Matt his validated ticket and change, looking embarrassed that he had talked so much.

''By the way, Joe, are we the only passengers?'' asked Carrie.

The conductor rubbed his nose with a knobby knuckle. ''Yep, that you are. Of course, if you're just countin' heads, there's me and Tim, and the fireman, and that new brakeman.'' He chuckled and shook his head. ''Poor freezin' lad is hangin' on the caboose ladder chippin' ice off the brake wheel right now.''

''In this weather?'' she blurted out.

''Well, hell, yes, miss. It's his job, you know. Started out as a brakie myself.'' The conversation at a standstill, the old man looked at Matt and touched the bill of his cap. "Well, guess I'll be movin' up to the cab," he said, and ambled away.

Alone again with the sound of the clicking wheels, Matt eyed Carrie, who looked as if she was going to burst forth with more accusations. "No . . . don't even mention it. I've read enough melodramatic propaganda for one night," he warned, meeting her insistent eyes. He stared her down, then turned and peered out the window, feeling the wheels rumbling beneath the floor. He could see clearly, for moonbeams shimmered over the gradually curving tracks and silvered a slash of rails that vanished into the darkness. Their swaying legs almost touching, Matt and Carrie rode for minutes in icy silence, before something caught his eye.

Aided by the headlight's gleam, he saw one of the snow cornices the conductor had told them about on the long curve. Jagged and windswept, it hung over the tracks like a bird of prey with huge outstretched wings. Down the line, he spotted another. The train highballed ahead, and he watched as snow clots tumbled down the distant cornice and spewed onto the tracks.

"Now what's so interestin' you can't take your eyes off that window?" Carrie piped as she studied his handsome, intent face.

"See for yourself," he said in a dark tone.

She sat forward and twisted to peer from the window. "Why, that's nothin' unusual. That huge boulder is just Indian Head Rock. Wait a minute . . . you're starin' at one of them snow cornices, ain't you?"

The moon gilded the huge ice shelf and surrounding slopes beautifully. Scarcely believing his eyes, Matt saw a chunk of the cornice tear off and crash onto the tracks. Many small evergreens were buried in powdery snow.

"God help us," Carrie cried, "it's going to cover the rails!"

As the brakes screamed she swung her gaze to Matt's face. Before she could speak, the car pitched forward and she and Bandit shot off the slick seat toward Matt, who instinctively reached for her when she landed between his legs. Shocked and angry, he realized the terrified lad atop the caboose had tightened the brake wheel too hard. Soon the link and pink couplings would break apart.

He cradled Carrie's head and bent forward, shielding her body with his. Fiery sparks flew up from the tracks. The train hurtled ahead, locked in a wild skid. "Dammit!" he swore. "That fool boy panicked. The cowcatcher could have plowed through the snow, but from the sound of those screaming brakes, there's going to be all hell to pay."

Fire sparking from the rails, the shuddering train screeched to a halt, followed by an impact that dumped Matt to the floor, beside Carrie. With sickening certainty, he realized their car had broken loose, for he felt it glide backward and stop. For an instant there was silence and he wrapped her in his arms, hoping they had escaped harm. Then a sound like a mighty wind chilled his blood.

From the protection of his arms, Carrie looked through the window and whispered, "Lord . . . it's like the gates of hell have been opened!"

Tall trees cracked and splintered like twigs; huge boulders plowed down the long slopes. The heart-shaking sound built to one great roar that made the earth tremble. He met her terrified eyes, and they clung together, helpless in the face of the swiftly approaching avalanche.

She watched the snowy sea thunder down the mountainside, spewing a barrage of debris before it. "Why now?" she muttered, her teary eyes glassing over. "Sweet Jesus, why now?"

Matt shook her head with both hands to get her attention. "Carrie, get down!" he screamed over the earsplitting roar. As the avalanche plunged closer, already banging the car with broken trees and rocks, he shoved her down. The car rocked—then sharp pain and darkness flooded over him.

Chapter 2

Matt shook his head and groaned. Groggy, he peered through the darkness at his immediate surroundings. To his surprise, he was sprawled across the car floor. His sore head awkwardly rested against a seat base. Propping himself up on one elbow, he scanned the car and saw that its drapes and lights hung down vertically while its walls ran at another angle. Borne on a night breeze, snow spit through a smashed windowpane and sifted over him.

More alert, he explored a lump on his skull while he recalled moon-silvered snow and splintered trees. Finally, the sound of rocks smashing the car and Carrie's terror-stricken face tumbled into his mind. My God . . . where's Carrie? he wondered, now totally awake.

His heart thudding, he stood and raked his gaze over the shadowy car again. Alerted by Bandit's whines, he focused his attention down the aisle, where he noticed Carrie's boot and his Stetson near a seat base. Hope surged through him as he struggled down the tilted aisle, bracing himself against the seats. When he reached the ruined hat, he tossed it aside and, kneeling on one leg, looked into the opening.

Bandit stood guard by Carrie, whining and licking her face. Matt scooted toward her, crumpled, still form. She moaned, and his spirits lifted. "Carrie . . . thank God you're alive, you tough little spitfire," he murmured. Moonlight shot over her pale face and parted lips while he cradled her body and looked for cuts, then swept his hands over her torso to search for broken bones. When she shivered, he gathered her icy hands in his and pulled her closer.

Roused by the movement, She fluttered open her eyelids. "Mr. . . . Mr. Worthington?" she whispered.

"Carrie, how did you get way over here? Are you all right?" he asked in a concerned tone.

She winced in pain. "I . . . I don't really *know* how I got here, but I remember somethin' about tumblin' and slidin'. I guess I'm all right, but I'm so stiff . . . and my foot—faith, my foot is hurtin' like hell!"

He laughed and massaged her stocking-clad foot. "I imagine you sprained your ankle. You probably hooked it around the seat base when you lost your boot. It feels like it's swollen."

"Ooh, yeah—don't touch it!" she warned, sucking in her breath.

"Sorry."

Carrie struggled up and surveyed the damaged car. "Why do you think we're still alive? Mary, Jesus, and Joseph," she blurted, "it looked like the whole mountain was fallin' on us."

"I don't know why we're alive. Perhaps since our car was disconnected, we took a lesser blow."

She ran her gaze over him. "Are you all right, Mr. Worthington? You . . . you look fine. Your tie is loose and your hair is floppin' over your eyes, but you still look as perfect as a jar of home-canned peaches on the shelf. In fact," she quipped as her spirit surged back, "you look like you're goin' to the governor's ball or somethin'."

"Carrie, for God's sake, will you stop calling me Mr. Worthington? Matt will do. And to answer your question . . . my head is, as you would say, hurtin' like hell! There's a knot on the back of it big as a rock."

Her teeth chattered faster than the hard snow pecking the windows. "Oh . . . I see," she whispered meekly.

"Hell, Carrie, I didn't mean to holler at you."

"That's all right . . . but I'm freezin'." She patted Bandit, then turned her head and listened to the wind whine through the cracked panes. "Brr, this place is icy! How long do you think we've been here?"

He peered through the window and muttered, "I don't know. But judging by the moon, it can't be too late—and obviously we haven't frozen yet."

"Yeah, but we've got to get into a tight place fast or we're goners," she predicted in her low, husky voice.

"That's right, but *where* in this godforsaken line of tracks?"

She looked at him thoughtfully. "Matt, do you recall we passed Indian Head Rock a minute before we saw the snow cornice?"

"Yes, I remember seeing it. What of it?"

"Well, I just remembered an old man who lives out here—his name is Botsie Klavanicks."

"Botsie Klavanicks?"

"Yeah, he's a prospector—somethin' of a hermit, too. He makes leather goods just to keep goin'. Da and I have been at his cabin to buy bridles. If we could make it to his place, we'd be all right."

Matt arched his brow. "Do you really think you could find his cabin in this wilderness?"

She nodded her head, ignoring his skepticism. "Yeah, and this is the good part," she added, flashing her gaze over him. "It's close to the railroad line, a little north of Indian Head Rock. We'll just retrace our route. If we stay close to the tracks we can't get lost."

"That, my dear, might not be as easy as it sounds," he snorted, cupping her quivering shoulder. "I doubt you can put any weight on that foot."

"Oh, don't worry about me. I'm used to walkin' a lot, and Da says I'm tough as a pine knot." She hugged Bandit to her side and ruffled his ears. "Bandit's tough, too—we can make it." Her eyes pleading, she studied his face. "Please, let's do it! The windows are broken out and it's gettin' colder by the minute. We can't just sit here like ninnies and freeze. And we *have* to get out and check on

the others anyway. They might need our help this very
minute.''

He knew they were truly marooned. It would be a long
time before the Denver and Rio Grande could get the huge
snowplow out of the Denver roundhouse. Undoubtedly, a
search party would ride along the tracks, but once it got
into the deep drifts, the horses would flounder. Any plan,
as farfetched as it might sound, was worth a try.

"Come on, *Matt*, what do you say?" she prodded.

He eased on her lost boot and met her hopeful gaze.
"All right, my girl. Since you're so game, we'll give it a
try. I only hope this old hermit is as close as you think."

A gunshot cracked the air as Matt blasted off the rusted
padlock with Carrie's .45. After the acrid-smelling smoke
drifted away, he handed her the pistol and kicked the
planked door open. He grinned at her and brushed snow
from his hair. "Hell . . . after the cutoff, it was easy!"

She pocketed the warm pistol and pushed back the
squeaky door. *"Right,* if you call wadin' up a steep incline
through knee-deep snow easy."

"You were the one who wanted to come," he retorted,
scanning her wet clothes. "What happened to your posi-
tive attitude?"

Aggravation seeped through her. "It froze to death about
a mile down the tracks, Mr. Cheerful."

The aroma of musty linen and kerosene assailed her
nostrils as they entered the dank cabin. Moonlight spilled
into the dim interior and highlighted a lamp on a table.
Her arms outstretched, Carrie threw down her walking
stick and fumbled her way to it. Bandit trailed her steps.

Matt lingered at the threshold and examined the
moisture-swollen door. "Where do you think the old guy
has gone?" he inquired.

"Who knows?" she moaned while she slipped off her
soggy head shawl. "Who knows where a crazy old man
would go with snow waist-high in the path to his house.
Maybe he's given up on findin' the mother lode; maybe

he's gone to California, where there's always rumors of another rich diggin'. At this minute I really don't care.'' Patting the table, she found what she was looking for—a box of matches. Soon soft, golden light flooded the cluttered cabin. She shielded the small flame with her hand and called out in a cranky tone, ''What are you waitin' for? Come on in before the light blows out.''

Matt jerked the door closed, muting the sound of the sharp wind, then turned and eyed the rest of the cabin. ''Lord, wherever he is, he must be coming back. Look at all this stuff!'' He watched as Bandit busily trotted around the room, poking his nose into every corner.

Carrie grunted in response and clicked a glass globe over the flame. ''Yeah, it's a mess.'' Her ears ached from the cold, her throat was raw, and every crease in her boot bit into her swollen foot like a knife blade.

Matt stripped off his overcoat and continued the inspection, looking at the leather-draped rafters and a tangle of guns and fishing poles near the fireplace. ''What a pack rat! The old guy has used every inch of space.''

With a dry laugh, she gazed over the rest of the jumbled cabin. ''Yeah, his housekeepin' never won any prizes I knew about.'' An iron skillet with congealed bacon grease sat on the blackened hearth, and old tools cluttered every corner. A sagging iron bedstead occupied the center of the room.

''Let's get a fire going,'' he suggested. ''It's cold enough to hang meat in here.'' Soon orange flames whispered about the kindling and filled the room with the comforting scent of woodsmoke. With a concerned gaze, he eyed Carrie while she guzzled water from a tin dipper and said, ''I know you're exhausted, so why don't you lie down?''

She splashed the dipper into an ironstone crock and sighed. ''Think I will. For the first time since I've been back from Denver, all I care about is lyin' down. I feel like I could sleep a week.'' She guessed the bedding would be dirty, but it didn't matter; she would lie on top of the covers.

When she reached the bed, she slid out of her jacket and plopped down. Bandit trotted to her and clawed at the mattress until she picked him up and nestled him by her side. Her facial muscles tense, she closed her eyes and tried to relax, but all she could think of was the scene she and Matt had seen after struggling from the railroad car. Their car and the two behind it were crazily tilted and rammed like toys into a huge snowbank; the first half of the train lay at the bottom of the steep ravine. The men in the cab and the young brakeman probably hadn't had a chance to move or even breathe. Anger cut through her at the injustice of it all. When she opened her eyes a tear ran down the side of her face.

Matt glanced at her and frowned. "What are you thinking about now?"

She sat up and tugged the boot from her good foot. "Nothin', Matt," she answered, thudding the boot on the floor. "I ain't thinkin' about nothin'!"

"You were thinking about the railroaders, right?"

"What if I was?" she blurted out.

"What's the use of torturing yourself, Carrie? There wasn't a thing we could do. I know you hated leaving them there, but we had to keep moving, or die ourselves."

Tired to the core of her being, she sighed heavily. "All right, all right, you win. I won't talk about it, or even *think* about it for the time bein'." She stripped off her damp stocking and added, "I've got enough problems without fightin' you all night!" When she tried to yank off her other boot, it wouldn't budge. She frowned. "Matt, help me with this boot!" she ordered crossly.

A smile lit Matt's face as he studied her. Her slender arms were braced behind her; one foot was naked, the other booted. "Well, thank God you've taken off that jacket," he commented, viewing her striking figure for the first time.

"What's wrong with it?" she huffed.

He bent and lit a cheroot in the flames. "It's ugly as a crate full of cross-eyed turkeys. That's what's wrong with it.'' He rose and walked toward her, his eyes riveted on her lithe body.

She rolled her eyes and snorted. ''Lord, Matt . . . bein' a Worthington you probably can't understand this, but some of us have to make do with what we've got.''

Step by slow step, he moved toward the bed. Carrie's plain white blouse clung to her like a second skin, revealing her generous breasts and trim waist. Even with side combs dangling from her curly hair and her eyelids heavy with sleep, she glowed with warm beauty. ''What's your story now,'' he asked good-naturedly, ''stoking up for another argument?''

Steaming, she glared at him. ''An *argument?* My, now that does sound temptin'! Let's get an early start at first light when we're both fresh. Now, help me get this consarned boot off!''

Matt laughed and drew closer, causing Bandit to growl. ''Now what's got into him?'' Carried wondered aloud, then turned her attention back to Matt.

His cheroot clenched in his white teeth, he knelt before her gently tugged at the boot, carefully observing her reaction. Tears brimmed in her eyes, but she clenched her jaw and forced herself to hold them back.

At last, she could stand no more. She groaned and met his gaze. ''It's no use. This ain't goin' to work!''

A thoughtful look clouded his face, then he smiled brightly. Quickly, he slid out his pocket knife and sliced the old boot from her swollen foot. ''Now, how's that?'' he asked while he skinned off the damp stocking. He trailed his strong fingers over her foot and frowned. ''By the looks of things, you need some pain medicine. I wonder if the old boy has a jug stashed somewhere.''

''I saw him offer Da some twenty-rod one time. Try lookin' behind that little door by the hearth,'' she said without thinking, trying to ignore the shiver of sensation his touch had provoked.

Matt rose and opened the tall, narrow door. Like a shot, Bandit bounded from the bed and poked his head into the opening. "Well, well, it looks like Botsie lives pretty high off the hog," Matt commented as he shoved the dog out of the way. "Right beside this bacon is just the article I'm looking for." He pulled a brown liquor jug from the closet and prized out the stopper. The powerful aroma of alcohol wafted its way toward her.

Matt glanced at her and smiled. "Want some liquor? It'll help." His concerned tone was as smooth as a silvery sunset.

A frown tightened her brow. "Faith, would you listen to that . . . now you're after tellin' me to get drunk."

"I'm not *after tellin'* you to do anything you don't want to do . . . but it *will* make you feel better," he promised, returning to her side. Plunking the jug on the floor, he gently trailed his warm fingers up her leg.

The phrase "No, I most certainly do not want any liquor!" hovered near her lips, but the pain in her foot made her reconsider. She looked down at his elegantly weathered face, which now held an expression of bland innocence. "Oh, all right, just this once! I guess only a fool would hurt when there was somethin' to help them."

He offered her the jug and smiled. "Good decision. Here you go, little lady."

"Remember, this is for medicinal purposes only," she sternly proclaimed. She swallowed deeply, and was promptly seized by a coughing fit. She gasped and sank back into the mattress. "Lord, the stuff is awful!" she spluttered. "How do people drink it?"

With a chuckle, he thumped the rosy ashes from his cheroot, then took a swig of the liquor himself. A moment later he brushed his fingers over the lump on his head. "Damn, I think this stuff is helping my headache," he commented. Again he feathered his fingers up her leg.

Carrie heard Bandit growl from across the room. Tired as she was, an uncomfortable feeling welled up from the pit of her stomach. She needed to put a stop to this foolishness right now.

"Feel any better?" he murmured.

"Good Lord, Matt! What, may I ask, are you doin'?"

He glanced at her innocently. "Trying to make you feel better! I hope you don't think I'm doing anything else. I've felt enough silky legs that yours wouldn't be a novelty, you know." He stood and slid his hard palm over her neck. She instinctively pulled away, even though she found his strong hand warm and comforting. "Good Lord, I think you have a little fever . . . probably caused by all you've been through. You need rest, liquid, and some hot food in your stomach." His face tense with sudden concern, he pulled the soft, threadbare cover over her body.

Carrie felt the liquor crash into her brain. God forgive her, she was actually beginning to think he might not be all bad. Worse than that, she had let her guard down a bit. Tightening her resolve, she reminded herself that Matt was a rich, privileged Worthington—and her enemy.

He waved his cheroot at the canned goods along the wall. "How about a bite to eat?"

"Yeah, now that I'm feelin' better, food sounds good." His deep, rich voice rippled through her senses like sweet honey. Soft and intense, it shook her emotions like a wind stirring dead leaves, and its velvety resonance made her feel warm, drowsy, and wonderful. The new feelings both excited and disturbed her.

Forcing herself to relax, she watched Matt paw through a box of cooking pans near the hearth. Soon a pot of beans bubbled on the grate and bacon sizzled in the skillet, their aroma making her mouth water. She sampled the twenty-rod again, and by the time supper was ready and he had finished his cheroot, she glowed with well-being.

Nestled in the soft quilt, Carrie ate her simple meal with relish and washed it down with more liquor. The room was warm and cozy, her stomach was full, and her head was light. She reckoned she felt as satisfied as Bandit, who now lay stretched on the hearth fast asleep. She had just turned up the jug for another nip when Matt gently took it from her clenched fingers, saying, "For medicinal purposes only—remember?"

"Why'd you do that? I'm feelin' much better."

He set the jug down and slid her a dark look. "I think you're feelin' drunk, Carrie."

She eyed the ceiling and smirked. "Drunk, is it? I've nivver been drunk in my life!" she boasted.

"Well, you are now. One good thing about it—you've got enough liquor in your fine white hide, you should be feeling no pain until tomorrow."

Snug beneath the quilt, she sprawled out and sighed with disgust. "You know, Matt . . . I think I could hear what you were sayin' better if you'd shut up!"

With a chortle, he stripped off his suit coat and unbuttoned his shirt. Within seconds, all of his clothes except his snug trousers and boots were on the floor. Firelight gilded his craggy features and well-defined torso, and she marveled at the way his furred chest tapered into a flat belly and sleek buttocks. Suddenly very warm, she twisted over and jerked the quilt higher. He chuckled, then crossed to the footboard. She could feel his eyes linger on her blanketed form.

Suddenly she could stand no more. She flipped the bedding aside and sat up, her brain reeling with the quick movement. "Will you kindly behave yourself, man?"

His face perplexed, he frowned. "What the hell are you talking about now?"

She gritted her teeth, trying to ignore the firelight playing over his broad chest, accentuating the smooth, masculine planes and shadows. "Now, don't play innocent with me. First you ply me with liquor, then you strip yourself like that. What am I goin' to have to do—light a pot of burnin' pitch to keep you away?"

"Oh, for the love of God—"

Her eyes roamed downward and she felt a hot flush sting her face. "Blood and thunder, don't go tellin' me you don't know what you're doin' displayin' yourself like that, you . . . you male Jezebel!"

He unbuckled his belt and removed it. "Well, just keep your eyes shut tight, little girl," he ordered, his face rock

hard, "because I'm fixing to take off something else, too."
He chuckled as she slid under the quilt, fast as a lizard
shooting under a rock.

She heard him blow out the lamp and stride to the window. Hidden in the shadows, she carefully peeked from
the cover and watched his moonlit face as he peered at the
darkness. For several minutes he studied the silvery snow,
his broad back to her, and then he turned and glanced at
the bed. "If you're through with your tirade, I think I'll
turn in, too," she heard him say.

Now as still as a mouse, Carrie clung to the far side of
the mattress and pretended to be asleep. Soon two boots
hit the floor. Faith, what would be next? she wondered.
She sighed with blessed relief when the old springs creaked
with his full weight. If he were a normal human being, he
would be asleep in a matter of minutes after their arduous
day—then she could go to sleep.

Soon she heard Matt's regular breathing and she drifted
into a smooth, liquor-softened state while scenes from the
avalanche shimmered before her. One last, comforting
thought shot through her mind before she tumbled into
blackness: the worst had to be over. After today, what else
could happen?

Chapter 3

⟨∽◡◡∽⟩

S unlight shot through the flour-sack curtain and flooded
Carrie's face. Stunned, she raised her aching head and
eyed the hearth, where a fire popped. The lingering aura
of woodsmoke and kerosene tinged the room. His nose
between his paws, Bandit still slept on the warm stones.
Her queasy stomach made her ease back on the pillow and
consider the situation. "Lord," she muttered, "why did I
drink so much?" Snuggled under the blanket, she wiggled
her sore foot to test its strength. As the fog lifted from her
brain, she patted the rumpled quilt beside her. Matt's side
of the bed was cold and empty. Where could he be?

Her heart jumped when the cabin door creaked open.
The sun at his back, Matt stood silhouetted in the doorway. Bundled to the ears, he smelled of the cold and the
spruce-scented mountains. A rifle rested over his broad
shoulder and a small, skinned hindquarter drooped from
one hand.

Carrie braced her arms behind her while Bandit scampered to the door. "Faith, you scared me, man!" she exclaimed.

He slammed the door, then fended off the dog, who
sniffed at the fresh meat.

She yawned and blinked at him. "What have you been
doin' out so early?"

"It's not that early—and I've been getting our breakfast," he replied, leaning the gun in a corner.

29

"Breakfast, is it? It looks like a great chunk of nauseatin', bloody meat to me."

"*This*, my dear, is a venison hindquarter," he announced, tugging off his muffler with one hand. "The rest of the deer is hanging from a tree near this cabin."

She rubbed her bleary eyes and watched sunlight streak the floor. "You know how to shoot? I thought editors just sat in their office and ripped other people's work apart."

His face amused, he dropped the meat on a wooden counter, then took off his coat. "I'm sure a lot of folks share your opinion. I have a ranch outside Crested Butte . . . I raise my own meat and kill my own game." As he picked up a notched butcher knife, he looked at Botsie's gun rack. "I thought I'd try one of the old boy's rifles this morning. That bacon is only going to stretch so far, you know." He glanced at the rack again. "The fellow can't have left for good. No one leaves that many good shooting pieces behind."

She smoothed back her tousled hair. "He's probably followin' up a rumor about another diggin'. You know how it is with us poor folks—livin' on hope all the time."

Matt slapped the leg bone against the counter while he hacked at the meat. Thoroughly cheerful, he whistled as he worked.

Carrie rubbed her tender head and sighed. "Could you be a wee bit quieter?" she pleaded.

He grinned and rearranged the meat, then began slicing it into steaks. "Oh, yes, you're a tad under the weather from drinking, aren't you?"

"There'll be none of that, now! *You* were the one who encouraged me to drink all that vile liquor."

"So that's it," he observed in a condescending tone. "You're having a serious guilt attack about imbibing so freely. Well . . . I must admit I *did* want to get you drunk," he added playfully.

She slid out of bed and clenched her fists. "Why, of all the unbelievable gall! God in heaven, you have the brass to stand there barefaced and tell me that, do you? I've heard all the rumors about you! How many other helpless girls have you liquored up, hopin' to take advantage of them? Faith, I wish I were a man so I could knock you clear around the cabin.''

A deep rumble burst from Matt's throat and shook his broad chest. Tears of laughter streaked his cheeks as she limped between the bed and the fireplace, thinking she might explode with impotent rage.

"I wanted to get you drunk to ease the pain and shock of the wreck, you little ninny,'' he finally was able to explain.

She felt her throat tighten up. "Oh.'' In crisp business-like tones she announced, "It seems I've lost sight of my original goals. Personally, I feel continuin' this conversation would be tiresome and useless.''

He tossed down the knife and rubbed his hands on a rag. "Hell, Carrie, I liked you better drunk.''

She snatched up her jacket and hobbled to the bright window. "Yesterday at this time my only thought was takin' you to my father and presentin' you with some of my articles. Luckily, the piece I was workin' on remained dry,'' she added, pulling some crumpled papers from her jacket pocket. "We have a lot of ground to cover and, the good Lord knows, I need your help. Let's get started. Who knows when they'll dig us out?''

Matt heaved a great sigh. "Lord, woman, will you never stop with your everlasting social work? An avalanche would have slowed down most females, but not you!''

A flame of anger darting through her, she plopped down the jacket and opened the curtain. Brilliant sunlight bounced from the crusted snow and caught her attention. The crisp day danced with light and the blue sky stretched for miles. She hoped the clear weather would speed the rescue party's progress and help it find Matt's marked trail. For the first time that morning, hunger nagged at her stomach, telling her the day was half gone already.

Fueled with fresh zeal, she turned and faced him with her scribbled papers. "So far, you've greeted my work with criticism. So be it. Da has never been able to give me much, but he *has* given me the will to fight. And I'm not goin' to lose the only thing I have. Actually, I enjoy a good fight, and if I can change you—rich, egotistical capitalist that you are—I can change anybody.''

"What a little reformer you are!" he stormed. "With that look of righteous indignation stamping your features, a fiery sword wouldn't look out of place in your hand. What are you going to do next? Chop up all the saloons in Crested Butte?''

She sucked in her breath, then crossed her arms and stared at the rough log wall. How dared he talk to her like that? "If you think I would waste my breath giving you an answer—you're dead wrong Mr. High-and-Mighty!

Matt shook his head in disgust, then started cutting up the venison again.

Two hours later Matt shot Carrie an amused glance and moved to the crackling fireplace with several steaks. "Look, you may be able to keep up this silent war without any nourishment," he quipped, "but I need to eat." After dredging the meat in a flour keg, he arranged the iron skillet on the grate and slapped the steaks into the hot, greased pan. He looked at her again and lowered his voice, so it was as smooth as a sandy creek bottom. "Why don't you come to the table? We'll talk while we eat. I can hear your stomach rumbling all the way over here. If I look hard enough, maybe I can find some coffee.''

A sharp retort trembled on her lips, but the thought of a cup of hot coffee to ease her headache sounded awfully good, and she *was* terribly hungry. There would be time to work on her writing later. Her mood a little brighter, she gave him a tight smile. "Think I'll call a truce and take you up on that. I've never had a man offer to cook for me before—it would be kind of different.''

He smiled and rummaged through the canned goods until he found some coffee. While the steaks sizzled, she observed him. The sunlight cast a warm glow over his rugged face. She saw strength and endurance there, just as she found finely disciplined power in his body. She girded up her emotions as the coffee permeated the air with its wonderful aroma. Lord, she was feeling all liquid again. The man was attractive, dangerously attractive, she thought. With him looking like that, she would have to guard her every thought and move.

Her stomach rumbled audibly when she finally pulled her chair to the table. Ravenously hungry, she watched Matt splash coffee into her battered tin cup. The room, which now smelled of cooked meat, had warmed up nicely and the venison steaks were done to a turn. Bandit lay on the hearth contentedly gnawing a meaty bone.

"Now what were we talking about before we started fighting again?" Matt asked between bites. "Oh, yes . . . something about livin' on hope, wasn't it?"

She swallowed a piece of steak and scanned his amused face. He looked so perfect, so confident. Those playful brown eyes were shadowed with an awareness that would shake the heart of any woman, and in his square jaw she glimpsed that special determination that gave him such a masculine aura.

But the warm feelings she'd harbored just a while ago had dried up. Faith, why did he have to look so self-satisfied? she wondered. And why in the world did his name have to be Worthington? That ruined everything! "Don't look so damn superior, Matt. You wouldn't have any idea what it's like to live on hope. You wouldn't know what people of my class have to do, would you?"

He stopped chewing and stared at her. "No, but I have a feeling I'm going to find out."

She plunked down her fork and squinted at him. "Well, first of all, you can't plan for the future because there's nothin' in the future but more of the same misery. You do your best—but you never quite make the grade. And if you're sick, death is the poor man's doctor. Old John thinks he's bein' generous because he pays for the miners' funerals!"

"There are ways to break out if you would trust some-one to—"

"Now don't go tellin' me about trustin' people. No, if a poor fellow goes around trustin' too many people, he ends up with the short end of the stick."

Sadness washed over Matt's thoughtful face. "Are you talking about someone in particular?"

"Indeed I am—that foreman at the Silver Queen—meaner than hell with the hide rubbed off, he is. When Da signed up, Clayright said he could trust him to take care of his needs. Later, when Da told him the lads was droppin' from the heat, he said, 'Let them drop. Men are cheaper than ice . . . there's a dozen waitin' at the gate when one goes down.' " Carrie gulped some coffee and eyed Matt again. "The men's hands bleed, the dust ruins their lungs, and the young lads are stooped like old men. A lot of the older ones are like Da—their hearts ain't so good anymore. But if they speak up to ask for a lighter job, Clayright says, 'Get out!' "

Concern clouded Matt's eyes as he leaned back and fin-ished his coffee.

"No, trustin' other people is for fools," she went on. "You're better off trustin' your own brain and muscles. That's all you got to keep yourself and those you love goin'." She took another bite and began again, her mouth half full. "You know, there are some advantages to bein' raised poor, though. I noticed it gives you a real clear view of humanity."

He studied her with amusement. "Anything else you noticed?"

"Indeed I have. The world is divided into the rich and the poor, and the rich do the dividin'. And another thing—just when you think you got it made, one more son of a bitch comes along to knock you down."

His face broke into a smile. "Do you have a specific son of a bitch in mind, or are we just talking about sons of bitches in general?"

She jabbed her fork at him. "All you Worthingtons are

sons of bitches—but I'm talkin' about old John. He's the biggest.''

He laughed loudly. "So I'm sort of a *junior* son of a bitch, right?"

She tugged at her ear and nodded slowly. "Yeah . . . that's a pretty good way to put it." When he laughed again, her voice tightened up. "I'll bet *you* never carried your shoes to keep from wearing them out, Mr. Editor."

"No, I always had plenty of everything," he answered good-naturedly.

"That's for sure! And there's one thing you Worthingtons will never run out of—false promises."

Stony-faced, Matt stood and walked to the window.

Annoyed, she stared at him while her dog sprawled at her feet. "Well, spit it out, man. What are you thinkin' about?" she prodded.

He turned, his countenance dark. "I was thinking how helping you is like trying to free a snarling fox from a trap. And did you know you're the biggest snob I ever met?"

She placed both her spread-out hands on her bosom. *"Me,* a snob?"

"Yes—*you,* a snob. If a man doesn't meet your acid poverty test, you're ready to condemn him flat-footed. Do you think a man's soul automatically rots when his bank account reaches a level set by you in your all-knowing wisdom?"

She jumped to her feet, but he strode back and, cupping her shoulder, sat her down. When she tried to rise, he held her fast and ordered, *"No,* you sit here and listen to me for a while, you hardheaded little mick!"

Rebellion flashed through her. "Hardheaded little mick, is it?"

"Yes, that's exactly what you are! You're opinionated, stubborn, have a temper like a colicky mule—and at this moment you have a big head from that twenty-rod you were slamming down last night!" Before she could reply, he rumbled, "Did you ever think about asking questions instead of stomping over the countryside with a big pistol, abducting editors?''

She clenched her hands. *"Questions?* What good would that do? I'd have no more chance than a kerosene cat in hell doin' that! Who'd answer *my* questions?''

Matt smiled tightly. *"I* would, you vile-tempered little wampus cat—if you would just ask like a decent human being!''

She looked away. "All right, then, Mr. Editor—pray tell, what *should* I do?''

Matt stood and poured them each another cup of fragrant coffee, then sat down again. After taking a big gulp, he looked at Carrie seriously. "I still think you're wrong about John's negligence, but if I were in your place, I'd try to form a union for the miners—to make sure they always get their rights.''

She cupped the warm coffee in both hands and blinked her eyes. Why was he telling her this? Wasn't he a Worthington? Didn't he get a revenue from the Silver Queen?

He glowered at her and shook his head. "If you're thinking what your face says you're thinking, no, you're dead wrong. I don't get a dime from the Queen. The *Courier* and the ranch pay for themselves. Yes, John raised me, but I won't see any money from the mine until he's gone—maybe not even then.''

"I still don't understand . . . your name is Worthington . . . you—''

He slammed his fist on the rickety table and rattled the plates. "God in heaven, woman, can't you get over that name thing? I'm trying to talk to you like one human being would talk to another, but you're making it trickier than saddling a grizzly bear!''

Bandit dropped the bone and stared at him.

"Don't you suppose I've thought of a union?'' she retorted as she pushed the cup aside. She stared at him and in a superior tone added, "The things are illegal. Or didn't you know that?''

A vein stood out on Matt's forehead. "No, they're not—

not anymore. The Massachusetts Supreme Court legalized them and the rest of the United States has followed suit. There's an organization called the Knights of Labor that has thousands and thousands of members now.''

She leaned forward in the squeaky chair and widened her eyes.

''A union is just a group of workers who have banned together to fight for what they want anyway,'' he explained. ''It's pretty hard to keep something like that illegal for long.''

She grinned and chuckled. ''Yeah . . . I see what you're talkin' about. If everybody works together, it makes their side so strong no one man can fight them, no matter how rich he is.''

''Exactly.''

As Matt went on to explain the situation, her spirit blossomed like a morning glory on an east porch. Faith, listen to the man, she thought. He could talk like the Lord's own angels. She listened intently while he told her how unions worked. During her short span she had noticed that after the first blush of youth most people had more of less given up on life. It was easy to tell; you could see it in their eyes. But Matt was different—he was intelligent and vibrantly alive.

A surprising thought bobbed up in her mind like a fishing cork—Holy Mother, it didn't even bother her anymore that his last name was Worthington. She studied him as the bright daylight streaked his face. The laugh lines around his eyes told her his intelligence wasn't of the bloodless, bookish type. True, the man was book-read; but better than that, he was horse-smart!

''But the men are so tired when the day is through,'' she finally interrupted, ''they don't want to come to any meetin's.''

He reached across the table and put his large, bronzed hand over hers. When he caressed it with his long thumb, warmth shot up her arm. Soon her skin was all shivery with delightful sensations. She tried to pull her hand away, but he held it tight. Why did she feel so faint? she wondered. And why were hot ripples shooting up her arm like fireworks?

"That's a sacrifice they'll have to make to get ahead," he said, finally releasing her hand. "I've cleared brush all day, then written editorials at night."

"Yeah, but that ain't like doin' it day after day. It grinds you down plumb smooth—your spirit, too. By the time the lads are fifteen, they've kind of given up already." Her pulse raced and she had the scary feeling she was losing control of her emotions.

Matt looked at her tenderly and smiled with such warm intimacy, she felt shaken. "But you didn't give up, did you?" he asked, his voice husky and vibrant, his eyes alight with some deliciously exciting emotion.

Blood stung her cheeks. "No, I believed deep down I could do better. I figured if other people could pull themselves up, I could, too. Besides, I'd like to think I could make the world a wee bit better—not just let it push me around."

He reached across the table again and rested his dark hand on her arm. Smiling, he gently caressed her skin. "That's my brave girl!"

She smiled back and tried to control the butterflies in her stomach. Lord, why was her arm glowing with that pleasurable warmth? And why did her joints feel so weak? She also felt afraid, as if part of her old tough self were floating down a stream, out of reach. If this kept up, what would she be like when the rescuers found them?

Matt watched Carrie hobble around the cabin, tightly gripping her scribbled papers. His tail wagging, her dog followed her steps. They had finished their supper and the aroma of fried meat filled the room. The wind moaned outside, and light from the kerosene lamp pooled in the center of the room.

He studied her halting gait and wondered what he could do for her ankle. While he watched, she paused by the lamp. He let his gaze swim over her. Her green eyes shone like emeralds and the backlighting sparked her hair with glossy, copper highlights. Her precious article was proudly clenched in one hand as she read it to herself. Soft and voluptuous, she exuded a warm, feminine confidence that pulled at his heart.

He assessed her thoughtfully. She was more than courageous and original; she was like no woman he had ever known. Dovie was gorgeous, but she was spoiled and vain. And Jenny, despite her churchgoing ways, was very self-centered. Carrie had shown him a woman could plan and act as decisively as a man. With some education and direction, she would be something to behold. Her warmth and zest for life enticed him, but their backgrounds mixed like kerosene and fire.

"Matt, I want you to give my work a fair readin'," she announced suddenly. "You've found some excuse to ignore it for two days. If I'm going' to get all the miners on the Slope to think about unionizin' this spring, I'll need some good material for printed handouts."

His gaze rippled down her body, from her springy red hair to her dainty feet. He had never seen a union organizer who looked like this. "You're going to unionize the *whole* Western Slope this spring?"

"What's wrong? I thought you were interested in this."

"I am—but do we have to write a complete union creed in one day? I feel like I've been marooned with Samuel Gompers instead of a gorgeous woman."

"Well, somebody has to keep all the big mine owners like old John in check."

Matt considered her words. Surely conditions couldn't be as bad in the Silver Queen as she claimed. Or could they? Dark, uncomfortable thought about the man who had been his substitute father nibbled at his mind. The little minx had raised some disturbing questions, questions he would rather not think about. "And that somebody is going to be you?"

"Do Chinamen eat rice?"

He shook his head and laughed, but the proposed mining union still troubled him. With Carrie running the show, who knew what would happen? She would dig up more snakes than a dozen men could kill.

"Come on, Matt. I want you to read this," she prodded.

His attention drifted to her crumpled, dog-eared papers as he considered her writing ability. "That's the problem . . . your work is so disorganized, I *can't* give it a fair reading."

"What do you mean by that crack?"

He paced back and forth as he eyed her. "Well, you need some instruction." In his own mind he admitted her work was better than he had indicated. Despite his best efforts to ignore the emotion, he harbored excitement about her potential. "Perhaps after you've studied more your work will gain some credibility and depth. You're sharp as a razor, and in no time I could teach you—"

Wait! What was he thinking about? He suddenly remembered that Jenny took care of things at his Crested Butte office, and he knew that she and Carrie would get along like a gut-shot grizzly and a snarling bobcat. How could he get Carrie's mind off this confounded reforming business? It would be nice to talk to a woman instead of a union leader for a while.

Her eyes gleamed with interest. "Could teach me what?" she probed.

His gaze darted around the room as he searched for something to divert her attention. "Nothing, Carrie, nothing," he mumbled.

"But I heard you say somethin' . . . I know I did. I—"

He snapped a flour sack from the cabinet and ripped it down the side. "I said, come here and let me wrap your ankle. We should have done this earlier. You're limping around like a hamstrung filly." He studied her and wondered why her color was so high and her eyes so bright. "Are you all right, girl?"

"Yeah, I'm just tired and a little hot."

"Well, *come here,*" he ordered again. She looked doubtful, so he strode to her and pitched the crumpled papers on the table. "Now, you and that nub-headed dog drift over here," he commanded once more as he moved to the table. He scraped back one of the chairs and pointed at it.

Her ample bosom swaying, she walked toward him while her dog trailed behind.

"Here, put your foot on this seat," he rumbled. She placed her small foot on the seat and pulled up her skirt. Even as hunger nipped at his loins he realized she had to be unaware of her tempting pose. Since she wore no makeup, those moist pink lips and smoky eyes had to be natural. And after all, could the girl help it if she had been given some extra helpings of silky white flesh in all the right places?

"What do you know about doctorin', Matt? Is that one of your sidelines, too?"

He ripped a strip from the flour sack and cocked his brow. "No, it isn't, but I've wrapped plenty of horses' legs. I figure it's about the same."

She chuckled while he bound the strip around her ankle. "You know, that's one way we're alike, you and me. We see things the way they really are, and leave out all the fancy bits." She watched him while he worked. " 'Course, there are lots of ways we're different—like you bein' rich and me poor."

Her comment brought him back to earth. He tied up the strip and tossed her skirt down. He lit a cheroot and squinted through the smoke at her. "You know, Carrie, there are different ways of being rich. You may have had more than I did."

Disbelief stamped her face. "Like *what?*"

He spit a piece of tobacco from his tongue. "Like a mother and a father."

Her features darkened and she flashed, "You had a mother and a father. You weren't hatched, were you?"

He smiled and rubbed his stubbled chin. "No, but my father died before I could remember him, and my mother ran off with all his money and a good-looking gambler soon afterward. Just stayed in Colorado Territory long enough to dump me on John."

She blushed and mumbled, "I'm sorry to hear that."

"Don't be," he replied, walking to the fireplace. "A hard bed makes a strong back."

"A hard bed? Yeah, I know all about them hard beds! I wish you knew what me and Da have come through already."

"What are you talking about? Go on, tell me about it." He leaned against the rough wooden mantel, noting her flushed face with concern.

Her dog sprawled out to watch while she limped around the cabin. "All right, since you ask . . . I will," she began. "Ireland used to be a sweet, lush country, and in the springtime the livin' was good and meant somethin'. Then all the crops started to wither and die." She looked at him hard. "And that ship comin' to New York was a livin' hell. Oh, you wouldn't know anythin' about steerage, would you, Matt? When you went to Europe you went first class, didn't you?

"Well, let me tell you about it," she continued. "There's a whole world beneath those gilded salons. People packed in like cattle, all coughin', and the frightened babes cryin' . . . everythin' smellin' like vomit and stale food. Sleepin' on bare, five-foot planks in tiers of four—"

Surprise shot through Matt. Why was she so disturbed? He already knew she seldom gave in to physical or emotional pain. Something was wrong. "Carrie—"

"Oh, let me go on! You wanted to know about it." She hobbled about, her hands on her hips. "Then there was the immigrant train. Wooden benches, too short for anyone but a child—everythin' stinkin' of sweat and tobacco. Feelin' lost and confused—every bite of food costin' ten times what it should. No one considerin' you worthy of the least respect.'' She whirled and clenched her fists; tears glistened in her eyes. ''We sat for three freezin' days in Kansas. They switched us off for a load of cattle.''

He scanned her red face, knowing she was sick. With two strides he crossed the room, took her into his arms, and caressed her back. Frowning, he smoothed back her damp hair and felt her hot forehead. ''Carrie, you're sick, love,'' he said softly. ''We've got to get you into bed. You're burning with fever.''

Chapter 4

C arrie gazed at Matt through a bleary haze when she heard him set the liquor jug by the bed. Over his shoulder she saw Bandit stretched on the hearth, his head turned, his eyes sad. She tugged up the quilt. Flames crackled in the fireplace, but she shivered convulsively. Pain pinched around her head and streaked through her limbs. Her weak muscles resisted all movement; her dry mouth tasted sour and bitter. She was so tired she could scarcely raise her arm, scarcely accept the coffee Matt held out to her. His strong hand closed around hers, pressing the warm cup into her hand.

"Drink this, love. I added a splash of Botsie's twenty-rod. It should make you feel better."

"What time is it?" she whispered through cracked lips.

"Around three, I'd say. You've been sleeping." He traced his thumb under her aching eyes.

She listened to the wind howl outside the cabin. "Is it snowing?"

He dragged a chair to the bed and sat down, his face worried. "Yes, some rough weather has blown in since sunset. Another blizzard, I'm afraid."

Her ears buzzed, and his voice sounded fuzzy and far away. He slipped his warm hand behind her neck and lifted her head. She tried to sip the coffee, but her stomach threatened to rebel, so she pushed it away, then collapsed. Matt took the cup and placed it aside. Running a hand through his tousled hair, he paced by the bed.

Suddenly she pushed away the quilt with a trembling hand and wiped her damp hairline. The room had suddenly become as hot as it had been cold. "Matt," she murmured, plucking at her blouse. "I'm so *hot*. Help me . . . I've got to get this off, got to get cool . . ."

He raised her limp torso, unbuttoned the blouse, and slipped the garment off. Her full, white breasts spilled free, their deep cleavage sliced with a dangling religious medal. Clenching his jaw, he unbuttoned her skirt and tugged it past her feet. Her white cotton petticoat quickly followed the same route. She lay in her mended bloomers, still perspiring. When he pulled the cover over her breasts, she eased it back a bit. "No, let it be . . . I'm on fire," she breathed.

His face dark, he felt her neck and laid his hand over her heart. "You're burning up, love. We've got to get your fever down somehow."

He strode to the hearth and found a battered pan. Pushing open the door against the wind, he went into the blustery darkness without his coat. Carrie felt the icy draft, heard his purposeful steps as he left the cabin, saw his concerned face when he returned a minute later with a rounded bowl of snow. After he kicked the door shut, he gathered a rag and carried the snow to the bed. He splashed twenty-rod on the material, then, ever so gently, rubbed the snowy rag over her fevered body, replenishing the snow when it melted down.

The icy snow and Matt's strong hands eased her aching muscles. All night he labored over her body and caressed and cooled her limbs, her torso, her hot brow. He spoke to her tenderly like a child and told her stories, trying to divert her. His smooth, deep voice reassured and comforted her, strengthened her.

His hands were like a strong, velvety balm. As they swept over her arms and legs, she sensed them imparting strength and power. She felt the occasional brush of his fingers as they slid past her breasts—the pressure of his thumbs as he kneaded her back. His almost unbearably tender touch sang through her body. She relaxed and sank into the mattress, letting him soothe her, take care of her.

Her fever broke as pink streaked the sky. After Matt had found some dry quilts and changed the bed, he gently dressed her cool body. He sat by the bed and brushed hair from her face as she dozed. Later, he tucked the cover under her chin and prepared to move away. To his surprise, she grasped his hand and held it fast. "What's your hurry, Mr. Editor? Stay a while," she murmured.

The next day, an icy wind whined down the slope, ushering in the last of the storm. Inside the snug cabin a fire crackled peacefully and pungent coffee simmered on the hearth. While Carrie gained strength, Matt relaxed in a chair beside her bed and studied her work with a serious eye. Feeling her stare, he looked up and noticed her tense face. With a heavy sigh, he shook his head and sailed another finely written page onto the bed.

Propped against the headboard with a pillow at her back, she picked up the paper and pressed it to her bosom. "Well, what do you think?"

He drew in a deep breath of air, which was scented with woodsmoke. "I think you have a wonderful, vivid imagination."

She dangled her limp hand from the bed and rubbed Bandit's furry head. "Yeah, I know that . . . but the writin'?"

He raked through his hair and glanced at her expectant face. "I'm afraid you have a terrible problem with grammar. You must have missed the basics in your younger years."

She raised her brows and chuckled. "Well, that stands to reason, 'cause I had to steal my education in Ireland."

"You had to steal it?"

Defiance sparked in her green eyes. "Yeah. They have hedgerow schools in the country for the poor crofters' children. A teacher will set up with a hedge behind him as a windbreak, and his students will bunch up around him on the clover. All the pupils were boys, but I used to sneak up on the other side of the hedge and listen.''

''You sprawled on your belly and listened to the teacher through the hedge?''

''Oh, it wasn't so bad,'' she said with a sly smile while she smoothed out the wrinkled sheet. ''It was kind of nice to lie there smellin' the clover and listenin' to the bees and meadowlarks. 'Course, when the boys found out I was there, they'd always chuck rocks at me and run me off.''

Matt grinned as he imagined the scene. He picked up another page. ''And when you got here at Crested Butte?''

''The teacher was too busy to help me catch up, so I had to piece things together the best I could. It was the same in Denver.''

He tugged at his ear and glanced at the creased page. ''Well, unfortunately you never got the pieces together. You don't know the difference between a restrictive and a nonrestrictive clause, you can't punctuate, and you have a lot of trouble with parallel construction.''

Her face clouded. ''Well, you sure dumped the whole load of hay on me at once, didn't you?''

''Don't you want to learn?''

''Yeah, I want to learn . . . but I don't want to be whipped in the face with a wet sack!''

Silent, he cocked his head and listened to the wind rattle the windows.

With a great sigh, she blew out her breath and crossed her arms. ''All right, all right, go on, what does that last one mean—that parallel construction thing?''

''It means that words that do the same work are easier to read if they are similar in construction,'' he explained, eyeing her serious face. When she didn't respond he added, ''Doesn't the daddy pig, the mama pig, and the baby pig sound better than the daddy pig, the mama pig, and their young piglet?''

Her eyes brightened up. ''Oh, is that all those big words mean? I like the way you teach grammar. I'll be able to learn this stuff real fast!''

"I'm glad you think so, because you'll need the time to work on your spelling." He sat forward. "Did you know you use words that aren't even words? Look at this." He held a paper in front of her with his thumb under a word. "What the hell is that word supposed to be?"

Disgust tightened her mouth. "Why, that's *cheneuvered*. It's a combination of cheated and maneuvered. You know . . . John Worthington has cheneuvered his way into wealth by keepin' the miners down. Faith, I'm surprised a man of your intelligence didn't understand it."

"Oh, I got what you meant by the context—but cheneuvered is not a verb."

"Why ain't it? I made it up. Why ain't it just as good as a verb that was made up five hundred years ago by some old monk in a long gown?"

"Well, it just isn't. You can't invent your own language."

In a softer voice he added, "Without a doubt you're the most unique writer I've ever read—you have quite a dramatic flair. I'm sure you would be brilliant on the stage. But not everyone has your colorful verbal skills, my girl." He ran his finger under a long passage punctuated with large exclamation marks. "And look at this. The logic in this would never hold. It's just pure Irish blarney."

With a twinkle in her eye, she smiled. "What if it is? You know what blarney is, don't you? Blarney is the truth the way it should be—not the way it really is."

He sat back and crossed his long legs. "Ah, yes, you poetic Irish, descended from a race of gods, warriors, and heroes."

Her countenance darkened. "Are you makin' fun of me?"

He laughed and watched the lamplight strike red highlights in her hair. "No, I'm not making fun of you. Where did you come from in Ireland anyway?"

She smiled again and her eyes took on a dreamy look. "Killarney."

"Do you miss it?"

She inched up on her pillow and smoothed back her hair. "Oh, yes. 'Course, I was just a young girl when I saw it last, but it was so beautiful. There are lots of little lakes and glens. And the wee lambs dot the green countryside like white flowers."

Heaving a long sigh, she closed her eyes.

"And the smell of the place . . . There always seemed to be a soft mist floatin' down from the purple heights all tangy with the scent of sea and heather." Her eyes still closed, she began to hum, then sang:

"Murmurs passed along the valley like the banshee's
    lonesome croon,
  And a thousand blades were flashin' at the risin' of
    the moon."

The warmth and intensity of her voice flooded the melody with special appeal.

Matt rolled his eyes and chuckled. "You Irish. Always singing about battles, death, and graveyards. Don't you know any happy songs?"

She opened her eyes and arched one brow. "Of course we do! An old story says Finn MacCool's fiddle was so lively he could throw the enemy's warriors to the ground with one tune." With an injured air, she scanned him again. "Don't you know wherever there's an Irishman there's always lots of laughin' and singin' and lovin'? Why, one time I saw a red ladybird on a stalk . . . and stopped and make up a little song about it."

He watched her smile as she scratched her dog's ears. A sudden tenderness that surprised him welled up in Matt's chest. He grinned and brushed his finger against the side of her creamy cheek. "Carrie O'Leary . . . so wide in soul and bold of tongue."

"That's pretty!" she said with a warm smile. "Who wrote it?"

"A man I had the great pleasure of meeting one time. I printed his work in the *Courier* once."

"And who might he be?"

"Tennyson."

"Tennyson? Where does he live—Crested Butte?"

Matt laughed until tears rolled down his cheeks.

Carrie crossed her arms and stared at the rough log wall. "You're makin' fun of me! You think I'm real stupid, don't you?"

Matt wiped his eyes, then gently turned her stony face toward him. "No, I don't think you're stupid at all."

She glared at him. "Then why did you laugh at me?"

"I wasn't laughing at you. I laughed at what you said because it was terribly funny."

Her face perplexed, she blinked her eyes.

"Tennyson is a famous English poet, love. He's very old and he lives in London. Didn't you take literature in Denver?"

"We've been studyin' grammar. We ain't had no literature yet."

He chuckled once again.

She clenched her fists and pushed herself up in bed. "See, there you go again laughin' at me. Why don't you just go on and tell me I'm stupid?"

"Because you're not! You're not stupid at all. You're ignorant—but you're not stupid."

The springs creaked as she leaned forward and tried to push the bedding aside. "Ignorant, is it!"

He eased her back and covered her up with the thread-bare quilt. "Just settle back and let me explain a few things, little hothead. You're ignorant because you haven't been exposed to the world of books or had a chance to meet anyone who might broaden your horizon."

She gazed at him doubtfully.

"In fact, you're keen as a razor. You're definitely not stupid." He reached out and caressed her cool hand. "Don't you realize how special you are? Any dull-spirited dunce could learn who Tennyson was if he stayed in school long enough." He caught her worried gaze and squeezed her hand, trying to emphasize each of his words. "But it takes a real special person to make up a song about a red ladybird on a stalk.''

A thoughtful look played over her face. Finally, she crossed her arms and fixed him with a hard look. ''Do you really mean those words you just said?''

He grazed his finger over the tip of her nose and smiled. ''Yes, Carrie. I mean them with all my heart and soul.''

Two days later Carrie got up and explored Botsie's larder. Then she walked around the cabin, looking at everything on the cluttered walls. When she found a yellowed calendar behind a gunnysack, she shoved her hands on her hips. ''Mother Mary, today is a holiday. We've got to celebrate.''

Matt looked up from a seed catalog he had discovered while desperately searching for something to read. ''Celebrate? What are we going to celebrate?''

''Small Christmas. It always comes on January sixth.''

He flipped another page. ''Christmas is over.''

''It ain't if you don't want it to be. There's an old saying, Matt—neither make or break a custom.''

''Well, I don't think anyone would ever notice if we skipped this one just once, do you?''

''I'd notice. It's bad luck. Besides, you can be the black-haired stranger. It's awfully good luck if you share Small Christmas dinner with a black-haired stranger.'' With some surprise, she noticed his countenance fall.

''Am I still a stranger to you?''

She pressed her lips together and shook her head. ''Oh, you know what I mean!'' Nervously, she pushed the flour-sack curtain aside and rubbed the icy pane. Outside, gentle snow swirled down and drifted into the misty evergreens. ''We need to cut a little tree, too.''

''We do?''

She wagged her finger at him. ''We sure do. I ain't had no tree this year, and I want a tree. I know there's an ax under some of this junk.''

''You've been sick and it's snowing.'' He eyed her papers, scattered over the table. "I thought you were going to revise today."

Smiling, she looked outside again. "I'll do it tomorrow. Just look at this day! The snowflakes look like puffy feathers from heaven, and God's decorated everything with shiny icicles. The writin' will be here tomorrow, but today will never pass this way again."

He chuckled and eyed her bare foot. "What are you going to use for shoes? We cut up your boot, remember?"

She glanced around the room and snapped her fingers. "I saw an old pair of boots around here someplace. I'll stuff paper in the toes and wear them."

As she clomped around the cabin in the clumsy boots, Matt slipped on his overcoat and gloves.

"I like the way you've included God on your side," he remarked while he helped her into the rest of her things. "You know, you might have a future in politics, too."

She stuck out her tongue at him and tied on her head shawl.

"Go on out," he said with a laugh. "I'll find the ax and join you."

The cold air rushed over her and nipped her cheeks as she opened the cabin door. Bandit shot in front of her and raced toward the trees, making big loops in the snow. She chuckled at his antics, then surveyed the silent landscape and crunched toward the tree line. Snowflakes whispered down on her shoulders, and once she was in the trees, frozen pine needles snapped under her boots. Like silvery nets, fine strands of ice webbed the stiff undergrowth. Hearing a twig crack, she looked to the side. Bright against the dark trees, a russet-colored doe froze for a moment, then darted to safety.

Carrie blinked snowflakes from her lashes and looked back at the cabin, whose eaves sported long icicles. Matt closed the door and jogged toward her, the ax in his hand. When he caught up with her, they wound their way into the forest until they found a small, perfectly shaped tree.

Stripping off his overcoat, Matt went to work. She

sucked in a breath of the crisp mountain air while the ax cracked into the tree trunk. "Ah, smell that spruce, man," she exclaimed. "The fragrance is enough to stir a statue's heart."

Inch by inch the ax clipped into the tree trunk, shooting wood chips to the side. One of the chips sailed behind her, drawing her attention to a bush of red berries, which glistened against the snow-powdered undergrowth. Happiness bubbling inside her, she trudged toward them, startling a family of sleek rabbits. Bandit barked and ran after them, spraying up powdery snow with his back paws.

Behind her, she heard the ax thud into the snow and seconds later something soft hit her back. With a little cry she whirled about. A mischievous grin plastering his face, Matt stood behind her, packing together another snowball. This time he splattered the snowball at her boots and made her fall backward near the berry bush.

The battle on, she scrambled up and chased after him. They ran from the trees and trailed over the smooth slope like children, yelling war cries and hurling snow. Hands on his hips, Matt laughed when Carrie tried to negotiate a quick turn in her oversized boots and rolled down a gentle slope in a cloud of snow.

A minute later she was on her feet, Bandit at her side. "Laugh at me, will you, you black-haired rascal?" she hollered, hurling snowballs faster than ever. All at once Matt dodged behind a tree and disappeared into the forest. Her heart thumping, Carrie walked the tree line, glancing into the dark forest. Suddenly two arms grabbed her from behind. With a huge growl, Matt sat down in the snow and brought her with him. "You've been captured! Give up!" he ordered.

"Oh, no, not yet!" Twisting around in his arms, she gritted her teeth and tried to rub snow in his face. Bandit tugged at his sleeve. At last he pinned down her arms and hugged her to his chest. "All right, all right, you're getting too hot. I concede the battle," he rasped. "You and that hound from hell are too tough for an old man like me anyway. Let's go inside and fix that damn tree of yours.''

She studied his amused face. ''All right, then, as long as you know you've been bested. I found some tea and spices while I was pokin' around. I'll fix us somethin' to warm up.''

Carrie ripped a strip of material from Botsie's red long johns. ''Here,'' she ordered, handing the limp material to Matt, ''drape this on the tree. We'll swag these red strips over the branches. After we add the berry twigs and those shiny snuff-jar lids, our tree will look real pretty.'' An intimate mood had welled up between them as they worked on the tree. Exhausted by his romp, Bandit slept in front of the rosy fire.

Matt sipped some of the hot spiced tea, which smelled of cinnamon and cloves, then clinked his mug on the hearth. He looked at her as he punched the tip of his pocket knife into a silvery lid. ''I still think you're going to a lot of trouble for nothing.''

''You ain't got no Christmas spirit at all, have you?''

''I guess not.''

''Well, what's wrong with you? Ain't you got no happy holiday memories or anythin'?''

He threaded string through the hole and tied the lid on the tree. ''No, not really. I was always stuck in some Eastern boarding school during the holidays when I was a kid.''

She walked toward him with another strip of material. ''I'll bet the place was as fancy as a king's palace.''

''It was cold as death . . . and the headmaster was a bald-headed old man with bad breath.'' He glanced up while he punctured another lid. ''How about you?''

She tossed the material aside and sighed. ''Oh, yeah, I remember some fine holidays in Ireland. There was always somethin' good to eat, and the kitchen smelled of butter and cinnamon. The turf fire was glowin' and everythin' was all warm and cheery.'' Her face softened. ''I remember Mam's shiny copper pans, and luster jugs, and blue willow dishes." She walked to the fireplace and held out her hands. "Our little house was thatched with wheat and straw. It was wonderful how the wind and rain played over the lime-washed walls."

Matt loved the way her face glowed when she spoke about her memories. "My best holiday, I ran off with another boy who was marooned at the school," he said.

She widened her eyes. "You didn't come back to Crested Butte? You didn't come back to your uncle?"

He looked up and tossed the knife aside. "No, John was always too busy with mine business. He worked right through the holidays and didn't want any company." He shook his head and grinned. "Anyway, this other kid and I slipped off and rented a hotel room for the night. Money was no problem. We said we were brothers and wrote a phony note that our father would be arriving later." He rubbed his stubbled jaw. "We ordered stuff sent up from the dining room and ate and drank until we were sick. We also bought a lot of silly stuff for each other and wrapped it up. We got a hiding when we got back to school—but it was worth it."

Her face darkened. "Why, that's sad, Matt. Real, real sad."

He shrugged and went back to the tree. "Sad? Well, I'll admit it can't compare with the luster jugs and the turf fire's glow—but I never thought of it as sad."

"I'll never forget my best holiday," Carrie began, picking up her spicy-smelling tea. "It was winter and we were just arrivin' in America. When the ship neared the shore everyone poured out on the deck. Our hearts were so high. We could see the twinklin' shore, and we could smell it. We were slidin' right past the tall buildings and the settin' sun was strikin' them, makin' them all rosy and soft. Everyone was laughin' and talkin' like old friends. Men jostled children on their shoulders and women cried. And Mam's face was so young and pretty I thought my heart would bust right open."

Transported by her warm, husky voice, he could see the

emigrants' faces in his mind's eye. "I've heard about your trip west. I imagine your high spirits began to wane after you reached shore."

She moved from the fire with the tea. "Yeah," she answered, placing her cup aside. "We had to pass through immigration. Sometimes my stomach still draws up when I remember the smell of that long, dark building." She looked him straight in the eye. "It was musty and stank of unwashed bodies, and medicine—and fear. The doctors separated me and Mam from Da when we went through for medical examinations. I noticed a boy from Dublin sittin' down cryin' his eyes out. When I asked him what was wrong, he said they were sendin' his mam back. They were sendin' everybody back who was weak or coughin' or sick. He said they just put a little pencil mark on her papers and that was all of it."

She stared past Matt into the shadows. "When Mam and me got in that little cubicle, the doctor checked her papers when her back was turned. I stared at that little check, thinkin' how that faint little mark blotted out a whole lifetime of workin', and prayin', and tryin'. After the doctor walked away, I erased that mark. Mam never knew she had been rejected and we walked from the end of that dark buildin' into the light."

Matt felt his throat tighten, but the pain felt good, like prickly feeling returning to a numb hand. "And she died after you came to Crested Butte?"

"Not right away. She got to see America . . . and she got to be with us several more years."

"I guess things have been pretty hard for you."

"Oh, they ain't been too hard," she replied, picking up her tea again. "Hard is livin' in a house where there ain't no love . . . and nobody havin' any feelin's for anyone. *That's* hard."

Her innocent words sliced into his heart. He thought of the distance between him and his uncle. True, John wasn't his real father, but he was the only father he had. When he noticed her sad face, he moved toward her. "What's wrong?" he asked, clasping her shoulders.

"Oh, I was just thinkin' about Da. He's got to be worryin' about me."

"What do you think he's doing?"

She frowned. "I know what he's doin'. He's got the sickness."

"He drinks to forget?"

"He drinks to forget; he drinks to celebrate life. The sight of a bird on the wing or a bunch of flowers can set him off." She eyed Matt softly. "Do you have anyone waitin' for you?"

He thought of John, busy with the mine and his investments. Then he thought of Jenny. After an introduction at a social event, she had skillfully entered his life, offering to do all his boring paperwork and solving a host of other minor problems. He pictured her angry and frustrated that he hadn't been in town to escort her to a recent party. "No, I don't have anyone waiting for me," he finally said.

Chapter 5

The kerosene lamp flickered light over the cluttered dinner table, and the aroma of camp biscuits, vegetables, and savory meat filled the cabin. Outside, a blustery wind howled down the mountains. Several nights ago, when her body had raged with fever, Carrie wouldn't have believed she could have been so hungry. Seated at the table, she watched Matt place a pan of hot biscuits before her, then turn and grind out one of Botsie's cheap, dried-up cigars that he had been smoking. She knew how much he hated the bent stogies, but she also remembered how happy he had been to discover them after the last of his expensive cheroots were gone. Making a terrible face, he scraped his chair to the table.

"Here, have some of this—it'll warm up your toes," he urged, gurgling the last of the twenty-rod into her cup. "The old boy's cigars are terrible, but his liquor is fairly drinkable."

She laughed and glanced over his shoulder at their little tree, standing in the corner. Firelight played over the red streamers and shiny lids. For some reason, it was the prettiest tree she had ever seen in her life.

With a frown, he put down the liquor jug. "Carrie, since I brought the idea up, I need to talk to you about something. You do realize unionizing is a risky business, don't you? You could get hurt—badly."

She looked at his concerned face. "What's life if you

don't take a few risks? Haven't you ever wanted to put your heart and soul behind somethin' that was good?''

He forked into his food. ''What you're describing, my girl, is a commitment—and no, I've never been that moonstruck.''

''Well, why not? You're real smart and I know you ain't afraid.''

''Are you suggesting I become an evangelical idealist like you?'' He grinned and chewed his food.

''I don't know what them big words mean, but I *am* suggestin' you care about people.''

''I've found people rarely appreciate it. Seems like high hopes and dreams have a way of crashing about your feet with a resounding thud.'' He shifted in his chair. ''Why stir up more troubles for yourself? Life has enough conflict without creating more.''

She leaned forward. ''Well, I feel real sorry for you, then. If you ain't made one of them commitments you were talkin' about, you ain't really lived.''

He sipped his twenty-rod, then chuckled. ''I haven't, huh?''

''No, you haven't. Don't you know that if you really believe in somethin', and put a little grit behind it, you've got a good chance of doin' it? You ought to jump in the big middle of life and rub it all over you.''

His face doubtful, he took another bite. ''It sounds wonderfully exciting, but I'm afraid I don't believe in miracles anymore.''

''Well, you should.''

''I see you're going to take the plunge no matter what I say.''

She squared her shoulders and picked up her knife and fork. Arching one brow, she slowly replied, ''Yeah . . . just watch my smoke!'' She cut into the juicy venison roast and put a large bite into her mouth. When the savory meat melted against her tongue, she blinked at his amused expression. ''Holy Mother, this is wonderful. Where did you learn to cook like this?''

He swallowed and grinned. "I taught myself. Didn't want to be old bachelor who didn't know how to stir up some vittles if I wanted them."

Her heart dipped at his words and to hide her dismay she tossed a meat scrap to Bandit, who lay at her feet. Why had his words hit her so hard? Despite his cynical ways, she had begun to feel a disturbing tenderness for him; still, his personal life wasn't any business of hers, was it? "Did you say bachelor?" she asked, straightening herself in the chair.

He studied her while he smeared peach preserves on his biscuit. "Well . . . yes. I never really met a woman I wanted to marry."

"I think we're really talkin' about commitments again, ain't we?"

"You're very observant. Experience has taught me a lot about women. When I was back east at school, I noticed all the belles were interested in one thing—finding a rich, docile provider. And I never met a Denver woman who wasn't more interested in the cut of her gown than the newspaper business."

"You must have met some fancy women while you were travelin' over in Europe, too."

"I did. I met a famous English music-hall singer I'll never forget. She was the talk of London while I was there."

A fiery blush stung Carrie's cheeks while she ate. "Well, somewhere along the way you must of . . . well, you know . . ."

His eyes twinkled as he bit into the biscuit. "Yeah, I have . . . 'you know' . . . and I guarantee you, that type is interested in only one thing—money."

"I see," she replied. Conflicting emotions rolled through her mind like a summer storm. Her days with Matt had left her confused. Helping the miners had been foremost in her mind for months—now other, vaguely understood needs troubled her heart.

When he took her hand, Bandit eyed him and growled. "What's the matter with that hound?" Matt asked.

She laughed. "I think he's jealous of you!"

"Good God Almighty—a jealous-hearted dog," he cracked as he glared at the mongrel. "Listen, you may think you've got a lot of fur on your brisket, old man, but I've still got the floor here. Mind if I squeeze off another round?"

They laughed at Bandit's downcast eyes; then Matt looked straight at Carrie. "What are *you* looking for in a man? Surely you'll marry someday."

Carrie was speechless. To make matters worse, his touch made everything inside her feel as if it were melting and swirling together like the preserves on her hot biscuit. And Mary, Jesus, and Joseph—why was there a rhythmic pulse throbbing between her thighs like a ticking clock? The sensation shocked, thrilled, and frightened her at the same time. She had to say something fast . . .

She took a big gulp of the twenty-rod, which brought tears to her eyes. "Oh, I ain't never goin' to marry," she finally blurted out. "I figure somethin' like that would just slow me down—interfere with my goals." With her free hand, she ate heartily, dismissing the subject.

He grinned and continued to caress her other hand. "Has anyone ever told you that you're a bluestocking, love? Not that you really could be, though. All those feelings you keep so well suppressed are bound to erupt one day."

She frowned, but felt the alcohol burn into her stomach and give her courage. "I have my feelin's just where I want them. You know, if I'm goin' to get this union thing goin', I can't have some man holding me back 'cause I ain't got his white shirt ironed yet!" She pulled her hand away from him and began eating again.

"Well, you do have a point, I suppose," he replied, digging into his own food. "There's more to life than peeling carrots and squalling babes, right?"

"Mother Mary, that's right. You need some kind of fire in your innards to really live."

He nodded thoughtfully and finished his plate. She wondered why he had scrutinized her so while they talked and why his eyes now held a strange, unreadable expression.

All at once he stood and walked over to her, extending his big hand. He pulled her to him as she rose, then kissed the top of her head. She felt weak and swoony, and the blood roared in her ears. She could feel his hard chest pressing against her, and his heart stroking as he spoke. "Carrie O'Leary, you're a fierce, fine-looking woman, who never plowed around a stump in her life. You hit every problem straight on. Well, you hardheaded little mick, I wish you the best of luck with all your desperate enterprises. Now it's late. Let's get some sleep."

Fitful dreams plagued Carrie's mind. In her nightmares she relived the avalanche and the freezing trek to Botsie's cabin. She moaned and fought for consciousness, but the dark images held her fast. Gradually she became aware of the comforting warmth of Matt's hand on her shoulder. Drawn to him like a starving man to food, she scooted closer to his hard chest. Pressed against him, she relaxed and savored the rhythm of his strong heart beating in the darkness.

His warmth and throaty reassurances satisfied a deep, primitive need she hadn't known existed. She curved her arms around his neck and nuzzled his shoulder. An inner voice whispered caution, but her dreamlike state and her urgent need drowned it out. His tangy masculine scent was an enticingly persuasive lure. His firm lips brushed her forehead and sent a ripple of joy straight to her heart.

Matt heard the wind wail through the rustling spruce. Inside the tight cabin, the scent of good food and woodsmoke lingered in the air. Heavy sleep almost tugged him under again, but a feeling he didn't really understand urged him to comfort Carrie. Jenny, who waited for him in Crested Butte, weighed lightly on his sleepy mind; besides, he had never wanted a woman as badly as he wanted Carrie. He wanted to crush her in his arms and drown in her soft, womanly scent. She had bewitched him with her lovely face, her delightful mind, and her fighting spirit.

When she sighed and wiggled against him, the unexpected action triggered a need as strong as the howling blizzard. Hard desire thundered up from his vitals, demanding surrender from the first woman who had truly fired his heart. "Damn it . . . come here, you little wildcat," he murmured.

His voice was as rich as melting butter. Her eyes flew open. "Matt . . . I . . . I don't know," she stuttered, her voice still slurred with sleep. "Faith, we just met, and we're so different! And if you think I'm a loose woman just because I never had anythin' . . . why, I'd rather die than—"

"Good God, Carrie, you run on like a addlepated professor! Why don't you just shut up and enjoy yourself?"

His lips seared her mouth while a languorous heat smoldered over her body. With profound relief, she realized it was too late to wonder what was right and what was wrong. She discovered she welcomed the confrontation as a young recruit welcomes his first skirmish. When he deepened the kiss and teased her lips apart, passion jolted through her like sheet lightning. Secret doors blew open and banged back in her mind, revealing bright new worlds of pleasure.

As he explored her mouth, she felt her body racing out of control. These new feelings were so sweet, so sharp, so strong. Sweet Mother of God, what was happening to her? Startled, she felt that pulsing flame between her thighs again. And to her greater surprise, warm pleasure glowed even between the cheeks of her bottom.

Prolonging the deep kiss, he trailed his strong fingers down her back until he kneaded her buttocks under her hiked-up skirt. Finally he eased his lips away and raised his head. "Feels good, doesn't it?" he whispered in a sexy growl.

"Yeah," she rasped, "kind of achy and sweet all at the same time."

Most of her buttons had already worked themselves loose; the rest popped open when he brushed over them. His gaze devoured her full, satiny breasts, now exposed in the darkness. While he savored their weight in his hand, her heart fluttered like a butterfly trapped in a flower cup. As he teased their coral crests between his fingers, sharp need shivered through her. Groaning, he lifted his moon-silvered face and studied her eyes. "Carrie, you're so lovely."

"Matt, I've never done this before . . ."

"Don't worry about it," he murmured as he eased his thumb over her nipple. "I'll give you extra points for inexperience."

His warm fingers skipped fiery prickles over her sensitive skin. Somewhat surprised, she discovered his hands were hard and callused—those of a working man, not a scholar. As he continued to gently tug at her nipples, her resistance dissolved like a sugar cube in steamy coffee. When he pushed aside her religious medal and lowered his head to her breast, she gasped and clamped her thighs together, thinking she would die with pleasure. "Matt, slow down, I think I'm goin' out of control or somethin'," she whispered anxiously.

He raised his mouth and chuckled. "Don't worry, everything is working the way it's supposed to."

As he lowered his head again, powerful feelings exploded through her veins like hot quicksilver. "First the liquor, now this . . . guess I'm fated to do all my wild livin' the same week." She sighed. Then her emotions skittered out of control. His fingers eased her skirt higher and sizzled a path up the insides of her legs. She glowed with an exultant feeling she couldn't express—but when he tugged at her mended bloomers, she jumped and grabbed his hand. "What in hell do you think you're doin'?" she growled.

"Trying to make *love* to you, you ornery little wildcat.

It works better with the clothes off, you know. Now be still, for God's sake—and quit squeezing your legs together!''

He jerked down her bloomers and slid them out of the way. A tidal wave of excitement rolled over her. She now lay bare and exposed beneath her skirt—and she burned with a wild, forbidden yearning she couldn't describe. Bursting with pent-up need, she kicked the bothersome garment to the foot of the bed and clasped his back. With a sigh, she stroked his corded muscles and worked her way to his firm buttocks. In turn, he nuzzled her sensitive breast, devouring her slippery smoothness. And, inch by inch, his confident fingers searched up her thighs for all the moist, secret places that would give her pleasure.

When he caressed her womanhood, she sucked in her breath and groaned. ''Mother Mary, it feels so good I may faint or die or somethin'.''

Even through his trousers she could feel the heat of his hard maleness as it pressed against her thigh. ''Hell, Carrie . . . you've got too much grit to faint, and you're just too plain ornery to die. Besides, you're just beginning to live.''

His mouth teased and lightly nipped her nipple while his stubbled jaw worked against her breast. When he roughly reclaimed her mouth, new fire flamed deep within her. Her guard completely down, she wondered why she had ever considered him her enemy. She realized her beating heart was his for the taking.

Spurred by his savage kiss, she responded in kind and hungrily met his insistent lips. Soon his hard tongue twined with hers and he rolled over to pin her where she lay. Her eyelids fluttered open in surprise and she watched rosy firelight gleam over his determined face. As she scanned his rugged features she realized she couldn't stop now, even if she wanted to. She eased her mouth away from his and confessed, ''God above, I just met you, and I feel like I've been waitin' for you all my life.'' While she studied his smoky eyes, she added, "Go ahead, enjoy yourself. The Lord knows, myself is all I have to give you."

He quickly slid out of his trousers and tossed them on the floor. No longer frightened, she let her body have its own way as he gathered her into his arms again. Like a team of stubborn horses, her willful passions raced wild and free. Fiery waves of sensation which began in her breasts, darted across her belly and down her legs. Gaining intensity, they whipped through her feet and shot back to her heart.

Soon there was a flurry of movement and confusion, and she felt her wadded skirt beneath her back and the threadbare quilt against her hips. "Carrie, relax your legs, love," he ordered. While he relentlessly teased the seat of her desire, an aching arousal bordering on pain swelled in intensity and demanded release.

Lost in exquisite pleasure, she savored the next moments, all filled with sweet caresses and soft words. His moist breath tickled her ear and his long leg rode hers as he whispered, "That's it, love, let yourself go. Believe what you feel inside!" At last, the artful movement of his fingers prompted her to yield utterly. Soon he crushed her body into the mattress with his possessive weight.

In her fevered excitement she was unaware of all his movements, but a shocking hardness and a smooth, wet warmth against her thigh soon gained her attention. His matted chest thudding evenly, he positioned himself and lowered his torso to her bare bosom. She could feel him slide into her, huge, slick, and powerful. At first she gasped and inched away.

Then he whispered, "My God, *trust*, Carrie . . . trust someone for once . . . I'll see we both enjoy ourselves."

Her trembling arms and legs moved instinctively, and trusting more than she had ever trusted in her life, she pulled him toward her. He grazed her damp face with kisses as he continued stroking her with his fingers. All the powerful feelings he had evoked built to a bursting point, and she wondered how long she could endure the delicious torture.

Throbbing with desire, she clasped his tight buttocks. "Matt . . . I . . . I need—"

"I know what you need." He seized her mouth as he raised himself a bit to protect her from his weight. Then he slid deeper into her tight warmth. With a hoarse moan, he eased away and thrust forward. Quick pain flared between her legs, but a throbbing pleasure rushed up to smother it. Carefully, but forcefully, he moved against her, leisurely skimming over her womanhood, carrying her to ever-rising planes of ecstasy. Just when she thought she would explode with sensation, he eased off, then began again, making her pleasure go on forever, until she could stand no more. Hunger gushed from her heart like a mighty river and, her spirit singing, she felt herself pulse about his hard maleness in endless minutes of sweet release. Only after she had reached joy's last lofty peak did he take his own shuddering pleasure. Then her senses exploded and her heart soared high and free, like a runaway kite that had swirled into the windy sky.

Still sleepy, Carrie raised her head and scanned the blackened fireplace, where charred logs shattered into embers. Stretched on his belly, Bandit lounged nearby. When her bewildered gaze traced Matt's form, each of the night's events rolled into her brain with a sickening thud. "Oh, Lord," she whispered while she eased her head down again, "I'm lying beside a naked man. Mary, Jesus, and Joseph—I've made love to a naked man!"

Wide awake now, she recalled every moment of their lovemaking. In broad daylight everything seemed so different—so sordid. All at once she remembered that her bloomers were lost under the cover. She edged a nervous glance toward the other side of the bed. Gloriously nude except for a bit of strategically placed quilt, Matt slept deeply, his matted chest moving rhythmically. Tears pricked her eyes while she tugged the covers higher and pondered the long-range effects of her abandon. "The **livin' truth be told**," she groaned, "I've totally ruined my life for all time. I've lost sight of my goal to help the miners. Worse than that, I've made love with a man whose very name I hate."

Sighing hopelessly, she wiggled her sore ankle. Her toes snagged the lost bloomers wadded at the foot of the bed, but she knew she couldn't retrieve them without rousing Matt. He moaned and instinctively edged his leg over hers; she was caught like a fox in a trap. "Lord, I've done it now," she breathed. "His eyes will be flyin' open next."

As she studied his handsome face and considered the situation, a shaft of anger shot through her. He had taken advantage of her—plied her with kind words and deeds while she was sick with the fever, then got her liquored up again. She remembered his advice to "trust someone for once" when they had made love. She had obeyed, and look where it had got her! Dear Lord, why hadn't she *trusted* her own experience? Soon her anger hardened into bitter, hurt pride.

Matt's eyes flickered open and he looked at Carrie. Her silky hair was tousled, her eyes bleary, and her clothes rumpled—yet she glowed with beauty. "Good morning," he drawled. When she greeted him with icy silence, he blinked and glanced at her again. The morning sunlight fired her soft hair with glorious highlights and intensified the whiteness of her skin. He grinned as she modestly lowered her heavily lashed eyes. "Are you thinking about last night?" he rasped, tracing her chin with his lean finger. "Come on, don't be shy."

One of her creamy breasts jutted provocatively from her open blouse and invited him to caress its smoothness. But when his fingers brushed her silky nipple, she yanked her blouse together and met his bewildered eyes with a glare. Before he could open his mouth, she squirmed away and swung her legs over the side of the mattress. "Carrie . . . what's wrong? Last night I thought—"

"That's your problem, Matt, you think altogether too

much—and plan, and plot," she interrupted as she hit the floor and limped away, humiliated beyond words. How could she have let all her discipline slide away in one night?

He stared at her in surprise. "Damn, will I ever live long enough to understand women? What's wrong with you now, you little heller? I haven't even had time to greet you with a morning kiss and you're already mad enough to stomp snakes. And what's this about planning and plotting?"

She shoved her blouse into her skirtband and met his eyes. "Don't you *know?* After last night, every man, woman, and child in Colorado will know I'm a shameless hussy when they look at my face. Mam always warned me against somethin' like this happenin', and now I've broken her trust. I've acted like the commonest doxy who ever walked shantytown."

He looked at her and shook his head. "Is that all?"

She clenched her fists and mimicked his voice. " 'Is that all,' the man says."

"Hell, Carrie it's not like it was branded on your forehead or something and—"

"Oh, I know as a confirmed bachelor you ain't thought of it," she cut in, "but as far as marriage goes, I've lost my most precious commodity."

"I thought you didn't want to get married."

"I don't. But if I did, I'd be ruined, wouldn't I? What decent man would want damaged goods?"

"I would, if I loved the woman."

"I said 'decent man,' Mr. Worthington." Matt's face hardened, and he propped himself up and started to pay attention. "I know you'll never offer me matrimony," she went on, hobbling around the bed. "What use would the editor of the *Crested Butte Courier* have with a miner's brat?"

"We have to talk about this, Carrie," he ordered. "We were both asleep and it just kind of happened, didn't it. I think—"

"Just kind of happened?" she thundered.

Hearing her loud voice, Bandit got up and shook himself, then looked at her with puzzled eyes.

Matt flopped back and crossed his muscled arms behind his head. "Hell, Carrie," he mumbled, his face serious, "when we went to bed I had no idea we were going to make love!"

Bitter laughter cracked from her lips and she froze in her tracks. "Is that a fact?" she retorted. "Lord, I've never seen such a man for lyin'. Sweet Mother of God, you're hopeless!"

It was now even more obvious to Carrie that she had made the biggest mistake of her life. Undoubtedly, she would have to pay for it by enduring his gibes for as long as they were together. "I think I'll get my pistol and blast you on the spot," she threatened, shaking her fist for emphasis. "After hearin' the whole sordid story, no jury on earth would convict me."

Matt raised up on one elbow and watched her snatch a poker from the hearth.

"And I may have been weak last night," she confessed in a shaky voice, "but I guarantee there will be no repeat of last night's events." His eyes glittered, and she realized his good mood had spun off like a whirlwind.

"Carrie, I find it hard to believe you're the same woman who responded so passionately only a few hours ago."

Suddenly she stabbed the poker into the floor, making Bandit dart under the bed. "Do you, now?"

He relaxed in lazy splendor and regarded her with hooded eyes. "You know something, Carrie . . . if my memory hasn't failed me, *you* were the one who woke *me* up last night."

His artful thrust hit home. It *was* really all her fault that she had lost a grip on her discipline and humiliated herself. At a loss for words, she pivoted and stared into the smoky fire. Tears stung her eyes while she jabbed at the logs until fresh flames licked the unburned wood.

Although she couldn't back down on her accusation, she decided his position did indeed hold truth. And hadn't she been forewarned that he wasn't the type of man who made a commitment easily? She sarcastically told herself she had lost her bloomers, but she hadn't lost the last remnant of her dignity—yet. She masked her features, then whirled and clanged the poker on the hearth stones. Cool composure would have to carry the day.

He sat up and stared at her. "What in God's name happened to the woman I held in my arms last night?"

"Oh, I'm the same woman—I just started thinkin'," she said as she moved from the fireplace. "And would you be so kind as to cover yourself up!" she ordered primly as she reached the window and looked outside.

Hearing no movement, she spun around again. Damn him! He hadn't moved a muscle. And her request that he cover himself had been completely ignored. "Blood and thunder—do you really think your muscled flesh might soften my resolve, you black-haired rascal? Last night I may have folded, but last night you stacked every card," she declared.

His frown dissolved into a grin, and an urge to claw away that overconfident grin exploded within her. Then she considered those muscled legs propped against the footboard and remembered how they had . . . Lord, I've got to stop it, she thought. But even as she tried to gather up her emotions, little ripples of pleasure stirred her vitals. "Dear God above! Am I losin' all reason? What is happenin' to my poor brain?" she muttered. Why did her insides flutter like a damn bowl of jelly every time she looked at the man?

Matt reached for his discarded suit coat on the floor and found a cheroot and matches. "Carrie, why don't you give up preaching . . . and just stay with lovemaking? That's one area where you don't need any lessons," he added while he lit up. A sly grin splitting his face, he tossed the coat aside and swung off the mattress.

Her eyes shot wide open in surprise. Sweet Mother of God! Matt was strolling toward her—stark naked. A grinning man with tousled hair and no clothes was leisurely ambling toward her! In desperation she searched for Bandit and found his nose peeking from the droopy bedding. "Bandit, come here!" she ordered. The dog eased out on his belly, but when he saw Matt he raised his ears and shot back under the bed. "Bandit, you crazy mutt," she hollered, "it's a naked man with a cigar you're lookin' at—not a grizzly bear!"

Her back against the wall, she turned her attention to Matt again. "Merciful heavens! Have you no shame, man? Ain't . . . ain't you cold?" Heated blood stung her cheeks. Her nervous gaze involuntarily skipped over his tall form, from his wide shoulders to his feet. Faith, why was he so good-lookin'? Why did he have to be so attractive, so downright gorgeous? "Look, Matt . . . last night it was different. Last night it was dark. Last night there was a quilt over us. Last night I didn't know what I was doin'. Last night . . ."

He whipped the cheroot from his clenched teeth and slipped his huge arm around her. Never taking his warm eyes from hers, he lowered his head. His body hovered so close she could smell last night's liquor on his breath, see the stubble on his square jaw, feel the man-heat from his hard maleness as it brushed against her. *Dear Lord*, the man's ready to make love this second . . . *do* somethin', *think* of somethin' to say, she thought while her brain whirred like a top. "Matt . . . as I was sayin' you . . . I . . . I . . ."

"Let's talk later," he whispered in a velvety murmur. "We have better things to do now."

God, why did he have to do this to her? she wondered as his fingers sizzled their way to her hips. To her shame, that now familiar flame once again burst forth in her vitals; that honeyed, languorous sensation seeped through her blood like a potent drug. In a matter of seconds she knew he would carry her to the bed and she would submit; once again she would cast her goals aside and betray her upbringing for a bit of carnal pleasure. Just as his warm lips flickered across hers, a loud wail split the air outside the cabin. Again the long blast shattered the snowy landscape. Startled, she jerked her head back and blurted, "Sweet Jesus—what was *that?*"

A frustrated look slipped over Matt's face and he hung his head. "A train . . . it's a train whistle," he rasped. "I'm afraid our idyll is over. Like it or not, we're being rescued by the good citizens of Crested Butte!"

Chapter 6

⟡ ～⟡⟡～ ⟡

Carrie twisted out of Matt's arms, ran to the window, and pushed the curtain back. Scanning the slope's base, she saw that the steep path to the cabin teemed with activity at the cutoff. A huge, wedge-shaped snowplow with a high, peaked top loomed from the tracks. Two engines and a passenger car trailed the shiny metal plow. Bells clanged. Flags waved. Whistles screamed. Exuberant miners scrambled from the car, while section hands swarmed up the slope like busy ants. Shouting and waving their arms, they attacked the path with shovels. Faith, they're nearly here, she thought when she spotted burly Jack Penrose. The Cornishman, famed for swinging a sledge at fifty strokes a minute, shoveled snow like a high wind scattering leaves. She squinted against the sun and glimpsed an older man awkwardly helping a younger woman from the car.

"Get your clothes on, man. They have a snowplow down there, and a passenger car. The whole world is comin' up that slope! There's a tall, gawky preacher with them, and some fancy woman with blond hair." Matt's eyes shot open at her last statement. She could have sworn his tan faded a bit. With a groan, he slung his cheroot into the fireplace and snatched up his discarded clothes. In record time he jerked on his trousers and buttoned his shirt. Carrie raked through her tangled hair while he flopped on the bed and tugged on his boots. "Why in God's name did you tie that handkerchief to the tree?'' she asked, her voice ground to a razor's edge.

"I wanted to be rescued!''

"Rescued? Faith, we're being invaded!''

A minute later the first miner up the slope banged at the door and made Bandit bark. Seconds later, other noisy men joined the miner. Matt shrugged into his jacket, but before he could answer the door, it sprang open and miners spilled into the room, letting in an icy draft. Their heavy boots scraped the floor as they whistled and laughed, showing tobacco-stained teeth. Red-faced from drink and the cold, they whooped joyously and slapped the stunned pair on their backs. Bandit raced in circles and barked wildly.

"Yahoo! We done it, boys!'' came a raucous cry.

"Dad blame,'' another hollered, tossing his derby into the air, "I was afeared they was goners!''

"Carrie, my beautay . . . damme, what are you doin' 'ere with 'im?'' Jack Penrose blurted, his open face awash with surprise.

Carrie rolled her eyes at the great bear of a man. "It's a long story, Jack . . . too long for tellin' now.''

"Where's Joe, and Tim . . . and the fireman, and that new kid?'' asked a bearded man. "Diggin' out the train?''

Matt sighed and looked him in the eye.

"Hold on a minute, Mr. Worthington. You mean it was somethin' worse than a bad drift?'' the man asked, his face saddening.

"Yes, I'm afraid so. There was a full-scale avalanche, boys. The men are in the cab . . . unfortunately it's at the bottom of the ravine.''

"Oh, no—not ole Joe!'' lamented one miner. Groans and oaths filled the room, and the men broke into muttering clusters.

A stooped old-timer tugged on Jack Penrose's sleeve. "Hey, what'd he say?'' he asked loudly, squinting up at the big man.

" 'Twas an avalanche, dad! All them railroaders was wiped out," the Cornishman hollered.

A commotion at the open door drew everyone's attention. Matt looked over to see Jenny Parker stamping her feet. The racket sent Bandit into another barking fit. Shaking snow from her long cape, Jenny swept into the room. "Did I heard someone say avalanche?" she wailed. "Oh, Matt, how horrid!"

With concerned whispers, the men stood aside and made a path for her and Reverend Parker, who rasped for breath. Jenny tossed her blue cape aside and hugged Matt's neck. A modest, like-colored gown skimmed over her slender figure. Rice powder whitened her face and rouge delicately pinkened her cheeks and lips. After she had chucked aside a fur muff, she slid her fingers over Matt's arms.

"Jenny, how in hell did you get here?"

She fluttered her lashes demurely. "Why, Matt, when you didn't meet me for supper, I went to your office. On the way back to the Elk Mountain House I met the stableboy. He told me you got on the train with some woman just before dark. I've been worried sick about you. Why, you missed the church potluck dinner."

"Sorry, Jenny . . . I was delayed by an avalanche." Laughter rippled among the miners.

Carrie's eyes narrowed. Something about the woman's churchly attire just didn't set right. Although her dress and manner were demure, Carrie sensed they masked a different persona. Wait a minute—Matt had called her Jenny . . . Jenny, was it? Fire raced through her as she realized this lovely Dresden doll with the pale face and long lashes was the same woman who had thrown away her letters. Suddenly something exploded in her brain. Surely this woman couldn't be his assistant. He had made it sound like Jenny was an old lady. Obviously there was a connection between the two, if Jenny's behavior was any indication. How could he have made love to her with such passion when he was Jenny's lover, too!

"Reverend Parker," Matt went on, "I certainly didn't expect you either."

"Are . . . are you all right?" the reverend asked in a tentative manner. "You gave us quite a start. The telegraph wires have been humming like bees. That first night the key man at Crested Butte didn't get a wink of sleep. When he sent the swamper to the saloon to fetch food, the old man told everyone what was going on."

"Where did Gunnison find that snowplow?" asked Matt while he moved away from Jenny. "There can't be more than one or two in the state."

"Well, it wasn't an easy task. They finally located one way up north. And wasn't that lucky for you, my son?"

"Mmm, right—lucky for me!"

Reverend Parker glanced at Jack Penrose, who beamed like a schoolboy. "Jack was at the saloon. He organized some miners to join the section hands when the Denver and Rio Grande finally got the plow to Crested Butte yesterday. I'm afraid my little girl talked him into taking us along."

A frown wrinkled Matt's brow as he studied the Cornishman. "I still don't see how you found us."

" 'Twas nothin'," boasted Jack. "I was ridin' in the cab, and with the weight of that big plow 'oldin' us back to a snail's pace, I spotted your flag right easy. I remembered ole Botsie 'ad a cabin here . . . but he's been out of town for a month. Coo, when I saw your smoke—that just about clinched it."

Carrie thought Reverend Parker had a tired, sour look about him, and an air of self-righteousness that clung to him like mildew. Obviously the man endured his Christianity like a daily dose of castor oil.

She looked back at the preacher's daughter, who had sidled up to Matt again. Despite her wholesome airs, the woman's eyes looked as hard as an old maid's biscuits. Couldn't anyone else see it? She pegged Jenny as one of those unfortunate persons who had never really loved another human being in their life. She watched the woman bat her lashes at Matt. It was plain Jenny had somethin' itchin' that needed to be scratched. Just how much scratchin' Matt had done ripped the lid off a whole new box of problems.

Jenny moved her gaze toward Carrie. "Matt, who is this . . . this person . . . and why are you together?"

"This is Miss Carrie O'Leary, Jenny. She and I were . . . were investigating a story."

"Investigating a story? My, how interesting!" Jenny's eyes flashed. "Father dear, don't you think you and Jack should escort the rest of the men outside? They can clear away more snow . . . and someone has to tell the engineer about those poor railroaders."

"Yeah," mumbled one man. "There's a sad job to be done yet."

The reverend finally noticed her prodding stare. "Ahem . . . oh, yes, yes, perhaps you're right!"

Jack Penrose ushered the murmuring men outside. "C'mon, lads," he ordered " 'Op to it, now. We can't waste the 'ole bloody day, can we?"

After Jack had closed the door, Jenny adjusted her lace cuffs. "Well, Miss O'Leary . . . now that they're gone, let me introduce myself properly. I'm Jenny Parker," she announced, walking about the cabin with her arms crossed in front of her. Receiving no reaction, she continued. "I've been Matt's assistant for three years, and if I do say so, I now know a great deal about the newspaper business."

Carrie murmured, "Too bad you've been too busy buyin' clothes and fixin' your hair to do anything about it." She scanned the woman closer. She was pretty the way a brilliantly marked coral snake was pretty: all cool and poised—and lethal. And were those tiny lines around her eyes?

"Can't you think of anything to say, dear?" Jenny shook her head and moved behind the table. "Oh, how silly of me. That's all right. You wouldn't be interested, would you? I'd almost forgotten how few of the miners' children get a chance for any higher education."

"I beg your pardon, miss," interjected Carrie. "I've been to school . . . but I'm gettin' over it just fine." Her eyes gleamed. "I can think almost as good as I did before I went to Denver."

When Matt's lips twitched upward, Jenny glared at him. "Oh, Matt, that's not funny!" The blonde slid her gaze to the rumpled bed and pressed her lips together. "I must say this looks . . . looks . . ."

Her jaw set, Carrie moved toward the woman. Bandit trailed behind her. "Is 'suspicious' the word you're lookin' for? Are you thinkin' what you'd do yourself?"

Jenny looked hurt. "No, of course not, but as the Scriptures say—I think the half has not yet been told."

"No, but you'll probably invent it, won't you!"

Jenny looked like someone had just thrown a bucket of icy water in face. *"Well!* I never. . . . You know what I think?" she snapped. "I think you arranged this whole thing so you could get Matt to yourself!"

As cool as an undertaker's smile, Carrie petted her dog's head, then stated, "Now that's the first nice thing you've said to me since you came in the door. Arrangin' an avalanche is quite an accomplishment. Mother Mary, *think,* miss! I know it will be a little unnatural at first, but you might like it."

"That does it!" Jenny exclaimed. "I won't endure this person a moment longer than I have to. I'm going outside to ask Father how long it will be before we can leave this wretched place." Eyeing Carrie, she flung on her cape and stalked out.

Matt watched Carrie standing there looking wicked, wanton, and tousled. Loose auburn hair tumbled over one shoulder and green fire flashed from her eyes. He strode forward and wrapped her in his arms while Bandit looked at him jealously. "You're doing fine, brat. Sorry I didn't have time to warn you about Jenny."

She squirmed and tried to shove him away. "Sorry, is it? No, I'm the one who's sorry I ever got mixed up with the likes of you! You let me think she was an old woman, not . . . not what she is."

Matt grinned as he held her at arm's length. "Love, I'm afraid you came to that brilliant deduction yourself. I never said anything of the kind. Of course, if you can't stand the competition . . ."

Carrie's eyes snapped. "Competition? Competition from that stiff, lacquered piece of wood? I'd as soon be in competition with a mud turtle! Faith, it gives me shivers just to think what I'd see if that powdered mask fell away. And you'd better check her birth certificate, if she hasn't burned it!" She twisted away and paced to the window, jerking back the flour-sack curtain.

Matt moved behind her and glanced out the window. Near the cabin, Jenny and her father were in a heated conversation. Down the slope he spotted the miners clustered around Jack Penrose. He peered at the sky, now darkening with new snow clouds, then watched Carrie blink away silvery tears.

She turned and glared at him. "For all I care," she plunged on, "the blacksmith can yoke you two together and sell you to the devil as a team!"

He bit off the end of a cheroot and spit it on the floor. His dark gaze flickered over her lush body while anger trickled through him. Even now, a part of him ached to caress her silky hair and comfort her—but after those words, it would be a frosty Friday in August before he did.

"First I hear about this famous music-hall singer you admire so much; now I find out you've been enjoyin' a bit of entertainment right here in Crested Butte!"

He lit the cheroot and squinted at her. This clever, willful child had to be taught a lesson. A man couldn't call himself a man and countenance words like he had just heard. "You should try writing," he drawled in a bored tone, aiming for her sore spot. "You do have a way with words, you know."

"What do you think I've been trying to do?" she

spouted. "There's always some editor or editor's assistant like Jenny standin' in my way. Someday I'll learn all about journalism and I'll start my own newspaper!"

"I think the possibility of that happening is rather remote, my girl." He scanned her angry face and leisurely puffed smoked into the air. "You know, you sound to me like you're just mad at yourself."

"I am! I'm mad at myself 'cause I let down my guard for a man who's slick enough to be involved with two women. I expected more of myself. I thought I was a better judge of character than that. You almost had me believin' I'd been wrong about rich people—and you ain't nothin' but a rich philanderer yourself!" Defiance boiled in her eyes as she looked at him. "Why did I ever think for one minute that I liked you? Damn you! All that talk about unions and your kind deeds when I was sick were just a ruse to win my trust." He started to speak, but she cut him off. "I'll not ask for your assistance again. With God's help, I'll go on alone. My body might be addicted to you, but my mind ain't."

Jenny's entrance interrupted Carrie's speech. She slid off her cape, then slumped down on the bed and covered her face with white hands. "Dear Lord, it will be another fifteen minutes. If Miss O'Leary speaks to me again so harshly, I will die." She looked beseechingly at Matt, who had reclaimed a place by the mantel. "As my employer, how can you let her talk to me in such a vile manner?"

"You don't need my help, Jenny. You're a big girl now, remember? With all your writing skills, surely you can come up with a few words in your own defense." Coolly amused, he studied her shocked face. Despite her frequent pleas that he marry her, he had sidestepped the matter. She had eagerly offered her charms, and he had accepted. As an amusing diversion after a hard day's work, she fit the bill, but the thought of actually marrying the woman struck chills down his spine, and he was damned if he'd fight her battles for her.

"Oh, how can you be so cruel after all I've done for you?" She moaned and clenched a lace hankie against her brow, her other hand clutching at the rumpled quilt. If she had touched a rattlesnake she couldn't have gone whiter. Gasping, she sat up and slid Carrie's bloomers from beneath the quilt. She looked as if she might explode as she shot to her feet and held them at arm's length. "And *what*, my I ask, are these?" Satisfaction spread over her face at Carrie's blush. "Cat got your tongue, dear? I have a feeling your feet aren't the only part of your anatomy that's bare, Miss O'Leary!" When Carrie said nothing, Jenny rattled on. "And for a person of my breeding to discover something like this—"

"Hold on! You're puttin' your thumb on the scale a little, ain't you, miss!" Carrie interrupted. She moved menacingly toward Jenny. His hackles raised, Bandit followed behind. "You know what I think, Miss Parker?" she added. "I think you're not so holy—you're just self-righteous!"

Jenny spluttered and glared at Matt. "Matt, how *could* you—and with this little Irish baggage!" She shook her finger at him. "Don't think I'm going to ignore this. I *can't* ignore it . . . why, it's my Christian duty to root out sin wherever I may find it!"

He coughed and suppressed a smile. "Root out sin? That's a good line," he said, remembering the torrid afternoon she had met him in the storeroom in her underclothes. He watched Carrie and Bandit approach Jenny like wily bobcats and wondered if the blonde could move as fast as she lied.

Carrie looked at the woman holding out her bloomers as if they were lice-infested. "Just a minute, miss. I think your mouth is spinnin' faster than your brain again. Let's go over that part about rootin' out sin once more. I can splice together some lies to make a truth, but who wants to limp in on that? 'Deed, I did enjoy Mr. Worthington's company on an intimate basis last night, as I'm sure you've done on numerous occasions."

"Why, not really—er, I mean no—no, certainly not! That's a sick, desperate thought."

"That's right. When your ship is sinkin', the truth is always the first thing to go overboard, ain't it?" Carrie proclaimed, sidling even closer.

"No, I don't lie! I'm against sin in all its forms."

"You're against anything that someone else can do better than you, ain't you?"

"Oh, shut up! You're talking to me like I'm an idiot."

Carrie puckered her lips and looked thoughtful. "Well, yes," she agreed. "If you act like an idiot, people tend to treat you that way."

"If you and that beast come a step closer, I'm going to do something drastic!" Jenny warned, flitting her gaze about the cabin.

"There you go again, miss. Never cock your pistol unless you've got a bullet in the chamber . . . and remember, when your back is against the wall, silence is the fool's best friend. It's worth a ton of fancy chat."

Jenny's eyes glassed over and the skin around her mouth went chalk-white. "Auggh—I hate you! I'll make you sorry, you little hussy!" she screeched. Her eyes wild, she wadded the bloomers into a ball and sailed them into the fire.

Carrie's mouth formed a horrified O as she rushed for the fireplace. She tried to rake the bloomers out with the poker, but the well-worn material burst into colorful flames. Spinning on her heel, she flung down the poker and went for Jenny. With the strength of three, she shook the frightened woman so hard, hairpins shot from her lacquered hair. At the same time, Bandit tugged at Jenny's skirt and tried to pull her down. Matt rushed over and slipped between the struggling women. "God Almighty, Carrie, you'll throttle her! Restrain yourself!"

"*Restrain* myself? Mary, Jesus, and Joseph—the woman threw my flamin' drawers in the fire!" Jenny burst into theatrical sobs as Matt wrenched her skirt from the dog's jaws. Carrie eyed the pair with distaste when Jenny heaved herself on his chest. "A good-lookin', lyin' man and a blubberin', spiteful woman," she declared. "That's the trouble with fools—they always come in pairs. Well, you're good enough for each other, and you can *have* each other!"

At that moment, Reverend Parker and several of the miners burst into the cabin with puzzled looks on their faces. "What in merciful heaven is wrong with Jenny?" the preacher asked.

"Oh, nothing much," Matt answered awkwardly. "Just a case of nerves, I imagine. Are you ready to go, Carrie?" he added in a sharp voice.

While Carrie slipped into her jacket and oversized boots, Jenny pushed back the curtain and glanced at the sky. "Oh, dear," she sniffled, blowing her red nose into the lacy hankie, "here I am in velvet and it looks like we're in for another flurry."

Carrie slung on her head shawl, then pushed ahead of the others and clomped over the doorsill. With stormy eyes, she raked Jenny's trembling form and observed, "Flurry? Lady, you're underestimatin' things. We're goin' to have a damn blizzard!"

Chapter 7

Her fingers clenched, Carrie tore into the roast chicken that sat on the counter. "I'll beat you yet, Matt Worthington, you smooth-talkin' rascal," she vowed, slinging a drumstick into a picnic basket. She had traded her woolen skirt and white blouse for a light cotton frock, stitched at home. Her mind racing, she pushed back her hair and continued her work. Two whole months had slid away since the debacle at Botsie's cabin, but Matt's memory still burned in her mind. She gritted her teeth and pulled off another drumstick, wishing it were one of his legs.

"If you think you can break my spirit, you overeducated rascal—you're dead wrong," she muttered while she peered through the kitchen window. A gentle breeze trembled the budding trees and ruffled the bright wildflowers. In the distance the snowy Rockies glistened under the sun. Apple trees had greened and the fields warmed—the old season had slipped away like water through sandy ground, but Matt's rakish features and warm voice still lurked in her heart.

Turning, she wiped her greasy hands on her apron and scanned the shack she and Shamus called home—a kitchen, two bedrooms, and a collection of shabby furniture and broken dreams. Asleep, Bandit sprawled under the oilcloth-covered table. She looked at her dog and sighed, thinking that most of the folks she knew were like him—just interested in eating and sleeping. To add to her depression, two more miners had perished since the avalanche. Obviously John Worthington didn't care. No, he wheeled from one spending spree to the next, as if the devil were after him with a sharp stick.

Hands on her hips, she circled the littered table, then paused to sail a wad of paper across the room. She shoved a gnawed pencil behind her ear and kept pacing. Did anyone care? she wondered. Had the whole Western Slope sunk into a pit of apathy? Was everyone blind and deaf? And why were her plans always blocked? How could she get folks interested in a union when they just wanted to eat and sleep? She leaned against the cluttered counter and rubbed her temples. Surely she could think of something to rouse people. Ideas were like grasshoppers: if a person whipped enough weeds, he was bound to turn up a few.

Shamus O'Leary slammed the squeaky screen door. "What are you thinkin' about, me darlin'?" His broad face beaming, he sauntered into the kitchen with some purple lilacs. A short, thickset man, Shamus wore a faded linsey-woolsey shirt and tweed britches. Red suspenders hugged his ample belly and brogans shod his feet.

Carrie watched Shamus move to the counter while he fingered the flowers, whose sweet, heavy fragrance tickled her nose. "Nothin', Da. I was just dreamin'," she lied.

"Mmm . . . dreamin', is it? I'm well acquainted with the problem meself," he rasped, shoving the flowers into a tall glass. He trickled a dipper of water into the glass, then thoughtfully eyed her face. "The way you were tearin' up that bird and talkin' to yourself," he added in a gravelly voice, "I thought you might be thinkin' of a certain newspaper editor, who'd blind the holy angels themselves."

"No, Da! We've gone over this forty times since the accident! Why do you keep bringin' it up? He's a Worthington, ain't he? I never felt anythin' but contempt for the man. Why, I—I can hardly remember what the scoundrel looks like." She stared out the window again, thinking she would say a long prayer before she went to bed. Shamus clasped the glass and shuffled to the table. He looked as if he wanted to say more. Instead, he plunked the flowers down and eased into a rickety chair.

Carrie studied him. Now why in God's name had the old man brought up Matt Worthington? She ran a hand over her arm as blood warmed her cheeks. Would she ever forget the touch of the man's hand, or the way his eyes sparkled when he smiled? Angry for letting her mind wander, she reined in her emotions. Damn Matt Worthington, anyway!

Promising herself she wouldn't think of the rogue, she gazed at her father again. Soft light silvered his curly hair as he sniffed the feathery blossoms. When he caressed the lilacs with his callused fingers, she felt guilty about her sharp words. Nearby on a crude bench, his mended jacket and battered derby lay ready for an outing. Why did he want to go on a picnic near Botsie's cabin anyway? What in heaven was the old fox planning? His story of a spring frolic didn't fool her. He obviously had something up his sleeve. Love pricking her heart, she eyed him more closely, and realized he was melancholy. Her voice tender, she joined him and said, "You're thinkin' of Ireland, ain't you, Da?" She edged her chair to his.

"Aye, that I am," he confessed, looking somewhat embarrassed. " 'Tis a queer thing . . . but when the air's so light, and the earth's so fresh, me old heart aches a bit. Of course, 'tis a foolish thing, and a man would be well served to avoid it!"

"Maybe you'll see Killarney again."

"Nay, crossin' the great sea is for rich men, darlin'. When your mam and me came over, it took all we had. I've cast me lot . . . I've got to make me fortune here."

His words added to the mounting pressure she already felt. How could he make his fortune here when John Worthington was squeezing the life out of him?

Shamus's eyes misted as he looked at Carrie. "You look just like her, girl . . . God rest her lovely soul. I can see her in me mind's eye the day we left, holdin' to your hand. 'We're leavin' home,' I says. 'No,' she says. 'We're goin' home. Wherever we're together is home.' " He swallowed hard and shook his grizzled head. "Blood and blunderbushes, what a fine woman she was . . . and so strong! We had such dreams . . . 'tis a sad thing I turned out so poor!"

"Hush, Da!" Carrie blurted. "Now you'll be after tellin' me you're a failure and all. 'Tis a frightenin' thing to think a man's value can be measured by the coins in his pocket."

"Aye, 'tis plain you're speakin' of Mr. Worthington himself now. The blaggard's so stingy-hearted he'd skin a flea for the hide. And him spinnin' around in his new carriage, while the lads are droppin' for lack o' ice when they come out o' the steamin' pits. Why, the hoist floor's so rotten I cross meself every time I step onto it!"

"Merciful heavens, why don't the men speak up, Da? Why do they put up with it?"

He heaved a deep sigh and shook his head. "Well, you see, that's what's so bad about bein' poor. A man who's held his hat in his hand all his life don't know how to speak up. He's afraid o' losin' his job an' failin' his family. Why, with a hundred Chinamen waitin' to take his place, he's scared to death. So he just takes his chances o' gettin' killed, hopin' it won't happen."

She pulled the pencil stub from behind her ear and slapped it on the table. "But there are other mines!"

"By the time a man's been here three months and been paid in that worthless script, he owes his soul to the Silver Queen's company store. Aye, those are the sad facts, lass. No matter how hard I work, we'll always be as poor as lizard-eatin' cats, and you know 'tis God's own truth."

Carrie scraped back her chair and stood, rousing Bandit. Anger blazed through her at the injustice of it all. Her heart ached as she looked at Shamus's dejected form. "Poor, is it?" She caressed his curls; then, her hands clenched behind her, she paced toward a potbellied stove. Bandit followed and stretched out on the cool tiles by the stove. "You're just lookin' at the dark side of it, Da," she said over her shoulder. "To tell the truth, I haven't minded bein' poor." She turned and studied him. "I always had you and Mam, and we had each other. What else could I want?"

Shamus raised his head and managed a smile. "Me darlin' girl . . ."

"Besides, when you're poor," she went on, "your mind is your own." She snapped her fingers at him. "It's—it's liberatin', that's what it is! If society's demands don't make sense, you can just chuck them aside like a hunk of spoiled meat and go on with your own rat killin'. Why, some folks are weighted down with riches, and they ain't happy. No, Da, I'd say I had a definite advantage, bein' poor. It sharpens your wits and makes you think."

Shamus scraped his white-stubbled jaw and chuckled. "Aye, that's one way o' lookin' at it. O' course, bein' poor is so damn time-consumin'." He scanned her, concern washing over his ruddy face. "But, darlin', tell me . . . didn't you miss the fancy dresses and the pretty dancin' shoes?"

"No, never." She raised her brow and grinned. "Besides, I had no place to wear them." They both laughed as she sat down and rubbed his knee. "Mother Mary, who wants to be dressed up like some stiff, helpless doll, afraid of spillin' somethin' on yourself? I'd rather be doin' somethin'—usin' my mind." She waved her reddened hand at the papers littering the table. "Like writin' on somethin'."

Pride flashed in Shamus's watery eyes. "Aye, and I know you're speakin' the truth now, darlin'. You always were a little preacher and could twist words faster than the devil on payday."

"I love the way the words bounce around in your head, and surprise you the way they shoot out," she said. "And perhaps 'tis prideful, but I want to write somethin' that holds, and makes people laugh and think, and helps them keep on fightin'. And someday, I'd like to see those words wrapped up in a fine leather book, or standin' all black and crisp on the front page of a newspaper.''

He chuckled at her enthusiasm. ''Aye, 'twould be a great thing, darlin'.''

She walked to the counter and tossed the disjointed chicken into the picnic basket. How could she have been so selfish? she wondered. In the tin cabinet she found bread and hard-boiled eggs and she added them to the basket. Surely a spring outing wasn't that much to ask, considering the man had supported her with his own sweat all her life. Pulling a dish of fruit toward her, she eyed Shamus again. ''Well, what are you waitin' on, Da—*Christmas?* Get your jacket on.'' Love warmed her voice. ''It'll be noon if we don't get goin'!''

Chapter 8

Shamus stretched his legs into the grass while he rested against the flowering pear tree. He looked tremendously pleased with himself as he surveyed his surroundings. Nearby, bees buzzed in the clover and birds warbled in the trees. Farther out, two mounts drank from the rushing creek. Beyond the creek, green foothills rolled into the shadowy trees. On the horizon, silvery mountains stood out against a blue sky. Shoving back his derby, he leaned forward and stared at the creek.

There he goes, lookin' at that water again, Carrie thought as she rolled onto her side. She brushed bread crumbs from the quilt and studied him suspiciously, then sat up. What in the world was wrong with him? Why was he so moody, and why had he walked the creek bank five times since they arrived? "Da, what are you thinkin' about?" she hollered. "I can hear the wheels grindin' in your head way over here."

"Now that the sun is right, look how that gravel bar sparkles," he answered. "Looks like it could be sprinkled with gold dust."

She squinted at the sun-dappled creek, which babbled around the gravel bar. *"Gold dust?"* Irritation rippled over her and washed away her warm feeling for him. That, she thought, was his silliest idea yet! No man alive could celebrate life more than Shamus O'Leary, but why did he always have to be such a dreamer? Why did he come up with these fantastic notions, and always seek solace in a whiskey bottle when he was inevitably disappointed? "Oh, Da, 'tis more of your Irish dreamin', and you know it!''

With a shrug, he stretched his short arms and rose. "Let's ramble to the water and look," he suggested. "Carrie, since you're closest, fetch a glass out o' the basket for your old da." Shamus sauntered to the creek while the horses eased away to crop grass. At the water's edge he dug up a handful of sloshy sand and examined it. As soon as Carrie arrived with a short, wide-mouthed glass, he scooped up more sand and poured it into the container. He spun the slush, making its whispering sound mingle with the creek's soft noise.

Carrie watched the mixture slide over the glass rim. "What are you lookin' for, Da?"

"I'm lookin' for gold, me darlin'. If there's any flour in the slush, 'twill sink to the bottom. The lighter sand will wash over the top."

A frown tightened her forehead. "Flour?"

Shamus raised his bushy brows. "Aye, gold dust. If we had a pan, the color would stick to the rough bottom."

She shook her head. "Da, you know the gold played out in these parts long ago."

" 'Deed it hasn't, love. This whole side o' Colorado is striped with silver and gold. Don't be forgettin', Three Arrows was one o' the richest diggings in the state."

"What makes you sure you'll find it here?" She eyed the slush as it dribbled over his hand.

Shamus stood and squinted upstream. "See how the river slows down and levels out afore it gets here? When a current slacks off, it leaves colors in low places. Aye, if there's any color in this creek, 'twould be here."

Doubt welled up inside her. "We've walked this land before. There was no talk of gold then. Are you after tellin' me this happened while no one was lookin'?"

"Blood an' thunder, Carrie . . . I'm after tellin' you the avalanche changed the way the creek flows," he explained patiently.

She widened her eyes. "You've been thinking about this for days, haven't you?"

"One month and twenty-seven days, to be exact, love. A man gets a whole new hand o' cards with a landslide."

She laughed and reappraised him. "Why didn't you say anythin' before this, you rascally devil?"

"I says to meself, Shamus, no use overburdenin' the child with another worry. She's been disappointed so much you'd be an idjit to do it again."

"Lord, Da, it looks like every man in Crested Butte would be up here."

"Aye, it does, and the smart ones might, if Clayright hadn't been nippin' at their heels twelve hours a day so they could scarcely drag themselves to bed."

With a deep chuckle, he knelt and swirled the glass until all the water spilled out. Carrie squatted by his side as he stuck his thumb and forefinger into the slush and pulled out a pinch of drag. While the creek babbled and the birds twittered, Shamus rubbed the gritty mud between his fingers. Soon gold flecks popped from the muck.

Carrie's heart thumped. "Is . . . is it . . . gold?"

"We'll see in a moment, darlin'." Shamus gazed skyward and crossed himself, then lowered his head and pinched the flecks. Standing, he threw his derby skyward and let out a whoop of joy. The curious horses raised their heads while he danced over the gravel bar. She clasped his shoulders, trying to calm him.

His face bright with ecstasy, he rasped, "Irish dreamin', is it? What do ye think o' yer Irish dreamin' now?"

Tears streamed from her eyes as he pulled her across the gravel bar. "Da, listen!" She held his wild eyes with hers. "How . . . how do you know it's not pyrite?"

"Pyrite? It's not pyrite, me darlin' girl, because it's soft. Pyrite is hard and brittle. Pyrite blinks an' winks . . . gold gleams with an even light." He wrapped her in a bear hug, swung her off the ground, then eased her feet onto the sand again. "Oh, Carrie, we've found a rich placer full o' flood gold."

She pushed him to arm's length and shook him. "Da, what are you talkin' about now?"

He squatted and studied the creek again. His eyes flashed like a young boy's. "Where the flour is this rich, there *has* to be a pay streak on the bottom o' the creek. You know, love—gold that's sunk through the sand and is restin' on bedrock."

She put her hands on her hips and sauntered to his side. "Well, not bein' a fish, tell me what you're goin' to do about it."

He stood and clasped her shoulders. "We'll just dam up the water and slice out the wonderful stuff."

"Wait a minute, in your excitement I think you're forgettin' one thing," she stated, wagging her finger. "Who does this land belong to? It's awful close to Botsie's, ain't it?"

Shamus chuckled and rubbed his chin. "Aye, but it misses his place by a good three-quarter mile. If he'd been home instead o' at Cripple Creek, the old scallywag would have already found it. When he gets back he'll be sick as a skunked dog and dig up every foot o' his place! If he finds nothin', I'll make sure he never goes wantin'."

"So you're goin' to slice the gold out like butter, are you, now? Begorra, can it really be done? How much could we take out?"

"Workin' from first light till dusk, forty to fifty dollars a day. Oh, Carrie, we're goin' to be rich as Horace Tabor himself. And I'm thinkin' that's just the beginnin'!"

Happiness sizzled through Carrie. This was wonderful! She could buy newspaper space from Matt instead of begging for it. She would have hundreds of notices printed and she would stick them in every door in town. She would call public meetings about the union and she would see Denver lawyers. Why, she would stir up such a fuss, Matt would spit out his cigar and Jenny would choke. And John Worthington? Why, that rascal would have a heart attack. *Thank God*, she could make people listen now.

Her father shook her arm. "Carrie, quit dreamin' and

look at me. This flour had to come from some place. I'll
bet me teeth the avalanche uncovered a blowup. That,
me darlin' girl, is the real pot o' gold at the end o' the
rainbow.''

"There you go again, Da. Talkin' so I can't understand.''

"O' course, I keep forgettin' you're a toplander," Shamus said as he raked through his windblown hair. "A
blowup is the end o' a protrudin' vein." He eyed her
thoughtfully. "Let's amble up that hill," he suggested,
pointing at a nearby rise. "By the lay o' the land, it stands
to reason there was a wash-off. Look for a float, darlin'—
that's a chunk o' quartz broken off the blowup. It'll be
pink and rusty-lookin'.''

Fueled by fresh zeal, she lifted her skirt and ran up the
incline. Soft earth spilled into her old slippers as she
climbed and scanned the hill. Her father picked up rocks
and thudded them aside while he trailed behind. She
scrambled ahead and searched harder than ever.

A backbreaking hour dragged by, but at last she dis-
lodged some cloudy quartz from a cluster of bear grass.
"What's this, Da?" she hollered back at him, holding the
warm quartz up in the air. "It looks interestin', don't it?''

The wind tugging his hair, Shamus hurried to her side
and took the quartz. Squatting on the grassy incline, he
smashed it with another rock. When the quartz cracked in
half, he spit on it and rubbed it on his pants. Soon yellow
flecks glinted in the bright sunlight. With a great whoop,
he hugged Carrie. " 'Deed there's a vein up there, love.
I'm sure o' it now. It'll take a few weeks, but we'll look
till we find it.''

She sank down on the green hill and pulled her father
to her side. Honeybees droned nearby. Far below, the
horses cropped tall grass near the rushing creek. Full of
happiness, Carrie pulled at some wild clover and watched
puffy clouds float across the blue sky. Her father pushed
himself up on his elbow and kissed her hand impulsively.
Twirling a long-stemmed clover, she winked at him mis-

chievously. "Well, Da, I see you're too excited to come up with a name for this bonanza, so I guess I'm goin' to have to do it. Why don't we name her the Shamrock, after this clover?"

"Aye—the Shamrock it is!" When she sighed, he stared at her with troubled eyes. "Carrie, darlin', what in the world could be wrong now?"

"Oh, it will be a hard burden to bear," she announced in a droll tone.

"What burden are you talkin' about, girl?"

"Bein' rich, of course. But if your mind is set—I suppose I can put up with it!"

A bell jangled as Carrie slammed the assayer's door. Her nose wrinkling, she scanned the cramped, sulfur-scented office.

Seconds later, Shamus strode in and banged his fist on a little table. "I've come to have me gold assayed," he proclaimed.

Brass lamps pooled light on the cluttered counters and drew Carrie's interest. She trailed her fingers over the smooth chemical vials while they waited for service, then tucked in her old work shirt. With a sigh, she turned and walked to the gold-lettered window. There on Elk Street grim-faced miners hurried to work. After a moment, she crossed the light-streaked floor and, spreading out her stained skirt, claimed a counter stool.

When no one came, Shamus jerked open a shabby drape and hollered into the storeroom, "Ain't no one here? I said I've come to have me gold assayed."

A small, bald man finally pushed back the ringed drape and eased into the room. Spectacles perched on his nose and a white apron lapped around his thin frame. "Gold, you say?" he softly echoed.

"Aye, gold it is. Me name is Shamus O'Leary, and like I've been tryin' to tell you, I've come to have me gold assayed."

The slight man coughed and smiled. "Why, Mr.

O'Leary, there hasn't been any gold in these parts for years now."

Shamus shoved back his battered derby and slapped two bulging pouches on the counter. "Is that right? Well, what is this stuff, then?"

The little, dried apple of a man opened the pouches and scanned the contents with disbelief. "Oh, yes . . . yes, I see what you mean."

"Well, can you do it, man?" Shamus asked, hitching up his tweed pants.

The assayer eyed the drape with a troubled air. "Yes . . . yes, of course. All right . . . I'll take the gold now," he informed them in a squeaky voice. "I'll be working in the back." The little man looked over his hunched shoulder, then snatched up the pouches and slid behind the drape like a beetle.

Shamus dragged out a stool and plopped down. A smile split his face as he rolled up his sleeves and studied Carrie. "Now, what was wrong with that fellow, darlin'? I've never seen such a nervous little man."

"He looked like he was about to bust with the news. I have a feelin' after today that mountain will be swarmin' with the general riffraff, Da."

"Let them swarm! I staked off the claim with strong stobs, with me name and the location boldly marked. If any claim jumper wants me land, he'll have to walk through a load o' buckshot first. I'll be usin' this dust to buy a good tent and supplies. After today, Shamus O'Leary will be livin' by the creek, protectin' his claim."

She cocked her head and frowned. "What good will protectin' it do if we can't work it? Right now we've got seven dollars to our name. Minin' requires money."

"True, if you're wantin' silver, it does. Silver has to be blasted out and expensive shafts sunk. With placer minin', we can do it ourselves! Me and Botsie will get sluice boxes and long toms, and pan the whole damn vein. With the flood gold, and the pay streak, we'll be ridin' a gravy train with biscuit wheels!" Shamus beamed and raised his bushy brows. "Darlin', right now I feel so good I'm jealous o' meself!"

Carrie laughed and sauntered to the plate glass window. She scanned the traffic on Elk Street. At the street's end a long mule team wound up the hill to the Silver Queen. Across the way, women with arm baskets entered the busy general store. Closer by, boys rattled hoops over the planked sidewalk. With a weary sigh, she glanced at the wall clock. What in heaven was keeping the assayer? When she looked through the window again, alarm flooded through her. *There* was the assayer. And he was slipping out of the Elk Mountain House Hotel, looking as guilty as an egg-sucking dog! She widened her eyes as he dodged transport wagons and hurried across the street.

He couldn't even wait until tomorrow. Obviously he had told everyone at the hotel about the gold, but she knew someone special had paid him to report the strike. When he slipped around the corner, her gaze shot back to the hotel's entrance. Lord, Matt and Jenny were coming out, too—and they were coming right her way, making a bee-line for the assayer's office. Carrie glanced at her work-stained clothes, then at Jenny, who was dressed beautifully and painted up like a new saloon. Miners and business-men now streamed from the hotel, stopping angry team-sters.

Before she could speak, a door slammed at the back of the shop and rattled the chemical vials. Whirling, she looked at Shamus's confused face. "Da, that sneaky as-sayer has told everyone in the hotel about the gold and they're all pourin' across the street." As Shamus's chin dropped, Matt and Jenny opened the belled door and spilled into the office.

Carrie felt herself blush. As always, Matt looked the picture of perfection. A fine Stetson topped his handsome head and a well-tailored suit showed off his massive form. The garment made her want to run her fingers over his shoulders. His face tense, he scraped the bolt across the door as the shouting men stomped up the office steps.

Jenny looked as if she had just stepped out of the pages of a ladies' magazine: frilly lace edged her muslin dress; a jaunty, flower-trimmed bonnet perched atop her golden curls; and white gloves encased her slender hands.

"The assayer told us you found a placer," Matt said forthrightly.

Carrie glanced at her father. "Yes, Da found a whole mountain of gold. I'm surprised that sneaky little man didn't write it up for the newspaper."

"Actually, that's my job," Matt drawled. "What *did* happen?"

Shamus climbed off the stool and strode to Carrie's side. "Well, sir, from what Carrie's told me, that's neither wheat, corn, nor turnips to you, is it? Bein' a Worthington, you're not interested in the likes o' us. Why should we talk—"

"Was it real gold?" Jenny interrupted.

"No, it was hen's eggs we painted up yellow to fool everybody," Carrie shot back. She wondered if Jenny had bought up all the ignorance in Crested Butte and sent to Denver for more. And why was her face so pained? Was her corset pinching, or was the thought of Carrie being rich just a mite distasteful? Carrie looked through the pane as the noisy miners opened their ranks for John Worthington. Silvery hair crowned the man's head and a brocade vest hugged his ample belly. His pocket watch swung like a gold pendulum as he crossed the dusty street.

After the man hoisted his girth on the assayer's porch, Matt opened the door a bit. Wiping his flushed face with a monogrammed handkerchief, Worthington squeezed into the office. The crowd roared its disapproval when Matt shot the door bolt.

The wealthy man eyed Shamus with distaste. "Clayright says you've been out for a week, O'Leary. What's all this foolishness about finding gold? If you're not on that hoist tomorrow, you're fired."

"Well, sir, that would be a grand trick, because you

can't fire a man who doesn't work for you. I'm turnin' in me resignation right now."

"What a foolish man you are. No doubt this harebrained scheme of yours will fall through, and both you and your daughter will starve. You'll have nothing to back you up."

Shamus chuckled and tugged at his whiskery ear. "I have nothin' to back me up now. If I injure meself I'm out of luck, ain't I?"

"I've often thought of setting up a miners' fund for just such events," Worthington proclaimed loftily.

"Aye, and someday you may even do it!" Shamus grinned at Carrie. "I've noticed there's a big difference between what is and what ought to be."

Color blotched the heavy man's face. "Why . . . I've never heard such impertinence. I—I—"

"Go on with what you were saying, sir," Shamus broke in. "Don't let me interrupt you with a good idea."

A long paper in his hand, the white-faced assayer clicked back the drape and stared at the group. "Mr. O'Leary . . . come here," he croaked. Silent, Shamus walked to him and grabbed the document from his limp fingers. With a great whoop, the Irishman swept Carrie off her feet. "This deed says it assays out sky-high, me girl. Our troubles are over!"

The noisy miners pressed their curious faces against the glass and stared into the office. His face aglow, Shamus unbolted the door and waved the document in the air. A hush ran over the crowd. "I'm a rich man, lads, and I'll be standin' every man jack o' you to a drink at Finnigan's Saloon." He chuckled and thumped the document. "I'm sure me credit will be good!" The miners broke into a roar, then hoisted Shamus onto their shoulders and carried him toward the saloon.

When a warm hand clasped her shoulder, Carrie turned to face John Worthington's stormy eyes. "I'm afraid your troubles aren't really over," he said smoothly. "Have you ever heard of the annex law, Miss O'Leary?" Her heart dipping, she stared at Matt's concerned face, then back at his uncle. "No, I thought not," Worthington continued. "Well, my dear, to make a long story short, it means I'll have your mine in less than a month."

Hairpins between her lips, Carrie pinned up a droopy lock of hair. Finished, she lathered her smooth arms and legs with rose-scented soap. As she moved, her bare hips squeaked against the brass bathtub. At last she rinsed with warm water and glanced around the steamy hotel room. Bright Oriental rugs carpeted the polished floor. Pink-flowered wallpaper set off a canopied bed and cherrywood nightstands. The cozy room even boasted two velvet chairs and a writing desk. Mary, Jesus, and Joseph, she thought, slinging back a loose curl, this was heaven. She could scarcely believe it. She, Carrie O'Leary, was now living in the Elk Mountain House Hotel!

She flicked away some bubbles and scanned the frivolous objects dotting the room. Shamus had bought them all. Tall and brass-rimmed, a huge mirror towered near the bed. Bandit sprawled at its base and watched her. She met his curious eyes with a frown. "Look at this place, Bandit. It could be a flamin' store. Why does Da have to waste his money on foolish gifts every time he brings gold dust into town?" The dog yawned in response.

Carrie floated the perfumed soap on a towel and glanced at the desk calendar. A red circle drawn around tomorrow's date, March 30, caught her eye. "Holy Mother," she muttered, "himself out spending money like old man Tabor, and our time is nearly up." The law books scattered on the desk all said the same thing—if John Worthington could prove the Shamrock's gold vein originated on his property, he could take the mine. Carrie didn't know if he could prove it, but she knew who did.

A tingly dread sang through her body while she thought about the problem. She had to see Matt Worthington—today. Tomorrow would be too late. The very thought of confronting him at his office made her sick. It was too risky. Jenny might walk in and see her sacrificing her pride. Like it or not, she had to get dressed and go to his ranch house. She crossed her arms over her slick breasts. "Peony, come on in and bring that bucket of hot water. It's gettin' chilly!"

The door opened and a young Chinese girl toted a bucket of water into the room. Oriental pajamas hung on her slender form, and loose slippers slapped against the floor while she crossed the room. "Peony will wash Missy all over," she proposed, sloshing water over the bucket's rim. Her jet-black braids jiggled and white towels swung from her shoulder as she brought the water to the tub. "I'll do a good job!" she added, splashing the warm water over Carrie's back.

Carrie uncrossed her arms and looked at the girl's expectant face. "Thank you ever so much, Peony, but I can bathe myself," she kindly explained. "That's why I had you wait outside the door."

The girl frowned, then trickled out the remaining water. "Ohh, Missy Carrie is a very beautiful lady—she'll make a man person so happy," she exclaimed as she stared at Carrie's full breasts. She unfurled a white towel and added, "Peony dry Missy now, put oil on—"

Carrie brushed the girl's brown hand away. "Faith, I can do *that*. Now scoot, go on with you. And stand up to that mean hotel manager who keeps bossin' you around!"

With a crestfallen air, Peony backed out of the room.

Now that, thought Carrie, was the trouble with these Chinese who worked at the hotel. They were always trying to wait on a person like a baby. Alone at last, she stood and dried herself, then stepped from the tub.

When she reached the bureau she pulled out a shift and gazed into the tall mirror. This was the first time she had seen a full reflection of her nude body. Fascinated, she dropped the sheer garment and lowered her hand. Would she make a man person happy, as Peony had suggested? Afternoon light slanted through a lacy window and high-lighted her creamy breasts and long, silky legs. She trailed her hands over her smooth hips and flat stomach. Then, feeling foolish, she padded away, her wet feet sucking against the bare floor. But something pulled her back— something made her look again.

She considered her face. The tense look was gone; a few added pounds had softened her countenance. She touched her moist skin. A blush rode her cheeks and her complexion glowed with freshness. Her best feature, her expressive eyes, sparkled with vitality. All at once, that foolish feeling came over her again and she dropped her hand.

Get dressed, commanded a stubborn inner voice. You won't save the Shamrock standing naked before a mirror! Mentally shouldering her responsibility, she slipped into the flimsy shift. Tightness knotted her throat while she studied her reflection. Despite their good luck, things had never seemed worse for her and Shamus.

She glanced at the dog, noticing that his curious eyes trailed her movements. "You know, Bandit, unless I can sort things out, we'll lose the mine. Then we'll really be in a pickle, won't we? Since Da has resigned from the Queen, we ain't got a thing to fall back on—just like Worthington said." She slammed a drawer. "Damn the whiskey-drinkin' Irishman, anyway," she mumbled under her breath. "Damn him and his stubborn pride!"

She kicked a silken slipper across the room and strode to the dresser. While she searched for her bloomers, her mind rehashed their heated argument of two weeks ago. Her heart thudded now, as it had then.

Fourteen days ago the noise of the rushing creek and the chirping birds filled the spring morning. Tall and lanky, Botsie Klavanicks worked in the distance, occasionally glancing at Carrie and Shamus as they spoke.

"But, Da, why do I need to move into town?" she kept asking.

His knuckles white, Shamus stabbed a shovel into the creek bank and turned around. "I'll not have ye' livin' here at the Shamrock in a tent when John Worthington has threatened us. Besides, we have money to do better.''

''What about our house?''

''If you're talkin' about that tar-paper shack we've been livin' in since we came to Colorado, you can be forgettin' about it.'' He threw down the shovel. ''I'm tackin' boards over the windows tomorrow and you're movin' into town with the quality folks where you belong! It's safe there, and with me fortune, you have a position to keep up.'' He wiped sweat from his brow, then shoved his red handkerchief away. ''I'll not have the ladies on the Ridge thinkin' bad o' you.''

''Da, don't let this dab of money make you foolish. We've never worried about what a few old biddies on Ridge Hill were thinkin'! But you *should* be worryin' about what John Worthington's thinkin'—our time is almost out. We need to find out about this annex law. The days keep flyin' by, and you keep sayin' 'tomorrow'!''

He stooped and scooped up some slushy mud. ''I have no time for messin' with such foolishness when there's gold in this slush just waitin' to be taken out,'' he asserted, letting the muck trickle through his blunt fingers.

She watched him pick up the shovel and walk to Botsie. ''Lord, I love him, but that man will never change,'' she murmured. With a flash of insight she realized he was afraid to match wits with John Worthington—the problem was on her shoulders.

Carrie pounded her fist on the dresser while her thoughts drifted back to the present. She couldn't be giving in, she had to get hold of herself. Half blinded by tears, she found some bloomers in the tumbled drawer. Yes, Shamus O'Leary would always be the same, she realized as she wiggled into the silky underpants. He would always be the same stubborn Irishman, standing like a big boulder in a stream, letting life rush around him. Why be angry with him now? It was too late to do anything but save the Shamrock herself.

Easing out of the reflective mood, she noticed it was

four o'clock. Instantly, she plopped into the vanity chair and released her hair. A tortoiseshell brush, a gift from Shamus, flew through her shiny locks. Two minutes later, color glossed her lips and stained her cheeks. She stood and assessed her potential. Would Matt consider her as attractive as Jenny?

Regret shot through her when she remembered he had never seen her in anything but rags. Suddenly her slender hands clenched into fists. You're doin' it again, and you've got to stop it, she ordered herself. What was wrong with her, anyway? She wasn't going to the ranch to display herself; she was going to get vital information!

Her jaw set, she tugged a riding habit from the cedar-scented armoire and laid it on the bed. The rust-colored garment, selected for practical reasons, came from a dress shop down the street. She caressed the plush velvet with her work-worn fingers. The smartly cut outfit was the first nice ensemble she had ever owned. After loosening all its buttons, she shrugged into the jacket, then stepped into the divided skirt.

As she slid a pair of stiff ladies' boots from the armoire, the scent of fresh saddle soap tickled her nose. She hugged the boots to her waist and daydreamed about the extra dress she might have one day. "I might have an extra dress if Da doesn't spend all his money on foolish things or lose the Shamrock before the month is out!" she mumbled.

The dreary thought brought her mind back to the problem at hand, and she swiftly pulled on her boots. Why was she so nervous? True, this would be her first private meeting with Matt since they had been marooned, but she had already convinced herself she was over him. Yes, she thought while she twirled before the mirror, this visit was business—strictly business!

Chapter 9

"**H**ave a seat, sir," the butler said in an unctuous voice. "Mr. Worthington will be with you in a few minutes."

Matt nodded and watched the butler back across the room. His face grave, the servant closed the tall library doors and disappeared. Matt glanced around the well-appointed library, then walked to a window glowing with late afternoon light. The lacy panels rustled as he opened them and scanned the smooth lawn below. Stately trees and graceful fountains dotted the grounds. In the distance, far beyond the estate's wrought-iron gates, men swarmed into the Silver Queen.

He frowned and dropped the panel. The sight reminded him that he had just spent the morning trying to get into the mine, only to be blocked by the superintendent. With a sigh, he turned and paced about the library, eyeing a lacquered Chinese chest and a large writing table. The place had a perfectly untouched quality that suggested wealth and immunity from life's petty problems. The gleaming furniture and parquet floors, which smelled of lemon oil, stirred his memory.

Yes, the room and the scent were familiar. The library was a replica of John's old study in Denver. He remembered the furniture from his childhood when his mother had left him alone while she held whispered conferences in the hall. He picked up a small picture of his mother and studied her beautiful likeness with a pang of guilt, for he suddenly realized he felt nothing.

As an ormolu clock above the marble fireplace chimed three times, John Worthington entered the room. The butler closed the doors behind him with a soft click.

Matt replaced the picture and looked at his uncle. Fat larded the heavy man's jowls and midriff, but he carried himself with dignity. His starched shirt and expensive braided suit spoke of wealth and authority.

"Nice to see you, my boy," Worthington commented, sticking out a hand heavy with rings. As he advanced, his diamond stickpin shot off stars of light. "Edwards told me you wanted to see me. What brings you to the Ridge?"

Matt pumped his soft hand, then sat down in a velvet chair. "I want to talk to you about the Silver Queen."

Worthington opened a globe bar and clinked out a brandy decanter. "The Silver Queen? You've never been interested in the mine before." He looked at his nephew and smiled. "Want a brandy?"

When Matt shook his head, the man splashed some liquor into his own glass and eased into a chair. His manner friendly, he asked, "Now, what could you want to know about the Silver Queen?"

Matt lit a cheroot and filled the library with its sweet scent. "Well, first I want to know why Clayright wouldn't let me in this morning."

Worthington chuckled. "He has orders to keep everyone out except those who work in the mine. We're opening a new room and it's dangerous in there. Why would you want to go in anyway? You've seen it all before."

Matt studied his uncle's earnest eyes. "I want to write an article about the Queen," he finally said.

The heavy man shrugged his shoulders. "Matt, I don't think there's any way you could get a story out of that hole in the ground. And the people who work there . . ."

"Yes, go on?"

Worthington sighed and sipped his brandy. "Well, they're immigrants, aren't they? Most of them came to this country because their own countries couldn't offer them work. Most of them are illiterate and somewhat backward.''

"And you're offering them a better life?"

"Yes . . . yes, I am," Worthington answered in a soft voice. "I pay them more than they could get in their homeland. And I don't cheat them . . . I do all that the law requires."

"What about provisions for accidents?"

"Well, I don't have everything worked out on that, but I'm making plans. There's always a certain risk with any type of manual work, isn't there? Their families have no cause for complaint. I give them a big shindig once a year and pay for funerals from company funds."

When Matt stared at him silently, the man began speaking in an intimate tone. "This is the nub of the thing, Matt—the men are dissatisfied with life in general. In their hearts they know they'll never amount to much, so they all grouse to make themselves feel better. If they have no skills—it's my fault. If they have poor working habits—it's my fault. Everything is always the mine owner's fault to them, and it always will be. Drinking and complaining are their only outlets." The tycoon finished the brandy and set his glass on a polished table. "Why all the interest in the mine? You've never brought up these kind of questions before."

Matt exhaled a stream of smoke and crossed his legs. "I know. That's what I'm worried about."

The older man laughed. "That little redhead has got you stirred up. That's all that's wrong with you, son. Hell, she's a tempting morsel . . . enjoy her. Just don't take her seriously. The woman has no idea what she's talking about. I've been operating this mine successfully for years and providing a decent livelihood for men like her father at the same time." He winked at Matt and reached across to slap his leg. "And another thing . . . when the chips are down, stick with your own kind."

"Why, John?"

"Have you ever heard of the Molly Maguires?"

"Yes, I have."

"Well, then, you know how that secret society of miners drove the big owners crazy back in Pennsylvania. The authorities barely managed to stamp them out in seventy-five. They were a wild, violent bunch—not the type of people you would want to be associated with, I would think."

Matt studied his uncle's sincere face and weighed his words. Perhaps Carrie's claims *had* been overblown. He knew she was a hothead and given to exaggeration. And even though he and John had never been close, he really didn't want to believe the man whose name he shared was as bad as Carrie claimed.

Worthington smiled and stood up. "Any more questions?"

Matt slowly rose and stared down at him. "Yes," he drawled. "I'd like to know if you were able to annex the Shamrock."

The heavy man shook his head. "All right, that's a fair question. Let's go out on the veranda and get some air. I'll tell you there."

Matt's ranch house loomed into view as Carrie's mount galloped around a curve. The old place sat back from the leafy road and was silhouetted against an orange sky. Surrounded by trees and looking pleasantly overgrown, the log home nestled between shadowy hills. Chimney smoke and a flock of chickens met Carrie's gaze when the horse loped closer.

A breeze caressed her face as her mount thudded down the last stretch of road. While her horse crunched over the gravelly cutoff, Carrie tried to ignore her tingly nerves. "Blessed Mother, please give me strength to face that smooth-tongued devil again," she prayed.

She finally halted the whinnying mount. Crocuses splattered the ragged yard, their purple petals highlighted by the sunset. The white chickens squawked and scattered into the dusk when she slid from the saddle and tied her horse.

Her heart churned as she knocked on Matt's door. The thought of asking him for help nipped at her pride, but she wasn't doing this for herself—she was doing this to save the Shamrock. When she received no answer, she rapped again, miffed that her great sacrifice should be thwarted. "He's probably out cavortin' with that painted-up preacher's daughter," she muttered, banging as loud as she could.

Again she waited. Her spirit stirring, she turned the knob and opened the door. The silent entry engulfed her as she half closed the door. She glimpsed her reflection in a wall mirror and jumped. "Mother Mary, I look a mess." She smoothed her hair into place and pushed up her tight sleeves.

Her boot heels clicking against the planked floor, she stepped into a large room. A warm, masculine aura enveloped her. The scent of wood smoke drew her attention to a rock fireplace topped with deer antlers. Whispering flames lit the room with a soft glow and gilded the dark furniture.

She scanned the gun cabinets and sporting scenes on each side of the rosy hearth, then stooped and touched the bearskins on the floor. "Now, doesn't he live fine? This place is full of nice things," she muttered, walking backward. All at once she bumped into something hard. When she turned she discovered a cluttered desk that dominated a window spot and commanded a view of the dusky mountains.

On the desk she spied a box of cigars. Beside the cigars a law book lay open with marked passages. Her heart thumping, she gripped the book and riffled its pages. In order to catch the waning light, she edged to the large bay window. While the birds warbled on the other side of the pane, she found a red-marked section about annex laws. Her hands trembled as she began to read. "Section seven of the Annex Law states—"

"Well, well, if it isn't Miss O'Leary herself!" boomed Matt as he closed the door behind him. "Here I was, feeling as lonesome as the devil in church, and you show up."

She jumped and dropped the book.

"Do you always let yourself into unlocked houses?" he went on.

A joyous warmth rose inside her as she studied him standing in the shadows. "Do you always sneak up on people while they're readin'?"

He laughed and sailed his battered work hat at a wall bracket. "I'm afraid you have it backward, sweetheart. You see, since this is my house and you invaded my territory, that makes you the sneak."

Her eyes devoured him as he removed the globe from a desk lamp. With the scrape of a match, he lit the wick and soft light pooled over his flannel shirt and tight suede pants. It played over his thick hair and touched his eyes, making them glint roguishly. When he clicked the globe in place, his light blue shirt flashed against his tanned forearms. Holy Mother, the handsome devil would look good in a gunnysack shroud, she thought.

He clasped her arm in his warm hand. "Don't look so nervous, Carrie. Come on, sit down and relax. I've been expecting you."

"Expectin' me?"

He grinned and led her to a blanket-draped sofa. "Yes, of course. Here, I think you'll find this comfortable."

She sank into the sofa, feeling her mouth dry up.

His gaze tracing every curve, he took in her form-fitting outfit. He lingered on the low neckline where the tops of her generous breasts swelled over the soft velvet. "Carrie, I must say you're looking luscious. And you seem to be in a better mood than the last time I saw you, at the assayer's office . . . or on the day of the rescue."

The rescue scene flashed through her mind. Mother Mary, where did he get the nerve to mention *that*? She remembered the humiliating ride back to town. She had traveled wet and bedraggled with Jack Penrose in the cab, while Matt and Jenny lounged in the passenger car like royalty. Once in Crested Butte, Jack had mercifully whisked her away before Matt could talk to her. Feeling her confidence wane, she forced her thoughts back to the present and tried to look calm. "I seem to remember you bein' in a sour mood that day, too," she finally said.

"Oh, was I? If you think *I* was in a bad mood, you should have heard Jenny." He sat down beside her. "She grumbled all the way back to town."

"What about the reverend?"

He rolled his eyes. "Lord Almighty, he was so swollen up, I thought that tight preacher's collar might burst right open."

To her surprise, she felt the corners of her mouth twitch upward, and she laughed despite herself.

Their impasse broken, Matt laughed, too. Then he rubbed her fingers and studied her face. "Yes, I'm feeling much better now, especially since I believe a little bargaining may be in order," he teased.

A blush warmed her cheeks as his hard thigh brushed her leg. His eyes twinkling, he kissed her upturned wrist where a pulse scampered. With slow ease, he pushed up her soft sleeve and caressed her arm. The action made torrents of pleasure ripple through her. Her hungry body devoured his touch.

She had to get away from his hands. She clenched her fingers, then stood and began pacing. Maybe if she got herself good and mad she could remember she hated all Worthingtons and everything they stood for. More importantly, maybe she could forget he was turning her insides to jelly.

Matt went to the window. An amused look on his face, he sat on the desk edge and watched her for a while. Finally, he shot her a hard look and lit a cigar.

She stared at him and said, "Do you have to smoke that thing?"

"You don't expect me to sit through your tirade empty-handed, do you?'' He snuffed out the match and exhaled in frustration. ''Carrie, will you cease that infernal pacing and tell me why you came here?''

She stopped and raised her brows. ''Why else? To try and find out about old John.''

''Are you sure?''

''Of course I'm sure.''

''Well, *calm down*, and let's talk things over.''

Frowning, she reseated herself on the couch and watched him move to the fireplace. Nearby, a cluster of bottles and bright crystal ringed a table. ''Sherry?'' he offered. ''Oh, I'm sorry,'' he added with a dry grin. ''Considering your habits, perhaps you'd prefer something stronger.''

She stared into his dark eyes. ''I think we went over this at the cabin.''

''Yes, so we did . . . but it's here if your nerves should feel the need.''

''I don't know about *your* nerves, but *my* nerves are just fine—and my head is goin' to stay clear, too.''

He laughed and poured brandy into his glass. ''You're really something. Did you know that?'' He gulped his liquor. ''I admire your courage. Most women in your position would be teary-eyed, but there you sit as cool as a fruit salad on ice. I've never met a woman like you before.''

She watched light flicker over his proud, strong face. ''I know you ain't. Due to my upbringin' I've never had the privilege of indulgin' in feminine weaknesses.''

He chuckled, tossed his cheroot into the fireplace, then flashed her a warm smile that left her shaken. Carrie knew the question in his eyes was so plain she should have felt insulted; instead, she only felt warm and good. Lord, she thought as heat rushed up from her bosom, I must be slidin', slidin' straight into hell on greased skids. Now wait a minute . . . she was supposed to be in charge of this situation!

All at once she sat forward and stabbed her finger at

him. "Don't be gettin' the idea I came here because I like you. This visit is strictly business!"

He polished off the brandy and clinked his glass by the others. Never lowering his amused eyes, he walked to the sofa. "Business? That word means dealing, doesn't it? That information about John would be very costly," he teased. "But I might be persuaded into trading a bit of gossip for a kiss."

She favored him with a sidelong glance. "I expected you to say somethin' like that, considerin' the bastard you are."

"God Almighty, you are determined, aren't you?" he rumbled as he sat down by her.

She lifted her chin and said, "A person never knows what they'll have to do in this hard world."

He touched her loose hair. "My God, you're beautiful. Did you know, with the lamplight shimmering over you, you look like some kind of fallen angel? Your hair is like fiery amber, and your figure is enough to make a man dizzy. But despite your tough airs, you still remind me of a lovely, angry child."

His eyes darkening, he cradled her head and brought his lips within inches of hers.

The look in his eyes shook her heart and melted her joints with desire: every inch of her skin glowed with tingly warmth. As he brushed the curls from her face, a deep satisfaction stole through her body.

"Carrie, we belong together," he murmured.

His brandy-laced breath stirred her blood. Before she knew what she was doing, she snuggled closer and savored the warmth and smell of him. At once a buoyant euphoria flooded over her, leaving her light-headed with excitement. When he took her lips, a shudder of joy darted through her. "Matt?" she murmured, pulling away.

His eyes dark with passion, he raised his head. "Yes, love?"

"I want you to know I ain't enjoyin' this or nothin'."

He lifted a brow and stared at her with surprise. "For

someone who's not enjoying herself, you're sure giving a good performance.''

''Why, you scoundrel, I ought to—''

''You know what your whole trouble is?'' he cut in. ''You talk too damn much.'' He fiercely covered her lips with his.

She moaned and caressed his jaw, feeling the fine stubble under her fingertips. Then she twined her hands in his thick hair, thinking it felt like heavy silk. He deepened the kiss and triggered sensations that engulfed her breasts and left her womanhood aching with pleasure. The sharp feelings startled and confused her. Could these delectable feelings make her soft and weak? Were they pointing her away from her goals? In view of all that had happened, how could she be making love to anyone named Worthington? Hadn't she learned her lesson the first time?

With gentle confidence, he slipped his fingers into her hair and caressed the nape of her neck. Sweet sensation spiraled within her belly. Before she had time to consider her worrisome thoughts further, he plumbed the depths of her warm mouth, leaving her weak with ecstasy. In response, she returned the kiss and thoughtfully traced his firm lips, surprised at her own inventiveness. His moist lips tasted like brandy and felt silky to the tip of her tongue. He returned her intimate caress with his tongue and then eased his mouth away. ''Carrie . . . my little love,'' he whispered.

His hand brushed over her breast. Her nipple hardened and soft, exquisite pleasure burst inside her like rosebuds. His skilled fingers made her think she would explode with desire. A leaping flame rushed through her damp body like a whirlwind. ''Matt . . . I could go on lovin' you all night,'' she whispered.

He unbuttoned her bodice and slipped it off. His hands strong and sure, he hooked his thumbs in her shift straps and tugged them down. Her large creamy breasts spilled free. Inch by inch, he nuzzled her neck with tingly kisses while his fingers teased her nipples.

She moaned again and pressed her face against his shoulder. His touch galvanized her skin with such sensation she was aflame with the need for release.

As she floated on a smooth sea of passion, he gathered her into his arms. Never taking his insistent mouth from her lips, he lifted her from the couch to the bearskin rug.

When she realized she was on the floor, her passion cooled as if a dark storm cloud had drifted over her. The hard reasoning part of her mind flared up again. Did he really care for her, or was this just another Worthington trick? After all, her pride was all she had, and she needed to guard it well. It wasn't too late—she could still save herself. Maybe she had surrendered her body once, but her heart bridled at the thought of doing it again.

"Carrie, what's wrong?" he muttered.

"This is just another rich man's trick, ain't it?"

"No, of course not. What's the matter with you?"

She eyed him while she pulled up her shift and leaned against the sofa. Why did something have to be the matter with her? Why did *he* always have the correct answers? And why did he think he owned her just because they'd made love once? On second thought, she decided they hadn't really made love—they had just found physical release.

"Now don't go givin' me that sermon about education and trustin' people again," she said. "Makin' love is one thing . . . I don't know what to call this." She closed her eyes and sighed. "Maybe I do, and I just don't want to think about it."

Matt propped himself up on one elbow and looked away wearily. A muscle twitched in his jaw. Frowning, he sat up and leaned against a chair.

Carrie stared into the ruddy fireplace, her eyes bright and tense. "Well, you know I'm right," she added.

Silent, he regarded her tenderly, then hugged her close. "Carrie, why can't you believe I have feelings for you?"

She shrugged away and eyed him silently, feeling tears

tighten her throat. "There's just too much difference between us."

He heaved a deep sigh. "Well, if we can't talk about us, let's talk about John. I spoke to him today. There has been a delay in the case," he said slowly. "The law states he must irrevocably prove the vein originated on his property, and the ground is too broken up for him to do that quickly. Thank God you have more time, but you'll need someone to help you."

Outrage bubbled over in her heart. "Damn you, Matt! Why didn't you just tell me I had more time right away?"

Strikingly composed, he stood up and ran a hand through his tousled hair. Then he strode to the window and propped his boot on the low, wide windowsill.

She snatched up her bodice and shrugged into it. Her hands flew over the buttons and popped them into place. "Holy Mother, what a rotten bastard you really are. To think only moments ago I was restin' in your arms. Are you sure you're even human?"

He turned, his face hard. "Yes, quite human, I'm afraid. And so are you, whether you want to admit it or not. A while ago I asked why you came here, and you lied. I went on with this game about the bargain to ease your conscience, but you know you could have asked me about John right out."

He walked toward her, his eyes hard. "Why can't you accept the fact you have the same instincts as the rest of the human race? Why are you afraid of your feelings? And Lord . . . why can't you accept the fact that you want me as much as I want you?"

"That's just your own swollen vanity speakin' now, man!"

Matt grinned. "I had considered that—but we still have the problem of those unforgettable words: 'Matt, I could go on lovin' you all night.' "

Her throat tightened up again.

"Carrie, you need to face some facts about us, just as

you need to face facts about John. And you need my help.''

''Mary, Jesus, and Joseph! Do you think I'd ever ask for or accept help from you! Our sessions would start at the desk, but they'd end up on the floor, wouldn't they?''

He shook his head grimly. ''Just as I thought. You're too stubborn to let anyone help you.'' His eyes angry, he went on. ''John is giving a ball for all the senior-level workers in the Queen, like he does every year. Businessmen from Denver come, and if you'd attend, you might meet some influential people who could help your cause.''

''Like who?''

''Like Martin Henderson—the biggest banker in Denver.''

''Tell me about him.''

''What does it matter? I'd take you, but you wouldn't go, would you? You're so set against anyone who has money you'd cut off your nose to spite your face.''

She gathered her things and strode to the door, looking at his dark face. ''You're wrong. If it will help the miners, I'll go. But I sure ain't goin' with you. And I want you to know,'' she promised with a shaky voice, ''that there's one thing that will see me through everythin', no matter what old John tries to do, and that's my anger at the Worthingtons—you in particular.''

She put her hand on the knob, tasting her own salty tears. ''And you remember that son-of-a-bitch thing? Well, I had the order wrong. *You're* the chief son of a bitch, Matt Worthington!'' With that, she slammed the door behind her.

Chapter 10

The sun had slipped behind the jagged horizon and colored the sky reddish-orange. Carrie squeezed Jack's hand as they neared the Worthington mansion. Its windows sparkling, the house glittered like a gem against the sunset. Light and music spilled onto the manicured lawn.

"Carrie, I dun't know about this . . . this place looks awful grand for the likes o' me," Jack stammered. A new suit strained across his broad chest and stiff shoes squeaked with every step he took.

She lifted the hem of her newly acquired green silk gown and tugged him forward. Her taffeta underskirts rustled with each step. "Jack Penrose, don't go feelin' you're not grand enough for this place," she ordered. "You're as good as any man here. Hold your head up and remember that! Do you hear me, you big Cornishlug?"

Doubt washed over his angular face, but he grinned like a schoolboy. "If you say so, my beautay, but I'd rather be at the saloon with me mates."

Crickets chirped in the shrubs as they approached the door. Once there, Jack pounded the brass knocker. While they waited, Carrie adjusted her neckline and smoothed her upswept hair. When no one came, she gave the door several sharp raps herself.

From inside the mansion she heard noise, voices, and the tap of heels on marble. At last, a tall, supercilious servant whisked open the door.

The fiery chandeliers in the entry made Carrie blink, while the aroma of a perfume stew assaulted her nostrils. Dressed in assorted pastels, groups of ladies dotted the inner room like flowers. Jewels twinkled from the richer women's throats and hands. Carrie was glad Peony had added a chartreuse plume to her hair and adorned her smooth neck with a like-colored ribbon. When she caught a glimpse of herself in a tall mirror, she paused for a look.

Her eyes widened at the image the glass flashed back. The peacock-green dress made her bare arms and creamy cleavage stand out dramatically. The snug bodice and bustled skirt magically transformed her figure: her bust had never appeared so full, or her waist so small. With a backward step, she assessed the exciting power that looking elegant bestowed. Her heart raced when she thought about Matt being in the next room. Surely even *he* would be affected.

The Chinese girl had powdered her mistress's complexion to a porcelainlike fairness, and darkened her long lashes until her eyes looked enormous. Rosy color enlivened her cheeks and glossed her lips. Carrie chuckled, glad she had rescued the browbeaten Peony from the angry hotel manager earlier that week. It had been worth it just to see the big bully's expression, but Peony's cosmetic expertise was an added bonus. Carrie stretched out several springy spit curls, then nervously ran her fingers over the lustrous bodice. A blush stung her cheeks as she considered the low neckline. Faith, she was half naked!

Turning from the mirror, she noticed several dressed-up miners who nodded at her. "See, Jack, there's some of your friends there."

He glanced at the men, who moved beside their women like awkward black crows. "Aye, their wives and sweethearts drug 'em 'ere, too. They all look as miserable as me, dun't they?"

At the back of the large room, a string band tuned up for another dance. Nearby, a table supported a rich buffet, spread on a snowy cloth.

As the pair strolled forward, the guests parted for them, their eyes bright with interest. It seemed to Carrie that all the men stared at her like a pack of hounds looking at a smokehouse door, the women whispered behind spread fans, then murmured and smiled in acknowledgment. Were they smiling to be polite, Carrie wondered, or because they knew Matt had made a fool of her? With a huge effort of will, she decided to enjoy herself, no matter what. "Look happy, Jack—smile!" she whispered.

"Lud, I dun't know 'ow . . . my mouth 'as gone dry."

She squeezed his arm. "Come on, pull up your socks, man!" Tension frosted the air like an icy fog. Her throat tightened, but she prayed for courage, and imagined a steel case around her heart. She channeled all her strength into a performance.

"*Damme,*" Jack swore, " 'ere comes ole Worthington 'imself!"

Dressed to the teeth, John Worthington moved in on them like bad weather. "Miss O'Leary, I'm a bit surprised to see you here tonight," he commented, ignoring Jack.

"I'm a bit surprised to be here myself," she shot back.

Worthington smiled at some cronies gathered at his elbow. "I hope you don't think that just because the decision on the annex has been delayed a bit you've won the war, my dear."

She idly scanned the room as she spoke. "It's the truth you're speakin' now. There's one thing I've learned about rats. Soon as you get one hole stopped up, they'll shoot out another."

The silver baron silenced his chuckling friends with a sharp look. "You seem to have something on your mind, Miss O'Leary," he continued. "I'm wondering if you'd care to share your thoughts with us."

She looked him in the eye. "All right. I was wonderin' how many men you had to work overtime without pay to finance this little affair."

His jowl twitched. "Overtime without pay? That's ridiculous. I promised just last month I'd never do such a thing!''

She smiled at Jack and rubbed her temple. "Now, why is it I get the feelin' that promise will hold together like a dirt dauber's nest in a thunderstorm?''

He laughed as Worthington and his group stalked away.

Suddenly she caught a glimpse of Matt, and her stomach did several flip-flops. He made a striking figure—his virile aura seemed to fill the large room. Arms crossed, he leaned against the marble fireplace and assessed her with a knowing grin. Jenny stood triumphantly at his side, her practiced smile cold enough to freeze a statue's heart. Brighter than a cat's eye, her overtrimmed dress barely skirted bad taste.

Carrie glanced at Matt again; she had never seen him looking better or more confident. Light from the chandeliers pooled over his freshly washed hair and strong features. His superbly tailored suit coat displayed his broad shoulders and trim waist to the best advantage, while his white shirt set off his tanned face and strong hands. Trousers made from the finest wool outlined his powerfully corded thighs.

His grin spreading into a smile, he left Jenny and maneuvered between the dancing couples. Time hung like a heavy mist while he moved toward Carrie. She watched his muscles ripple under the fine coat and her heart thudded with delicious anticipation. As he neared, his musky cologne hit her nostrils and stirred memories of their lovemaking. Telling herself she wouldn't be softened, she stoked her anger with memories of their last meeting.

When he lifted her hand to his mouth, his eyes twinkled mischievously. "Well, well, Miss O'Leary . . . how do you enjoy being a woman of fashion?'' he asked, pressing a kiss on her hand.

"Oh, I suppose it's all right if you have nothin' else to do,'' she replied in an offhand manner.

Jenny sauntered to Matt's side and raked Carrie with a cold stare. "Why, Carrie,'' she purred, clinging to Matt's arm, "that dress is lovely on you . . . but don't you think it's a bit low-cut, dear?"

"You know what your trouble is, woman? You think by the inch and talk by the yard. The Lord knows, that thing you're wearin' would sicken a buzzard!"

Matt laughed and untangled himself from Jenny, whose face had turned redder than a turkey wattle. "I think it's about time we sampled the buffet," he suggested, tucking Carrie's arm under his. He extended his hand toward the table. "Shall we?"

Jack stood by helplessly, confusion clouding his eyes.

Matt glanced over his shoulder as he strolled away. "Come on, Cousin Jack—and bring Jenny with you!"

"I see you brought Jenny as your guest," Carrie said to Matt in a low tone.

He glanced back at the woman. "She's not my guest. She brought herself."

"Well, she's attached herself to you like a cocklebur to a wool sock, ain't she?"

Grinning, he eyed Carrie playfully. "Why, I'm flattered you noticed."

The music faded away as they reached the buffet. Silver gleamed; crystal twinkled; candles flickered. Carrie had never seen so many delicious-looking foods at one time. Her mouth watered at the variety. A baron of beef and mounds of smoothly braised chicken breasts dominated the table. Fruit balls, glazed pastries, and nuts mounded heavy silver platters.

Matt released her arm and nodded at a chef standing behind a stack of creamy, gold-rimmed china. As the man carved a slice of beef for her, Carrie watched a pack of awkward girls corner Matt. Their proud mothers stood behind them as they closed in. With a wise smile, she met Jenny's eyes as the woman pulled away from Jack. Soon the band struck up a lively tune and Matt escorted one of the girls to the floor.

"Look, Jack, isn't that disgustin'? He's certainly makin'

a fool of himself, ain't he?" Carrie huffed as they took their plates and sat down, leaving Jenny behind.

"I dun't see what's wrong with it," Jack mumbled. " 'E's jest dancin'."

Carrie rolled her eyes as several miners shuffled up to take Jack to the punch bowl. She watched Jack guzzle the spiked punch for a while and realized he had completely forgotten her. Then she spotted a group of men standing around a tall, distinguished gentleman. They seemed to be hanging onto his every word. Dressed in a stylish suit, the man radiated confidence and authority. *Of course,* she thought, it had to be Martin Henderson.

Gradually the man turned his head and met her gaze. Silver streaked his thick hair at the temples and his blue eyes gleamed with intelligence. She blinked in embarrassment, but he smiled warmly. Then he spoke to a companion and moved toward her. Why was her heart beating so fast? After all, she hadn't done anything wrong, and the man looked like a real gentleman. Telling herself she should forget Matt and enjoy herself, she lifted her chin and smiled.

A twinkle in his eye and a glass of red wine in his hand, the tall banker approached her. With some surprise, she noticed his gaze lingered on her eyes, not her bosom. She liked his respectful air and elegant bearing. As the banker neared, other men broke off their conversations and drifted behind him.

"Miss O'Leary," the courtly financier began, "if I may be so bold, let me introduce myself. I'm Martin Henderson from Denver. When Worthington invited me to this little affair, I nearly turned him down. Thank God I reconsidered. I must say, meeting you has been worth the inconvenience of the trip many times over. I understand you're the little spitfire who's making a fool of John."

She cocked her head. "No, I just tell the truth as I see it. Old John does a fine job of makin' a fool of himself."

Everyone roared. Some of the men lit cigars while others spiked their punch from private pocket flasks.

"Beauty and wit in one lovely vessel," Henderson went on. "What a rare and wonderful coincidence. You must have a fine mind. I've heard about the wonderful work you're doing for the miners."

She nodded and smiled.

He handed her the wine. "Here you are, my dear. I begged Worthington out of some of his better stock."

Her gaze locked with his, she sipped the wine.

"I myself am interested in helping the less fortunate," he explained in a smooth tone. "I'm sure we have many common areas of interest. If you should ever need assistance in Denver, please telegraph me at the Cattleman's Bank."

Carrie looked over Henderson's shoulder and noticed Matt standing by the fireplace looking as if he might burst. His face darkened while he lit a cheroot. A flame of rebellion flared inside her as he purposefully headed her way. Why, he was acting like she was his private property!

Tossing down the rest of the wine, she plunked the glass on a polished table, then smiled into the banker's face. "Now that's somethin' I'll be rememberin', Mr. Henderson. Yes, it is!" The wine shot through her veins and loosened her tongue. "And who knows when I'll need to go shoppin' . . . or feel the need for a bit of—*relaxation?*"

The others laughed, but Henderson gazed at her respectfully.

"Enjoying yourself?" Matt questioned, clasping her wrist. The cheroot dangled from his mouth; anger hardened his face. Resolutely, he pulled Carrie to the floor and maneuvered her between the dancing couples. Only his eyes showing his displeasure at Matt's rudeness, Martin Henderson discreetly backed away. Their faces disappointed, the other men followed. Some of the dancers laughed and stared openly. Warmth from their bodies and the bright chandeliers flushed Carrie's cheeks as Matt tugged her around the onlookers and ushered her to the other side of the room.

Carrie tried to ignore the shiny-faced women who stared in malicious delight. "Have you lost your wits, man?" she rasped at Matt.

"No, have you lost yours? Henderson is the biggest womanizer in Denver. He was practically drooling. And you seemed to be enjoying every minute of it."

She clenched her fists. "Has your brain fossilized altogether? You told me I should meet him."

"I didn't tell you to make a fool of yourself."

"The man's interested in my mind!"

"He's interested in taking you to bed!"

"It's just like you to think something like that. Why don't you go back to that sly-eyed Jenny Parker who's been circling the room like a hungry buzzard all night?"

"Why, Carrie," he exclaimed, "is that the sharp voice of jealousy I hear so clearly?" An insufferable smile spread over his handsome face. "I thought you'd renounced all claims to my worthless person."

"Me, jealous of you? I wouldn't waste a second thinkin' about you or that snippy Jenny Parker," she stormed.

"Snippy she may be, but Jenny doesn't give a damn about my last name. Why are you so waspish?"

Hands on hips, she leaned forward and whispered in his ear. "Waspish, is it? Funny, you're after usin' that particular word, because right now I feel madder than a two-stingered hornet. How dare you interrupt my conversation. Holy Mother, you have more nerve than a three-day toothache!"

He studied her with a bored air. "I was just trying to keep you from making a fool of yourself."

She backed off and shoved her hands on her hips again. "Matt, you *idiot*—you snooty, stuck-up, high-toned excuse for an editor—I hate you!"

He exhaled cigar smoke from the side of his mouth, then grinned crookedly. "What's your problem, girl? Why don't you quit beating around the bush and say what you really mean?"

For several seconds she thought she might actually burst,

but a sudden clamor from the front hall stopped her retort. The music scraped to a halt and a hush fell over the crowd.

"Carrie!" Botsie Klavanicks stamped across the shiny floor with mud-caked boots, hair hanging in his tired eyes. He looked as if three more steps might do him in. Carrie gasped and rushed toward him.

"Carrie, come quick," he cried. "Shamus has been hurt—bad!"

Chapter 11

Mealtime sounds floated up the hotel's stairs while Carrie rested against the banister. The aroma of roast beef made her mouth water, but she presently had no time to enjoy lunch. Breathing heavily, she smoothed down her wrinkled blue dress, then tugged her father's weight one step higher.

"Oh, me knee, watch me knee, darlin'. You're goin' to kill me!" Shamus exclaimed as he hopped up the stairs on one leg.

Perspiration stinging her eyes, Carrie gripped his large waist. "Go on, get a hold, Peony! We need to put him in my bed." The Chinese girl pulled up her loose pants and tried to hoist Shamus from the other side.

He rubbed a bruised hand over his trousers and massaged his knee. Bandages swathed his head and arms; a heavy leg cast banged against the metal treads as he moved one step higher. "If I just had a wee drop o' whiskey, 'twould help me leg."

Carrie stared him in the eye. "There's no use bringin' that up again, Da. I'm followin' the doctor's orders, and there will be no drinkin' for you unless it's for medicinal purposes."

"Blood an' thunder," he moaned, "and how bad would I have to be before you'd give me a drink?'Tis a comfortin' thought to know with me last breath I might be gettin' a sip o' whiskey!"

"Don't be tryin' any of your Irish charm on me, man.

I've heard it all my life. We've been up all night without food . . . you should be thinkin' about eatin', not drinkin'.''

"I should be thinkin' about gettin' back to me mine."

"No, Da! Come on, lift your weight and help us."

Suddenly Shamus clutched at his chest and winced. "Wait a minute, darlin'. It's me heart—it's pullin' again."

Alarm surged through Carrie. "Are you all right, Da? Rest a while—take it easy. We'll slow down." Holy Mother, she thought, what a time for his heart to start acting up.

After a few minutes, Shamus breathed deeply, then wiped his moist brow and nodded at her. "I'm all right now—let's get up to the room."

She and Peony gave one last tug and heaved him to the top of the landing. "Get that door open, girl," Carrie ordered, still clenching her father's waist. Groaning, the pair dumped Shamus onto the bed, beside the peacock-green gown. One of his arms dangled over the side of the mattress. Bandit bounded from his spot by the window, then sprawled on the floor and licked his master's hand.

"Don't worry, Missy. I take good care of him," Peony promised.

With gentle hands, the girl removed Shamus's boot. Instantly, he relaxed into the soft mattress. "Ohh, every bone in me body is hurtin'!" he complained. "And it makes me head ache to think o' no one watchin' the Shamrock but Botsie. Why, any child could come out there and take it away from the old fool."

Carrie moved the ball gown to a chair, then trailed her fingers over his hot brow. "Peony, get that window open . . . and wet a rag for his face."

When the girl opened the pane, a welcome draft floated into the stuffy room, carrying with it the scent of flowers, and of the good earth warmed by spring sunshine.

Carrie wiped her father's brow with the cloth and searched his worried eyes. "Now, let's go over this again, Da. The doctor had you so loaded with laudanum last night, you weren't makin' sense. You said it was dark when the accident happened?''

"Aye, nearly . . . it was about sundown. I was movin' one o' the wagons—we'd had it by the diggin' all week, fillin' it with quartz. I was goin' down the hill and tried to brake.''

"And?"

He heaved a great sigh while he patted the dog. "Well, you know what happened then, girl. The damn brake handle busted off like a dry twig. The team went crazy, the wagon turned over, and I was pitched on me head.'' He looked at her crossly. "O' course, there was no one to bring me in but Botsie.'' He rubbed his bruised side. "Ohh, I thought the jabberin' fool was goin' to kill me. He hit every bump on the road—and took half the night doin' it, too.'' Shamus scanned the room as if he were searching for something. "If I'm goin' to die, all I ask is a wee drop o' whiskey to ease me partin'.''

Carrie slung the rag aside. "You're not goin' to die!''

"Aye . . . I think I shall. Ahh, well, I've lived a happy life in me own way. I just hate to be tricked out o' me mine before I go.''

"Tricked out of your mine? Sweet Jesus, what are you talkin' about now?''

He scowled and eyed a rosewood cabinet in the corner. "Everythin' seems kind o' fuzzy . . . but if I had a wee drink, I could think better.''

Carrie stalked to the cabinet, opened it, and rummaged through its contents. At last she found a bottle of cherry brandy. She frowned while she splashed a half jigger of liquor into a glass and strode to the bed. "Bribe me, will you, you old rascal? This better be good!''

Her father swirled the brandy and smiled. "Ahh, 'tis a gorgeous girl you are, lass, a gorgeous girl.'' He tipped the glass, swallowed, and sighed. Happiness flickered over his seamed face as he sparked his eyes at the open window. He inhaled deeply. "Ahh, that sweet scent reminds me o' Ireland. I always loved the smell o' early mornin' when the fields were heavy with clover.''

Frustrated tears stung Carrie's eyes. ''Da, you're ramblin' again! We ain't talkin' about Ireland. You were tellin' me about bein' tricked out of your mine!''

He swept his gaze back to her. ''Aye, so I was,'' he replied, struggling up against the pillows.

Fists on hips, she glared at him as if he were a naughty child. ''Well, go on, then—go on with what you were sayin'.''

''It was the brake wheel, darlin'—it snapped off too easy. I think it was sawed, or the bolts loosened.''

''Now you're tellin' me Worthington tried to kill you?''

''I suppose I am . . . but if he succeeds, the man can take little from me,'' he observed. ''I don't regret leavin' earthly goods, for I never had any. As for position—I have none o' that either.'' He slurped the last of the brandy and set the glass aside. ''Aye, if Worthington kills me, he only speeds me through the gates o' paradise, where I'll see your blessed mother's face. I just hate him trickin' you out of your inheritance!''

She cocked her head. ''And just how are you knowin' it's Worthington who did it?''

''Mary, Jesus, and Joseph! Who else could it be, darlin'?'' His face flushed, he struggled to get up. ''Who else would be bold enough? And who else has enough money to hire someone to do his dirty work for him? I'll just be gettin' me pistol and goin' to the Ridge meself.''

''You'll not be goin' anyplace.'' She eased him back, then signaled Peony, who paddled across the room and pulled up the coverlet. ''The doctor said you needed to stay put . . . to mend.''

Color splotched his cheeks. ''I can't be restin' in the bed like a lord when that man is plannin' me downfall. I'll be havin' a talk with him, right now!''

She shook her head and stood her ground.

''But he's trickin' us, girl,'' Shamus insisted. ''He's trickin' us, I tell you.''

"You can't be makin' accusations without facts to back them up, Da. The brake handle could have just worked loose."

"Aye, but it didn't! I'm careful about that kind o' thing. Someone slipped out there and worked on it!" He tried to get up again, but she pressed him back. "Let me be, lass. I need to get back to me mine!"

"No, Da, you'll be stayin' in bed behavin' yourself! But just to set your mind at ease, I'll go and check on this business myself." She pointed at a straight chair and locked eyes with Peony. "Pull that chair to the bed and watch this old scalawag, girl. And look out for his stories—the rascal can tell you things that would make a hangman cry!"

Shamus struggled up again. *"One day,* me girl . . . I'm stayin' in bed one day, then I'm goin' back to—"

"Peony, don't give him any more liquor," Carrie ordered, cutting off his words. She put her hand on the doorknob. "And don't let him out of bed! Do you hear me?"

"Yes, Missy . . . but you've been up all night and had no food. You must eat before you go to the Shamrock."

"All right, all right, I'll eat a bite—and I'll send somethin' up for the two of you."

A frown wrinkled her brow as she shut the door behind her and hurried down the stairs. True, John Worthington was a stingy-hearted, mean-spirited miser, but was he capable of killing a man to take his claim?

The scent of coffee and freshly baked peach cobbler made her stomach rumble. Faith, I'm so hungry my teeth are itchin', she thought. Telling herself she just had time for a quick bite, she walked into the nearly deserted dining room and seated herself at a table by the hearth.

The cozy room glowed with an aura of warm life. Bits of Oriental china and dried flowers decorated the walls. Overhead, bright copper pots and strings of peppers hung from the beamed ceiling. Before a lace-draped window, a row of potted greenery reached for the sun. A fresh-faced young girl took Carrie's order and quickly returned with a tray of food, which included a salad, a plate of roast beef and vegetables, and a sugary cobbler.

Just as Carrie crunched into the crisp salad, the sound of purposeful footsteps rang from the hotel's entry. Seconds later, Matt strode into the dining room. A fancy vest flashed against his white shirt and dark trousers covered his muscled legs. As always, a sharply creased Stetson crowned his head.

Carrie's heart sank. Why did he always have to catch her in some ragged work dress?

With concerned eyes, he watched her eat. "I heard you've been up all night. How are you doing?"

"I was doin' fine until you came in."

Matt sat down, then signaled the serving girl and ordered cobbler and coffee.

From the corner of her eye Carrie scanned him as he took off his Stetson and placed it aside. She was irretrievably lost in sin. Yes, that was it. It had to be. If not, why was her body taking on a soft, sensual glow while she watched him eat? Why, she should have hated him that very second—just the way she had hated him at the ball. Wasn't his uncle trying to kill her da? Frowning, she hardened her resolve.

Matt pushed his half-empty dessert bowl aside and picked up the steamy mug of coffee. He studied her face. "Why didn't you let me go with you last night? And why won't you tell me how Shamus is doing?" he asked between sips of coffee.

"There wasn't a need for you to go to the doctor's office last night. And to answer your second question—Da's about as good as could be expected after John's thug rigged up that accident for him."

"Rigged up an accident?"

She cut into the roast beef and started eating. "That's what I said," she replied with a full mouth.

His eyes stormy, he slammed down the coffee. "Carrie, that accusation is about as serious as a snake bite. Would you care to talk about it?"

She ripped apart a crusty roll. "Da says someone fiddled with that brake handle. Now, I wonder who that could be?"

Matt rested his large hand on her arm. "Has anyone checked into this yet?"

"No one's had a chance to, but I'll be goin' that way as soon as I eat." She pulled her arm from his fingers and buttered the bread. It wasn't fair, she thought. The warmth of his hand satisfied some deep need in her—and she so wanted to stay mad at him!

"Mind if I go along?" he asked, pushing the empty mug aside.

Why was he being so damn nice? she wondered. And what right did he have to look so all-fired concerned? She thumped down her knife and glared back. "You've sure changed your tune. Last night you were bitin' my head off."

"Last night you were making a fool of yourself over Martin Henderson."

"Oh . . . and you were just bein' social with all those silly young girls, huh?"

A sour look rolled over his face. "You didn't answer my question."

"Suit yourself about goin'. The roads are public and I can't stop you. But if you think I'm just some helpless female . . ."

Matt laughed. "Helpless female? No, actually, I was hoping you could help me." He grinned as she hacked at her cobbler.

"Whenever you're ready, my rig is just outside the hotel," he offered graciously.

"So, there, you've seen the wagon for yourself," Carrie announced while she rinsed her dirty hands in the creek. Light washed over the mountainside and filtered through the freshly leafed trees that surrounded her. Outside the trees' shade, chirping birds flitted from bush to bush and insects droned in the tall grass. The scent of sun-warmed greenery and wild flowers filled the balmy air. Downstream, Matt's unhitched horses drank from the bright water that babbled over the rocky creek bed.

Matt watched a small opalescent rainbow shimmer over the water, then studied her face. "I don't know. The brake lever was broken, all right. But who's to say it wasn't half rotten already?"

In hearing distance, Botsie looked up from his work and frowned.

Carrie stood and slung shiny water droplets from her hands. "Well, I know! Both of these wagons were in good condition when Da bought them just a few months ago."

Matt broke a lacy twig from a tree. Seconds later, he frowned and sailed it aside. He felt sick and disappointed inside—and he half believed her. But a proud, loyal part of him refused to accept her allegations.

For an instant she met his eyes, then turned and stared at the capsized wagon, lying only yards away. "I'm going back and look again," she declared. Resolutely, she strode past Botsie, who poured muck into the long tom.

Matt glanced at her while she stooped in the flower-strewn grass to examine the brake lever. Two orange butterflies sailed from the wildflowers and landed on her skirt, which belled out around her. As she brushed them away, her breasts strained under the worn dress, and the wind ruffled her loose hair, making her look younger than ever. This fiery young woman had prompted him to reexamine his life. He listened to the rushing creek and considered her words. Was there a wild chance she could be right? Could John have actually engineered such an accident? His mind troubled, he strode to her side.

She picked up the brake lever and held it out. "Still not convinced?" she challenged. "One part of this was sawed. There ain't no jagged edges, and nothin' breaks off like this without help."

An empty feeling washing through him, he took the wood and examined it. "Don't you think Shamus or Botsie would have known if someone came out here?"

Shielding her eyes, she studied the digging on the hill-side. "No, not if they came at night. The wagon was up the hill from their bedrolls—and pannin' gold all day makes a man sleep awfully hard."

"All right, say we accept your theory that someone did tamper with the brake lever. Why do you insist John was behind it? Why couldn't it have been any wild-eyed claim jumper?"

"Because most wild-eyed claim jumpers just come in blastin' buckshot," she responded. "They couldn't figure out somethin' like this."

His thumb moved over the sawed brake lever. "Using the law to get what he wants is more John's style. Why would he do this when he can use the annex law?"

She picked up a rock and sailed it aside. "Can he?" she asked, looking him in the eye. "You yourself said the vein was so broken up he was havin' a hard time provin' anythin'. This is just his way of makin' sure he gets what he wants!"

Her words made sense. Worse than that, they made him very uneasy about his uncle's integrity. He rested his booted foot on the wagon wheel and peered at Botsie as he moved down the creek. "You know, this *does* mean another problem for you, Carrie."

"Another problem? That's all I've been havin' lately. Which problem are you talkin' about now?"

He tossed the brake lever into the lush grass and walked to the other end of the wagon. "I doubt that Shamus will be able to work the mine for a long while."

"He won't," she answered, slowly tracing Matt's foot-steps. "You should see how broken up he is. But what does that have to do with anythin'?"

"Have you considered how you're going to support yourself and Peony and take care of your father's bills while he's recovering?" He looked at Botsie's clumsy ef-forts with the long tom. "I doubt that old man can make enough to feed you."

The wind, which carried the scent of crushed grass and

flowers, tugged at her hair. She glared at him. "I've got a little savin's. I can make do."

"Can you? It may take your father a long time to mend." With a sigh, he chose his words and plunged ahead. "I've got a business proposition. I'm ready to offer you a job as my assistant at the *Courier*."

Tears filled her eyes. "I don't want any handouts."

"You're not getting any. You're going to work that stubborn red head off for me."

Anger flashed through her eyes. "Do you think I'd work in the same office with Jenny?"

"You don't have to. I fired her last night after the ball."

She stared at him with puzzled eyes. "You did what?"

"I fired her. I decided it was time to make some decisions."

"I don't understand."

"You don't have to."

Quickly, she moved away and turned her back. "I don't know, it still sounds like a handout to me."

"Aren't you the same lady who told me she was going to learn about journalism?"

She turned around, her face miserable. "Yeah, but I didn't know I'd have to learn about it from you!"

He crossed his arms and laughed. "Knowledge has its price, my dear."

Tears swam in her eyes again. "Seein' I have Da and Peony to take care of, I'll accept your offer—but I want you to know I'll be workin' on a temporary basis only. Oh, there's another thing," she added in an embarrassed tone. "Don't think because I slipped a couple of times I'm goin' to be an easy mark. There will be no . . . no . . . well, you know."

He let his gaze travel over her gorgeous face and lush figure. For a long minute, he stared at her silently. "Fine . . . we'll keep things on a professional basis. Be ready to go to work day after tomorrow."

* * *

Dressed in a simple blue shirtdress, Carrie walked down the planked sidewalk toward Matt's office. Her nerves on edge, she took a breath of cool air and glanced over Crested Butte's steep roofs toward the mountains. The morning sun had just pushed the shadows away and softened the mountains' hard edges with a rosy glow. A new dawn, she thought: a new dawn and a fresh start. Feeling responsibility settle around her shoulders like a heavy mantle, she dropped her gaze and put her hand on the *Courier*'s doorknob.

Matt looked up from his work with a grin as she came through the door. He was wearing a smudged print apron and calico print sleeves safety pinned over his white shirt. The friendly, warm look in his eyes touched a vulnerable spot deep within her.

"Well, you're here bright and early. Want some coffee?" he asked, handing her a fresh mug he had just poured and cooled.

"I suppose so." She swept her gaze over the cluttered office, liking its cozy atmosphere and the smell of fresh ink, paper, and coffee.

"Good. That's the first thing you have to learn about the newspaper business. It runs on nerves and coffee."

She chuckled and took the warm mug; then her gaze strayed to a large piece of equipment.

Matt poured himself coffee from a battered pot, then moved to the press and lovingly rubbed his hand over the toggle levers. "I see you're looking at the press. As the advertisement says, the Washington handpress is the pride of the Western pressroom. It is elegant in appearance, quick, simple, and powerful in operation."

She grinned. "To me it looks like an old iron winepress with a big leg shootin' out the front of it."

"That's just about what it is." He drank some coffee and placed the mug aside. "It's a descendant of the original flatbed press invented by Gutenberg in the fourteen-hundreds. The first wooden screw presses were little more than winepresses."

Curious, she set down her mug and wandered to it. "It's huge. How does the thing work?"

"You sure asked that question at the right time. I'm just finishing an advertising job." He reached over to an equipment table and picked up a blackened roller with upright handles on each end. "After you've set your type and locked it in a form, you ink it up with this roller." He whizzed the roller over the set type. It made a squishing sound. "It's just like rolling paint over a table."

She grasped the roller with both hands and pushed it over the type several times herself. "Yeah, or like spreadin' jelly out for a jelly roll." She laid the roller on the equipment table. "Well, that was easy. What next?"

He picked up a large sheet of clean newsprint and placed it on a large, wooden frame. "Next, you place a sheet of paper on this hinged wooden tympan."

"The tympan? It looks like a window, don't it?" she asked, tapping the frame with her fingernail.

"That's right. To use your language, you slap the window with the paper over the type, then slide the whole thing under the platen."

"And what might that be?"

"The platen is just this heavy weight that presses the paper and inked type together." He slid the bed bearing the form to a position beneath the platen.

"It looks like a big square skillet lid, don't it?"

He laughed and shook his head. "If you want to think of it as a gigantic skillet lid, go ahead." He put his hand on a smooth metal bar. "Now all you have to do is pull this bar and the platen will press the paper against the type and make an impression."

"What are these funny things right here?"

"They're toggle levers. They keep the platen from twisting and smudging the impression when leverage is forced down." He placed her hand on the bar. "Go ahead, pull the bar."

Feeling a surge of excitement, she followed his order and printed a crisp advertisement for Hellman's hardware store. "Well, blood and thunder," she exclaimed, staring at the sheet, "this is just like pressin' out butter molds or somethin'. I didn't know it was all so easy."

"It isn't quite as easy as you think." He picked up his coffee and took another gulp. "Take a look at that California job case over there."

"You mean that tall case with all the little drawers in it?"

"Yep. You have to know where all the type is without thinking"—he grinned wickedly—"unless you happen to be one of those rare people who can naturally read upside down and backward." With a frown, he raised his voice. "And you need to make sure you get every piece of print back in the right drawer. Don't misplace it. Type is expensive, and all the foundries are back east."

She rolled her eyes and sighed. "Yeah, yeah, yeah, I'm hearin' you." She picked up a narrow metal stick. "What's this funny thing?"

"That's your type stick. You clamp your type into that before you put it on the form."

"Why?"

"The type stick will show you the exact line of type. You can see if you need to add spaces to justify the margin."

She frowned and sighed. "Umm . . . now we're gettin' into all that little dull, nitpicky stuff, ain't we?"

He laughed again. "If you think setting type isn't as much fun as writing colorful stories, you're right—but you need to learn all of the business, even the dull, boring parts."

She opened one of the job-case drawers and ran her fingers through the heavy type. "I'll never learn where all of these letters are."

"You ought to be glad we're printing in English. There are only twenty-six characters in the Roman alphabet. How would you like to learn the twenty thousand or so in the Chinese language?"

She wagged her head. "No, thank you!" Her gaze

moved to a stack of newsprint in the corner. "What about that paper over there? Where do you get it?"

"Getting paper is a real problem. All the paper mills are back east with the type foundries. If the train gets switched off, you're dead in the water."

As he picked up another sheet of newsprint, she paced to a leather couch by the window. Outside the quiet office, some freight wagons creaked down Elk Street. She sat down on the couch and watched him place the sheet on the tympan. "How much do you make off this paper?" she inquired suddenly.

He frowned and folded down the tympan. "Not much. If you're looking for money, you won't get rich in this business. Anyone who considers themselves literate would pay a dollar for a month-old Eastern paper. They'd pay almost that much for a recent copy of the *Rocky Mountain News* or *San Francisco Chronicle*, but for the *Courier*, they pay ten cents. As you can imagine, I don't clear a lot of profit."

"Why do you do it, then?"

"I like to write. Of course, journalism in the West carries worse problems than financial woes."

"What do you mean?"

"Well, let me give you a few examples. Someone shot a cannonball through a publisher's window in Georgetown. A lunatic kidnapped William Byers in Denver because he didn't care for his editorials. And a bunch of idiots tarred and feathered an editor in Utah."

"You don't mean it?"

"Every word. They didn't have any tar in a little Kansas town, so they just covered an editor with sorghum molasses and sandburs before riding him out of town on a rail." He put his hand on the bar and printed another advertisement. "Sure you want to be a journalist?"

Was this a test? Was he trying to scare her? "Yeah, I'm sure. Stuff like you just mentioned don't scare me a bit— neither does hard work."

Matt grinned and whipped off his print apron. "All

right, then. I need to go out and rustle up some more subscribers. Try printing up a dozen copies of this advertisement.'' He took off his stained print sleeves and tossed them aside. "And for your first assignment, write up a story about the new meat market that's opening next week. The facts are on my desk.''

He strode toward the door and grabbed his Stetson from a hat tree, then walked to a shelf of books. One at a time, he pitched her a grammar book and a copy of Shakespeare's plays. "After you've studied the first three chapters of this grammar book and done the exercises at the end, stretch your soul and start reading *King Lear*. Oh, yes, the storeroom needs straightening up, too.''

She raised her brows at him. "Anything else, master?''

"Yes—spend some time with that job case. Get so familiar with it that you can slap type on that type stick without even thinking.'' He paused at the open door. "I'll be back about six o'clock. I'll review your story over dinner tonight. Do you think you've got enough to keep you busy until I get back?''

She glared at him. "I don't know. If I have any time left over, I'll paint the office.''

"I thought you weren't scared of hard work.''

"I ain't—but I ain't an idjit either.''

Matt chuckled and closed the door behind him.

Chapter 12

By seven o'clock the Elk Mountain House Hotel was full. The dining room was fragrant with the heavenly aroma of coffee and buttery, sugar-sprinkled pie crusts; the clatter of rattling dishes floated from the kitchen. A pigtailed girl carrying a huge silver tray had just served dessert. Matt looked up from his flaky apply pie and scanned Carrie's face. "By the way, how's your father?"

"Oh, he's healin' up pretty good, but he's still weak and washed out and his heart is actin' up a little. Besides that, he just keeps worryin' about that annex law." She leaned forward and searched Matt's eyes. "You haven't heard anythin' about how John's doin', have you?"

"No—he's been tight as a clam about it."

She grinned and rubbed her nose. "Well, you finally did it, didn't you?"

"Did what?"

"Ain't that one of them clichés the grammar book says writers ain't supposed to use?"

He slid her a superior grin. "Well, what would you have said, Miss Shakespeare?"

Concentrating, she stared over her shoulder at the velvety drapes. "I'd say tight as a fat lady's garters, or tight as a pair of wet boots, or tight as a banjo string." She glanced at his amused eyes. "Let's see . . . how about tight as a hangman's noose or tight as a preacher's jacket? Want me to go on?"

"Can you?"

"Sure. The stuff just pops into my head."

"Great. Next you'll be telling me you're simply the instrument of a higher power."

He chuckled and took a bite of the juicy, cinnamon-scented pie. "Well, at least I know you've been studying that grammar book." He glared at her. "You *have* been studying it, haven't you?"

With a sigh, she tossed her fork down. "Yeah, I've been studyin' it, but I don't know that it's been helpin' me any."

"Why?"

"Well, it may help me spell and punctuate, but it can't help me think—and it seems that's what a person needs for writin'."

"Thinking and grammar aren't like oil and water. They can go together, you know." He smiled and nodded at a portly gentleman as he passed their table.

"Who's that?"

"Elmer Hellman. He runs the hardware store, and he's a big advertiser."

"I guess advertisers are real important."

"You bet they are. I couldn't make it just selling subscriptions."

She swallowed a mouthful of sweet pie and washed it down with hot tea. "That's because your paper is dull."

"I'm sorry—news *is* dull sometimes."

"No, you just make it that way. It doesn't have to be." Idly watching the golden juice run from the pie crust, she asked, "What happens when the news runs out? There can't be that much goin' on in Crested Butte."

"I look at my exchanges."

"What's that?"

"Just notices and clippings other papers send me." He finished the syrupy pie. "There's a great exchange system out here in the West. We all use each other's stuff and credit the source."

"That sounds pretty handy. Do the exchanges ever run out, too?"

"Sometimes. I've never resorted to it, but occasionally

editors invent wild tales about wompus cats or phantom Indians, or anything else they can think of to fill up space."

"Now, I like that!"

"Yes, I thought you would." He tossed his napkin aside and pushed back his chair. "We need to get some work done. Get out your article and let me see it," he added, taking out a pencil.

Her heart thumping, she tugged the folded article from her bosom and laid it in his hand.

His face darkened like a storm front. A vein standing out on his temple, he slapped the papers on the table and scratched out several lines. "What's this? A comment on the price of meat? This isn't an editorial, you know."

"Well, maybe it should be."

"An editorial on the price of meat?"

"Why not? For a workin' man the price of pork chops is a lot more important than what's goin' on in Denver."

He sailed the pencil stub over another line. "God Almighty, you've used a double negative here."

"Well, that don't matter noway. It just makes it stronger."

He read on in stony silence.

Carrie slumped back and crossed her arms. "Go on— go on and say it. I guess you think it's just awful."

After blacking out another line, he looked up and laid the pencil aside. "Yes, it is awful. The whole thing is a twisted literary deformity, but it's also fascinating in a strange way. You have a stunning grasp of the common vernacular and use words like I've never see anyone use words." With a scowl, he held up the papers and jabbed his finger at a circled passage. "You use them like a stick to bludgeon the reader into submission."

"Yeah, but I entertained them while I was bludgeonin' them. That's better than just plain bludgeonin' them to death with dullness." She cocked her head and grinned. "Don't you know you have to make them laugh first— even if you want to stomp their heart out later? Why, every gospel-sharp and jackleg politician knows that. I think all those fancy schools you went to sucked out all your common sense. Folks are kind of lazy about thinkin'—you have to ease them into it.''

He smiled condescendingly and shook his head. "I'm well acquainted with the uses of humor and satire—but we're talking about a news story."

"And I'm talkin' about gettin' people to pick up the *Courier* and read it. You need more feature articles. And your news items need colorin' up. Why don't you let me touch up your stuff a little?"

"*You* touch up *my* stuff?" His eyes fiery, he shook a finger at her. "Do you mean fictionalize a news story? Don't you know you never put your opinion in a news story!"

"Well, you give your opinion all the time."

"That's because I keep it on the editorial page!" He blew out his breath and stared at her. "You know, you should write dime novels or bodice rippers. That sex-in-the-coach-box-with-the-devil-riding-postilion stuff would really be your meat."

She fell into silence. "If I didn't know any better, I'd think you were makin' fun of me again."

"I'm not making fun of you! I'm just frustrated with you."

"You're really frustrated because your paper is dull and it ain't sellin'."

He glowered at her.

She leaned forward and winked. "I've got an idea. Why don't you let me write a little column for you? We could put it in the right-hand corner of the front page so folks could see it real good."

"You've been on the job one day and you're ready to write a column?"

Sighing heavily, she raked back her hair. "This is the problem, Matt. Your stuff is so wordy it's hard to read. I could kind of translate it for the common man."

He fished out a cheroot. "You're thinking of a large credit, no doubt?"

"Yeah, yeah, that would be good. And we could call the column Carrie's Comments, or something like that."

He turned sideways and crossed his long legs. "Ahh, yes, Carrie O'Leary, writer and raconteur. As truth's local authorized agent, I suppose you'll want to give public readings in the firehouse next. To hear you talk, you're journalism's last hope."

His face bright with amusement, he toyed with the cheroot. "My sweet child, do you actually think I'd give you free rein to verbally terrorize the citizens of Crested Butte with your opinions? People read newspapers for facts."

She stared at him, wondering if there was any scheme she could forge, or lie she could spin, to get him to buy the idea.

"They also read them to be entertained."

"I've been editing this paper for seven years."

"Yeah, and how many years have you been doin' it wrong?"

"Facts are the most important thing we have to sell!"

"Good—let's be kind of stingy with them, then. We don't want to run out!" She sighed. "Look, Matt, I'll make you a deal. Let me write that column, and if you haven't sold more papers in one month than you've ever sold before, I'll quit and not bring it up again."

Lamplight gilded his hard face as he stared at her.

"Well, say somethin'. It's so quiet I can hear your fingernails growin'."

He lit the cheroot and took a long draw. "It will be a feature piece, Miss—not an editorial column. And I will check and double-check every work, comma, period, and exclamation mark in it. No fireworks or bastardized superlatives. If you try to slip something past me, you'll be out the door faster than a jackrabbit with its tail on fire." His face dark, he took another long draw and leaned forward in the creaky chair. "Forever!"

Light from a kerosene lamp flickered over Carrie's damp face while she struggled with the print stick. Matt took her sweaty hand and twisted it around. "No—you hold the type stick like this."

She glowered at him and clamped another piece of type into place. "You're a hard master, Matt Worthington."

"I'm just trying to make sure you do it right. I've never seen anyone who was so inept with type. You actually look like you're in pain while you're working with that stick."

"Well, I *am* in pain. I'm in pain from listenin' to you all day. Do this, Carrie, do that, Carrie, have you cleaned the storeroom yet, Carrie? I've run my legs off tryin' to please you for weeks now."

He filled up the print stick and studied her anguished face. "Feeling like slave labor?"

"No. The slaves got to rest while they were clampin' on and off their leg irons."

He laughed and picked up another type stick.

Sighing, she ambled to the equipment table, then turned around and glared at him again. "I've had to learn a whole new language in three weeks. Quads and quoins, outs and overs, hellboxes and sheep's hooves."

"That's a sheepfoot," he said with a chuckle.

She rolled her eyes and sighed. "Well, at least I made you laugh. It wouldn't hurt you to do more of that, you know. We could use more laughter around this office."

He smiled and cocked his brow. "Oh, yeah?"

"Yeah. Don't you ever whistle and sing or anythin'?"

"No."

She shook her head and groaned. "Mother Mary, you're a hopeless case. I suppose I'm actually goin' to have to teach you a song to cheer you up." She moved toward him and raised her chin. "Here, you watch me while I sing—then you try it."

Tossing back her shiny hair, she began to sing. Matt was transfixed as she moved about the room, her light blue shirtwaist a frame for her creamy complexion and bright hair. She sang unselfconsciously, with great depth of emotion, and her voice carried a sweet plaintive tone that touched emotions he'd barely known existed. He had to get hold of himself. Finally, the last words of this poignant melody came rolling off her tongue like golden coins.

> "I thought, O my love, you were so—
>   As the sun or the moon on a fountain,
>   And I thought after that you were snow,
>   The cold snow on top of the mountain."

Matt dryly commented, *"That's* supposed to cheer me up?" Grinning, he walked toward her. "I think if I wanted to make someone laugh I might do this." Without warning, he grabbed her waist and started tickling her.

She squealed and tried to pull away, but he held her fast and tickled her until tears seeped from her eyes. "Please, no," she gasped. "I'm losin' my breath!"

"I thought you wanted more laughter around here."

She broke free and ran past the desk, knocking a carelessly stacked pile of notices to the floor. Her eyes wet with tears, she dropped to the floor to pick up the papers.

Matt stooped by her side and clasped one of her small hands, feeling warmth stir his loins. He thought of their weeks together, standing close while they set type or worked with the press. Every day he had see the fire in her eyes and smelled the soft scent of her hair. Lord, how had he resisted the temptation to ravish her on the spot? The experience had been excruciating. Even now, it took all his resolve to keep from kissing her rosy lips. He leaned forward . . .

Quickly, Carrie rose and started piling the notices on the desk. "Wait a minute—look at this," she exclaimed, looking at the last notice. "This is just what I need for my column." Standing, she held up a picture of a lovely, dark-haired woman in a low-cut gown. " 'Dovie Benningfield, famed music-hall entertainer, will tour Colorado in August,' " she read.

Matt's heart lurched. Damn, why hadn't he thrown the thing away when it came in? Rubbing the back of his neck, he slowly stood.

She glanced at him. "What's wrong, Matt? You look real peculiar. Do you know this woman or somethin'?"

"No, no, I was just surprised to see it."

Satisfaction spreading over her face, she studied Dovie's picture. "This is just what we both need. We'll get lots of mileage out of this. You can write it up for the stuffed shirts and play up the lady's musical refinement. I'll write it up for my column and tell the miners how pretty she is. Everybody will love it."

"Sure, sure, everybody will love it," he echoed in a faint voice.

Preoccupied, he walked back to the press; then the sound of running footsteps seized his attention. Before he could turn around, a brick crashed through the *Courier*'s window, splintering glass over the floor. Like a shot, he rushed to the door and jerked it open. A blurry form clattered down the planked sidewalk and dissolved into the dark night. Instantly, Matt whirled to check on Carrie. She had picked up the brick and was reading a note that had been bound to it with a piece of rough twine.

"Here, give that to me," he ordered, taking the note from her.

She snatched it back, crumpled it up, and threw it on the desk. "Why should I? It concerns me."

Boiling with anger, he paced to the desk and smoothed out the note. His jaw tight, he held it close to the lamplight and read: "Get that O'Leary woman out of your paper's office—or she's going to get hurt!"

Finnigan's Saloon smelled of tobacco, whiskey, and sweat. Their faces rosy with drink, happy men lined the long, crowded bar. Seated at round tables, other grimy laborers clinked glasses and ruffled cards. Surrounded by miners, a piano player banged out a lively melody on an old upright. In a sheltered corner of the saloon several miners and their wives ate dinner—a simple one-item special that Finnigan's offered nightly.

Carrie and Peony had just seated themselves when Jack

Penrose walked past. "Do you two mind if I join you for a bite of supper?" he asked.

"Make yourself at home," Carrie replied.

After Jack joined them, the trio ordered stew and corn bread and started eating. When they had finished the meal, Jack began complaining that there wasn't anything to do in Crested Butte during his few hours away from the mine.

Carrie watched a miner snap open the *Crested Butte Courier* and run his blunt finger under a headline. "Look at Will Larkin. He reads all the time. You could try readin'."

Jack shifted his gaze to the miner. "I like that column you write. But Mr. Worthington's writin' is 'ard to read."

Nodding her head in agreement, she watched as Will walked to the table.

"Carrie, what's this word?" he asked.

Roughly, she took the paper and scanned the word he pointed at. "That's 'insufferable'," she answered tiredly.

Will tugged at his ear and grimaced. "In-suf-fer-able . . . What the hell does that mean?"

In a kinder voice, she explained, "It means somethin' that's too much to bear, Will."

"Ohh, I see. Like workin' in the Silver Queen?"

Jack laughed and slapped his leg. "You said a mouthful there, my friend."

The miner guffawed and stabbed at the paper again, repeating, "In-suf-fer-able, in-suf-fer-able." Several of the men gathered around to see what he was laughing about. "Why does Matt Worthington use big words we can't understand?" Will asked. The others murmured similar questions, then looked at her with curious eyes.

While the miners waited for an answer, she proceeded to the bar and rested her arm against its cool marble surface. "Matt Worthington uses big words because he don't think workin' people are interested in readin' newspapers, lads."

Thumbs hooked in his suspenders, a short, sandy-headed miner declared, "I'd be interested in readin' a paper if there was somethin' in it for me."

The drinkers along the bar stopped talking and looked at Carrie. "Me too," another piped up, "if the words were plain enough to understand."

"Gol durn, I wish we had us a good paper," wheezed an old-timer. "I don't give a good goddamn who's givin' tea parties on Ridge Hill!"

Everyone laughed and nodded.

"Carrie, you know how to write. Your column is real good. Why don't you write us a whole paper we could read?" suggested Will. "I'd buy it, and so would everybody else."

Peony beamed at her mistress while the crowd cheered.

Carrie's heart lifted—then her spirits quickly dropped. "To make a paper you need a printin' press, lads . . . and that little item costs a pretty penny."

Will scratched his head. "What if every miner who works in the Queen threw in some change on payday? Would that be enough?"

"Every miner?"

"Yeah," he answered with a crooked grin. "We could all spread the word, and I'd be in charge of takin' up the money. The press would belong to all of us." He turned and eyed the warm, crowded saloon. "It would be our newspaper, boys, and Carrie would write it so we could understand it. We wouldn't have to be ignorant no more."

A roar punctuated with long whistles went up from the grimy crowd.

Jack sauntered to the bar and thumped down his fist. "Now you're talkin', lads! We'll name it *The Miner's Press* because it belongs to us. Carrie will write you a paper that will make you laugh, and make you cry—and educate you, to boot!"

The men laughed and stamped their feet. Their faces plastered with tobacco-stained smiles, two burly miners hoisted her atop the bar. She waved her hands to silence the noisy miners, then looked down on them. "Slow down, lads. You're goin' a bit too fast," she warned. "Where are we goin' to buy this press? And who the devil is goin' to set the type? I've learned a lot of things since I've been workin' at the *Courier,* but I ain't learned that."

Will grinned from ear to ear, showing a shiny gold tooth. "It's easy as pie. Matt Worthington can help you with everythin'!"

Matt tossed down his inked print roller and stared at Carrie. "You want to do *what?*"

She sauntered to his desk and plopped down in a swivel-based editor's chair. "I thought I made myself clear," she said, spreading out the skirt of her low-cut, blue gingham dress. "I said I want to buy a press. Where can I get one?"

He shook his head and snorted with derision. Lord, he wondered, what would the little heller think of next? A muscle twitched in his jaw. He wiped his hands on an inky rag and threw her a hard look. "Why the hell do you want to buy a press, anyway?"

She propped her small feet on the desk and looked at him as if he were addled. "Well, why do you think? I want to start a newspaper."

He whipped off his white print apron, then strode to a potbellied stove where a pot of bubbling coffee scented the air. "Oh, you do? First you want to write a column, now you want to start a newspaper. What are you going to do next—run for Congress?"

She jumped to her feet and glared at him. "I didn't come here to be insulted, I came here to ask a simple question." Her eyes flashing, she lifted her chin.

Silent, Matt only scowled at her.

When he didn't speak, she stalked to the door.

"Oh, don't get your drawers in a knot," he rumbled. "Sit down while I explain a few facts."

After she had coolly reseated herself, he poured two cups of coffee and placed one in front of her. "All right . . . To answer a simple question with a simple answer," he ground out as he perched on the edge of the desk, "you order your press from A. B. Taylor and Company." He opened a bottom desk drawer and slammed a thick book down in front of her. "You'll find the press on page seventy-eight. They manufacture them in Chicago and ship them west by rail."

Her face aglow, she ruffled the pages with her thumb. "How fast could I get one?" she prodded.

He smiled tightly. "Well, if you telegraphed the order and sent a check on the first eastbound train—maybe six weeks." He swigged his coffee, then grinned. "I hope you have a wad of money in your sock, darling, because you're going to need it."

She glanced up from the dog-eared book and blinked. "Oh, money's not a problem. The miners are all chippin' in—we talked about it last night. It will be their paper. And they don't know it yet, but after expenses are paid, half of the profit will go to a widows' fund I'm startin'." She smiled sweetly. "And don't be worryin' about that column. I can write it and anythin' else you want for the *Courier,* and still have time left to write my own paper."

He plunked down his coffee. "Tell me, Carrie, why do we need two papers in Crested Butte? What's wrong with the *Courier?*"

"They can't read it," she said while she scribbled down the manufacturer's address. She tossed the pencil aside and met his gaze. "The words are too big, and you don't write about things they're interested in."

"But you're going to?" he asked, raising his brows.

"Yeah, they like my column because they can read it. Now I'm goin' to write them a whole paper they can read." She smiled up at him. "Outside of you, how much competition have I got?"

Frustration tightened his voice. "Well, *outside of me—* not much. Every time the railhead shoots forward, a bunch of little papers pop up like fleas on a dog's back. Way out there where it's nine miles to water and ten to hell, there are even a stubborn few who set up in tents."

She smiled again, pleased. "Now, ain't that interestin'. Who are they?"

"Mostly misfits. Lawyers, preachers, politicians, land speculators—anyone with a drum to thump—just your kind of folks."

Her eyes danced with defiance.

"You thinking about joining them?" he added in a hopeful tone.

"Yes, if I have to," she shot back. Before he could speak, she carried her coffee to the window and turned her back to him. "I know you're gettin' ten cents for the *Courier*."

"Yes. Why did you bring that up?"

She whirled about and grinned impishly. "Well, I'm goin' to ask seven cents so I can undersell you."

"Hell, lady, that kind of news goes down like a dose of kerosene!"

"This is a free country, ain't it?"

He studied her as she drank her coffee. Despite his anger, admiration warmed his heart. This was one lady who would never give up on anything. "Yes, it's free," he finally answered. "But before you can use the free enterprise system, you need something to sell. All I've heard about are dreams."

"And what's wrong with dreams?"

"Nothing, if you have the wherewithal to back them up! Even if you get a press, how are you going to afford the paper and print?"

She frowned and shook her head. "There you go draggin' up more problems again."

"All right, let's say by some miracle you do overcome those little hurdles. Where are you going to print this fabulous seven-cent paper of yours?"

Her half-empty cup in hand, she sauntered toward him. "Matt, I'm an old hand at makin' do. When I get my equipment, I'll print the paper in an outhouse if I have to! Until then, I'll pay you rent and use your stuff."

"Use my stuff!" He stood and clenched his hand. "God Almighty . . . and you told me *I* had nerve."

"I'm offerin' you a sound business proposition, man. I thought you might like to make a little on the side. Of course, if you're afraid of the competition . . . "

"Afraid of competition from *you?*" He flashed her a grin. "Tell me, who's going to edit this paper for you—or do you plan to write it in your own colorful dialect?"

"Oh, since I started my column I've been studyin' a lot. I know how to use all that grammar stuff when I want to now."

He shoved a pencil behind his ear, then sat down on the desk and stared at her speechlessly.

"Well, come on. Say somethin'," she prodded. "What do you think?"

"A woman running a newspaper! Lord, how did you come up with that idea, anyway?"

"I didn't. The miners came up with it, and I just couldn't let them down." She placed her cup on the desk and walked to the press. "But I did some readin' in the *Rocky Mountain News*. There's a woman named Caroline Remmy who edits a paper in Durango called *The Record.*" Her eyes wide, she stared at him. "And up in Oregon there's a woman named Abigail Duniway who writes a paper. She's been clamorin' for women to get the vote since 1871."

"What are you going to clamor for?"

"Mine safety, better wages, sick pay, a walkout, and a union." She shook her finger at him. "If I see somethin' that needs writin' about—I'm writin' about it!"

"Well, you better be a dead shot, darling." Anger threaded his voice. "This isn't like back east. You've already received a threatening note." He nodded at the patched window. "Doesn't that put the fear of God in you? If you really get someone riled up, they won't throw a brick through the window, they'll aim a bullet at your head!" He put his coffee down and walked to the press, beside her. "I've been spit at, punched at, and shot at," he continued. "Think you're up to that?"

She looked at him seriously. "I think so. You know what's the best thing about havin' nothin'? You ain't got nothin' to lose. And I'd rather go down writin' somethin' that will help somebody than be holed up someplace, safe but scared."

"You're not afraid of the devil himself, are you?"

"Guess not—'cause I figure he looks a lot like you."

He burst out laughing. "God Almighty, woman, you could talk a hungry dog off a meat wagon!"

Seeing her chance, she grabbed his arm and tugged at it. "Come on, Matt. You've got to do it. This paper will make the miners feel like they really count!"

He stared down at her while she pleaded with her eyes. "Don't you understand, man?"

"I understand I'm a fool for even considering this. If I *do* agree to this little enterprise, there's going to be a list of rules!"

Ignoring his words, she beamed up at him, her face wreathed in smiles. Then she seated herself behind the desk and began to scribble out a story.

His jaw tightened. "Carrie, what the hell are you doing?"

She eyed him hotly. "I'm drivin' a stake. I'm fixin' to get published!"

Chapter 13

Carrie rose to get a pencil from the other side of the desk, then smoothed out her long black skirt and reseated herself. Lamplight flickered over her intent face as she turned another page in the grammar book. She mumbled to herself while she underlined a passage. "Use 'very much' instead of 'very' as a modifier of the past participle in a passive verb phrase. Wrong: We were very surprised at her answer. Right: We were very much surprised at her answer." She snorted and flipped another page. Holy Mother, what a load of muck, she thought as she shoved up the sleeves of her pink blouse.

When she heard the tap-tap-tap of Matt's boot heels, she jumped and slammed the book closed, then shoved it under some papers on the desk.

Matt opened the door and sailed his Stetson toward a hat rack. He was dressed simply, wearing a white shirt open at the collar and dark trousers. "Have you written that story about the McFalley twins that you promised to give me before supper?" he asked. "I have to set the print on it tonight."

She glanced up and toyed with her lace collar. "Sure. There wasn't much to it." She picked up the scribbled paper and began reading woodenly. " 'Mrs. Dora McFalley, wife of Timothy McFalley, gave birth last week to twins. The infants, Timothy and Kenneth, are both doing well. Mrs. McFalley says she hasn't had time to contact relatives back East.' " Carrie sighed and looked up. "It goes on like that. You know, a lot of dull stuff about kin-folk and how long they've lived here.''

Matt grinned. ''Hold on! Back up a sentence or two. What was the last thing you said about Mrs. McFalley?''

''I said she hasn't had time to write relatives back east.''

He snatched the grammar book from its hiding place. With a wide smile, he flipped through the book, seeing places she had underlined. ''Praise the Lord. Could it actually be possible you've been reading my grammar book? And could you have actually dropped that colorful contraction *ain't?*''

She shrugged her shoulders. ''What if I have? You've been naggin' me about it for weeks now. I'm so used to followin' all your writin' rules I'm beginnin' to talk like you—and I hate it!''

From the desk drawer she pulled out a list entitled ''Matt's Rules.'' At the bottom of the long page, written in red ink, were the words *Don't Use Ain't!* ''Da said I was beginnin' to sound like I lived on Ridge Hill, and I believe he's right.''

She moved to a pile of newspaper stacks and picked up a copy of *The Miner's Press.* ''If I keep writin' and talkin' like you, pretty soon my paper is goin' to be as dull as yours.'' She pointed at a story she had written last week. ''Just listen to this.'' She began to read.

'' 'A man was wounded in an altercation in our city on Wednesday evening. The particulars were not related to this reporter.' '' She shook her head. ''That's terrible! Now, wouldn't it sound better if I'd written this? 'John Miller was plugged while he was cattin' around shanty-town Wednesday night. If anybody knows anythin' about this scrape, they ain't talkin'.' ''

Matt laughed and lit a cigar. ''Well, forgive me, Carrie. I didn't mean to stifle your originality by teaching you English grammar.''

She carried the paper to the desk and sat down again. ''It's not all your fault. Part of it is mine for tryin' to copy you. That kind of style is all right for your people, but it doesn't work for me and mine."

"Why not?"

"Well, I promised the miners I'd use language they could read, and I'm lettin' them down. When I mention somethin' about the union, they seem to ignore it. I think it's just because they can't understand it." She tore the thin newspaper in half and threw it on the floor. "From now on I'm writin' like I want to write." She looked at his scowling face. "Oh, when I write a story for you, I'll use good English like you taught me, but I'm goin' to make *The Miner's Press* stout and excitin'."

"Exciting?"

"Yeah, we need a good knifin', or a shootin' or somethin'."

He chuckled again and sat on the edge of his desk.

She pawed through a basket of news notices beside him. "Here we are takin' shifts eatin' supper and stayin' up late and we still don't have anythin' good to write about. Even these exchanges from other papers are dull as dirt. Just a bunch of marriages, births, and deaths."

She stood and strode to the press, stopping suddenly. "I know—I'll write a long story and keep it goin' so they'll have to buy more papers to find out what happened."

"Good idea. That's called a serial piece," he informed her while he slipped behind the desk.

"I'll make it funny so they'll be sure and read it," she went on. "But I'll ease in some stuff about the union a little bit at a time." She looked at his amused face. "You know, when a man's not used to thinkin' for himself, you can't give him a big idea all in one chunk—and that's what I've been doin'. You know how you told me editors sometimes make up wild tales when they don't have any news stories? Well, I think I'll write a story about a big fat grizzly bear that cheats all the other animals until they ban together to fight him. Of course, all the miners will know I'm talkin' about old John."

He rocked back in his chair, puffing away on his cheroot. "That's quite inventive, Carrie. You are acquainted with the libel laws, aren't you?"

She arched her brow and grinned. "As far as I'm concerned, grizzly bears is grizzly bears!" She wiggled her fingers. "Ohh, I can hardly wait to write it."

Smiling, he took out his pocket watch. "Well, it's getting late. I suggest you finish this issue of *The Miner's Press* first—but before you do, I need to talk to you." Standing, he looked at her seriously.

She widened her eyes and stared at him. "What about?"

"About the mine."

"You . . . you want to talk about the Silver Queen?"

"Yes. In fact, I'd like to talk about some of your thoughts right now. I don't subscribe to all your ideas, but you've made me consider things I'd never thought of before."

Joy surged through her. Maybe he was beginning to come around, to accept her views. This could be a real milestone in their relationship—a real breakthrough. She remembered how close they had been when they made love. Wouldn't it be wonderful if they could be that close mentally, she thought. "Like what?"

"Well, it seems that when the boys go into the mine, they never come out—they're locked into one occupation the rest of their lives."

"Oh, yes, that's right . . . and they go in so young. You see, most of them come from large families and they start workin' to help their dad feed the little ones. It's the script that keeps them in such debt. They just keep sinkin' into a pit they can't get out of."

He tugged at his ear and looked thoughtful. "You know, I think I'd like to publish an article about the Queen written by you."

Her heart leaped. "I've written several articles like that for the *Press.*"

"Yes, and to be truthful, they were good. In the interest of an open press, I'd like to give the folks who subscribe to the *Courier* a chance to read your views."

Quickly, she scanned the messy desk, looking for a piece of clean paper. "Fine. I'll get us some paper so I can write things down. This may be a long talk and I want to make sure I don't forget any of my points." With a sigh, she glanced at the storeroom. "There isn't anything to write on here. I'll have to go to the storeroom to get some paper."

She picked up a kerosene lamp, then pushed aside some curtains and fumbled along the narrow, dark hall of a room. But when she reached the open paper cabinet she found the shelf empty. Hearing Matt's steps, she placed the lamp on a shelf and turned around. "What are you doin' in here? I'm gettin' paper."

"I remembered I moved the box. I was afraid you'd never find it." He squeezed by her, and she could sense the warmth of his body, so close to hers. She caught her breath while he stooped and rummaged around on the bottom shelf until he found an unopened box of paper. He rose and attempted to push by her again, and she felt the pressure of his broad chest as he brushed against the front of her blouse. She felt alarmingly light-headed from holding her breath so long. She suddenly realized he had stopped moving.

She looked up and found her lips inches from his, his eyes intent on her face. With only the slightest hesitation, he laid the box on the shelf and took her in his arms.

"Matt, we've both been good . . ." she protested. "I think we've set some kind of record, workin' together and all."

He muttered, "Well, records were meant to be broken, weren't they?" And then his lips took hers.

She tasted a trace of tobacco in his mouth, felt his hard manhood ridged against her as he gathered her closer yet. Gradually, one hand moved to her breast and teased it through the thin material, making her gasp with pleasure. With a superhuman effort she pulled her mouth away from his and sighed. "We can't be doin' this again, 'cause we'll both regret it afterward."

"You may regret it—I won't." His lips covered hers once more.

What was love anyway? she wondered while the fire built inside her. What she had thought all her life, or this wild hunger she felt for Matt? Unbidden tears slid down her cheeks.

He paused to glance down at her. "What's wrong, love?" he whispered. Before she could stop him, he kissed the tears away.

Happiness flashed through her heart. Like a thirsty man drawn to an oasis, she clasped her hands behind his head and pulled him closer. Why was she so afraid? Things were going wonderfully. Matt had opened up and was finally listening to her. They were on the edge of working everything out, on the edge of finally understanding each other better. "Nothin', Matt, there ain't nothin' the matter. I just made a decision."

As his lips found hers in the shadows, he deepened the kiss and probed the recesses of her mouth with his hard tongue. Deftly, he unbuttoned her blouse and slipped his hand inside her lacy shift. With sure confidence, he cupped her breast in his warm hand, then eased his lips away to scan her face. "Ah, love, how beautiful you are," he uttered. When he reclaimed her mouth, his fingers tenderly rolled her nipple, arousing her further. In response, she met his tongue and trailed her hand down his trousers.

When he moaned, she gently drew away and opened her eyes. The orange light from the kerosene lamp whispered over his glossy hair and high cheekbones while desire flamed between her thighs. The strength she found in his features frightened and excited her at the same time. Need trickled down her spine like ice water at the sight of the raw hunger in his dark eyes.

Her body aching with passion, she pulled his head down and surrendered to his lips again. As the hot seconds melted away, her hand was drawn once more to the insistent urgency of his manhood. She could hear his ragged breath and feel his pounding heart. He unbuttoned her skirt and the garment slid to the floor with a whispery rustle. Groaning, he tugged down her bloomers and kneaded her bottom. His sure fingers worked their way forward until they nestled against their moist destination.

A moment later, the office door slammed. Carrie stiffened, her heart racing wildly. His face alert, Matt looked at the square of light at the end of the dark passage. Then Carrie heard soft, familiar steps in the office.

"Missy? Missy, are you here?" came a frightened voice.

"It's Peony," Carrie whispered. With frantic haste, she adjusted her bloomers and blouse, then jerked up her skirt and fastened it. Smoothing down her hair, she walked to the end of the dark, narrow storeroom. Steeling her nerves, she entered the softly lit office.

Her face white, Peony stood near the desk like a forlorn child.

Carrie heard Matt's footsteps behind her as she took the girl in her arms. "Peony, what's the matter? What's wrong?"

Tears welled in the girl's almond-shaped eyes. "It's Mr. Shamus, Missy. He real sick. The doctor thinks he had heart attack."

Sudden tears stung Carrie's eyes. She felt like a great vise had closed around her heart. "Go back to him," she whispered. "I have to talk to Matt for a second, then I'll run right after you."

Covered with a sheet, Shamus rested on Carrie's bed in the Elk Mountain House. Deep lines creased his lips, and smudges brushed his lower lids. Softly crying, Peony sat at the foot of the bed. Bandit sprawled at her feet.

Da may be dyin' and I can't do a thing about it, Carrie thought. Her lashes wet with tears, she sat beside her father and watched lamplight flicker over his haggard face. "Da, will you see Father Newly?" Carrie whispered.

After a pregnant silence, Shamus finally spoke in a gravelly voice. "Me beliefs have not always agreed with the church, but the little priest seems kind enough. Ask him to come in."

She stood and signaled Peony to get the priest. The Chinese girl slipped into the hall, and moments later a gray-haired priest entered. Carrie led Peony from the room. "Tell me what happened," she said, touching the girl's slender arm. "I didn't want to talk in front of Da."

Peony's eyes glistened. "It was Mr. Worthington's man, Missy—a lawyer, I think. He came up to the room about bedtime. I couldn't understand everything, but I know he told Mr. Shamus that he had lost the Shamrock." She began to sob.

Carrie held her close. "That's all right, you're doin' fine. Go on, tell me what happened next."

"Well, Mr. Shamus, he gets very mad and he shouts and shouts. The man puts papers down on table—very hard—and he leaves. Right after that, Mr. Shamus slumps over and holds his chest—he whispers for me to get Dr. Pritchard. I run as fast I can. When we come back, he gives Mr. Shamus some medicine that makes him rest and go to sleep. Then I ran to the *Courier* for you." Her black eyes brimming with tears, she asked, "Where is Mr. Matt now? Why did he not come?"

"He's printin' *The Miner's Press*. I asked him to do it." She shook her head. "There's nothin' he can do anyway. You said the doctor was comin' back—maybe he can tell us how Da is gettin' along."

Peony wiped her eyes while she watched Shamus and the priest through the open door. "What kind of person would tell an old, sick man such bad news?"

· "I think we both know the answer to that question, girl—a mean, small-hearted man like John Worthington. But he's too cowardly to bring the news himself: he hires people to do his dirty work." She heard the priest's rising voice and knew he would soon be finished.

After praying, the priest cleared his throat and patted Shamus's arm. Concern flickered over his face as he moved toward Carrie. "Shamus has a good heart and a great love for you, my dear."

Tears filled her eyes.

"Mr. O'Leary hasn't visited the church in years, but he has a great appreciation of God's handiwork and a great practical faith. Surely God knows of his love for the woods and the vales and all the wild, hidden things."

She nodded, mute.

Genuine sympathy deepened the man's clear blue eyes. "I'll come back later." With that, he touched her hand and left.

Peony took her place at the foot of the bed once more. Sighing, Carrie sat down again and lifted her father's gnarled hand. "How are you feelin', Da?"

"I'm feelin' terrible," he rasped, "and why shouldn't I be—I'm dyin', ain't I?"

"No, you're not dyin'." She tried to mask her emotions. "Do you think God wants a stubborn old Irishman like you?"

He moaned and touched his chest, whispering, "Ohh, I feel like I've been run over by an ore cart."

She laughed and wiped her eyes. "Hush, save your strength. You don't have to entertain me, you know." She moistened a rag in a bedside bowl and sponged his brow. Then she kissed his callused palm.

He squeezed her hand and murmured, "Well, there's one thing that eases me partin', darlin'."

Ever so lightly, she ruffled his silky curls. "What's that, Da?"

He eyed a whiskey bottle on the bedside table. "This is the way every Irishman should die, stretched out beside a bottle o' fine whiskey. Now, if you would only give me some."

"Oh, Da." She sighed and smiled.

"Miss O'Leary, may I come in?"

Carrie jumped at the voice, then turned and saw Doc Pritchard at the door. Tall and lanky, the bearded doctor wore a dark frock coat. She stood and offered him her chair. "Yes, please, come in."

She moved back to the door and watched the doctor examine her father. At last, the doctor spooned some medicine into Shamus's mouth. He then lifted the Irishman's head and offered him a glass of water. Silent as a shadow, Peony took the glass when Shamus finished drinking.

Doc Pritchard pulled the sheet up to his patient's chin, then snapped his bag together and looked at Carrie. He pushed up his loose spectacles as he walked toward her.

"Miss O'Leary, there's really nothing else to be done . . . he'll slip away easy," he explained in a soft voice.

The words stabbed through her heart. "Slip away?" she whispered hoarsely. *"You mean he's dyin' and you can't do anythin' for him?"*

"No, I can't. His heart is so damaged it's scarcely beating. He's truly living on borrowed time."

"How . . . how long does he have?"

The doctor raised his brows. "Oh, perhaps the rest of the night." He glanced at Shamus. "I'm surprised he isn't gone already."

Carrie felt like her throat would burst with tears. "Yeah, he's a stubborn old man, all right."

He sighed and patted her shoulder. "I'll come back later to verify the death. You'll need some privacy now."

She watched the doctor disappear, then, blinded with tears, went to Peony. "Go downstairs and sit with Botsie. I saw him down there by himself when I came up."

As soon as the girl had left Carrie numbly returned to the bedside chair. Shamus rolled his head and looked at her. "That medicine is workin'," he rasped. "I feel high as a kite."

She rubbed his cracked hand. "Da, are you thinkin' of Ireland?"

Tears misted his eyes. "Aye, I can see it with me heart now. I can smell it, and I can feel the warm earth in me hand. I had fine times there when I was young."

Listening to his words, she imagined the young boy

who'd ventured forth boldly to meet life, never guessing the trials he would encounter.

His voice rallied. "Carrie, the air was so keen after a sudden spring sower and so heavy with lilacs, it made your head reel." He coughed and stared at her while she wiped his lips. "But I'm ramblin', ain't I?"

"No, go on! I want to hear about Mam."

Happiness flickered over his face. "Our first year was hard and we was thin as rails. But that first icy winter we made love every night and we were happy, for we had each other and our dreams." He glanced up sharply. "That's important, Carrie. You need somebody to love. Some people go through life with no more than a thimble-ful of joy."

"Yes . . . I know."

"Bury me by your mother, God rest her lovely soul. She's worth a dozen Irelands." He squeezed her hand once more. "Which brings me to another point."

"What's that, Da?"

"This Matt Worthington. If you love him, don't be denyin' yourself. Don't die without really knowin' love."

She tried to speak, but her lips trembled.

"I think he's different, girl. He and old John may have come off the same shoot, but they're as different as corn and cabbage."

"Da . . ."

"Hush now, I'm gettin' in me dyin' words, ain't I?"

She swallowed her tears and nodded.

"And don't be forgettin' the lads in the Queen: you're all they have . . . and take care of that poor Chinese girl." His face paled. "I want to sleep now," he said in an easy, relaxed way. He closed his deeply sunken eyes. "Give your old da a hug."

She held him so tightly their bodies seemed to melt into one. Maybe if I hold him close enough to my heart he won't die, she thought desperately. When he was asleep, she spread her hand over his heart and, feeling a faint beat, moved to the window.

Tears flooded her eyes as she prayed for strength. On the other side of the window a red sunrise bled into the dawn sky and highlighted the trees by Finnigan's Saloon. The emptiness inside her ached like a bruise. Shamus was dying, and nothing she could do would bring him back. Her throat tight with emotion, she glanced at the bed and noticed that his right hand clutched the sheet. Her heart began to pound in her ears.

The moment she touched him she knew he was gone. She had left him for barely a second, and he had slipped away as easily as a raindrop from a green leaf. Her eyes wet, she fled from the room and stumbled down the stairs. With the air of lost children, Botsie and Peony huddled around an empty table. Tears choked Carrie's throat; she couldn't look at them. She had to get out, had to get some air.

Once outside, she clung to a porch post. A cool dawn breeze caressed her damp cheeks. Dizzy, she glanced across the street and saw Matt striding toward her in the dim light. Rage blossomed deep inside her. Damn the Worthingtons anyway! Shamus would be alive if John hadn't sent a man to tell him news that had crushed his poor heart.

Matt reached the porch and touched her arm. "I finally got the *Press* printed—just like you wanted. How's Shamus?"

She stared at him, then swallowed her tears and looked away, down the silent street. "He's dead."

He tried to take her in his arms, but she eased away. Pain darkened his eyes. "Carrie, I'm sorry. I'm very sorry."

"I know you are, but it won't do any good."

He scanned her face. "You're thinking about us, aren't you?"

She moved to another post. "Yes . . . things have changed."

His face tense, he cupped her chin. "Since last night?

What do you mean things have changed? You said you'd made a decision. I thought—''

"I know what you thought, but it won't work. Too many people are standin' between us now!''

He frowned and dropped his hands. *"Who's* standing between us?''

Her fingernails bit into her palms. "Seventeen hundred miners and my father's ghost.'' She clenched her teeth and eyed his troubled face. "Did you know John sent a man to tell Da he had lost the Shamrock?''

Matt dropped his gaze.

"Hope was the only thing keepin' Da goin', and John ground out that hope like he was crushin' an insect under his shoe.''

Matt's eyes flashed. "Look, I know you blame John for your father's death, but I didn't choose my last name.''

"No, you didn't choose it, but your name will always be Worthington, won't it?'' She wiped her eyes. "I'm movin' my stuff out of your office today. I won't print any more papers until I get my own press.''

"You don't have to do that,'' he said tightly.

"Yes, I do. At best, us workin' together is an awkward situation. At worst—it's downright foolish. I think we proved last night we can't work together on a business basis.''

A muscle twitched in his jaw. "There you go again. Listen, Carrie—''

"Sweet Mother of God! Do you think I can share an office with you when your uncle killed my da?'' She glared at his rock-hard face and shook her head. "You're ready to publish my article, but you still won't take a stand, will you?''

"No, I can't—not when you expect me to blindly believe everything you say!''

"You'll never believe it until you see it with your own eyes, will you? Your family loyalty is just too strong, ain't it?''

She watched as he turned to walk across the street. "I

dare you," she hollered after him. "I dare you to find out what kind of man your uncle really is. And you can start by takin' a good look at that hellhole he calls the Silver Queen!"

Grubby miners packed the huge building housing the Silver Queen's only shaft. Steam hissed from the shaft opening and floated to the beams, forty feet above. Far across the wood-floored building, an engineer kept his eyes on two large dials and maneuvered levers on a hoisting engine. Its bell ringing, a cage clanked up from the deep shaft, bringing a group of grimy laborers.

Dressed in shabby clothes, Matt tugged down his derby and eased behind the patient men who waited to descend into the steam. Carrie's words had haunted him for the past two weeks. *I dare you to find out what kind of man your uncle really is,* she had said. While the men inched forward he thought of her small, black-clad form at Shamus's funeral. Proud and distant, she had refused to meet his eyes even as he had longed to comfort her.

One of the men nudged him forward, bringing his mind back to the present. His face smeared with grime, Matt scanned the scruffy miners about him. A friendly-faced fellow caught his eye and spouted in an Irish brogue, "You're doin' a double shift, ain't you?" Torn trousers encased the man's stout legs, and his feet were shod with thick brogans. A felt skullcap crowned his head. "I see you ain't had time to clean up. Why'd you come up? Get a bite to eat?"

"Yeah," mumbled Matt.

The Irishman moved closer and grabbed his arm. "Bejabbers, you're green as corn, ain't you? How far down you workin', two thousand?"

Matt watched miners pour from the cage and listened to the cable creak around the engine spool. "Yeah, two thousand. First time I've been down that far."

"I thought so. Well, stick with me, mate." He shoved

out his thick arm and shook hands. "Me name's Tim Delaney."

"Johnson, Tom Johnson," Matt rumbled over the noise.

A bell rang, and the men pushed Matt and Delaney into the cage—an iron frame with a rotten wooden floor and open sides. The stench of tobacco and whiskey clung to the miners' close-packed bodies.

As the cage lurched downward, Matt glimpsed a huge room dotted with shirtless men. He heard the sound of muffled voices and swinging picks. Seconds later, blackness closed in, and the sides of the shaft shot up around him.

Delaney elbowed him. "We're comin' to the fifteen-hundred-foot level next."

Matt felt the men tense while they braced for the stop. Soon a big, main draft flashed into view and the cage rocked to a halt. The miners, all wearing long johns, held candles and lamps. Narrow gage tracks crisscrossed the floor. Several miners jumped the gap between the cage and the draft, giving the remaining men more room. Delaney chuckled as Matt wiped his face. "What's wrong, man? I thought you were a miner. Hot, ain't it?"

Matt shoved the handkerchief into his pocket. "Hot as hell."

"Mary, Jesus, and Joseph. Now I *know* you're green. It's only a hundred here. At two thousand feet it'll be twenty-five degrees more. We couldn't take it without the blowers and the ice."

"We had plenty of ice at Mount Davidson. How's the situation here?"

The cage plunged into the blackness again and Delaney cleared his throat. "Bad, real bad. Worthington's awful tight with the ice—lost two haylofters last week because of it." His voice tightened. "Heat stroke, you now. The lads was laid out like cods. I drug them into the cage meself. Pity of it, one of them was only a boy."

An acrid taste filled Matt's nose and mouth. "What's the rest breaks for this level?"

"We're supposed to have half an hour o' work and half an hour o' rest—but it don't work out that way."

"Oh?"

"Yeah, Clayright sets us quotas, you know. To meet your quota, you gotta work most of the rest period. That's why them new fellers passed out last week."

Light from the two-thousand-foot level flickered over the miners' tense faces while the cage bumped to a halt. The Irishman nudged Matt again. "Let me give you some advice, mate. Strip off them clothes real fast. Move slow, and stay up next to that blower pipe."

Matt nodded and jumped from the cage with the other men. Their shuffling footsteps echoed about the cavernous room as they claimed their tools.

Delaney shed his pants. "Another thing—drink lots o' water and chew ice if you can get it. That's what us old hands do to keep goin'." He picked up a lamp and glanced over his shoulder. "The little ice we got is in them barrels over by the blower pipe."

Matt stripped off his pants and looked at the men around him. Limp drawers and breechcloths draped their shiny bodies. The miners' thick muscles gleamed pale against the bluish ore as they worked. Swinging heavy picks, they assaulted the walls, which glittered with copper pyrite. Here and there, quartz crystals twinkled like gems.

With the odor of rotten wood and laboring men filling his nostrils, Matt hoisted a pick and began work. By the time the saliva had thickened in his mouth, he noticed Delaney at his side again. The wiry Irishman tugged Matt's blistered hand from the pick and closed it around an ice chunk. "Pace yourself, man, pace yourself. You've got to at this level, if you're goin' to last."

All at once, the timbers groaned and dust floated downward. Matt stared up at the high ceiling. "God Almighty, what's happening?"

Delaney wiped his sweaty brow and grinned. "Worthington uses old salvaged timbers to save a dollar. Rotten as a hunk o' ripe cheese, they are. I should know, I put a lot o' them in." He ripped a strip from one of the nearby timbers, then crumpled the wood and tossed it away. "See? They groan all the time. What we keep our eye on"—he pointed to several rats eating lunch scraps—"is them!"

"Rats?"

"Aye, tame as dogs, they are. They know when the rock is movin'. They can sense it or somethin'. When we see them skitterin' about, we run for the hoist."

Matt spied a grappling hook next to his discarded pick. "That hook—what's it for?"

Delaney spit on the ground and looked embarrassed. "Well, you know, man . . . it's for the sump."

"Go on."

"Blood and thunder, ain't you seen them pull nobody from the sump yet? You *are* green, ain't you? Sometimes when we come topside, the ride up cools us off too fast. We try to watch everybody, 'specially the green lads, but sometimes they faint and tumble from the cage. Then they bounce down the shaft and fall into the sump." His face paled under the grime. "The water's a hundred and sixty degrees down there. We keep it all pretty quiet; it would just tear up the women folk. We asked Clayright to get some proper cages, but he said Worthington wouldn't allot the money."

Anger tightened Matt's throat.

"What's wrong? You looked puzzled or somethin'. Everybody knows this is the worst mine on the Slope." Delaney held up the stump of his index finger. "I lost me finger choppin' them rotten timbers down here last year. I pressed me suit and got fifteen dollars in a one-time settlement. Aye, he's a stingy bastard, all right." He stared at Matt with surprise. "Brace up, man. You better get used to it. We don't have a way o' fightin' him, you know."

Matt slumped down, his eyes fixed on the pitted wall.

"That's right. Sit down. Suck that ice. After you rest, I'll show you around some more."

Matt shook his head. "No, I think I've already seen enough to last me a lifetime."

Chapter 14

Louvered doors slapped behind Matt as he entered the Elk Mountain House barroom. His teeth clenched, he scanned the smoky room, which smelled of cheap perfume and sweaty bodies. A piano player pounded out a frisky tune—the place pulsed with buoyant good feeling. Miners and merchants stood side by side, lining a long brass rail. A large gilt mirror tilted from the wall reflected the drinkers' red faces. His sleeves circled with garters, a barkeep in a starched jacket slid shot glasses down the smooth counter so customers could pour their own drinks. Brass lamps twinkled on the wall behind him.

Now where in hell is he? Matt wondered. His gaze skipped over the rest of the room while he threaded his way into the crowd. Nearby, a table of curious miners eating hard-boiled eggs watched him. In one corner, a roulette wheel clacked; in another corner, Betty B'damn, Crested Butte's most famous courtesan, dealt cards for faro. Next to her, under a picture of a fleshy nude, a cardsharp pulled players in for three-card monte. The dandy shuffled the cards and flipped three of them on a green felt tablecloth. "Now watch this heart, gents." He raised his finger as Matt brushed past the table. "How about you, sir? You got enough sportin' blood to pick the heart?"

Ignoring the cardsharp, Matt finally spotted John Worthington seated at a table toward the back. His eyes glazed, the heavy man snapped down cards as he played solitaire. He clenched a cigar in his teeth; a glass of iced bourbon and water sat by his free hand. When Matt blocked his light, he looked up with a start. "Matt, for God's sake . . . what's that grime on your face? And why are you dressed like that?"

"For where I was going, this getup seemed to be the best attire."

Worthington laughed. "Where, might I ask, have you been?"

"I've been in a suffocating pit otherwise known as the Silver Queen."

Worthington took the gnawed cigar from his mouth with an injured air. "God, you didn't have to go to those lengths. I'd have taken you on a first-class tour."

Matt took a chair. "I didn't want a first-class tour. I wanted to see for myself this dangerous situation you've been spouting off about."

"Well, it *is* dangerous."

"Yes, I found that out, John, and I also found out why you didn't want me to see those new rooms you put in last year." Matt slapped a sliver of rotten timber on the table.

Worthington's face paled.

"God Almighty, the place is a death trap. A rotten hoist floor, rotten timbers, scarcely any ice. A—"

"Hold on, Matt," Worthington cut in. "When did you get so high-and-mighty?"

"Since I worked a shift at two thousand feet with a pack of poor bastards who'll be doing it for the rest of their lives."

The heavy man smirked. "Seems you had no complaints when money from the Queen sent you to that fancy Eastern school."

Matt crumpled up the rough wood. "No, I had no complaints. How was I to know what went on? On all our tours of your model room at five hundred feet, we were met with smiling faces and manly jokes. At thirteen, I didn't realize the poor devils were smiling because they were scared to death. Looking back over the years, I'd say you did a damn good job of keeping me *out* of the mine.''

Worthington threw down his cards. ''Yes, I did—because I cared for you,'' he said in an earnest tone. ''There will always be grumblers and loafers, and yes, there will be a few accidents along the way—most of them prompted by the men's own negligence and horseplay,'' he finished self-righteously, then swirled the ice in his drink and fell into a moody silence.

Matt shook his head and stared at the clacking roulette wheel. ''I refuse to accept that explanation.'' He leaned forward, clutching the edge of the table. ''Why didn't you allot money for some decent cages, for God's sake?''

His uncle slammed down the glass of bourbon. ''Don't you realize once I start giving in to their requests they'll never stop wanting? I have to watch every penny if I'm going to make a profit.''

''Tell that to some mother after they pull her boy from the sump.'' Matt ran his gaze over the tycoon's puffy face. ''I hear you're paying fifteen dollars for a lost finger now, John. Sure you can afford that much?''

Color splotched Worthington's cheeks as he picked up the cards again. ''Fifteen dollars is a lot of money to men like that.''

Matt noticed a familiar spicy aroma and glanced at the cigar jammed between the man's pudgy fingers. ''How much do you pay for a box of those Havana cigars? Have them shipped in from Cuba via Frisco, don't you?''

''Look here, I'm tired of this cross-examination! You have no idea how the Silver Queen stands financially. I'm being forced to take drastic measures as it is!''

''Like what?''

''Like gradually cutting wages thirty percent over the next six months.''

Matt clenched his hands. ''You know, you make me sorry my name is Worthington.''

''Wake up, man! I'm actually doing them a favor. If I

have to close the mine because I can't make a profit, they'll all starve."

"Right, but you'll keep right on buying those cigars, won't you!" Matt gibed as he stood and turned to go.

Worthington waved his stubby hand. "Wait, let's talk this out. Where are you going?"

Matt pushed through the crowd, then glanced back over his shoulder. "I'm going to see Carrie O'Leary about a story."

Night sounds filled her ears while Carrie strolled down the planked sidewalk bordering Elk Street. Insects chirped, distant thunder rumbled, and the voluptuous smell of rain hung heavily on the warm air. She stopped as she crossed the alley that ran between the barbershop and the general store. "Faith, Bandit, did you hear a noise?" At the alley's end a small streetlamp washed the dust with dim light. She paused to peer into the shadows, but found them empty except for a stack of crates at the general store's side entrance. His floppy ears pricked up, Bandit whined.

As she started on her way a faint sound claimed her attention again. Narrowing her eyes, she traced the dark doorways along the alley and listened to the night wind stir the dust. Outside of the wind and the distant music from Finnigan's Saloon, she heard nothing. She rubbed her damp palms on her skirt and slipped uneasily into the alley. "Mother Mary, I could swear somethin' or someone is here," she whispered, wandering to the shipping crates.

Bandit whimpered nervously and trailed her steps.

Her throat tightening, she glanced at a crowbar and a hammer carelessly left on top of the half-opened crates, then she studied the shadowy doorways again.

Very softly, a man's raspy voice called, "Miss O'Leary . . . I need to talk to you."

Her heart galloped while she waited to see what would happen next. Every instinct told her to *run*. She pushed herself away from the crates with shaky arms. "Come on, Bandit, let's get back to the hotel." She had taken only three steps when a thick arm brutally slammed her to the dust. She gasped and rolled over.

Through tear-blurred eyes, she skimmed the man's heavy body from his cheekbones to his brogan-shod feet. A kerchief covered his face, and a knitted cap concealed his hair and forehead. His shoulders were wide and thick, his balled hands rough and scarred. Her gaze jerked back to his face and she studied his vaguely familiar, contemptuous eyes. Weak and dizzy, she glanced at Bandit, who was standing guard, growling at the ruffian. Suddenly the man snatched up the discarded crowbar and hurled it at Bandit, who yelped piteously as the iron bar knocked him across the alley.

"Holy Mother . . . What have you done to Bandit!" Carrie tried to get up and go to him, but the man stood in her way, breathing heavily through the thick kerchief.

"That mutt can't help you now. He's dead."

An aching hollowness filled Carrie's heart. She had lost her final link to the past—to all that was old and familiar and warm. Now she was totally alone. She bit back a sob. "No . . . he ain't dead. He can't be!"

The ruffian yanked her forward. "Get up."

"No . . . I—"

He jerked her to her feet. "Yes, get up!"

With a dry chuckle, he released her hand, and she staggered backward and slammed against the side of the barbershop. Tears stung her eyes, but she rubbed them away and bit her lip. Don't cry, she ordered herself. Raise your head, look proud! By now the attack's first brutal shock had faded a bit. She gulped back her tears as courage bubbled up inside her.

The man glared balefully at her. When he touched her cheek, she pulled back and willed strength to her weak knees. I've got to get a rein on my emotions, she thought. She squirmed against the building, hearing splinters tear her skirt.

The man lifted her hair and let it slide slowly through his blunt fingers. She bit her lips and locked her legs. She felt sweat trickling between her breasts and down her sides. Finally his hot gaze flickered over her face. "Think you're smart, don't you? Writin' all that stuff in the paper."

Instinctively, she understood her life might depend on self-discipline. She drew in a breath of rain-scented air and spoke in an even tone. "I just write what I think is true."

The man grasped her wrist and she locked eyes with him. Humiliation tore through her, but she composed herself and lifted her chin a bit higher. She couldn't break now, no matter what. Blood roared in her ears and her heart tattooed a crazy rhythm.

Anger—and something else—darkened the man's eyes.

A tiny whimper bubbled from her throat as she struggled to pull away, but he held her fast. While the first raindrops plopped into the dust, the man forced her to her knees. Defiantly, she coughed up a mouthful of spit and hurled it at his face. The surprise made him loosen his grip for an instant, and she fell to the side and rolled away.

A second later, a possessive hand clenched her arm. A swift glance told her the hand belonged to Matt. His face a stiff mask of rage, he pulled her to him. The crowbar swung in his hand as he glared at the attacker. "Care to take me on—or do you just harass women?"

The man whipped out a knife and snarled, "I'll cut your heart out, rich boy."

Matt pushed Carrie to the side and studied the intruder's eyes.

The burly man stared back, searching for an opening, then he lunged.

Matt's feet slid over the soft pebbly earth while he dodged several crude attacks. Seeing his chance, he swung the crowbar and knocked the knife from the thug's hand.

His head down, Matt darted for the shiny blade; but as he stooped to retrieve it, the man wrenched away the crowbar.

Matt grasped the knife and eyed his opponent. "Looks

like we have a brand-new game here. Still have enough stomach for this?''

"Enough stomach to knock your head off.''

Matt jumped aside as the man swung wildly, using the crowbar like a bat.

When the attacker paused to get a tighter grip, Matt leaned in and sliced at the man's belly, missing it by mere inches. Fat raindrops thudded against the crates and splattered in the dust while they fought. The heavy air was filled with the sounds of their labored breaths.

His eyes alive with hate, the man finally swung the crowbar in a smooth arc aimed at Matt's head. Matt ducked and, with one hand, caught the thug's wrist; then, using all his strength, he forced the man's quivering arm upward. The intruder's eyes flooded with pain and the crowbar fell from his hand.

As the ruffian fell back, Matt glanced at Carrie. Her eyes widened, and he pivoted in time to see the thug retrieve the crowbar and charge forward like an angry bull. In an instinctive reaction, Matt sliced downward at the man's chest. The attacker moaned and dropped the crowbar, then clutched his chest and staggered backward. Blood stained his coarsely woven shirt. "We ain't finished with this yet!'' he yelled as he turned and stumbled from the alley.

Quickly, Matt took Carrie into his arms. "Are you all right, love?''

She sniffled. "Yeah, just scared to death. I was afraid I'd distract you if I tried to help.'' Tears mingling with the rain on her cheeks, she looked at the spot where Bandit lay, wet and still. "The bastard threw that crowbar at Bandit and killed him,'' she sobbed. How small Bandit looked—how helpless, how lifeless. She wanted to hold him and keep him warm and safe.

Disengaging herself from Matt's arms, she ran to Bandit, then scooped up his limp body and held it against her bosom. Her heart ached as she ruffled his drenched, tangled fur. She remembered the day Shamus had brought home the frisky, tiny ball of fluff and put him into her arms. And she remembered all the evenings she had relaxed by the fire's glow, secure in her parents' love, and laughed at the pup's antics. Her mother and father were gone—and now Bandit was gone, too. A great knot swelled in her throat. "I suppose he was just a worthless old dog," she said brokenly, "but he was family to me." She sobbed again. "I can't let him go. I keep rememberin' the way he used to crawl under the cover and snuggle up to my legs on cold winter nights."

Matt went to her side, stooped, and took Bandit. After a moment he clasped her hand and pressed it against the dog's chest. There, she felt a small, steady heartbeat. Joy flooded through her. "He's . . . he's all right?"

"Looks that way to me."

She gathered Bandit in her arms and called his name, waiting for a response. She was rewarded with a wet kiss. Laughing, she let her tears stream down her cheeks.

Matt shook his head and chuckled as Carrie sobbed. "It will take more than a crowbar to kill that ornery mongrel. Nothing was broken; he was just stunned. He's going to live to give me many more bad days. Come on, let's go to my office and get out of this rain." His eyes sparkled. "I have something I want to ask you."

Low-burning flames from a kerosene lamp lit Matt's office. Wrapped in a blanket, Carrie sat on the leather sofa, sipping a whiskey. Her wet clothes hung from the back of a straight chair near the freshly stoked potbellied stove. She hugged the fuzzy blanket around herself and looked at Matt, who stood, bare-chested, by his desk. "Umm . . . thanks for stirrin' up that fire. It feels good even though it is June."

Bandit sprawled near the warm stove, eating a leftover sandwich from the desk drawer.

Matt lit a cheroot and eyed the dog, then sank down on the sofa. "See what I mean? That dog's just fine. Right now he's looking at me like he'd like to tear out my throat.''

Carrie laughed and plunked down the whiskey glass. The liquor had warmed her insides and lifted her heart. Outside, the rain pounded and made the office feel safe and cozy. She glanced down at herself and sighed. "Well, despite all my good intentions, here I sit in my under-clothes, drinkin' liquor with you again." She made a face. "I still hate the stuff, you know."

Matt laughed at her.

Secret joy stirred in her heart while she watched him. At least something good had come out of the attack: it had forced her and Matt back together and got them on speak-ing terms again. And only God knew how much she had wanted that. Her brush with violence had made her see things in a different light—given her a new perspective. At this very moment her love for Matt was so strong it almost frightened her. She now clearly realized that their love outweighed all the differences that might stand between them.

He traced her chin with his thumb. "Are you sure you're all right? He didn't hurt you, did he?"

She gazed into his perceptive eyes. "No . . . just scared me—that's all."

Brandied sweetness floated from the cheroot while he caressed her hair. "You have no idea who the attacker was?"

She pressed her lips together. "No, but there was some-thin' familiar about him." A grin tugged at one corner of her mouth. "By the looks of all that blood, he'll be wear-ing a scar across his chest for the rest of his life."

Matt puffed on the rosy cheroot. "Fine, we'll have every man in Crested Butte take off his shirt so we can identify the culprit."

"I may not know who the man was, but I know who put him up to it."

His face darkened, and he rose and poured himself whiskey from the bottle on his desk. "I'm not ready to agree with you on that, but I do believe you now about the mine." He turned and looked at her. "I went into the Queen this afternoon."

Tears welled in her eyes. "I thought you'd never believe me."

"Yes, I've seen it all—seen the misery and the hopelessness. I talked to the men who work down there."

"That's right," she said, her voice shot with happiness. "Always talk to the man on the spot. He'll tell you what's really goin' on."

He gulped down the whiskey, then touched her face. "I'm afraid it's worse than you think. John is going to cut wages by thirty percent over the next six months."

"Thirty percent? Well, that will just about finish the men off."

"That's what I figured. Care to give me some details?"

She sighed. "Sure. Let's begin with the food. Since the miners are paid in script, they have to buy in the company store."

"Yes, I know."

"Well, here's somethin' you'd have no way of knowin'," she added in a tired voice. "Your empty guts are a mighty heavy load. At a cash store, a barrel of flour would be six dollars. In the company store it's eight dollars. At a real store, butter is nineteen cents. In the company store it's fifty cents. And price isn't the only difference. The *butter* in the company store is made with casein, gypsum, and gelatin fat."

"Go on, I'm listening."

She stared at Bandit, who now slept peacefully. "The price isn't any better for that swill milk the store operator pumps out. He makes two quarts into a gallon by waterin' it down; then he doctors it up with chalk and molasses. No wonder the little ones are sick all the time." She glanced at Matt while he ground out his cheroot, then went on, her voice razor-sharp. "You've also got the problem of housin'."

Matt finished his whiskey and placed the glass on the

floor. "Yes, I know. John owns most of the shacks in shantytown, doesn't he?"

Her throat tight with emotion, she nodded. "Of course. And most of the miners are behind in their rent right now. If they miss another payment, he'll evict them and take some other poor immigrant's deposit money." She swirled her whiskey, then finished it with a grimace. "He's got his foot on our necks and he knows it. We're in a losing situation with no way out!"

A crooked smile played over Matt's face as he gathered her into his arms. "Maybe not. Your union is still a good idea. You just need to organize it and push it." He brushed his lips against hers. "It wouldn't hurt, either, if you had someone to help you."

Her pulse thumped in her ears. "Like who?"

He turned and pulled a paper from the stack by the door. "Like me." With a snap, he folded the paper back and handed it to her. "Read the article on page three—it's yours."

With a soft gasp, she stared at the newspaper. "I didn't print last week."

"No, but I did. Peony brought me an article you wrote after Shamus died."

She could only gape at him.

Mischief glinted in his dark eyes. "Yes, it helps to have a good intelligence system—and those Orientals *are* clever, you know." He thumped the paper. "For God's sake—go on, read it!"

She scanned the paper and smiled. "Why, it's my serial—the Grizzly Bear story!"

"That's right, and John's going to explode when it hits the street tomorrow."

She grinned as she read the story, then looked up at him with narrowed eyes. "You didn't change anything, did you?"

He raked back his damp hair. "Not a word—didn't have to. It was perfect."

Her gaze flew to the top of the page. "Mother Mary, my name's so big! It looks pretty good, don't it?"

"You bet, and it will look even better in *The Denver Star.*"

"*The Denver Star!*"

"Sure. I sent it to a friend there. I'm sure they'll publish it. It's superb, love. Really first-rate—and funny as hell." He took the paper and laid it on the floor, then slid his warm hand under her hair. "I want to talk to you about your ideas some more, but first we have some unfinished business to take care of."

His strong hand trailed lower and found her breast under the blanket. As he touched her nipple she felt a languid heat smolder up between them. After he pushed the blanket away, he slipped off her shift and tossed it aside, then bent to nuzzle her neck.

His fingers felt like gentle flames as they skimmed over her skin. When he lowered his dark head to her breast, hot desire surged between her legs. Fevered and dizzy, she was carried away like a leaf on a swift stream. She moaned in glorious torment as sharp need swept through her. "Lord, I said I wasn't goin' to do this again . . . and here I am doin' it."

He raised his head and chuckled, "Carrie, you do nothing by halves. Your passions for life, for love—they all run deep."

She felt Matt's heart thudding against her breast while he traced her lips with his tongue. When he took her mouth again, some savage force inside her tore away from its mooring like a ship in a storm. Outside the window, the rain thudded down. In the back of her mind she heard the storm's music and she savored Matt's scent mixed with that of the rain.

As he entered her mouth, the kiss became more insistent. She moaned with pleasure while he eased her onto her back and slid down her bloomers. Tugging lightly, he worked them past her feet and dropped them to the floor. At last his fingers dipped into her moist womanhood:

taunting, teasing, and spreading a sensual glow through her limbs. Her bothersome conscience gave way to passion. Lost in ecstasy, she twined her fingers in his thick hair and dug her fingers into his bare back.

His mouth still on hers, he caressed her bud of desire and flicked his thumb over her nipple. When he sensed she was about to explode, he eased off and began the process yet again, stroking gently, insistently. Swiftly, he unbuttoned his trousers and leaned over her. She tensed as she felt his hot desire bob against her flesh.

"Don't be afraid, angel." His ragged voice was shot with warm concern as he grazed kisses on her face and nipped at her neck. "Let your body melt into mine."

She relaxed and arched toward him, allowing him to slide his hands under her bottom and pull her closer yet. With barely restrained hunger, he plundered her mouth in a hot kiss and eased into her pulsing warmth.

Carrie felt a moment of anxiety, but a warm, familiar pleasure throbbed up and lifted it away. When she had accepted him, he paused and lifted his face, searching her eyes. "Carrie, let go, angel."

Outside, rain pounded the earth with savage force, but, wrapped in an erotic trance, she lost track of time and space. Her body had melted into one fiery bundle of sensation. With a whimper, she rolled her head and moved against the pleasure that was almost too much to bear. When he found her rhythm and increased their momentum, she completely surrendered herself to his love.

She pulled him as close as possible, moaning in ecstasy with each carefully timed thrust; then once again she was on the precipice of desire's lofty peak. "Matt, please," she begged, her body straining, reaching. "Now, or my heart will stop." He plunged even deeper, until her breath came in short gasps. Only then did he spill himself into her, taking her to a sweet garden of pleasure where only they existed.

When her heart had settled to a normal beat, he eased her up and they sat side by side on the couch. He cradled her head on his shoulder and adroitly caressed her sensitive breasts. Like their tempestuous emotions, the storm had passed. The rain had slacked to a lulling rhythm and dripped from the porch in front of his office. She nuzzled close to the warmth of his body and felt happy and complete. For one brief moment she and Matt had been one body, one soul. During those precious seconds all their problems had dwindled into insignificance.

For the longest time they listened to the rain and floated in and out of sleep together. Finally Matt rose and tenderly wiped her love-sheened legs with a clean rag from the press. Then he found some blankets in the storeroom and made them a cozy pallet on the floor. Afterward, he blew out the light, laid her on the pallet, and fluttered kisses over her face.

She could see his face in the stove's soft glow. "Didn't you say you had somethin' to ask me?"

He threw her a warm glance and chuckled. "Oh, yeah. What would you say to becoming Mrs. Worthington?"

"Is this a genuine proposal of marriage, you gorgeous man?"

"You bet. If you can't stand being a Worthington, maybe I can change my name to Snodgrass or Bloodsworth."

She giggled and ruffled his hair, too happy to even answer.

He tugged the blanket over her bare shoulder. "Oh, you find those laughable? Well, how about Duckworth or Dingleson?"

"God help me, I do love you . . . and I'll marry you even though your name *is* Worthington."

He laughed and pulled her into his arms. "You know when I first realized I loved you, you little hellion?"

"No, when?"

"Well, I think I had a pretty good idea even before we left the cabin. You'd managed to touch a part of me I'd numbed up so I wouldn't hurt anymore. But when I saw you talking to Henderson, I wanted to strangle the man. I realized then how badly I wanted you—and needed you.''

She grinned and cocked her brow. ''Oh, yeah? Well, if you think I'm goin' to say somethin' mushy like that, you're a great fool.''

He laughed and kissed her fingers. ''We've really had some obstacles to overcome, haven't we?''

She smiled and winked. ''Yeah, like your hardheadedness about the mine.''

He widened his eyes. ''What—me hardheaded? What about your temper?''

''My temper? Surely you ain't talkin' about the way I stand up for my firm convictions?''

With a wide grin, he held her close. ''Well, all that's in the past. Thank God we're pulling together.''

''And I suppose you'll want to be the lead horse?''

''Well, I—''

''You know, whenever you're followin' the lead horse, there's always one thing you can depend on for sure,'' she interrupted. ''Every time you glance up, you're lookin' at a horse's rump.''

Matt laughed and nuzzled the side of her neck. ''Why, you little mischief. Is there a moment that nimble Irish brain of yours isn't turning?'' He brushed back her hair. ''As star-crossed as our relationship has been, it's a wonder we reached this point. We've had to battle everyone and everything—including a determined preacher's daughter.''

Carrie frowned. ''Jenny Parker? Just thinkin' about that woman makes me feel sick. Have you seen her lately?''

''No, actually I haven't seen her since I fired her. Can we stop talking now, Miss O'Leary?'' He held her close again and kissed her long and lovingly.

Fire burst inside her. ''Well, Mr. Worthington, I've always said actions speak louder than—oh!'' His lips captured hers, wordlessly promising a long night of earthly delights.

The sound of the office door creaking open jolted Matt awake. Moving instinctively, he covered Carrie with the blanket, then stood, tense and ready.

Carrie clutched the blanket around her torso, and propped herself up on one elbow just as Jenny burst into the office. Pale dawn light filtered into the room and illuminated the woman's ghastly appearance. The rain-sodden flowers on her straw hat flopped down over angry eyes; her torn, muddied clothes dripped water.

"Jenny! What are you doing here? What's wrong?" Matt asked.

"My, my, what a pretty picture this is," Jenny drawled.

Matt glanced at the wall clock. "God Almighty, Jenny, it's five-thirty in the morning. What do you want?"

She paraded around the office, stopping to eye Carrie's discarded clothes. Bandit barked when she neared the stove where he lay. "Oh, I'm just doing a little investigating. I saw John as he was leaving the Elk Mountain House late last night. He said you were upset, Matt; that you had visited the mine and were spouting some nonsense about discussing a story with Carrie. He said we needed to talk if I wanted to hang onto you."

She took off her ruined hat and threw it down, then glared at Matt. "I've been up all night looking for you! I went to your ranch and tried to get into your house. On the way back to Crested Butte my buggy slid off in the mud. I've been walking for hours in the darkness, the cold, and the rain while you've been getting warm and cozy with this Irish hussy!"

Carrie jumped up, still hugging the blanket around herself. "We're going to be married, you stump-tailed heifer."

Jenny laughed until tears streaked down her mud-splattered face. Then she looked at Carrie with contempt. "You little fool. You fell for the oldest line in the book. Why should he marry you when he's getting what he wants already? He's just priming the pump for more rainy nights ahead."

"Shut up, Jenny," Matt ordered.

Jenny ran her gaze over him. "Oh, yes, it would be rather embarrassing for her to find out, wouldn't it?"

He squinted at her. "What the hell are you cooking up?"

"What the hell are *you* cooking up, love? It's pretty hard to be married to two women at the same time, you know."

"He's marrying me, not you!" Carrie shouted.

Jenny thrust out her hand, which glittered with a huge diamond engagement ring. "Oh, he is? Well, what are we going to do about *this*, then?"

Carrie's heart dipped. "Matt didn't buy that for you."

With a snap of her purse, Jenny handed a large receipt to her. "Read this, dear. I've been carrying it with me in anticipation of this moment."

Carrie scanned the receipt for a diamond ring from Steiner's jewelry store. On the bottom of the dated receipt was Matt's large, distinctive signature. She dropped the paper and sank onto the couch, feeling like the whole world had crashed in around her.

"Carrie, I can explain this," Matt said.

She stood and snatched up her clothes. "Oh, don't bother. You told me you hadn't seen Jenny since you fired her. You lied to me!"

Jenny picked up the receipt and smiled. "Now you're catching on, dear."

Matt followed Carrie across the room, but she stalked into the storeroom and yanked the curtain behind her.

He paced in front of the curtain. "Don't you see what she's doing? Let me get rid of this viper and we'll talk."

"We're finished talking." The blanket sailed over the curtain and hit his head. Dressed in her underwear, Carrie stepped into the office carrying her blouse and skirt.

"Carrie, listen!" Matt shouted.

She shrugged into her blouse and buttoned it up, her fingers trembling. "Why? So you can tell me more lies?" She stepped into her skirt and fastened the waistband, then gathered Bandit in her arms and headed for the door. "Why should I listen when I can see the truth with my own eyes?"

Jenny sauntered toward her. "How many times has he tricked you now? Three or four? My, you *are* a slow learner, aren't you, dear? But, thank God, you do see the light at last, you poor child."

"Carrie, listen. Come back here, you little hothead!" Matt ordered.

Carrie whirled and jabbed her finger at him. "The sun will set in Galway Bay before I listen to you again. An old cat doesn't burn himself twice, you know!"

Jenny looked at Matt's stormy face and patted her hair. "My, my, my . . . she's certainly taking things hard, isn't she?"

Tears brimming in her eyes, Carrie slammed the door behind her.

Chapter 15

Matt entered Taylor's barbershop and scanned its gloomy interior. The shop smelled of leather, hair tonic, and soap. Seeing the place was deserted, he tossed his Stetson on a hat rack and picked up a copy of *The Police Gazette*. Then he made his way to an adjustable chair, sat down, and propped his boots on a velvety footrest. "Ned," he yelled, "are you still in the barbering business?"

Seconds later a small, dapper man eased into the shop from the back room and slipped on a white jacket. Dark, slicked-back hair crowned his head, and a thin mustache highlighted his face. "Mr. Worthington . . . you don't get your hair cut on Wednesdays."

Matt raised his brows at the barber. "Well, I'm getting it cut this Wednesday. That is, if you'll oblige."

Ned flipped open a glass case and snapped out a linen cover. "Oh, sure, yes, sir." He tied the cover around Matt's neck. "We've got a ten-cent special this week on shaves. You want a shave, too?"

Matt slapped the magazine in his lap. "Oh, why not? Just give me the whole works."

Ned chuckled and turned the creaky, swivel-base chair around so Matt faced a mirror. Rows of colorful shaving mugs flanked his dour reflection.

Ned snicked his keen shears in the air. "What's wrong, Mr. Worthington? You don't look too good today. Have you been gettin' enough sleep? Are you off your food or somethin'?''

Good God Almighty. Wasn't it enough he had spent hours fighting with Jenny after Carrie stormed out? Did he have to be cross-examined by his barber? ''Ned! You're a barber, not a doctor. Would you just go on and cut my hair?''

With a wounded sigh, Ned went to work. 'Well, I was just askin', you know.''

Silent as a mummy, Matt thumbed through *The Police Gazette* until he found a lurid picture of a man plunging a pair of scissors into a woman's breast. Lord, he thought, how I wish I were that man and Jenny were that woman. How could he ever explain to Carrie about that afternoon in Steiner's jewelry shop? He had already spent a half day looking for her. And even if he found her, he doubted she would listen to him. He had never seen her so mad.

''You're daydreaming, Mr. Worthington. Here, look out this window.'' Ned turned him so he could see out the plate glass window, then pushed his head down so he couldn't see anything at all. Whistling, the barber snipped and clipped, then dusted hair clippings onto the floor. ''Well, Lordy, Lordy. Here comes your uncle.''

Matt lifted his head and watched John Worthington stride across the street. Dressed to the teeth, the mine owner carried a stack of newspapers under his arm. By the look on his face, Matt knew he had read every one of them. Thirty seconds later Worthington stormed into the barbershop and slammed the door behind him, making the bell ring violently. He slapped the papers in Matt's lap. ''My God, have you read this piece in the *Courier?*''

Matt shot him a grin. ''What piece are you talking about, John?''

Worthington jabbed his finger at Carrie's front-page article. ''You know what piece I'm talking about.'' His face reddened. ''This—this Grizzly Bear thing!''

Matt ducked his head so Ned could cut his hair. ''Of course I read it. I set the type on it.''

Worthington tossed the *Courier* to the floor and hoisted up a thick copy of *The Denver Star*. He flipped through the pages, then displayed an article printed under a humorous cartoon. In the picture, a hideous Grizzly Bear standing in front of a mine complex stuffed small animals into his full mouth. "Well, how about this mess? Have you seen it, too?"

Matt guffawed when he saw the drawing. "Hey, that's a nice touch. I thought they'd print the article, but I didn't know they'd run a cartoon. Looks like someone in Denver has a sense of humor."

"You thought they'd print it!"

Matt glanced at Worthington. "Yes, I sent the article to them."

"This Grizzly Bear serial doesn't bother you?"

Matt laughed good-naturedly. "It's a humorous story, John. Why are you taking it so personally?"

Worthington's small eyes flashed. "Humorous story, my foot. It's vicious satire directed at me!" He picked up two other papers and shook them in the air. "I hope you know what you've started. It's in *The Advocate* and *The Register*, too."

"That many?" Matt said with a chuckle.

Worthington stabbed his short finger at the Denver paper again. "The *Star* says it intends to print the rest of the serial. What are you going to do about that?"

"I'm not going to do anything about it. I run my newspaper, and they run theirs." He tapped his uncle on the chest. "This Grizzly Bear thing is going to make me a lot of money, John. A lot of folks are interested in it."

Worthington glared at him. "So that's it. *That's* what you're interested in." With a dark glower, the heavy man moved to the door and opened it. "We need to have a talk, a long, long talk." His face grim, he slammed the door behind him.

Ned took the papers from Matt's lap, then swiveled him toward the mirror again. "Whew, I've never seen Mr. Worthington so mad," the barber breathed.

Matt chuckled, wishing, with a pang, that he could share the news with Carrie. "It'll do him good. John's had his way too long."

"Tell me somethin'. Did you mean what you said? Are you pushin' those Grizzly Bear stories just for the money?"

"Not really. I just explained things in a language John could understand."

Ned dusted prickly hair off Matt's neck, then picked a steamy towel from a candle-warmed hot tray. "Whatever you say, Mr. Worthington," he said as he laid Matt back and draped the towel over his face. While the barber whipped up lather and stropped his razor, two more customers entered the shop.

"Sit down, boys. I'll be with you as soon as I shave Mr. Worthington," Ned said.

"Oowee, look at that woman comin' across the street," one of the men remarked.

"Yeah, ain't she the most beautiful thing you ever saw?"

"Yes, sir! And that fancy dress she's wearin' didn't come from here," the first replied.

Suddenly anxious, Matt stayed hidden under the hot towel and listened.

One of the men laughed deeply. "She fills out that dress real fine, don't she?"

"Yeah," the other agreed. "In that getup she does a lot of talkin' without sayin' a thing! Wait a minute . . . she's comin' in here."

Matt's heart beat faster as a gardenia scent drifted to his nostrils.

He heard a smooth British voice say: "Hello, gents. Have any of you seen Matt Worthington? They told me at the hotel I could find him here."

Matt jerked the towel from his face and sat up, seeing a breathtaking brunette's reflection in the mirror.

"Matt, love," the woman crooned. "I've found you at last. I've come to spend the whole summer with you—and I have a wonderful surprise!"

* * *

The summer sun sank low and tinged the sky with soft reds. The scent of watermelon tickling her nose, Carrie lay on a quilt and gazed at the rosy sky. Her heart ached as she listened to the wind whisper through the huge oaks. Hearing laughing children, she rolled onto her side and watched the other Fourth of July picnickers. In preparation for departure, mothers folded blankets and snapped baskets shut while small boys with dirty faces sacked up marbles and put on their socks. As she watched, two older boys walked past talking about the fire that had ravaged Crested Butte the previous week.

The fire. Faith, when would folks stop talkin' about it? she wondered. Trying to forget, she lay down again and closed her eyes. But all she could think of was the fire— the fire everyone had gossiped about for days—the fire that had destroyed Matt's office. Her thoughts drifted back to that terrible day a week before. She could almost smell the smoke and almost hear the crackling flames.

After supper she and Peony had strolled to a shady spot near the edge of town. Gradually smoke drifted over the twilight sky, telling her a fire burned in town.

"Missy!" Peony had exclaimed. "What do you think is burnin'?"

"I don't know," Carrie answered. "But I can see the glow from here. Lets hurry back to town."

Once there she saw a man flash his white hat at a confused mob. "All you men—come on!" he shouted. "There's a fire! We need all the help we can get!" A frightened roar rose from the crowd. Soon, clanging fire wagons thundered down the dusky street.

Entering the smoke and noise of Elk Street, she and Peony navigated the sea of people about the office. All around them, men scrambled to join the long bucket brigade. Smoke and dust choked her throat as she pushed through the crowd searching for Matt.

Her heart thumping, she finally spotted him at the head of the long bucket brigade. Tousled hair hung in his face and black grime smeared his square jaw. She raced to him and grabbed his arm. "Matt, are you all right?" she cried.

His eyes blazed as he stepped aside and set down a brimming water bucket. "Oh, *I'm* fine, Carrie."

She sighed and leaned on his arm. "Thank God!" Her heart lurched when he tugged away and scowled down at her.

"Yes, I'm fine, but my office is burning and my press is ruined. Someone smashed it to bits with a sledgehammer. I saw it when I came back from the Elk Mountain House and noticed the smoke. I tried to get things out, but the flames got too bad."

She had never seen him so cold and distant.

He frowned down at her. "Someone had scratched a message on the press. It said, 'Worthingtons, get out.' "

Her spirits sank like a boulder plunging to the sea floor.

"As you can see," he went on, "I'm a little too busy to talk right now. I've been working on another unexpected problem—and then I came back to find my office on fire!"

Then Matt had turned his back, picked up the water bucket, and walked away. Perhaps she should have run after him, but her legs had failed her. Perhaps she should have tried to talk to him the next day, but pride had stilled her tongue. Hurt and wounded, she had turned away physically and emotionally. Even now the memory pierced her heart like a keen blade.

Jack Penrose sauntered up and eased down beside her, shaking her from her troubled thoughts. " 'Avin' fun, Carrie?" he asked.

She sat up and straightened her blue cotton dress. A sultry breeze fondled her skin. "Yeah, Jack," she said uncertainly. "It's been a good day. How about you?"

He grinned broadly. "I always 'ave a good time when I'm with you—but I just figured you weren't feelin' good. You didn't eat 'ardly anythin'."

Silent, she glanced to the east, where a dirt road sliced through a clot of spruce. Its windowpanes gold in the last light, Crested Butte lay at the road's end. To the west, sturdy oaks loomed in stark relief against the red sky. Closer to the picnic grounds, manzanita hugged the purplish earth. With a heavy sigh, she gazed through the dim light at his patient face. "Oh . . . I'm all right, Jack."

He studied her. "Luv, can I talk to you? I've been wantin' to all day."

"Sure . . . you know you can always talk to me." The sound of cicadas grew louder as the light dimmed.

"Well," he stumbled on, "I know you've been worryin' yourself sick about Matt Worthington's office burnin'. It wasn't your fault. You couldn't 'elp it."

She moved her gaze over the hills, which were peppered with spruce, then traced the red horizon. She was glad it was dim, glad he couldn't see her teary eyes. "Yes, I know," she answered softly. "But I'm sure he thinks that miners did it."

"What if 'e does?"

She sighed and looked away. How could she explain what that possibility meant to her? This new problem just pushed her and Matt farther apart. First there had been the awful scene with Jenny—now this. Self-doubt swept through her as she thought of the preacher's daughter. Perhaps she had been wrong about Matt and Jenny. Jenny's story about the ring sounded so convincing—but perhaps there was a slim chance she had been wrong.

While Carrie and Jack talked, fireflies sparkled near the earth and small boys darted past, trapping the fiery insects in jars. Two larger figures trailed the boys, prompting her to look up at them. A pair of girls walked toward her with baskets on their arms. Excitement brightened their young faces.

Jack stood as the girls neared them.

"Oh, Carrie," one of them bubbled. "Have you seen that new ring Jenny Parker is sportin'? My Lord, the thing is as big as a pigeon egg. Only a Worthington could afford somethin' like that."

The other giggled. "Yes, no wonder that pair isn't here. I suppose they have better things to do."

Carrie clenched her hand under the protection of her spread skirt.

"Jenny has such plans," the first girl continued. "Everyone was talkin' about it Sunday in church. Why, she even asked me to be a bridesmaid." She batted her eyes and twisted the tip of her lace collar. "You should see the patterns she's picked for the dresses. The material is comin' all the way from New York City."

Tears choked Carrie's throat. "Is that right?"

The girl smoothed back her hair. "Yes. I just hope it gets here in time."

Carrie stood and brushed crumbs from her dress. "What do you mean by that?"

"Well, don't you know? Jenny said they've set a date for late October!" Giggling, the girls ran off to chase lightning bugs.

While the first lamplight flickered from Crested Butte's windows, a deep, lonely feeling swirled through her. The final evidence of Matt's deceit had just been delivered with brutal force. She watched the loving couples as they walked toward their buggies, arm in arm. It seemed that everyone had someone except Carrie.

Jack eased his arm around Carrie's waist. "Dun't pay attention to them silly girls, luv." Compassion softened his eyes. "I know I ain't rich and smart like 'im, but I'll marry you."

"That's awful kind of you . . . but I don't know . . . I—"

"Don't worry," he broke in. "I ain't got nobody."

She swallowed her tears and gazed at the ruddy sunset. She would never love Jack like she loved Matt, but Jack understood her ideas in a way Matt could never understand them. Matt had worked one shift at two-thousand feet. Jack had worked the mines most of his life. And, more importantly, he would never break her heart. Maybe she could somehow make him happy in return.

He crushed her in his big arms. "Think about it, girl. At least we could look at rings. At least we could do that."

Her shoulders slumped as she studied his earnest face. "Yeah . . . I suppose we could."

Shyly, he kissed her, and a blessed numbness flooded up to smother the pain she had carried so long. His tentative lips left her empty, but, kind and gentle, they soothed her loneliness. She smiled at him, and his face glowed with happiness. "Yes, sir, I'm goin' to buy *you* a ring. It may not be as big as Jenny Parker's, but we'll show 'er she's not the only one in Crested Butte who can sport a gem."

Carrie and Jack walked past Matt's burned-out office and headed down Elk Street. The charred office stirred her memory. She thought of all that had happened in the three weeks since it had been destroyed, all the times she had glimpsed Matt about town, and all the times they hadn't spoken.

When she and Jack reached Steiner's jewelry shop, she pulled on his arm. "There's no need wastin' your hard-earned money on an engagement ring. Besides, you have to be at the mine soon."

"We're both 'ere together now. I say let's go in and take a look. If Matt Worthington can buy that snooty Jenny Parker an engagement ring, I can buy you one, too."

His innocent words cut into her heart. Stung, she pretended to admire Jacob Steiner's flower boxes to hide her moist eyes.

The morning sun filtered through the trees and highlighted Jack's stolid profile. "Girl, what are you thinkin' about?"

She looked at him standing there in his tattered work clothes and realized he had no idea the damage his words had done. There wasn't a mean bone in his body. How could he know she thought of Matt every waking hour? How could he know the memory of Matt's knowing eyes and infectious laughter still tugged at her heart? And how could he know she longed for the warmth and security of Matt's strong arms like she longed for life itself?

She smiled and adjusted his wrinkled collar. "You're just doin' this to be nice."

"I'm doin' it 'cause you're my best friend and always 'ave been. I'll not see you 'urt."

Tears welled in her eyes. Dear, sweet Jack, ready to give her his name to save her pride. He was a fine, decent fellow and many a woman had done worse. The least she could do was look at the rings and salvage *his* pride—they weren't walking down the aisle yet. "Well, all right," she finally replied. "Let's go in and see what this Mr. Steiner has to offer."

A doorbell jangled as they entered the small jewelry shop. Bright sunlight streamed through the cracks in the shuttered windows and streaked the floor. Her curiosity pricked, Carrie scanned the cluttered room, which smelled of paper and silver polish. Ticking clocks hung on the walls, and files and rags littered two worktables. A soft leather apron drooped over an old chair. At last her gaze rested on a small bearded man who stood behind a glass counter. A warm smile wreathed his benign face.

He extended an old, veined hand. "Hello, my friends. I'm Jacob Steiner. How can I help you?" Dressed in several layers of clean but mended black clothes, the frail jeweler wore thick wire-rimmed spectacles that hooked around his large ears. As he peered over the small half glasses, Carrie thought his full beard and protruding ears made him look like an inquisitive elf.

Jack cleared his throat and straightened his back. "We've come . . . we've come to buy an engagement ring."

"An engagement ring?" the jeweler repeated, lifting his voice with amusement. *"Ay-li-lu-lyu,* I just sold one recently. That tall, good-looking Mr. Worthington and a blond lady were here and—"

"Never mind about that," Carrie cut in. "Just show us what you have, all right?"

Jacob's dark eyes danced as he adjusted his spectacles. "And what is your name, my beautiful young lady?"

Carrie took a seat in front of the glass case while Jack eyed the room. "I'm Carrie O'Leary and this is Jack Penrose." She threw Jack a sidelong glance and motioned him to her side.

Jack leaned against the case. "We ain't got much money, you know."

The little jeweler brushed the statement away with a wave of his hand, then walked to the windows, threw open the shutters, and drenched the shop in light. "That's no problem, my friends." He returned to the counter and settled a tray of rings on top of the case. His gaze ran lovingly over his work. "I have something for every pocketbook here."

Filled with sadness, Carrie looked at the glittering gems, and realized that Matt had bought Mr. Steiner's largest ring. As long as she didn't choose a ring, she and Jack weren't really engaged, she told herself. Then a practical inner voice ordered her to face hard facts and toughen up. Girls like her didn't marry rich newspaper editors. They married their own kind. They married miners. She pointed at a modest setting. "Let's see that one." Her own voice rang cold and distant in her ears.

The jeweler handed her the ring. "All right, my dear."

She slipped it on and held it to the light, battling the painful emotions within her heart. "A big ring doesn't mean a good marriage, otherwise rich couples would all be happy—and we know that ain't so," she said.

The old man stroked his silky beard and regarded her warmly. "So much wisdom for such a young head. It's almost unnatural. Now, the other young lady wanted my showiest piece."

Another shaft of pain stabbed through her as she thought of Jenny pawing the jewelry. "I can imagine that."

"You know the lady?"

She held the ring so Jack could see it. "You could say we're acquainted."

"That one's too little," Jack complained. "Get a bigger one."

Jacob chuckled. "Thank God for gentlemen like you who keep men like me in business." He walked to one of the worktables and took a ring from a crumpled polishing rag. "Let me show you a piece I just finished. Perhaps it's a little larger, but we can size it." He slipped the ring on Carrie's slender finger.

Jack's eyes gleamed as the gem caught the light. "That one's beautiful!" He raised Carrie's hand and met her gaze. "I want you to have it, luv. Damn the cost." He glanced at the jeweler. "Can I pay it out, Mr. Steiner?"

The small man smiled and bowed his head. "Of course, young man."

Looking from the window, Jack spotted one of his friends on the way to the mine. "There's Bryan Kelley! I need to ask 'im about our shift, luv. I'll be back in a minute."

Carrie watched him stop the tattered miner in the middle of the street.

The jeweler laughed as she handed him the ring. "What a lucky young lady you are. Mr. Penrose is a fine man."

She swallowed and glanced at the ring. "Yes, he's a fine man—that's true."

A flicker of sadness played over Jacob's lined face while he studied her. "You should be happy, my dear," he said, wagging a crooked finger at her. "A man's willing to pay out for an expensive ring to please you. The other young lady had to buy her own ring."

Her heart thudded. "What do you mean?"

The old man put the ring aside. "Mr. Worthington came in to look at cuff links. The lady came in after him."

"Go on."

"Well, the gentleman found some cuff links he liked and bought them. Then the pair got into a big argument right in front of me. She said he had no right to fire her—and that he'd promised to marry her several years ago. He only laughed and told her she would have to buy her own ring.''

Jacob paused as Jack banged the door behind him and walked to Carrie's side.

"Please, Mr. Steiner, tell me the rest," Carrie urged.

He scratched his whiskery ear and grinned. "After he told her she'd have to buy her own ring, a light seemed to go on in her eyes. She said: 'That might not be a bad idea.' Mr. Worthington looked at her like she was crazy. She kept nagging him about everything so much he left. In fact, he was so mad he walked right out without the receipt for the cuff links that we'd both signed. The young lady shouted after him, but he kept on going."

"Lud . . . what happened then?" Jack asked.

Jacob widened his eyes. "This is the crazy part. She turned around and bought the most expensive ring I had. It just fit her. She's paying it out, of course, but she said she and her father had plenty of money. She also said a few folks around Crested Butte would be mighty surprised when they saw the ring." He rubbed his temple. "But I still don't understand it. Why would a woman buy an engagement ring for herself?"

Tears pricked Carrie's eyes.'

"There's something else that puzzles me, too," Jacob went on. "When she left, she took her receipt, Mr. Worthington's receipt, and tore another from my book." A frown plowed his brow. "Can you imagine that? She *stole* a receipt. What a puzzlement!"

Carrie's heart beat so loud she thought it might pop from her breast. Jenny had taken the clean receipt and placed it over Matt's, then pressed them both against a bright window and traced his signature. Obviously, she had just been waiting for a good time to spring the surprise so she could hurt them both. If the woman was this vindictive, she had probably lied to the girls about the wedding date, too. Happiness pealed in her heart like bells. Matt *did* love her. Then she remembered Jack was standing by her side. And with a rush of pain she remembered how bad things were between her and Matt at the moment.

"Luv—you're cryin'!" Jack took out a clean white handkerchief and wiped her eyes.

Jacob smiled and nodded his head. "That's all right. I understand. All brides cry. That's the way it should be!"

"Missy, may I come in?" Peony's muffled question penetrated the closed hotel door. "I have a tray for you."

Carrie burrowed under the warm covers, trying to think of some excuse to keep her out.

Before she could reply, the girl entered and closed the door behind her, her backless slippers slapping against the floor as she moved.

Peony placed the tray on a bedside table and glanced at her mistress. "Missy, won't you get up? You've been in bed too long. You need to eat." She moved to the windows and opened the curtains, washing the room with sunshine.

Carrie propped herself up. "Thanks, but I ain't hungry."

Peony walked to the bed and whipped the starched napkin cover from the food. Mouth-watering aromas floated upward from the tray. "Oh, no? Just look—biscuits and ham and eggs, and chocolate, too." She poured steamy chocolate into a china cup and smiled encouragingly. "Go on, Missy, it's good."

Carrie hadn't thought herself hungry, but when the buttery scent reached her nostrils, she found her hand reaching for a flaky biscuit. Peony smiled and seated herself at the foot of the bed. "Do you want me to tell you what has happened today?"

With a shrug, Carrie smeared butter and strawberry jam on her biscuit, then licked her sticky knife. "No, not particularly."

"Well, I will tell you anyway. Mr. John is gone. No one knows where he is."

Questions buzzed through Carrie's head, but she could

find no answers. "Well, how about that?" she finally replied. "Maybe things will improve around here."

A knowing smile brightened Peony's countenance. "Then there's Mr. Matt—"

"I especially don't want to know about him!" Carrie wondered if she would ever be able to rid herself of Matt's memory, which insisted on returning with bothersome regularity. In the warm privacy of sleep, her body had responded to his memory only a few hours ago. Even at this moment she had to discipline herself to concentrate on what Peony said.

The girl patted her blanketed leg. "Missy, I'm worried about you. You don't listen. You don't talk. What's wrong?" Her black eyes glistened with interest.

Carrie rolled her eyes. Who would want to hear her problems? God knew, *she* was sick of 'em. Then she thought again. Peony really wanted to help her—and in her own simple way she was a wonderful friend. Carrie took a bite of the fluffy eggs and decided to share her troubles. "I don't know—this whole marriage-and-passion thing seems so confusin'. I'm just all mixed up and miserable inside."

Insight illumined Peony's round face. "Ahh . . . so, now I understand."

Carrie cut into the pink ham and waited to hear her small friend's pearls of Oriental wisdom.

Peony spread her delicate hands. "My San Francisco lady told me all about it," she revealed in a conspiratorial whisper. "She said it's all very natural."

"So's diphtheria."

The girl covered her mouth and giggled. "Oh, Missy, you always make me laugh."

Carrie put her plate and cup aside and dusted the biscuit crumbs from her fingers. Dressed in a filmy shift and bloomers, she slipped from bed. After pausing to pat Bandit, she ambled to the window and watched midmorning traffic rattle down Elk Street. "I just don't know. Marryin' sounds kind of scary."

Peony walked to the wardrobe and opened its big door. She selected a frothy, light green frock, slipped it from the hanger, and gracefully moved to the sunny window. "I don't think it is scary if the right man-person asks you." She unbuttoned the dress and eased it over Carrie's head. With gentle fingers, she buttoned it and smoothed her mistress's unruly locks. "Missy, I—I think there is something else you need to talk about. Mr. Jack told me how sad you were when you left the jewelry shop."

Carrie turned away and picked up a brush. Silent, she tugged it through her thick hair.

"Missy?"

Her eyes full of tears, Carrie finally whirled about. She threw the brush at the dresser and rubbed her damp eyes. "Oh, Peony, my life is in a terrible mess!"

Compassion flooded the girls' soft face. "Maybe I can help."

Carrie breathed deeply and went on, her voice strangled with tears. "Matt and I had a horrible fight. I blew up . . . I wouldn't listen to him." Tears filled her eyes again while she stared at the slight girl. "Of course, Jenny just lied about everythin' to stir up trouble. I should have known. But instead, I said somethin' awful to Matt. To top everythin' else off, I'll bet he thinks miners burned his office." Fresh tears trickled from her eyes.

Peony dabbed at them with her own handkerchief. "Is there somethin' else?"

"Yeah, I'm worried about Jack. After I found out the truth about Jenny, I just couldn't accept his ring."

"I don't think you love Mr. Jack anyway."

Carrie grabbed the handkerchief and blotted away her tears. "I love him . . . but I love him like a brother. He just asked me to marry him to be nice—to save my pride."

The girl smiled gently and caressed her arm. "Missy, don't worry. Mr. Jack understands why you couldn't take his ring."

"Do—do you think he does?"

"Oh, yes! We talked about it. He's a very kind man-person. And he needs to marry a lady who loves him like a husband, not a brother.''

New tears fell from Carrie's eyes. ''I feel better about Jack, but that still doesn't fix things with Matt. I know I've ruined my chances with him forever.''

Peony reached out and clasped both of her hands. ''No, no. Mr. Matt is a good man. He will forgive you. But you must talk to him soon, or both of your lives will be broken. You must go today—you must tell him you love him.''

Full of doubt, Carrie eased down on the bed and patted Bandit, who stood loyally by her legs.

Peony pulled her up and held her at arm's length. ''Missy, I heard Mr. Matt has been shut up in his house for a long time. His heart is probably breaking for you right now.''

Carrie tried to smile. ''Do you really think there's any hope?''

Morning light streamed across Peony's radiant face. ''Oh, yes—don't worry. After your visit you'll feel like a new lady!''

Chapter 16

Carrie slipped from her horse and tossed her reins around a hitching post, scattering Matt's chickens. She took several deep breaths of the light, petunia-scented air to steady her nerves, then banged on the door. When she heard his loud steps resounding, she clenched her fists and locked her knees.

The door flew open. "Damn it, hold on a minute," Matt ordered irritably. Wrinkles creased his clothes and an unlit cheroot dangled from his mouth. He peered from the dim entry. "Carrie! My God, what are you doing here?"

She moistened her dry throat and tried to speak. "I came . . . I came to—"

"Well, spit it out."

She drew herself up and cleared her throat. "I came to apologize, you big jackass. Are you goin' to let me in, or do I have do it here on your doorstep?"

He bit off the tip of his cheroot and spit it out. Oh, Lord, why did you pick today?" She moved forward, but his arm shot out, forestalling her.

"Matt, what are you—"

A silky feminine voice floating through the open doorway stopped her in mid-sentence. "Matt, love . . . who's at the door?"

Anger exploded within Carrie. "It's Jenny—you've got Jenny in there!"

"No, Carrie, stay out!"

She ducked under his arm and sailed into the entry like a full-sailed man-of-war. "I know you're in here somewhere, Jenny. You might as well come out." As her eyes adjusted to the light, she spied the most beautiful woman she had ever seen.

Tall and voluptuous, she wore a low-cut, peach satin gown, more suited to evening than day. The puff-sleeved gown displayed white shoulders and smooth arms—and a daring amount of creamy cleavage. As she moved forward, gardenia blossoms flashed against her inky hair and perfumed the air. The woman's complexion was faultless, her makeup soft and skillfully applied. A riot of shiny black ringlets bounced from the back of her head as she stopped in front of Carrie and extended her jeweled hand. "Hello, darling—I'm Dovie Benningfield."

Carrie heard Matt slam the door violently. Heat radiated from her bosom and questions buzzed in her head like angry hornets. So *this* was the unexpected problem Matt had been working on! He had said she wouldn't understand, and he was right. What was the famous English singer doing in Matt's house? And more importantly, how had she got here? But instead of asking these questions, she took the woman's soft white hand and stammered, "Uh . . . hello, I'm Carrie O'Leary."

Carrie looked over her shoulder at Matt, who had flopped down in a leather chair. Wasn't one woman on the side enough for him? Was he keeping a harem now? "What's *she* doin' here? No, don't tell me—you two are talkin' about a story!" Sarcasm laced her words.

"Don't I wish," Matt said gloomily. "God knows, I could, write one." He lit the cheroot and puffed smoke into the air. "Think I'm going to send it to the *London Illustrated News,* too!" he added sarcastically.

"Oh, darling, how sweet," Dovie purred. "You didn't tell—"

He strode across the room and took her arm. "Look here, Dovie, you need to rest your voice. And why don't you take a nap while you're at it?"

She wrinkled her straight little nose and smiled. "Take a nap?"

"Take a nap?" echoed Carrie. "She needs to take a nap to rest her voice?"

Matt loosened his tie and opened his collar. "Yes, why not? It would be good for her. She hasn't adjusted to our American hours yet."

Dovie laughed and waved a lacy hankie at him. "Don't be silly. I've been in America for two months, and in Crested Butte for a fortnight at least."

Carrie frowned. This situation was smelling fishier by the minute. "You've been in town that long?"

The prima donna shot her a pointed look. "Yes, of course, dear. I've been right here, snug and cozy as a little squirrel."

Matt slung his cheroot into the fireplace and rubbed his stubbled jaw.

Hands on hips, Carrie sauntered to his chair. "Since when have you been interviewin' ladies in your house in the middle of the afternoon—and providing them with food and lodging to boot, Matt Worthington?"

He gave her a tight smile. "Since someone burned my newspaper office down. Or did you forget?"

She started to speak, but Dovie laughed and shook her head. Her ringlets bounced merrily as she crossed to Matt's side. "Oh, Matt and I have known each other for a long while." She caressed his wide shoulders with her slender hands. "We're very good friends, indeed."

Carrie squinted at him. "I thought you said you didn't know the woman when we were lookin' at that notice."

"Well, I . . ."

"Let me help you, darling," Dovie interjected. "It's obvious what's happened here. You've picked up a little playmate since you left London last year"—she looked at Carrie and smiled—"and now we all find ourselves in a rather unpleasant situation." She trailed her fingers over Matt's clenched jaw, then paced across the room, wafting gardenia scent in her wake. "Thankfully, I'm European and understand such matters.'' Her dark eyes flirtatious, she threw him a glance over her shoulder. ''I'm ready to forget and forgive, darling. It's all right. I understand!''

Matt rose and stared at her. ''No, I'm afraid you don't understand.''

Dovie laughed and glanced at her reflection in a glassed gun case. She smoothed back her sleek hair, and with a huge sigh, she slipped a perfumed hankie from her bosom and dabbed at her makeup. ''We've been over this before, love.''

''Yes, and we're not through going over it.'' A vein standing out on his temple, he strode to the singer.

By now Carrie felt as if she had interrupted a lover's quarrel, and the feeling sickened her. Here she was, ready to forgive Matt any misdeed he had committed with Jenny. Here she was, ready to shoulder the blame for the misunderstanding about the fire that had separated them. And here she was, ready to cast off her pride like an old, frayed slipper—only to be upstaged by an old lover! Well, if either one of them thought she would stand there like an orphan child while they talked about their precious affair, they were wrong! She lifted her chin and turned to leave, just as a loud wail issued from the bedroom.

''Oh, dear, now you've awakened Percy!'' Dovie fumed. Tossing her hankie aside, she whisked out of the room with a silken rustle.

Carrie glanced at Matt and raised her brows. ''Percy? Who the hell is Percy? Another Englishman?''

''I certainly hope he's one hundred percent English.'' With a pained look he rubbed the back of his neck and caught her eye. ''Carrie, you're going to see something you may find rather upsetting. I just want you to remember that—''

''Here we are,'' Dovie crooned as she reentered the room, carrying a plump baby boy. Outfitted in a lacy dress, the baby looked more like a fat ball of ruffles than an infant, Carrie thought. Pink flushed his little cheeks and a mop of black curls covered his round head. Dovie sidled up to Matt and pushed the baby into his arms, forcing him to catch the child before he slid to the floor. "There we go, my little lamb. Daddy will make you feel all better. See? He's asleep again." She glanced at Carrie, who felt the bottom drop from her world. "That's all it usually takes, you know. A father's touch is so soothing. I think babies can just sense it, don't you, dear?"

"Uhh . . . wh . . . where?" Carrie croaked.

"London, of course," Dovie shot back. "The Ritz, I think."

"When?"

"Last fall. September the tenth, to be exact. Percy was born in May. I was hardly recovered when we set sail." She ruffled the baby's black hair. "Aren't they a pair? The acorn doesn't fall far from the tree, as they always say."

Sweet Mother of God, thought Carrie, Matt was completely depraved. Here she was, ready to believe that Jenny had lied about the wedding date as she had lied about the ring. Maybe she *hadn't* lied. A man who had kept a woman and a baby secretly stashed in England might do anything!

Matt gave the baby to Dovie, then moved to Carrie and tried to take her in his arms. "Carrie, I know this looks bad—"

"Looks bad?" she said, squirming away. "I suppose you'll be tellin' me you're not the father."

"I want to tell you that, but I'm not sure the baby isn't mine."

With her arms crossed, she stared at him and tapped her foot.

He raised his open hands and shrugged. "Well, you don't expect me to put Dovie and Percy out until I'm sure, do you? If my memory is correct, *you're* the one who's always giving *me* those lectures on responsibility and commitment. Maybe some of your comments made an impression on me."

She rolled her eyes and snorted with derision. "Do you really expect me to believe that? Man, you've got so many women I'm surprised you ain't got some kind of chart to keep them straight.'' Hands on hips, she glanced at the top of his head. "You better check and see if you've sprouted antlers yet.''

Using every ounce of inner strength, she made it to the door without her knees buckling. She turned and glared at him. "Just as I was ready to admit I was wrong about Jenny, I find out you have another woman. And this one has somethin' real special—your baby!'' she stormed. "I may be a lot of things, but I ain't a home wrecker.'' She slammed the door behind her, hoping it would wake Matt's precious Percy.

Matt slung Dovie's carpetbag into the back of his rig, then stared at her while he knotted his string tie. "For God's sake, hurry up, Dovie. The Rio Grande leaves for Denver in less than an hour.''

A vision in black and lavender, she slammed the front door with a kid-gloved hand and stalked down the flagstone walk. Dressed in lace and ribbons, Percy nestled in the crook of her arm. "I still don't see why I have to go today,'' she complained. "My troupe doesn't begin rehearsals at Tabor's Opera House until tomorrow.''

Matt handed her up into the buggy. "You have to go, my dear, because you signed a contract and we don't have anything left to say to each other.''

Her head held high, she plopped down on the green leather seat and arranged her fringe-trimmed chapeau, nearly sliding Percy from her lap. He began crying. She hoisted the fussy infant to her shoulder and patted him on the back. "*Really,* Matt,'' she huffed, "I would think that as the baby's father, you'd be more understanding.''

Matt swung onto the buggy and picked up the reins. "I'm trying to keep an open mind about that, Dovie, but at this point I'm not ready to make a decision.'' With a frown, he snapped the reins and they lurched away, scattering chickens across the road. Dovie clasped the side of the jostling buggy and pretended to admire the forested land. Occasionally, her eyes darted to Matt.

For about five miles he focused only on the thud of the horses' hooves and the whir of the buggy wheels; then he glanced at Dovie while she arranged Percy's ridiculous bonnet. Her strong gardenia scent assaulted his nostrils and her painted face nauseated him. Lord, he thought, how had he ever got himself tangled up with the woman? He'd spent hours agonizing over what he should do. Once, he would have just sent Dovie on her way, but his association with Carrie had somehow changed him. He had to do the right thing now. But he needed time to figure out just what "the right thing" was.

Dovie threw him her best seductive glance. "Matt, how can you be so cold?" She batted her long black lashes coyly. "Why, you haven't touched me since I've been here. Don't you remember those wonderful nights we shared in London?"

He negotiated a sharp curve that prompted Percy to break into another gale of tears. "Yes, I do remember London. I remember downing a bottle of champagne at a first-night party and being introduced to you by a friend." He grinned. "You were dressed in red, weren't you?"

She quieted the fussy baby and smiled brightly. "Why, yes, I was."

Evergreens whizzed past them on each side of the dusty road. With a snap of the reins, he went on. "I remember you asked me home to discuss a story idea." Amused, he watched the wind whip silky hair away from her surprised face.

"Yes, yes, we talked until two."

"And I remember you begging me to stay so we could talk more at breakfast." He scanned her starkly outlined form. "And I remember you crawling into my bed about four." She almost looked embarrassed for a moment, but he quickly reminded himself that she hadn't been embarrassed since she was ten years old.

She smoothed back her sleek hair and lowered her eyes. "Well . . . yes, but—"

"God Almighty, what a night," he cut in. "The only thing lower than your nightgown was your morals!"

Blood leaped to her cheeks. "You make it sound like some kind of cheap affair. I told you I was coming to America."

"Yes, you told me you were coming." He jerked his thumb at the red-faced baby. "You didn't tell me you were bringing *him.*"

They rode for another long stretch in silence; then, looking very nervous, Dovie blurted out, "Matt, I want you to admit this baby is yours!"

He eyed the chubby infant. "The child might be mine— but I seriously doubt I could have sired a baby named *Percy.*"

"Well, I've never heard a gentleman talk like that!" She hugged the baby to her bosom and stared straight ahead as the outskirts of Crested Butte appeared.

"We—we need more time to talk about the situation!" she added in a desperate tone while Matt directed his horses toward the railroad platform.

He reined in the team and reached for her overstuffed carpetbag. "You have rehearsals to attend . . . and we've been over this dozens of times." He looked at the Denver train that sat on the tracks, building steam, then tossed her luggage at an old porter's feet. With a grin, he eyed a homeward-bound shift of miners who had stopped to watch the show. "Looks like you even have one of those great audiences you like so well. Now why don't you get out of this buggy like a big girl, get on that train, and go to Denver?" When she only glared at him, he added, "I'm not above carrying you, you know."

"You wouldn't dare!"

He winked at the amused miners and moved toward her. "Oh, wouldn't I?"

She squirmed and kicked her black-stockinged legs while he hoisted her from the seat. "Put me down, you

brute!'' Her eyes flashed. "I'll get on that train, all right,
and I'll find the best solicitor in Denver. I'm going to sue
you for breach of promise, Matt Worthington!''

He dumped her and the baby back on the sofa seat. "Go
ahead. Get after it. No one will ever believe you, but it'll
keep you out of my hair.''

"Dovie swished up the ramp after the porter, then
turned dramatically at the car door and glared at Matt.
"Just wait! I'm prepared to match wits with you any day!''

He picked up the reins and pushed back his Stetson.
"Match wits? What are you going to use for ammunition,
darling?''

The miners guffawed as she raised her chin and stormed
into the train.

With a huge laugh, Matt urged the team away. Already
he felt less pressured. Then he noticed a work gang un-
loading a large crate from the freight car. And wasn't that
a familiar figure signing a receipt for the goods? God Almighty—it was Carrie. Peony and Bandit guarded her
flanks. Snapping his reins, he rolled toward her, followed
by a gang of curious, laughing miners.

Her eyes fastened on the crate, Carrie watched two section hands open the sides with crowbars. When the men
had prized out the last nails, the boards slapped down on
the loading dock to reveal a new Washington handpress
and a tall California job case.

"So it finally came," Matt observed, looking over Carrie's shoulder.

She whirled about, her eyes fiery. "Who invited you to
this party?''

Peony frowned; Bandit growled.

Matt eased the reins through his long fingers as the
freight-car door slammed. "Just thought I'd see what was
going on.''

Carrie crossed her arms. "I thought you'd be busy with
Dovie back at the ranch.''

He tugged down his Stetson and watched the train slowly
chug away. "I'd say that problem is rapidly receding.''

With a smile, he eyed the spanking new press. "What a pretty sight! I've been itching to get back in the newspaper business. That must be the only press for hundreds of miles. You're going to share, aren't you?"

She rubbed her hand over the press and cocked her head. "I don't know. I have a lot of issues to get out. I'd say my press is goin' to be tied up day and night." She smiled at Peony, then glanced back at him. "Besides, the newspaper business wouldn't be profitable enough for you anymore. With a fancy woman like Dovie to support—and a baby, to boot—you'll be needin' somethin' real stable. I hear Harry Carter is tryin' to sell his dry goods store. You might check into that."

"I think I get your drift, love." He looked at her and rubbed his jaw. "Seems I remember when we were putting out two papers—I set the type on both of them. And I'm sure you haven't learned your California job case." He glanced at the excited miners, who were converging around the press. "Of course, I suppose a resourceful person like yourself has figured a way around that problem."

She smiled and hooked her thumbs in her skirtband. "Yeah, I have. I'm payin' someone else to do it. Will Larkin put out the word in the mine. He found a man who used to set type in Virginia. He's goin' to work for me at night when his shift is over." A murmur of approval rippled through the attentive crowd.

A muscle twitched in Matt's jaw. "I see. Well, it seems to me you're still in trouble." He smiled broadly and leaned forward. "Where are you going to print this literary masterpiece?"

Her eyes widened. "Oh, that's no problem. The miners chipped in so much that I was able to rent that old funeral parlor that went out of business last month."

He laughed and stroked his chin. "You're going to print a newspaper in a funeral parlor?"

"Yeah, it's goin' to work out real fine. It's got sinks for washin' type and everythin'. You know," she said thoughtfully, "you ought to give some thought to bein' more flexible—it makes life a *lot* easier.'' She eyed the patient miners, then added, as if in afterthought, ''Oh, I almost forgot. I'm afraid you're goin' to have a long wait on your press. The man at the factory wrote me and said production was at a standstill—somethin' about a strike. I got the last available one.''

''The last one?''

''Yeah, the last one. Life can sure take some funny turns, can't it?'' She grinned and shrugged, then faced the miners. ''Well, boys, what do you say we get our press to the funeral parlor so I can start printin'? I've got enough stuff written up to paper Colorado.''

A roar went up while a gang of men hoisted the press and the job case onto a huge railroad dolly. Some of the laughing miners hung onto the back of the dolly to break its forward momentum. Bandit barked as the men wheeled the new merchandise down the ramp.

''Someone pick up Carrie!'' a grizzled miner yelled.

Several of the miners lifted her to their shoulders. With a joyful smile, she waved her hand in a circular motion and pointed a finger in the direction of the funeral parlor. ''Blood and thunder, we're wastin' precious time, lads. Let's go!''

Matt could almost smell, almost taste the festive spirit in the air as he drove along beside the happy crowd. One bruiser lifted Peony's light form to his shoulder, and she and Carrie clasped hands. Another shouted, ''Let's sing 'Trafalgar Boy.' '' Then he belted out the first line of the old drinking song and the others chimed in, thundering each line as the leader yelled it out. Proud as a lord, Bandit pranced in front of the men who supported Carrie.

The noisy parade marched up Elk Street and lured white-aproned merchants from their shops. Beer glasses in hand, drinkers stumbled from the saloons. Dressed in scarlet and roped in pearls, Betty B'damn sauntered after them shouting, ''Give 'em hell, girl!'' At the other end of the street small children spilled from the schoolhouse.

Matt rolled along with the throng and watched Carrie

smile and wave. Despite his anger, he felt his heart swell
with pride. He saw the sun glint in her auburn hair, saw
how she reached out to the miners with her dancing eyes
and her wide smile. The men adored her and they always
would. He understood. They loved her because she had
given them a chance to dream again, to be alive again.
She was their symbol of hope—their angel.

His writer's mind buzzed with ideas while he followed
the parade. As ironic as it was, he realized the best way
to correct the abuses he had seen in the Silver Queen was
to help Carrie. Even if she didn't care about him, he still
cared for her—and her causes. Absorbed in thought, he
watched the men pull the press into the funeral parlor.
When Carrie's shining head disappeared into the dark interior, he tugged a pad from his vest pocket and scribbled
several lines with a pencil stub. "Colorado Angel . . .
Mountain Angel," he murmured, then crossed out the
lines.

He stared at the crowd for a moment, then grinned and
said, "Angel of the Slopes, yes that's it . . . By God,
that's it—Angel of the Slopes." He snapped the pad shut
and eyed the funeral parlor door, still packed with raucous
miners. "Deny me your press, will you?" he muttered.
"Well, that's all right. I'll use H. H. Hardin's press. I'm
going to make you famous, whether you want to be or not,
you hardheaded little mick!

Carrie stood and checked off another Friday from the
calendar, then plopped down again and looked at the date.
Four Fridays—four deadlines met. Immensely happy, she
glanced at the cluttered desk before her—a small picture
of Shamus sat in one corner. "Don't forget the lads," he
had said. Thanks to the new press in the corner, she had
been able to keep her promise. Four meaty editions of *The
Miner's Press* had flooded Colorado and trickled back east.

With a chuckle, she snapped up a copy of *The Denver
Star* and scanned her latest Grizzly Bear story. She laughed
at the wonderful cartoon above it. John Worthington, she

thought, wherever you are, I hope you've read this! A satisfied glow radiated through her. With the popularity of *The Miner's Press* and the big newspapers' help, triumph had to be right around the corner.

She watched Peony wrap twine around some papers destined for Gunnison. "Why don't you quit for tonight, Peony? You've put in a good day."

The small-boned girl tied off her knot and glanced up. "You should quit, too, Missy. You work too late every night. Soon your eyes will look like Mr. Botsie's." She pulled her lower lids down like the bags under Botsie's eyes.

Carrie laughed and picked up her pencil. "No, you go ahead. I have an idea I want to work on."

With a final admonition about work, the girl slipped through the curtains that divided the funeral parlor and disappeared.

Carrie took a deep breath and sucked in the scent of ink, newsprint, and excitement. She had good friends and a worthwhile cause that inspired her. Everything was more or less on an even keel. And she was pursuing her dreams. Yes, life was wonderful.

Well . . . at least part of the time. When she thought of Matt, pain still clutched her heart. The vision of him wrapped in Dovie's perfumed arms cut her like a keen razor. And the thought of him dangling the black-haired baby hurt even worse. But the pain was nothing compared to the need.

Committing herself to the miners' plight, she had shrugged aside the lonely ache and driven herself without mercy, trying to numb her emotions with work. And she had partially succeeded. But when her work was over, the old longing crept back like a wily animal.

With a huge sigh, she picked up her pencil and scratched it across some rough newsprint—then footsteps drew her attention. Troubled, she opened the desk drawer and eased out a loaded pistol. When the footsteps got closer and louder, she stood and pointed the pistol at the curtains.

"If you're here on friendly business, come on in. Otherwise, take off, 'cause I'm fixin' to blow your head off."

Matt laughed and entered the room, tossing his Stetson on her desk. "That's my girl—always prepared. I see the incident with that ruffian taught you something."

Her heart hammered like a locomotive. "Yeah, it taught me to be on the lookout for low-down skunks like you."

"What a welcome!" he said, looking amused. "Why don't we have a nice chat? We haven't talked in a long while; every time I see you, you sail by with your nose in the air."

"I'm surprised you have time for a chat"—she emphasized every word—"what with Jenny, and Dovie, and the baby, too."

He grinned and tugged at his ear. "All right. Let's take one problem at a time. We could have settled this thing with Jenny weeks ago if you'd let me explain what really happened in Jacob Steiner's shop."

"I know what happened there."

"Then you know why I lied."

She clenched the pistol butt. "Yeah, I know. I don't like it, but I understand why you did it."

He took a step closer to the desk. "How did you find out about the ring?"

"It doesn't matter." She studied his face. "Did you know Jenny's spread it all over town you two are gettin' married? She even mentioned a date and got bridesmaids."

"She's been nagging me to marry her for years. Guess she thought she'd tighten the vise with a little public pressure. I'm not presently, nor will I ever be, engaged to Jenny Parker."

Disdain pulled up the corner of her mouth. "Well, that's nice, since you've got another woman and a baby on the side."

"You're dead wrong, lady. But since you brought up Dovie, I'd like to mention that you could learn something from her."

"Oh, yeah? Like what?"

"She knows a man doesn't want to be constantly grilled and questioned—and she knows how to handle people, too."

"I suppose you admire her—have feelin's for her."

"No, I never said that!"

Her foot tapped the floor. "Well, why did you keep her and that fat baby in your house, then? And why did you say you didn't know her when I found the notice about her?"

"Let's take the notice first. If I'd told you I knew her, that would have opened a can of worms that I could have never resealed. As to the other . . . there is a possibility the child might be mine. Do you think I should have turned them both out?" He lowered his voice. "Carrie, I can explain—"

She flicked her hand in the air. "Oh, there's no need to explain. I'm sure it would be a colorful story, but it's one I really don't care to hear."

With an angry oath, he slammed his fist on the desk. "Hardheaded to the end! Are you going to put that pistol away, or do I have to talk around it all night?"

"And just why should I put it away?"

He sat on the edge of her desk and took out a cheroot. "Because I need your full attention. I'm going to make you famous."

"Right," she shot back, brandishing the pistol. "A famous whore! And why is it I feel I'm goin' to hear another sermon about trustin' your good judgment?"

He lit his cheroot and snuffed out the match. "You are. But if you trust me, I'll make your name a household word."

"Like measles?"

He chuckled, then, clenching the cheroot between his teeth, gestured dramatically. "No, like Angel of the Slopes."

"Angel of the Slopes? That sounds like a saint or somethin'." Irritated, she added, "If anybody knows that ain't true, it should be you."

"I didn't say you were perfect." He stood and grasped her arm. "But to the miners you're a symbol—a symbol of hope and courage."

She removed his hand, then put the pistol away and walked to a stack of twine-bound newsprint. Ignoring him, she tried to snap the twine.

He followed. "How would you like your union idea to take off like a high-flying kite?" His voice was low and persuasive.

"Holy Mother, what kind of question is that?" she answered in an aggravated tone. "You know I'd love it."

"Well, you need to make a tour of Colorado. You need to talk to every miner in the state."

She released the twine and put her hands on her hips. "Why can't I just keep on writin' like I've been doin'?"

"You *should* keep on writing, but you need to give speeches, too."

"Speeches? You want me to give speeches now?"

"Sure. You don't want folks to think you're a one-trick pony, do you?"

She crossed her arms. "And how am I supposed to give these speeches? I've never had any trainin' in that."

"Just say what comes into your head—the same way you do when you write."

"And what will the speeches do that the writin' won't?"

He took a long draw from the cheroot and smiled knowingly. "The people want to see you, they want to touch you. You're magic, and they want that magic to rub off on them."

He took out his pocket knife and cut through the tough twine. "We're not going to unravel this problem—we'll just slice right through it."

"Yeah, and what kind of knife are we goin' to use for that?"

"It's simple. We'll use you. Politicians do it all the time. Your personality is strong enough to motivate the miners.

It will override all the issues that are too complicated for them to understand or care about. All you have to do is stir them up with your words.''

''And what is old John goin' to say about this?''

He stared at her with shocked eyes. ''Do I hear Carrie O'Leary asking for permission? Who cares what he thinks? He's off God knows where, doin' God knows what. We don't need any of the mine owners' permission for this operation.'' He began pacing again, building up steam. ''We'll hit every train station in Colorado. We'll make twelve a day if we have to. You'll give a speech at each one and shake hands with every man there. Then at night you can write. We'll—''

''Whoa, *whoa.*'' She waved her hands. ''Do I get to eat and sleep, or do you have a plan to get around that, too?''

''I said it would be simple—I didn't say it would be easy.''

She sighed and shook her head. ''Holy Mother, you're beginnin' to sound like me!''

He puffed on his brandy-scented cheroot, his face aglow. ''We need some kind of goal for all the miners. What about a massive walkout? That would show the mine owners they were really serious. While the miners had the upper hand, union men could come in from back east and tie things up.''

Her heart started thumping. Damn. As she had known all along, the man was smart, real smart. Keeping silent, she weighed his words seriously for the first time. Exciting possibilities sparkled through her mind like fireworks. The thing might just work.

''Come on, what do you say?'' he prodded. ''We're not just talking about the Silver Queen. We're talking about thousands and thousands of lives. We're talking about all of Colorado.''

She sat down at her desk and leaned back, her silence louder than any speech.

He held her gaze. ''I'm still waiting for my answer.''

She tossed her pencil across the desk. ''You know . . .

there are several things that bother me about this operation.''

"Go on, then . . . let's hear them.''

"Well, number one—what are we goin' to use for money?''

He sat on the edge of her desk again and leaned so close she could smell his bay rum. Unwanted, a shiver coursed through her. "Have you ever heard of H. H. Hardin?''

"No, who is he?''

"He's the biggest newspaper mogul in New York City. I met him back east in school. I wrote him about you and he's interested in your story. He's already read your Grizzly Bear stuff in *The Denver Star.* ''

She raised her brows. "H. H. Hardin is goin' to give me the money?''

"Better than that.'' He grinned and winked at her. "To the tune of one hundred fifty dollars a day rental fee, he's going to supply us with a parlor car, a sleeper, and even a kitchen car—all the finest rolling stock in America.''

"How can the man afford to do such a thing?''

"He's one of the richest businessmen in America. He doesn't own one paper—he owns dozens of them.'' He shook his finger at her. "And he's smart, too. He knows the folks back east will eat this up with a spoon. He'll sell newspapers faster than he can print them. Next question?''

Curiosity buzzed through her mind like a restless bee. "I notice you keep talkin' about 'us' and 'we'. How do *you* come into the picture?''

"Me? Oh, I'm going to be with you every step of the way—to write your personal story. Hardin is giving me a big advance.''

"What about your ranch?''

"Your story is a writer's dream. I'm using some of the advance to hire a man to look after things until I get back.''

She grinned. "Are you usin' some of the advance to attach a nursery car to this rollin' circus for Dovie and the baby?''

His eyes flashed. "Dovie's in Denver! She said good-bye weeks ago."

"Is that right? Well, everybody who says good-bye ain't necessarily goin' home, are they?"

He sauntered around the desk, his face amused. "Since we're talking about extra passengers, where are we going to put lovable Cousin Jack—in the club car? I heard you two were engaged."

She clenched the edge of the desk. "Don't you talk about Jack Penrose. He's a good man."

"A good man, maybe . . . a problem, definitely. A fi-ancé lurking in the wings could take the edge off our working relationship, you know."

She mumbled, "You don't have to worry about Jack. I couldn't accept his ring."

"What did you say?"

She shot to her feet. "I said, I couldn't accept his ring! But don't be gettin' any ideas it was because of *you*. I just decided I needed some time to work, some time to think."

She studied him while he paced the length of the room, puffing on his cheroot. "Somethin' puzzles me. Why are you doin' this?"

He glanced at the floor, then back at her. "I'm doing it because I saw the conditions in the Queen with my own eyes."

"But at the fire I could tell you blamed the miners for burnin' you out."

"Would you believe me if I told you I'm not holding a grudge against one thousand seven hundred men because of a few hotheads?"

She stared at him silently, wanting to believe him, yet afraid. Could he be making the commitment she had dreamed about?

He finally raised his brows and shrugged. "All right, there's no use trying to fool you, is there? I'm doing this because it will stamp my byline across America."

He chomped on his cheroot and strode around the desk. "Look, do we have a deal or not?"

She raised her chin with derision. "Do you really think I'd sleep in the same car with you?"

He stopped in his tracks and graced her with a dry grin. "You don't have to. I'll sleep in the parlor car. I understand a steward comes with this rig, too, so we'll have our own personal chaperon, if that will make you feel any better."

She took the pistol from the drawer and slapped it on the desk. "And I've got another chaperon right here." She wadded up some newsprint and sailed it across the room. "Damn, do I have to bring you along to get the train?"

"Yep—Hardin's rules. The train and I came together—just like scotch and water, or pork and beans." His eyes twinkled. "You're a writer. Which do you like better?"

She met his amused gaze. "I've got a better one. How about pestilence and death?"

Chapter 17

$\sim\sim\infty\sim$

Matt knocked, then entered Carrie's sleeping car and placed coffee and a sweet roll on an antique nightstand. His eyes widened as he scanned the luxurious car. Clothes and crumpled papers littered the mahogany furniture and Oriental carpet. A ream of scribbled-on notes covered a small French desk set under a velvet-draped window. Jostled by the train's movements, some of the papers had spilled to the shiny parquet floor. A brass lamp still burned on the desk, warming a pot of rose-scented potpourri with its heat. Across the car, two wall sconces supported by brass angels blazed inside a sleeping alcove.

Attired in the same lavender shirtwaist she had worn the day before, Carrie slept in a nest of tangled satin covers. Her lips were parted. Her lustrous hair, which had been pinned atop her head, now flopped comically to the side; a shoe dangled from one foot, while the other foot remained bare. One hand clutched some ink-stained papers against her rising-and-falling bosom; her other hand dangled to the floor.

Torn between laughter and tenderness, Matt paced to the chiffon-draped alcove and shook her shoulder. "Time to rise and shine, love. It's five-thirty, and your first audience is anxiously waiting."

Flushed with sleep, she moaned and stretched. Dawn light shot in through a crack in the velvet drapes and gathered in her auburn hair. Outside the car there was the sound of hissing steam and muffled voices.

She finally opened bleary eyes and stared at his face. "Oh, no . . . it's mornin' and I'm still breathin'." She glanced at the coffee. "If that's poison, I'll drink it," she added in a thick voice.

Matt laughed. "How much sleep did you get last night?"

She tried to struggle up. "Not much. I kept writin' things I wanted to tell the folks today."

Suddenly the train whistle shrieked three long blasts.

Carrie shot to a sitting position and clamped her hands over her ears. "Sweet Jesus, is the engineer goin' to do that every mornin'? The man just took three years off my life!" She flopped back down, pulled a coverlet over herself, and closed her eyes. "If you need me, I'll be in bed the rest of my life," she said hoarsely.

He ripped off the silken coverlet. "You need to get up!"

She yanked the coverlet back up. "Could I do it when I feel a shade better than horrible?"

"No. It's daylight. It's the first day of the tour. And it's time for you to become a celebrity." He picked up a copy of the *Star* and looked at their schedule. "I'm sure a lot of reporters from the Denver papers will be here for your debut. You need to do well"—he pushed her eyelids open, trying to ignore the soft feel of her skin—"and somehow I feel you would give a better performance with your eyes open."

She opened her eyes and shoved back the covers. "What was your major at that fancy college you went to—ancient tortures? Mother Mary, you must have been at the head of your class."

With a chuckle, he moved to the window and pulled back the drape. He noticed pink still blushed the sky and dew still sparkled over the grass. Then he scanned the sleepy, dull-spirited throng milling around the railroad platform. Dressed in clean but outdated clothes, the local dowagers and businessmen had come to see the outrageous redhead who was raising brows all over the state. By the look of their cold, judgmental eyes, they would be hard nuts to crack.

Then there were the hard-bitten housewives, who had given up hope and were simply hanging on grimly. Around the edges of the crowd, the layabouts and no-goods squatted to roll dice and exchange gossip. He knew the type—they had put up their feet and turned off their minds. Finally, there were the miners—ragged, tired, hopeless, embittered men, whose very demeanor challenged Carrie to say anything to change their mind.

Matt heard Carrie put on her shoes.

"Lord," she groaned, coming up behind him, "they look like they've come to see a hangin'."

He turned and studied her frightened face. "Evidently these folks haven't heard about your magnetic personality yet. You need to stir them up some way."

"Fine . . . how are we fixed for whips and chains?"

He chuckled and clasped her cold hand. "You can do it. Just remember, this won't last very long."

"A beheadin' don't last very long either." She looked at them again. "Faith, what am I goin' to say to those people?"

He tossed back the drape and moved from the window. "You're the one with the gift of gab—just make up stuff as you go along. Get yourself worked up." He grinned. "Pretend you're mad at me."

She glared at him and grabbed a brush from the dresser. *"Pretend?"*

"Go on, shoot for their hearts—you've got nothing to lose."

"Nothin' except my life."

She took down her tangled hair and brushed it. He watched as she washed her face and dried it, then ate the sweet roll. He lit a cheroot while she gulped down the coffee. "Just trust me—you can do it," he said firmly as he ushered her toward the exit at the end of the car.

When he opened the door, a morning chill rushed into the warm, rose-scented car. Smiling, he found Carrie's shawl and draped it around her shoulders, then pushed her forward.

Her face anguished, she glanced back at him. "Matt?"

He narrowed his eyes and sharply nodded his head. "You know what you've got to do—now go out there and do it! Spit fire and spout rain!"

"Bein' famous has quite a hellish side to it, don't it?"

"You may be the next Abigail Duniway."

"No, I'll be the woman with the permanently bloodshot eyes."

Ever so slowly, she walked to the iron railing and gripped it tightly. The crowd remained perfectly silent. Then she leaned forward and started speaking. Her warm Irish lilt rolled out over the crowd like sweet honey; her eyes had turned the cool emerald green of the deep forest. As the sun rose higher, the people began to return her enthusiasm.

Puffing on his cheroot to cover his own nervousness, he watched her soften up the crowd. He could see their mood changing, their body postures relaxing, their faces smiling. When she told them a hilarious joke and earned her first belly laugh, he knew she would do fine. Before her speech was over, she had them laughing and cheering.

Matt leaned against the car, finally relaxed. He had been right to bet on her charisma and fighting heart. She was outrageous. She was wonderful. God, how he wanted her.

The Denver and Rio Grande grated to a halt outside another small mining town and screeched its whistle. Inside the Pullman car, Matt pushed back the velvety drape and peered out the window. Streams of miners scrambled toward the seventy-foot car like hungry cattle to a feeding trough. Their day's work done, the noisy men swung derbies and lunch buckets. Some tugged their wives' hands, while others boosted small children who covered their ears against the whistle's blast. Matt eyed Carrie and took a dog-eared notebook from his vest pocket. "Are you ready?"

Outside the steaming car, the miners chanted her name.

"As ready as I'll ever be. Is this Silver Crest?"

He looked at the depot siding, then scanned their front-page schedule in *The Denver Star*. "Yes, the last stop of the tour—and we're right on schedule."

She glanced into a gold-framed mirror and shook back her hair. Light shot through the windows lining the car's domed ceiling and struck fiery highlights in her loose curls. "Faith, I'm glad this is almost over," she confessed with a sigh. "After a month you'd think givin' speeches would be easier, but it ain't." She reviewed her notes, then tossed them on a dinner table already set with bright crystal and creamy china. "I don't need these papers anymore," she said, moving to the door. "What I want to say is in my heart."

"Do you want the newspapers?" Matt asked.

"Yeah, they seem to like that pretty good."

He opened the platform door and extended his hand. A din of excited voices poured through the door as the people caught sight of his tall, well-dressed form. "All right," he mumbled. "Let's go. After you, love."

Dressed in a simple white blouse and a navy blue skirt, Carrie stepped onto the train's back platform and waved her slender arm. A loud roar punctuated with long whistles rose up to meet her.

Carrying several newspapers, Matt eased onto the platform and watched the miners and their families crowd around the train. He unbuttoned his suit coat and leaned against the car, waiting for the magic to happen, as it had happened in dozens of other towns.

Their faces full of hope, the people fell silent when Carrie raised her hands.

"I'm goin' to say somethin' that I don't want you to miss," she stated with emotion. "You're worth somethin' and you should never forget it!"

Some of the miners laughed nervously, while others looked at her in a puzzled fashion.

"Tell me how much you think you're worth!" she went on.

An old-timer pulled back his lips and pointed at a gold tooth. "I got a twenty-dollar gold tooth here. How's that for value?"

She laughed along with the crowd. "I suppose it's fine,

but you're worth much more than that. You're all human beings with dignity and hope—and working together in a union, you can get the decent wages you deserve.''

"I thought you was goin' to tell us somethin' new," hollered a man with a hangdog expression. "We ain't got no education. We ain't got no money. We ain't got nothin'—and you know it."

Agreement rippled through the miners.

She shook her small fist at the man. "Yes, you do have somethin'. You've got yourself!"

The crowd settled down to pay attention.

"*Listen,*" she proclaimed, "there ain't no level ground. All of life is uphill. Life will go rotten on you quicker than a ripe persimmon if you don't fight back! Life is set up to beat you down, if you don't fight back. And if you think anythin' of yourself, you *will* fight back!" She looked at an old swayback horse hitched to a milk wagon. "How much did you pay for that nag, mister?" she asked the owner.

The crowd laughed while the man scratched his head. "Well, not much," he finally mumbled.

She shook her head and smiled broadly. "Just like I thought. You didn't pay much because she ain't worth much." She searched the faces in the crowd. "What gives worth to somethin' is what you're willin' to pay for it. What do you think your dignity and self-respect are worth?" Her eyes blazing, she leaned forward and clasped the fancy platform fencing. "They're worth everythin' you've got!"

Matt heard the crowd murmur and fall silent. He knew they were finally ready to listen.

"Don't you see, mine owners all over the state are chokin' the life from you because you're scared to fight?" Carrie asked. "Yeah, life is tough. It's tough to fight for what you deserve, but it's tough to lay back and see your babies sicken and die because you ain't got money to take them to the doctor, and your friends go hungry when they can't pick up a shovel anymore. You need a decent wage. You need sick pay. You need some kind of retirement.''

"Yeah," roared a burly youth. "We ought to string those rich devils up right now."

"No, no, no!" she shouted. "Quit carryin' that hate from the past around with you like a dead skunk. All it'll do is stink up the future." She gazed at the crowd. "You"—she pointed at the burly lad—"come up here. You look like a strong fellow."

"He is. He's the strongest driller we got," hollered an old man while the youth shouldered his way to the platform steps.

She took a copy of *The Miner's Press* from Matt's hand and passed it to the young man. "Let's see you tear this in half."

The youth ripped the paper apart and tossed it from the platform as the crowd laughed.

Then Carrie pulled two thick copies of a Denver paper from Matt's arms and gave them to the young man. "Let's see you do that trick with these," she said.

As Matt watched the youth struggle with the papers, admiration for Carrie flowed through him. He remembered how frightened she had been the first morning of the tour, and he knew how she had fought her fear and developed into a skilled orator. This is her strength, he thought. She can put things in such a powerful, simple way, everyone can understand them—and to her it's *just talkin'*. He grinned as the red-faced youth finally tossed the papers down in disgust. Only Carrie would have thought of this newspaper trick.

With a bright smile she hoisted the bulky editions over her head. "Mother Mary, this is only measly newsprint." She tossed the papers down, then held up one sheet and ripped it apart. "This stuff is so thin a baby could tear it to bits. But when you stack hundreds of sheets together, no one can tear them. You people are just like those sheets of paper. If you'll stick together you'll be strong. You can get what you want."

"Just how're we gonna do that?" a man yelled while the dejected youth left the platform.

"All right, I'm goin' to tell you. On October thirtieth every miner on the Western Slope is goin' to walk out of those black prisons. And you're goin' to stay out until the owners meet your demands."

A roar went up from the crowd, then a pinch-faced mother asked, "How're we gonna live if we ain't got no pay comin' in?"

"Save now. Put somethin' aside. Help those who ain't got anythin'. There's men comin' from back east. They belong to a union, and they'll help you organize. I want you to have a gatherin' tonight and elect some men to meet with these leaders after the walkout."

A young preacher held up his Bible. "Listen to her, she's right! Go home and eat your supper, and those of you who can, meet at the church house at seven-thirty."

Carried raised her hands again and the crowd whistled and cheered. "I want to tell you somethin' you can depend on like the rising sun. If you do nothin' you'll just get older and die, and your dreams will die with you. But you can become *somebody* if you'll fight. Yes, it's a risk—but you have to take a risk sometimes to get ahead." She surveyed the expectant crowd and asked, "What are you goin' to do on October thirtieth?"

"Walk out," several men said.

She shook her head. "No—say it so you'll feel it and believe it!"

"Walk out!" the crowd roared in unison. "Walk out! Walk out! Walk out!"

Smiling, Matt scooped up the papers and opened the parlor car door. Carrie was silhouetted against the glowing sunset. Her eyes shiny with tears, she smiled and waved at the cheering people for a long time, then turned and entered the car.

Matt clicked the door closed behind them, muting the sound of the noisy crowd. Inside the tight car, the aroma of savory food permeated the air and soft lights twinkled their welcome. "You were marvelous," he said.

Fatigue stamped her face. "I don't know," she answered,

wiping her eyes. "I've given so many speeches my throat is raw, and I still don't know if they'll really do it."

He laughed and tossed the papers aside. "They'll do it, but you'll have to write a big article right before the walk-out. They'll need reminding." He rubbed her shoulders while a white-coated steward placed a tray of food on the buffet. "You're just tired. You'll feel better after you eat," he suggested, pulling out her chair.

As she sank into the chair, her gaze swept the length of the long car, which boasted paneled walls and a parquet floor. "Yeah, I guess you're right. I didn't know makin' speeches could make a person so tired and hungry."

He eased into his velvety chair and flipped open a wine list with "Pullman Palace Car Company" emblazoned across the top. Before he could skim the list, he heard a sharp knock at the door. He glanced up as the steward admitted a tall man dressed in a Stetson and casual clothes. Swinging an envelope in his big hand, the man followed the steward to the table. When they reached it, the steward respectfully stood aside and announced, "This is the sheriff of Silver Crest, Mr. Worthington."

Matt stood up to shake hands, but the sheriff ignored him and instead turned toward Carrie. "Carrie O'Leary?" he asked.

She looked up in surprise. "Why, yes."

The sheriff tipped his hat and pressed the envelope into her hand. "Thank you, miss. I'll be goin' now." He strode to the platform exit and let himself out. After taking their wine selection, the steward, too, disappeared from the car.

Carrie stared at the envelope as the train slowly chugged away from the station and clickety-clacked over a switch crossing.

"Well, open it!" Matt finally commanded.

She ripped the thick envelope and slipped out an official-looking paper. Her face paled.

He frowned and studied her troubled eyes. "What is it?"

"It's a subpoena to appear in court in two weeks." Her voice wavered. "John Worthington is suing me for libel."

"Libel?"

"You heard me." Her face troubled, she eyed the long document again. "I knew somethin' was goin' to happen."

"Why?"

"Because I've been doin' too good, too long."

Matt rubbed the back of his neck. "Are you trying to tell me that good luck comes in unreliable dribbles, and bad luck in squirts and gushes?" he asked, trying to lighten the moment.

The steward returned and began to place fragrant dishes in front of them. She smiled tightly. "That's right—but maybe I can still win. I'm goin' to request the trial be held in Denver. Old John owns Crested Butte lock, stock, and barrel!"

Matt now realized what John had been up to for weeks. He also knew her statement carried some validity. A frown tightening his brow, he removed the silver cover from a dish of salmon and glanced up. "I'll go with you."

"Who said I wanted you to go with me?" she retorted. "Just because I tolerated you for this tour doesn't mean I want you hung around my neck forever."

The steward returned and, his eyes bright with curiosity, splashed white wine into their glasses.

She tossed the sharply folded paper aside and ran her contemptuous gaze over Matt. "Besides, haven't you got enough problems of your own?"

Anger seeped up from somewhere deep in his guts as he clicked the cover back in place. "What do you mean by that?"

"Well, Jenny Parker is still after your hide—and now I hear you've got another hornet's nest on your front porch."

The words had barely left her mouth when the nervous steward hoisted up his tray and slipped into the kitchen car.

Matt glanced at the harried steward, then frowned at

her. Her ingratitude and smug attitude nettled him. "What in God's name are you talking about?"

She helped herself to the salmon and stared back at him evenly. "I'm talkin' about that letter you got last week, in Leadville." Very deliberately, she leaned forward and waved her dinner knife under his nose. "You know—that letter from Dovie Benningfield, informin' you she's bringin' a breach-of-promise case against you?"

Surprise shot through him. "How the devil did you find out about that?"

She set her knife aside and grinned. "The steward told me."

He glared at the kitchen door. "That little man talks too much."

"Or maybe just enough." She scooped scalloped potatoes onto her plate and eyed him again. "The way I see it, you need to worry about your own business first."

Resentment flooded over him. Who was *she* to advise *him?* Hadn't he made all the arrangements for the tour and seen that everything went smoothly? In his heart he realized they were actually fighting about nothing—but the woman could be so damn infuriating! Squinting at her, he took some potatoes, then flung the serving spoon back into the casserole dish. "Yeah, the way you need to sleep with a pistol under your pillow every night?"

"How did you know that?"

"The steward told me," he said triumphantly. "He does make your bed every morning." He snorted with disbelief. "Why would you do a silly thing like that? Haven't I behaved like a perfect gentlemen? Do you think I'll lurch into your sleeping car like some crazed midnight stalker?"

"I didn't want you to get lonesome for Dovie and come lookin' for me. I believe in bein' prepared."

He clinked down his fork. "You believe in driving a man crazy! For weeks you've talked about nothing but miners' rights and unions. I feel like I've been touring Colorado with the head of the Knights of Labor!"

Color splotched her cheeks. "You gave me the idea in

the first place!'' She held her hands in a praying position and rolled her eyes heavenward, saying, ''Don't you remember, Reverend Father, you were the one who invented Carrie O'Leary—Angel of the Slopes.''

With a groan, he flipped aside his napkin and stood. ''Yeah, yeah, yeah, I remember, but I didn't know you were going to become a single-minded idiot. You used to be warm . . . feminine . . . funny. Oh, you put on a good show for the folks, but in private you're as much fun as a hanging judge.''

Her small hands clenched, she jumped up and glared at him. ''Well, that's the way with us saints. We tend to be a mite sober-sided, you know.''

''God Almighty, I didn't ask for a saint.''

Nodding her head wisely, she circled around him. ''Faith, you always find out what they really want, after you give them what they said they wanted, don't you?'' She shook her finger in his face. ''I know you. You just want what you've always wanted—which is sex.''

He waved the subpoena before her nose. At that point he wanted nothing more in life than to win this particular argument. ''Well, if you're right—I'll be getting it from you at the penitentiary, won't I?''

She snatched away the stiff document and crumpled it in her hand. ''Why don't you just disappear from my life?''

''Ohh, no, little lady. While you're on trial I'm going to stick by you like a tick on a fat dog. The libel trial of the Angel of the Slopes will make H. H. Hardin tons of money and stamp my byline in the mind of every reader in America.'' His arms spread in a dramatic gesture, he flopped down on one knee. ''I can see it now,'' he proclaimed with feeling. ''I'll center my last piece around the judge's verdict—the one where he asks you to pay a fifty-thousand dollar-fine and go to jail for the rest of your life.'' He stroked his chin. ''Umm . . . maybe I'll write an exposé for the scandal sheets, too! As your royal consort, I should have the inside track with the editors.''

She sauntered to the door that led to her sleeping car and turned.

"I'm goin' to bed now," she announced in a dry tone, "and when I close this door, I will consider our conversation *and* our business relationship finished." She glanced at a ticking wall clock and shoved the crumpled subpoena in her skirt pocket. "Before dawn we'll be in Denver, and I'll be free of you and this rollin' house of horrors." Her white-knuckled hand clenched the doorknob. "I'm not eatin' breakfast in the mornin', and don't bother sayin' good-bye. I'll be leavin' from the other end of the train."

He stood and jabbed his finger at her. "Don't think Hardin will bail you out of this mess."

"Yeah, a woman convict ain't as glamorous as a woman union organizer, is she?"

"You can take this lightly if you want, but you're in a real fix. I doubt there's a man alive who has the stomach or the money to get involved in this escapade."

She raised her chin. "Oh, you don't? Well, it just happens that I know one who does!" She slammed the door behind her.

How had he managed to get along with her this long? The woman could drive a man crazy with her stiff-necked pride and hot temper—especially if he loved her. With a colorful oath, he flopped down and slammed his fist on the table, rattling the crystal glasses.

Two days later Carrie sank down on Martin Henderson's Chippendale sofa and glanced around his well-appointed library. Evidence of the man's wealth dotted the room. An ornate silver service rested on the tea table in front of her. Book-filled shelves lined the room's walls, and a bright Oriental carpet stretched across its shiny parquet floors. A huge crystal chandelier hung from the scrolled ceiling.

Henderson leaned forward in his overstuffed chair and patted Carrie's hand. "Don't worry, my dear, everything is going to be just fine." He smoothed back the gray hair at his temples and nodded at the severely dressed man standing beside him. "Donald Simmons is the finest lawyer in Colorado." Adjusting the lapels of his expensive suit coat, he added, "With his brains and my money, we'll have you out of this scrape in a jiffy."

The tall, silver-haired lawyer glanced at a chiming grandfather clock, then sat down beside Carrie. The bespectacled man projected a dry, professional air. "That's right, Miss O'Leary. I've had some experience with criminal libel cases before. I'm sure you'd like to discuss your case. Where shall we start?"

Gowned in a black velvet bodice and a plaid taffeta skirt, she studied his shrewd eyes. "I don't know. Maybe you should tell me how the law looks at libel." Long ringlets jiggled from the back of her head as she talked.

Simmons cleared his throat and adjusted his cuff links. "All right, I think I can put everything in simple terms. The law demands that you take care with the things you say about people. An untruthful statement is called a defamation and can result in criminal liability."

Henderson poured fragrant jasmine tea from the silver service while the lawyer talked. Carrie noticed his perceptive eyes followed all of her movements and reactions. She accepted a delicate china cup and saucer from him and looked at Simmons again. "So slander and libel are the same thing?"

The lawyer stood and tugged off his spectacles. "No, they're not. Slander is spoken; libel is written. I'm afraid the penalties and damages awarded for libel ar harsher than for slander. You see, my dear, since it is written, libel is more long-lasting and widely noticed."

She widened her eyes and glanced at Henderson. "Widely noticed? I guess that description fits my grizzly bear stories, all right. By now half the people in America have seen them and laughed at old John."

Simmons put on his spectacles and stared at her. "Miss O'Leary, are you saying you wrote these stories to specifically satirize Worthington?"

"I'm afraid so." She sipped her tea, then set it down

and grinned. "I was tryin' to rally the miners against him—I needed somethin' they would read and understand. After the stories came out in the *Star*, lots of editors thought they were funny and used them."

The lawyer moved to a fancy mahogany sideboard and picked up a copy of the *Star*. "Well, I strongly advise you not to advertise that fact."

"But it's the truth."

He snapped open the paper and scanned one of her stories. "That's too bad. Your honesty might bring down this paper with you." The stiff paper crackled as he handed it to her. "See how the editor has cleverly placed the story on the Entertainment for Children page with some riddles and jokes. Most of the other editors have followed suit. By doing this, they are saying your articles are children's stories—not biting satire or, as Worthington claims, libel. You see, anyone who repeats defamation is also liable for it."

"So I have to . . . to lie to keep some other folks from gettin' hurt?"

He steepled his hands. "I prefer to say readjust your literary perspective. Don't you think your pieces would make fine children's tales?"

"Yes, I suppose so."

"And when you wrote them, didn't you have children in mind?"

"Well, I thought children would like them, but—"

"There you have it." He took the paper, folded it, and laid it aside. "You wrote the tales for children, and *that* shall be our defense."

Henderson lit a fat cigar and filled the room with its spicy aroma. He glanced at the lawyer, who had moved to a wall of thick law books. "You've done it again, Simmons. I knew you'd think of something."

Carrie spread her hands and looked at Henderson's distinguished features. "But that's really a lie. When I came to you yesterday, you said you'd help me because you believed in my cause. And when you took me to lunch today, you said your lawyer would get me out of this pickle—but you didn't say I'd have to lie!''

Apprehension clouded Simmons's face. "I'm afraid the only defenses for defamation are privilege and truth." Hands behind his back, he paced before the tea table and shook his head. "Knowing the content of these stories, I'm sure Worthington's solicitor will come down hard on malicious intent.''

Carrie frowned. "What does that mean?''

"It means that you knew your accusations against Worthington were false and you wrote them anyway.''

She laughed, then in a relieved tone said, "Oh, my accusations weren't false—they were true. And every miner in Crested Butte knows they're true.''

He glanced over his spectacles at her. "I'm afraid you'll have to prove that. And although some miners may agree with you, I doubt few would jeopardize their futures to back your claims. Besides, you would need an uninterested party, a very reliable source indeed, to confirm your accusations." He shot her a hard look. "Do you know a person like that?''

Matt's face sprang to her mind, but she pushed the vision aside. He had helped her promote the walkout, but that was one thing, and this was another. She knew he still wouldn't see the whole truth about John because his family loyalty was too strong. Could he actually testify against his own flesh and blood? She doubted it. And after their bitter parting, she couldn't ask him to make that painful choice. "Well . . . no," she finally replied. "I—''

"Just as I thought," Simmons cut in. He glanced at the library clock, then back at Carrie. "Miss O'Leary, you should stay with the defense I suggested. Anything else would be disastrous.''

"Isn't there anythin' else I could do?''

With his eyes closed, he took off his spectacles and pinched the bridge of his nose. "I suppose you could plead nolo contendere . . . you'd avoid an ugly trail that way.''

"Nolo contendere?''

"Yes, you would not contest the charge. You would be putting yourself at the mercy of the judge." He shoved his spectacles back on and smiled at Henderson. "I'm sure any judge would be favorably swayed by such feminine beauty. Of course, there would still be a very stiff fine."

She stood and raised her brows. "Wait a minute . . . if I did that, I'd be sayin' Worthington was right—that I *did* lie about him."

Simmons gathered up some documents and tapped the crisp papers against the tea table. "Yes, that's correct."

Hands on hips, she looked at him, then at Henderson. "I can't say that. I'd be goin' back on everythin' I believe. That's worse than lyin'."

Henderson puffed smoke into the air, then stood and took her hand. "Yes, but you would be saving your neck, wouldn't you?"

She eased back. "Mr. Henderson . . . I can't lie. I can't say I wrote those stories for children. And I can't say the things the Grizzly Bear did, really the things Worthington did, weren't true."

Simmons coughed and looked at the tall library doors. "I'm afraid I must go, Miss O'Leary. I'd hoped I could help you out of this kettle of fish for Martin's sake, but you leave me no defense."

Clenching her hands, she stepped forward. "How about truth? When did it become wrong to tell the truth?"

He walked to the door and glanced back over his thin shoulder. "It's not wrong, of course, but in this case it's not very expedient." His countenance uneasy, he eyed Henderson. "I'm sorry, Martin. I can't take this case."

"Don't worry about it," Carrie shot back. "Mr. Henderson told me how he believes in what I've written. We'll get another lawyer."

Simmons shrugged. "I don't know a man in Colorado who would take the case." With a nod at the banker, he exited and closed the door behind him.

Henderson looked at Carrie and gestured at the sofa.

"Sit down, my dear. I can see how distressed you are. Perhaps we can work something out."

She dropped onto the sofa and studied Henderson as he adjusted his fine silk tie and eased down beside her. An inner voice warned her to get up and leave, but then she remembered her back was against the wall. Where could she turn? Without Henderson, she wouldn't have a chance to win the case. And if she lost, others would get hurt, too. Perhaps her instincts were wrong—after all, the man had been a perfect gentleman. She looked him in the eye. "Mr. Henderson, I want to fight. Are you behind me? Will you back me up?"

"Of course, my dear. But I really think you should consider what Simmons told you." He took her hand. "I think you'll have to reconsider his suggestions. You must have a defense and someone to defend you."

She pulled her hand away and scanned the library wall. "Have you read any of those law books?"

He took a draw from his cigar and glanced at the wall. "Yes, quite a few. In fact, I studied for the bar in my youth."

Hope glowing within her, she walked to the shelves and pulled out a heavy volume, then turned to a chapter entitled "What Is Evidence?" Thoughtfully tapping her chin, she eyed his amused face. "Mr. Simmons said truth was a defense in a libel case, so my defense will be *truth.*"

Henderson laughed. "That's all very well and good, my dear, but if you insist on pursuing this reckless course, you still need someone to defend you."

She snapped the book together and smiled at him. "That's no problem. With your help, I'll defend myself."

Chapter 18

Two weeks later, a clerk opened the Denver County courtroom doors for Carrie and Martin Henderson. A murmur washed through the expectant crowd as all eyes fastened on Carrie. Matt slapped his notebook on the press table and watched her, remembering the dark, chilly morning she had stepped from the hissing Pullman car. Clothed in an old dress and a tattered shawl, she had stalked from the train and never looked back. Brave enough to go to hell alone, she had lugged her frayed carpetbag up the station steps and melted into the Denver crowds.

Ten days of colorful newspaper articles about the plucky redhead had fired the city's imagination. Now she was entering the courtroom like Cleopatra upon her barge. A peach-colored suit swept over her lush curves, and saucy curls bounced from her head while she paced into the packed room. Mantled with confidence and panache, she looked calm and undeniably gorgeous.

"There she is!" shouted a young man who clambered over his friends to touch her.

When Martin Henderson clasped her waist to guide her around the eager youth, the gorge rose in Matt's throat. He glared at the tall, distinguished man, hating his expensive clothes and polished manner. So this was her new protector! Damn, why had she chosen the most notorious womanizer in Denver? Was she too innocent to realize the man was simply biding his time before he made his move?

Chairs scraped back and bumped into one another as the Denver reporters scrambled for the press table. His temper rising, Matt watched Carrie and Henderson take their seats behind the bar; then he scanned the crowd.

Dressed in their finest, the perfumed matrons of Brown's Bluff whispered behind waving fans. On the other side of the room, a passel of quiet, gingham-clad mothers cuddled children and stared at the socialites. A group of noisy college boys lounged behind Carrie and passed notes, while a few working men stood at the back of the court-room. At last Matt spotted Jacob Steiner sitting by an older woman dressed in black. Lord, what was Jacob doing here? he wondered.

The reporter beside Matt nudged him in the ribs. "She's a looker, ain't she? I'd sure hate to convict her."

Matt eyed the jury, composed of conservative Denver businessmen. "I wonder if that sober-looking jury will feel as gallant."

Suddenly the tall courtroom doors flew open again and John Worthington entered. Dressed in a London-tailored suit, he strode down the aisle, his eyes locked straight ahead. Matt looked up when he neared, but his uncle walked past him without so much as a glance. Displaying not a flicker of emotion, he seated himself beside his at-torney, a tall, raw-boned man of fifty.

The crowd's gaze shifted to a massive door at the front of the courtroom as a wall clock chimed nine. In impres-sive tones, the clerk ordered, "All rise for his Honor, Judge Baker!" Garbed in somber black robes, the judge left his chambers and mounted the bench. An excited buzz rose from the seats.

Glancing over his spectacles, he pounded his gavel for order. "You may be seated."

Matt evaluated the judge. From the look of his silvery hair and stern features, he wasn't a man to be trifled with. Then Matt looked at Carrie again. Hands clasped in her lap, she sat solemn and serene, waiting for the proceedings to begin. But where was Henderson's fancy lawyer? Apprehension shot through him.

"All the witnesses have been sworn in, and I've read the briefs," the judge commented. He adjusted his robe and looked at Worthington's attorney. "You may proceed, Mr. North."

North stood and opened the trial with a statement outlining how he expected to prove Carrie had maliciously slandered Worthington. While he spoke, he paced in front of the jury box and gestured dramatically with his long hands. His eloquent statement finished, he glanced at the bench and reseated himself.

The judge tugged off his spectacles and addressed Carrie. "I understand you intend to defend yourself, Miss O'Leary. Why are you pursuing this course?"

Her eyes large, she slowly stood. "Well, I can't find a lawyer that suits me. Besides, I figure I know more about my side of the story than anyone else."

A few people laughed at her remark.

"Do you really believe you're capable?"

"Yes, sir . . . I think so. I've been readin' Mr. Henderson's law books and he's been coachin' me about plaintiffs and litigants and all that stuff." The spectators chuckled again. "Maybe you can help me out if I make a mistake." Loud laughter exploded through the crowd.

"I'm not here to *help you out,* Miss O'Leary," the judge roared. "And I seriously doubt your judgment in defending yourself. But since you've made this decision, go ahead with your opening remarks." He glared at her. "Please make them as plain and precise as possible."

Matt tossed his notebook aside and leaned back, torn between admiration, fear, and fury. He didn't need to write anything down. He knew he would remember everything for the rest of his life. Lord, it was going to be a long trial.

Carrie faced the jury and cleared her throat. "The plaintiff"—she pointed at Worthington's scowling face—

"said I wrote my grizzly bear stories with him in mind, and I maliciously slandered him. Well, he's half right!"

The jurors murmured and glanced at each other with puzzled eyes.

"I did write the stories about him," she went on, looking at each juror, "but I didn't slander him. Slanderin' is makin' up somethin' about somebody that ain't true. And every word I wrote about Worthington is true. I'll prove every mean thing that the Grizzly Bear did is really what John Worthington did." She paused, now that she had captured the jury's attention. "My defense is truth." With a little smile, she turned and looked at the judge. "Was that all right, sir?"

He raised his brows. "Very crude—but passable. All right, Miss O'Leary, take your seat." He glanced at North. "You may proceed, Counsel."

North stood and called first one literary light, then another to the stand. He questioned English professors and journalists, making them all admit Carrie's work was indeed satire. When the editor of *The Denver Star* came to the witness chair, the harried man barely escaped admitting he had printed a libelous work, even though he had placed it on the Children's Page. Her face impassive, Carrie declined her right to cross-examine the witnesses.

At last North looked at her and smirked. "As my next witness, I call Carrie O'Leary."

When she walked to the witness-box, a young man stood and yelled, "Give them hell, Carrie!"

She glanced over her shoulder and quipped, "Thanks. I intend to."

Everyone roared.

Judge Baker banged his gavel several times. "Miss O'Leary! You will not address remarks to the spectators. And you, young man," he continued, sternly eyeing the youth, "will remain silent or be evicted from this court!" He glared at North. "Very well, go ahead, Counsel."

"Miss O'Leary," North began, "in what way did you know John Worthington?"

She settled herself far back in the seat. "Well, old John owns the Silver Queen, and my father worked for him."

A smug smile spreading over his lips, North approached the witness-box. "Yes, but did you know him yourself? Did you ever question him about his thoughts or beliefs?"

"Oh, sure. I've talked to him a few times—but he never told me what he was thinkin'."

"You mean you wrote satirical articles about the man, but you had no idea of his opinions?"

She scratched her head and grinned at the jury. "No, but when you've got a sprayin' skunk under your house, you already know what he's thinkin'."

The jury laughed; the spectators guffawed; Matt coughed and kneaded his furrowed brow.

The red-faced judge hammered his gavel again. "Miss O'Leary, this is not a music hall. You will restrain yourself from entertaining the jury."

"I ain't tryin' to entertain them, sir. I'm tryin' to tell them the truth."

Judge Baker shot North a dark look. "Try another line of questioning, Counsel."

The lawyer pointed his finger at Carrie. "Isn't it true you hate John Worthington?"

She looked at Worthington's angry face. "Yeah. It's awful to say that about another human bein', but I guess I *do* hate him. But I didn't lie about him."

"Isn't it also true you've publicly stated that you consider him responsible for many miners' deaths and your father's death?"

She leaned forward and grasped the arms of the witness chair. "Yeah, I consider him responsible for the deaths of all the miners who died in the Silver Queen last year. And he as good as killed Da. His messenger boy told Da that he had lost the Shamrock. The shock made him have a heart attack."

Several of the Brown's Bluff matrons gasped and glared at Worthington.

"And still you persist," North challenged, "in telling

us you harbored no malicious intent when you wrote your articles?''

With a tremulous sigh, she looked at Judge Baker. ''Malicious intent means you set out with hurtin' somebody in mind. I never wanted to hurt John Worthington, I just wanted to wake up the miners, and show them he was squeezin' the life from them.''

The judge looked thoughtful. Matt watched while the man weighed her words; then he listened to North question her from every angle he could think of. Using simple but witty logic, she managed to hold her own and sidestep his accusations. A grudging pride swelled in Matt's chest.

The spectators guffawed as the skinny English teacher left the witness-box and hurried up the aisle. Their forces increased since the noon recess, the society matrons slyly smiled at the embarrassed man. Carrie's rooting section from the local college hooted and clapped. A number of prominent Denver businessmen, who had closed shop for the day, chuckled and nodded their heads. The raucous delegation from Crested Butte whistled and stomped the wooden floor.

''This court will come to order, or I will have all spectators removed!'' Judge Baker ordered.

Carrie glanced at the noisy courtroom, which was filled to capacity; then she sat down. So far she had cross-examined two supposed experts on satire and torn their testimony to shreds. Pleased, she swept her gaze to the press table and studied Matt.

Seemingly unconcerned, he scribbled in his notebook. His cool manner nettled her. It was unnatural for a man to be so detached. Look at him sitting there in that starched shirt and expensive suit, turned out like a preacher for a camp meeting, she thought. You'd think he would have the decency to at least laugh at her joke. No doubt while her future hung in the balance, he was revising his list of grammar rules.

Martin Henderson caressed her arm. ''You're doing very

well, my dear. You should be able to bring things to a head tomorrow. Just keep hammering away like you have today.''

She pulled her arm away and smoothed down her stylish dress. ''I can hear you just fine, Mr. Henderson. You don't need to keep touchin' me every time you say somethin'.'' She eyed his striped suit and diamond stickpin. Apprehension seeped through her: she felt as if Henderson were tightening the reins on their relationship. How long could she maintain the friendship without hopelessly indebting herself to the wealthy banker?

The judge finally restored order to the courtroom. ''Very well, Counsel,'' he said, looking at North. ''Are you ready to call your next witness?''

North stood and hooked his thumbs into his pants pockets. ''Yes, your Honor. I'm going to call a witness Miss O'Leary may not find so amusing. I call Miss Jenny Parker to the stand.''

Alarm jolted through Carrie. She didn't know what the lawyer had in mind, but she knew Jenny Parker meant trouble. She glanced at the back of the courtroom and saw Reverend Parker sneak in and sit down. And as she turned her head, Jenny sashayed into the room from a side door. The thin blonde wore a yellow silk walking suit, trimmed in black.

Feeling ire bubble up inside her, Carrie watched the preacher's daughter parade to the witness stand and take her seat. From the corner of her eye she noted Matt's surprised face.

''In what capacity is Miss Parker testifying, Counsel?'' the judge asked.

North stepped forward. ''She is here to testify about Miss O'Leary's character—or lack of character, to be more precise.''

Carrie shot to her feet and groaned with outrage. ''Your Honor, a blind woman ain't no judge of color. That woman knows as much about character as a dog knows about his father.''

The spectators roared again, but the judge silenced them.

"Miss O'Leary, take your seat," he commanded. "I don't want to send you from this courtroom." He looked at North and nodded. "Go ahead, Counsel."

North paced before the jury, his hands clasped behind his back. "Miss Parker, how long have you known Miss O'Leary?"

Jenny raised her thin brows and glanced at Carrie as if she were a small animal, beneath her exalted notice. "I've known of her since my father and I came to Crested Butte, about five years ago."

"Where did the O'Leary family reside?"

"In a shack near Three Arrows."

"What is her father's occupation?"

"Her father was a miner."

"Was?"

"Yes. Recently his heart failed after a drunken binge."

"Objection! That's a lie," Carrie hollered.

The judge glared at Jenny. "Do you know for a fact that Mr. O'Leary died from drinking?"

"No, not . . . not really," she stuttered, "but everyone says it's so!"

Judge Baker frowned. "That is hearsay, Miss Parker, and not admissible as evidence. Make sure you relate only the facts. Go on, Mr. North."

"Did Mr. O'Leary frequent saloons often?"

"He was the town drunk."

Carrie stood and shouted, "Objection, objection, objection! Move to strike that from the record! It's not pert . . . pert . . ."—she leaned over and conferred with Henderson—"it's not pertinent." Then she raked her gaze over Jenny. "That's right, attack a dead man who can't defend himself. Da drank, but he had more of the milk of human kindness in his little finger than your father has in his whole withered body!"

The judge thrust his head forward. "Miss O'Leary, I'm

letting that pass because I understand your desire to defend your dead father, but I'm warning you that my patience is at an end.'' He glanced at North. ''Miss O'Leary's objection is sustained. Go on, Counsel, and get to the point. Miss O'Leary's family is not on trial.''

The tall lawyer crossed his arms, then turned back to Jenny. ''Did you ever see any of the O'Leary family in your father's church?''

''No, of course not. Shamus O'Leary was always too drunk to go to church.''

''Objection,'' Carrie shouted again.

''Sustained,'' the judge said. ''Counselor, please make your point.''

''All right,'' North answered as he strode toward Jenny. ''Didn't Miss O'Leary leave Crested Butte for several years?''

''Yes, she came here.''

''Why do you think she came to Denver?''

''That calls for speculation,'' Carrie piped up.

The judge frowned. ''Overruled. I want to hear Mr. North's point.'' He nodded his head at Jenny.

''For the same reason most young girls who are hastily sent away come to a large city. I'm sure you can guess. My sensibilities forbid me from being more specific. Let us simply say another orphan was thrust upon society.''

''That's a lie, a bald-faced lie. I came to Denver to go to school, not have a baby!'' Carrie shouted.

''Hold your tongue!'' the judge thundered.

''Did you personally witness an episode of Miss O'Leary's loose morality?'' North asked.

Jenny stared at Matt and batted her eyes. ''Yes, yes, I did. Last winter the Denver and Rio Grande was derailed by an avalanche between Crested Butte and Three Arrows. Miss O'Leary was on that train. Seeing a need to care for the survivors' spiritual welfare, my father and I accompanied the rescue party.''

''And what did you find?''

"There was ample evidence that Miss O'Leary and the male survivor had been intimate." Jenny stared at Matt, and everyone in the courtroom looked his way.

The judge raised his brows. "Ample evidence? Miss Parker, you must be more specific."

Jenny modestly lowered her head. "Your Honor . . . I can't . . . I—"

"*Go on.* Someone's reputation is at stake."

She raised her head and took a deep breath. "All right, if you insist. We found Miss O'Leary and the male survivor in a cabin. There was only one bed in the cabin. By the look of the bedding—they had shared that bed."

"Anything else?"

Jenny glanced at the floor. "I . . . I inadvertently found Miss . . . Miss O'Leary's bloomers wadded at the foot of the bed, under the cover."

Everyone in the courtroom gasped; one of the society matrons slumped over in a faint. The members of the jury murmured and shook their heads. Several of the reporters jumped up and hurried from the courtroom, notebooks in hand. Carrie glanced at Matt's stormy expression, and disgustedly slumped into the chair by Henderson.

The frazzled judge looked at Jenny. "Miss Parker, may I remind you that you were sworn in before these proceedings began," he said solemnly. "If your statement is true—this is damaging evidence concerning Miss O'Leary's character. Are you sure you don't want to amend your testimony?"

"No, your Honor, I do not. I stand by my words, for they are true."

The judge glanced at North. "Do you have any more questions, Counsel?"

"No, I believe I have established Miss O'Leary's character."

Judge Baker studied Carrie's face. "Do you care to cross-examine the witness?"

Numb with shock and anger, she slowly stood and looked into Matt's eyes, petrified yet hopeful. When he nodded his head, her heart felt like it would burst, but she collected her thoughts and began to speak. "Miss Parker, are you in the habit of tellin' lies?"

"No, of course not!"

"All right, then . . . let me ask you another question. What is your relationship with Matt Worthington?"

"Why, he used to be my employer. I was his assistant at the *Crested Butte Courier.*"

Carrie paced in front of the witness stand, stroking her chin. "Umm . . . I see. And that's all you did for him?"

"Yes, of course. I certainly hope you're not insinuating what I think you are!"

"I'm just askin' a few questions," Carrie said with a grin. She neared the witness stand and looked up at Jenny. "Can you tell us about your plans for October twentieth?"

Jenny sat bolt upright. "P-p-plans? What plans?"

"One of your friends in Crested Butte said she would be serving as a bridesmaid on that day. Would you happen to know whose wedding date that might be?" Carrie asked, arching her brow.

"I'm sure I have no idea."

"Let me rephrase that question. Aren't you presently engaged to be married to Matt Worthington?"

Jenny looked down. She toyed with the pleats on her skirt, and readjusted her waistband. At length she straightened in her seat and said, "Not to my recollection."

"Perhaps I could call a witness to help you recollect," Carrie said, peering at Jacob Steiner, who sat at the back of the courtroom.

As he rose to walk down the aisle, Jenny sputtered, "There's no reason to get that jeweler up here—he'd just lie. Perhaps I was a little hasty announcing my engagement to Matt Worthington."

"I thought you said you weren't engaged to him! Which is it? Are you, or aren't you?"

Jenny sat in icy silence.

"You must answer," warned Judge Baker.

The blonde hung her head. "All right, all right! I'm not engaged to him . . . I just bought a ring and told my friends I was engaged to him. I . . . I made it all up."

The society matrons glared at her and whispered to each other behind open fans.

Carrie studied the surprised jury. "Doesn't it make you wonder, if she'd lie about one thing, how many other things she'd lie about?"

Jenny wiped her teary eyes with a handkerchief. "Er . . . perhaps I have been a little harsh in my judgment of Miss O'Leary's character. After all, the Good Book says we should be forgiving to those who are less spiritually mature than ourselves."

"But, Miss Parker, why the sudden change of heart?" asked the judge.

Jenny squirmed and batted her lashes at him. "Oh, I just see things in a different light now." Then she looked at Carrie with pleading eyes. "Miss O'Leary, may I step down now?"

"Seems to me you're mighty anxious to get out of that witness chair. Makes me wonder about your motives for testifyin' in the first place."

A faint sweat sheened Jenny's brow. "My motives are strictly honorable."

"You and John Worthington have always been close enough to share the same pillow. Are you sure you ain't just tryin' to tie a tin can to my tail?"

Jenny blotted her white face with the lacy handkerchief. "No, no. Certainly not." Her faint voice cracked. "Now may I please step down?"

"Please do." Carrie looked at the judge. "I think you've told the jury everythin' they need to hear." Motioning gracefully, she bowed the way for Jenny as the blonde left the stand.

From the corner of her eye Carrie noticed Matt smile broadly.

* * *

Late in the day, North concluded his presentation.

"Miss O'Leary, are you ready to begin?" Judge Baker inquired.

"I am, your Honor," she replied. "I call Mrs. Potter from Crested Butte for my first witness."

With great interest Matt watched Jacob Steiner help a frail woman in black to the witness stand.

"Mrs. Potter," Carrie began gently after the woman had been seated, "I need to ask you a few questions. Is that all right?"

Her face lined with grief, the woman nodded her gray head.

"Mrs. Potter, how long did your husband, Ned, work in the Silver Queen?"

The woman twisted her plain white handkerchief. "Fifteen years, miss. He's dead now."

"How did he die?"

"There was a small cave-in. Ore fell on his leg and crushed it. He later died of gangrene."

Matt noticed the judge's scowl.

"You didn't take him to the doctor?" Carrie asked.

"We couldn't, miss," the woman answered while she dabbed at her eyes. "We didn't have any money, only script—and the doctor wouldn't take script. But script's all that Mr. Worthington pays the miners, you know."

"You had no savin's?"

"No, miss. We'd used up all our real money. We was behind on the rent and we owed other places."

"Objection," thundered North. "This line of questioning is totally irrelevant. Obviously this woman is a coached witness. She's too poor to have paid her own way to Denver. And I'm sure Miss O'Leary has seen to it that train fare was only part of her compensation."

Carrie glared at North. "Just because she's poor doesn't mean she's a liar! Mr. Henderson here paid for all my witnesses' train fares so that this court could hear the truth." She looked at the judge hopefully. "Sir, I can tie this in with my case. I'm goin' to show the jury why I was forced to write my stories—and that they were true."

The judge nodded his head. "Objection overruled, and may I caution you, Mr. North, not to defame the witness. You just might find yourself in another trial. Proceed, Miss O'Leary."

Carrie gave the woman time to compose herself, then went on. "Mrs. Potter, who owns your rent house?"

"John Worthington."

"And tell us who owns the company store."

"John Worthington."

"Mrs. Potter . . . you said 'we' couldn't take him to the doctor. Do you live with someone else?"

"I did, miss—my son."

"You *did?*"

"Yes, he's also gone now. He died several months after his paw."

"How did he die?"

"He died in the mine, too. He fell in a scaldin' sump." Mrs. Potter broke down and started sobbing.

Carrie moved to the witness stand and put her arm around the woman. "I'm sorry I have to ask you these questions, Mrs. Potter—to bring up these painful memories. But I know you're a woman who understands love, and your love and courage may save another mother's son."

The woman nodded and wiped away her tears. "The poor boy lived for two days, but he finally died," she said softly. "He was just burned too bad."

"Why do you think he fell into that sump?"

The woman looked at Worthington. "The hoist was rotten. My brother saw it. When my boy jumped on the hoist, a piece crumbled under his boot and he fell."

Carrie paced in front of the jurors, commanding their attention. "Had anyone reported this rotten hoist to the superintendent?"

"Oh, yes, lots of times. Mr. Clayright kept sayin' they had to keep expenses down and couldn't fix anythin'. He said my boy was just clumsy."

"Did you ever receive any money from Worthington when your husband or your son died?"

"He paid for the funerals, but after that I received no money of any kind. I've been livin' with my brother since my husband and son died."

Carrie took the woman's hand. "Mrs. Potter, how old was your son when he died?"

"Thirteen, miss."

Several mothers gasped.

"Move to strike," shouted North. "How can any of these questions be relevant?"

Judge Baker shook his gavel at him. "No, Mr. North. I overrule your motion. Do you care to question the witness?"

North waved his hand and sat down. "No, of course not."

"Very well, you may step down, Mrs. Potter." Taking off his spectacles, the judge studied Carrie. "Miss O'Leary, this court has patiently listened to this sad story in the hope of serving justice. Now, please tie this unfortunate woman's testimony into your case."

Carrie helped Mrs. Potter from the witness stand, then she faced the judge. "All right, your Honor. You said you had patiently listened to her story. I've listened to stories like that all my life." As Carrie spoke, everyone in the courtroom fell silent, engrossed in her words.

Sighing heavily, she faced the solemn jury and continued talking. "And I was gettin' tired of listenin' to stories like that. In fact, I couldn't listen to them anymore! I had to do somethin'. Sometimes if you can make people laugh, you can make them think. That was all I was tryin' to do—make people think."

North shifted uncomfortably in his seat and spoke with Worthington. Seconds later he stood and said, "Your Honor, due to the hour I request a recess until tomorrow morning. I need to confer with my client at length."

The judge looked at his pocket watch, then frowned at North. "Very well. This court is dismissed until tomorrow morning at nine o'clock." As Judge Baker stood and gathered his things, the jury filed out and the spectators began leaving the courtroom.

Matt watched John Worthington stand and stride toward him, North at his side. His eyes emotionless, Worthington passed the press table and mumbled, "See me outside." Then he proceeded down the aisle with his attorney. Questions shot through Matt's mind. What could the old fox be up to now?

Matt caught Carrie's eye while Henderson lingered to talk to the law clerk. At first she avoided his gaze, but when he stood, she looked directly at him. He shoved a pencil in his vest pocket and fell in beside her as she turned up the aisle.

She glanced at him from the corner of her eye. "I'm surprised to see you here. I thought Dovie would have your hide tacked to the wall by now."

Amusement tugged the corners of his mouth upward. "Being a foreigner, she has run into some legal problems. But I'm sure Henderson has been more successful. No doubt he has you ensconced in his little love nest by now."

A frown marred her smooth countenance. "As a matter of fact, I'm stayin' at a nice, quiet hotel, and he's even paid for Peony to come to Denver so I wouldn't be alone."

Matt eyed Jacob as he left the courtroom with Mrs. Potter on his arm. "What's Jacob doing here?"

Carrie marched ahead. "Bein' the kind soul he is, Jacob just brought Mrs. Potter up yesterday. They're goin' back to Crested Butte today." With a grin, she turned around and added, "And since North surprised me with Jenny, isn't it handy he happened to be here?"

Matt tugged on her arm. "Where did you find Mrs. Potter? She was wonderful."

Carrie glanced back at Henderson, who was talking with the clerk. "I lived beside her for two years. Any more questions?"

"Yeah . . . what else do you have in your bag of tricks?"

Her eyes stormed up. "They ain't tricks—but I have as many witnesses as I need. Mr. Henderson has supplied me with enough money to pay their train fare."

"Carrie, there's gossip among the reporters that Henderson is tied up in some shady business affairs. Don't you know who he is? Don't you know what he wants?"

"He's a generous man who believes in the miners' cause." She looked at him disgustedly. "As to the other, I know what you're hintin' at, but I think you're just drawin' on your own experience."

He gave her a forced grin. "Do you really think Henderson is trying to help you?"

She stared at him defiantly. "Yeah, he's been pickin' me up every day, coachin' me on the law."

"Well, you're damn lucky if that's all he's been coaching you on."

"You've got your nerve, Matt Worthington! Besides, he knows I ain't interested in him!"

"Perhaps not, but he's definitely interested in you." Matt glanced at the banker. "He looks like a wolf watching a coop of chickens—and believe me, before this operation is over he'll have discovered how to get the door open."

Throwing Matt a look colder than an iceman's shoulder, Henderson strode toward them, then took Carrie's arm. "Is this reporter harassing you, my dear?"

She darted a quick glance at Matt. "No, no, he ain't harassin' me. We're—we're—"

"Old friends," Matt cut in.

"Yeah," she quipped, "very old friends."

Henderson smiled at Matt while he took Carrie's elbow with a proprietary air. "Well, that's the best kind, isn't it?"

Matt watched them exit the near empty room, then clenched his hands. His jaw tight, he trailed their path from the courthouse. He paused halfway down the busy steps and saw them wheel away in Henderson's expensive carriage. Soon the carriage blended into the noisy sea of traffic flowing up Main Street.

When he glanced back at the pillared building, he spied his uncle standing by a white column. With a drawn face, Worthington walked down the marble steps and extended his arm. Matt moved toward him and slowly clasped the older man's fleshy hand. "John? It's been a long time."

"Thank God we have a moment alone. I need to talk to you, my boy." Worthington glanced around at the people streaming into the courthouse for the next trial. "But not here. We need to really talk. We need privacy."

Matt studied at his uncle's troubled face. "We've had years to talk and we've never *really* talked before. What are we going to talk about now?"

Worthington dropped his gaze. "Something we should have talked about twenty years ago when your mother brought you to me."

Curiosity—and compassion—percolated through Matt as he stared at his uncle's anguished eyes.

"Meet me for breakfast tomorrow at seven," Worthington said. "I'm staying at the Chartwell."

Chapter 19

The aroma of coffee and freshly baked pastry floated toward Matt as he entered the Chartwell's restaurant. Curious, he scanned the dining room and searched for his uncle. Creamy china, set on lacy cloths, covered every table; potted palms in blue-and-white pots loomed in every corner. Its prisms bright with morning light, a crystal chandelier glittered from the high ceiling.

Matt edged around a white-coated waiter pushing a coffee cart. As he threaded his way into the heavily carpeted room, the sounds of clicking silverware and muffled chatter engulfed him. Men with morning editions and fashionable, perfumed ladies brushed past him as they exited the pleasant restaurant. Finally he spotted Worthington hunched over a newspaper at a small table in the corner. Another fine-tailored London suit hugged the man's thick shoulders and large middle.

Unbuttoning his dark suit coat, Matt walked to the table. "Well, John, I'm here and ready for some real talk."

Worthington glanced up and smiled. "Matt! I was just wondering if you would show. Glad to see you, my boy." He folded the newspaper and motioned to a young waiter carrying a silver coffeepot. "Give Mr. Worthington your complete breakfast, and hurry," he ordered as he tossed the crisp newspaper aside.

As soon as the boy had poured coffee and hurried away, Matt sat down and placed his Stetson on the chair beside him. Then he looked at Worthington's tired eyes. "What do you say *I* begin this conversation with a few questions?''

His uncle spread both hands and nodded. ''Fine, fine, go ahead.''

Matt leaned back and sipped his coffee. ''All right, where in hell have you been for so long? You disappeared faster than a boardinghouse pot roast after we had that argument about Carrie's articles.''

Worthington rubbed his nose and chuckled. ''Yes, I suppose I did. I just needed to be here in Denver—to take care of some business I'd let ride for years. I knew Clayright could take care of the Queen.''

''You're sure it didn't have anything to do with the fact that a certain redhead had made it very hot for you in Crested Butte?''

The older man waved his stubby hand. ''No, no . . . in fact, it actually ties in with the matter I wanted to speak to you about.''

''And what's that?''

''Your mother.''

Shock darted through Matt. ''My mother? No one has talked about her for years.''

The waiter placed two plates of food before them, poured more coffee, and discreetly backed away.

Matt watched Worthington eat and wondered what he would say next. A nagging voice told him he wouldn't like the answer. *''Well*, what about her?'' he finally prodded.

Worthington wiped his lips with the Chartwell's monogrammed napkin and glanced away. ''I hate to tell you this, Matt . . . but she's . . . she's dead.''

Surprising pain squeezed Matt's heart. The woman in the bronze gilt frame was finally gone. She had been a memory for so many years, he was astonished he felt anything at all. But it was there—a sharp loneliness close to his heart. ''How do you know?''

Worthington finally met his gaze. ''I set some detectives on the case. The last time I'd heard of Maggie, she had gone back to St. Louis.''

Matt shoved back his untouched plate. "Yes, after she left me on your doorstep."

"I wouldn't put it that way."

"What other way is there to put it? That's what she did, isn't it?"

Uneasiness rolled over Worthington's face. "Not exactly."

"John, just say what you mean."

"Your father and I grew up with Maggie in St. Louis. We were both very close to her."

Frustration tightened Matt's jaw. "Yes, yes, I know that."

Worthington tossed his napkin aside. "Well, perhaps you didn't know she was engaged to me at one time." Regret tinged his voice.

Matt's heart sank. He didn't want to hear the words that would follow—but he knew he must. "Go on."

Worthington pushed his plate back and stared across the busy dining room. "She still loved me when she married Tom. We'd had a silly argument."

"John, I find all of this rather tedious—"

Worthington caught his eye before he could finish his statement. "She brought you to me before she ran away with that no-account gambler who hypnotized her, because . . . because I'm your natural father!"

Matt stared at him, feeling totally empty inside. His teeth clenched, he stood and shoved his chair back. "You're lying. You're playing on my sympathy because you need my support at the trial."

Worthington sighed heavily. "How I wish I were lying."

Matt braced his arms on the table and leaned forward. "If you were my father, why didn't you tell me about it? Why did you pretend to be my uncle, and a rather cold, distant one at that? And why have I never seen my own birth certificate?"

Worthington gazed up with shiny eyes. "Sit down. I'll tell you about it now," he said softly.

Matt eased into his chair, feeling the energy drain from him.

"I visited Tom and Maggie the summer of fifty-three. Nine months later, you were born," the heavy man continued.

"How can you be sure Tom wasn't my father?" Anger edged Matt's tense voice.

Lost in his memories, Worthington stared across the room again. "They'd been to New York—had some tests. The doctor said Maggie was perfectly healthy. He put the blame on Tom."

"So you want me to believe Tom just accepted the fact you had cuckolded him?"

His eyes misty with emotion, the tycoon stared at Matt. "They wanted children so badly, I think he was relieved. The three of us just never spoke of it. Maggie burned the birth certificate. Can you understand?"

Matt blew out his breath and slowly shook his head. "Why didn't you tell me this years ago?"

"I couldn't, because Maggie made me swear I wouldn't. She said I could never tell you until she died." He blinked tears from his eyes. "After that no-account left her, I would have taken her back. I didn't care what she had done. But that fierce pride of hers wouldn't let her come back."

A picture of another proud woman flashed into Matt's mind. At that very moment, he decided he wouldn't let Carrie's pride separate them. He studied John's pained face. "What made you start searching for Maggie now?"

"I had to find out what happened to her before this business with the Queen went any further! She had a weak heart—I felt she might pass away young. That's why I've been in Denver conferring with lawyers and detectives." He placed his warm hand over Matt's fist. "Thank God I'm finally free to tell you that I'm your father."

Thoughts spun around in Matt's head like a whirlwind. Was the man unburdening a horrible secret that he had carried for years, or was he just manipulating him? And why had he picked the same time he was suing Carrie for libel to reveal Maggie's dark past? Matt pulled his hand away. How could this despicable man who had profited from the misfortune of others be his father? His father was Thomas Worthington, a war hero—a man he could be proud of.

"I know what you're thinking," Worthington blurted, reclaiming Matt's attention. "You're thinking about Tom, fighting giving up his memory. It's hard for me to compete with a ghost. Just remember, everything I did, I did for you."

Matt stood again. "Really?"

"Of course. I've had to make some hard decisions, do some hard things, but I did them for you." Worthington leaned forward as if revealing a great secret. "You'll inherit the Silver Queen—everything—when I'm gone."

A muscle throbbed in Matt's jaw. "Why, I didn't know I was in your will, John."

"Of course you are. Under the circumstances I just couldn't tell you. You understand, don't you?"

Matt looked at the Chartwell's exit. "I have to go. Court will be in session soon."

Worthington grabbed his arm as he moved away. "Matt, don't let that O'Leary woman ruin your life." He looked up imploringly. "The money is yours . . . everything is yours. Don't destroy your financial future."

Matt removed his hand and stared down at him. "I don't think I'd want to pay the *tax* on that kind of money, John."

Worthington rose while Matt walked away. "I put you in my will—and I can take you out," he stormed.

Matt paused and turned. "Then we both have some interesting decisions to make today, haven't we?" he commented. His words still heavy in the air, he left the fashionable restaurant.

Court had been in session for an hour, and another of Carrie's witnesses had just stepped from the witness-box. "Ohhs" and "Ahhs" rippled through the spectators like wind through ripe wheat when the handsome editor man walked up the aisle. Carrie saw Matt speak with the clerk, then give him a note. Sitting down, she brushed back her hair. Now what was this all about? she wondered as the clerk passed the creased paper to Henderson. After reading the note, the banker leaned toward Carrie, saying, "I strongly suggest a recess, my dear. Matt Worthington wishes to confer with you."

She stood again, feeling rather light-headed. "Your Honor, I request a short recess."

"Very well, Miss O'Leary. This court is recessed for fifteen minutes."

With a great sigh, she glanced at Matt, who strode toward her, maneuvering through the newspaper men, who rushed for the door.

"We're going outside and we're talking," he said as he took her arm.

Henderson stood. "All right. Perhaps we can use your help."

"Not you, Henderson! Only Carrie and I are going outside. You're staying here." Ignoring the man's glare, Matt marched her up the aisle.

"Would you let go of my arm?" she snapped. "I'm not a child who needs to be taken out of the room."

When they reached the tall doors, he pushed them open and nudged her into the vestibule. "No? Well, you're sure acting like one." Once outside the courtroom, he glanced around until he found a marble bench. "Here," he ordered as he plunked her down on the hard bench. He glared at some nosy socialites, then looked back at her. "Why are you trying to protect me? After our last night on the train, you were mad enough to kill me."

Hands on hips, she ground her teeth. "And I'm still mad at you—but I ain't mad enough to ruin your life."

He snorted with laughter. "Do you think I give a good goddamn if I'm dragged into this? You've already totally rearranged my life. What's one little court case?" he said in a loud voice. Some of the embarrassed dowagers rushed away.

Sudden happiness swirled through Carrie. "I thought you were still mad at me."

He threw her a lopsided grin and sat down. "I'm *always* mad at you—but you happen to be right about John and the Silver Queen."

She smiled and nodded her head. "I guess both of us are big enough to put our quarrel aside to help a whole town of sufferin' people."

"That's right. . . . Look, you've hog-tied Jenny, but you still haven't got the rope around John," he said, putting one hand on her shoulder. "Get me up there and you'll win your case."

She removed his hand and blinked at him. Were her ears deceiving her, or had she heard him correctly?

He grinned and tugged at his ear, then wagged a long finger at her. "You need a disinterested witness. Let me testify about the night I worked the shift at two thousand feet."

She stared at him and raised her brows. "You'd do that? You'd testify against your own flesh and blood—your own name? John would never forgive you, you know."

"I know. But I found out something this morning that turned my world upside down."

"For heaven's sake, what?"

"It doesn't matter now. But maybe I can make something good come from the news. Maybe I can help you win your case."

She studied his eyes, then shook her head in disbelief. "You're sure?"

He took her face in his warm hands and turned it toward an image of Justice over the courtroom door. A scale in her raised hand, Justice stood blindfolded. "Yes, I'm sure. Let's take the blindfold off that lady and show her the truth about the Silver Queen."

* * *

Minutes later the judge sternly eyed Matt while the clerk moved away with a Bible. Then he looked at Carrie. "Are you ready to question the witness, Miss O'Leary?"

"Yes, I am, your Honor." She walked to the witness stand and glanced at Matt. "Would you state your name and occupation?"

"Matt Worthington, editor of the *Crested Butte Courier* . . . or rather, former editor. I now write for the H. H. Hardin syndicate."

At the mention of the Worthington name, a murmur of excitement rippled through the spectators. Several of the jurors sat up and stared intently.

"By the way, I might mention that while I was editor of the *Courier*, Miss Parker was my assistant."

Sitting in the middle of the crowd, Jenny proudly glanced about the courtroom, then spoke with her father, who sat beside her.

Carrie crossed her arms. "Yes, she was tellin' us about that earlier. Do you have any comments you'd like to add about her performance?"

"Performance?" Matt scratched his head and grinned. "Strange you should choose that word." Steepling his hands, he leaned forward. "All I can say is that she was an excellent assistant. She did *everything* she was asked." He ran a finger around his collar. "How can I delicately put this . . . ? Let's just say she gave more of herself than any assistant I ever had."

The crowd exploded in laughter while Jenny and her father jumped up and ran out of the courtroom.

"Order! Order!" shouted the judge. He took off his glasses and rubbed his forehead. "Please. . . . Go on, Miss O'Leary," he added in a weary tone.

Carrie paced in front of the witness-box. "Mr. Worthington, as a resident of Crested Butte, are you familiar with the Silver Queen mine? Have you been in it?"

"Yes, I've been in the Queen many times . . . for brief periods at the higher levels. Recently, however, I made an extended visit to the two-thousand-foot level." Matt watched his uncle's face tense and darken. He knew Worthington was wondering what decision he had made.

"Why did you do this?"

"To gather information for a story about the Queen."

Carrie glanced at the jurors' interested faces, then back at Matt. "You'd never written an article about the mine before?"

"Only brief pieces—notices, you might call them."

She rubbed her temple. "Then why would you want to write a story when you had never been interested in doin' it before?"

Matt shifted his weight and cleared his throat. "Someone sparked my interest. Someone indicated the miners' lives were in jeopardy, due to the inferior equipment being used."

When North stood to object, Worthington tugged on his arm and motioned for him to take a seat. Matt knew his uncle was still betting on his loyalty—still betting he would never sully the family name.

"When you went down to investigate, how were you dressed?" Carrie asked.

"I was dressed as a miner."

"A miner . . . and you were a newspaper editor? Why were you disguised?"

Matt exhaled and crossed his legs. "Because I'd been barred from entering earlier."

"Who barred you?"

"Clayright, the mine superintendent. However, his orders came from John Worthington."

At these words Worthington leaned forward and glared at him. His face grim, North slapped a folder together and crossed his arms.

Carrie noted their actions, then brought her attention back to Matt. "Why were you not permitted into the mine?"

"Clayright said they were opening a new room—a new area of excavation. He said it was too dangerous at the lower levels."

"How did you get by Clayright? Didn't he know you?"

Matt grinned. "My face was grimy and smeared with soot. I wore a wide-brimmed hat, held my head down, and entered the gates with a press of men."

"So you descended to the two-thousand-foot level. What did you find?"

He raised his finger. "May I tell you what I found before the two-thousand-foot level?"

"Yes, of course."

Matt gazed silently at the jurors until all of them waited for his words. "First of all, I found the hoist to be rotten and in need of repair."

"What else?"

"At five hundred feet, at one thousand, five hundred feet—at all levels—the miners were working under the worst conditions. I noticed all types of jerry-rigged equipment and defective ore carts."

"And at two thousand?"

He leaned on one elbow and rubbed a thumb across his chin. "It was like Dante's inferno. The timbers in the new room were rotten. The miners live in constant fear that all the reinforcements will crumble and cause a cave-in. And due to the defective blowers and lack of ice, the men are forced to work in horrific heat. Despite this, they often work during their rest periods—and often pass out."

"Why don't they rest?"

Matt raised his brows and met Carrie's gaze. "They can't. They're trying to meet their quota, which is set by Clayright. If a man misses his quota several times, he is fired."

"So in your opinion," Carrie continued, "the abuses I attributed to John Worthington in my Grizzly Bear stories are justified?"

Matt looked Worthington straight in the eye. "They are totally justified. Since the men are paid in script, they soon find themselves in virtual bondage to John Worthington. Morally, he is guilty of gross neglect and exploitation.

Due to his negligence, God knows how many men have died."

"Thank you, Mr. Worthington," Carrie said as she turned to look at Henderson.

"Miss O'Leary," Matt called in a loud voice, "you forgot to ask my familial relationship to John Worthington."

Her face washed with surprise, she turned and stared at him. "All right, then . . . what relation is John Worthington to you?"

Matt pulled himself up and met his uncle's angry gaze once more. "Until very recently I thought he was my uncle. I now know, by his own admission, that he is my father." He spoke the words with measured ease.

The courtroom buzzed with surprised comments. Some of the spectators moved to speak with friends.

Judge Baker banged his gavel, then looked at North, who whispered in Worthington's ear. "Counsel, do you care to cross-examine this witness?"

North blanched. "No, your Honor—*I do not.*"

"You may step down, then, Mr. Worthington," the judge said.

After Matt left the witness stand and sat down, North began his summation. As the man spoke, Carrie sat rock still, her stunned face milk-white. Matt could read dozens of questions in her curious eyes. Questions that he didn't want to answer. Quietly, he started walking up the aisle.

Seconds later, Worthington rose and followed him to the back of the courtroom. "I'm always amazed at what a man will throw away for a pretty face," he commented in hushed tones when he caught up with Matt. "I've just witnessed the most pitiful display of ingratitude I've ever seen in my life. Mrs. Potter is obviously emotionally unstable and North could have discredited her testimony. If I lose this case it will be because of you. If you had any dream of seeing a penny from the Queen, you can forget it."

Matt paused. "I never wanted your money, John; I wanted your love."

"You had it, boy. But now you have nothing. You burned your coal, but you didn't warm yourself, did you? Don't expect anything but trouble from that Irish trollop." Matt's jaw tightened, but Worthington grasped his arm. "Everything I did, I did for you, and now you cut my heart out. What kind of son did I raise?"

Matt removed Worthington's hand from his sleeve. "An honest one, I hope." He stared at his uncle's hot eyes for a moment, then pushed open the tall doors and exited the courtroom.

Her sensibilities still shocked and numbed by Matt's revelation, Carrie stood to make her summation. The cost of his testimony staggered the imagination. She ached to talk to him, ask him questions—and comfort him. But obviously he had left the courthouse because he didn't want to talk to her or anyone else. Now she had to put her concern for him aside. She had to stand in front of the jury one last time and convince them she was right.

Her heart thumping, she walked to the jury box and clasped the rail. "Mr. North has regaled you with some fine words. I wish I had his eloquence. But I only have my own plain words and the feelin's I carry in my heart. Those feelin's are so strong and sharp I know they'll tumble out quickly. I only hope they make sense to you."

She paced in front of the box, her hands behind her back. "Mr. North has told you that John Worthington cares for his employees. The truth is Mr. Worthington cares only for himself. Let me acquaint you with a few facts. Mr. North has mentioned a proposed pension plan and sick pay and lots of other wonderful things." She pointed her finger at the jury. "The truth is old John has been promisin' the same thing for years—ever since he bought the mine, in fact. But he never delivers. Last year he came up with a reason he couldn't deliver. This year he came up with a reason he couldn't deliver. Bein' intelligent businessmen, you make decisions based on associates' past records. What do you think John will say next year?''

She faced the jury and raised her hand. ''Mr. North says Worthington is a good mine owner. With your own ears you've heard what Mrs. Potter said, and what Matt Worthington said.'' Hands on her hips, she chuckled. ''Faith, I know fathers and sons get crosswise sometimes. But think about it—the meanest day of your life, could you have testified against your own father if you didn't really believe what you were sayin' was true?''

She hung her head and sighed, then looked up. ''I realize John's not on trial here. I'm on trial. But I need to prove he's guilty so I can prove I'm innocent. I beg you in the name of all that's decent and good to declare me innocent of the libel charges against me. Because if you do, you'll be sayin' what I wrote was true—and maybe others will pay attention to my words.''

With a frown, she paced to the end of the jury box and ran her gaze over the concerned businessmen's faces. ''Mother Mary, don't think I don't know what you're goin' through. I've wrestled with it myself. The truth is a fearful thing to acknowledge, because you're acknowledging that greed and negligence exist—that there's a hard, crusted-up side of the human soul that cares only for itself. If you risk knowin' the truth, you're acknowledgin' there's a whole town of people whose daily companions are pain and fear. And you're acknowledgin' these same people walk with poverty and sickness on a regular basis.''

Raising her chin, she held the jurors' eyes. ''But those same people are still there, whether you acknowledge them or not.'' She moved to a spot near the center of the rail. ''By now you all know I'm not well educated, but once I got up enough nerve to read a play by Mr. Shakespeare himself. Referrin' to a poor, wretched man, he wrote, 'Is man no more than this?' Think about that line when you think about the miners slavin' their lives away in the Silver Queen. I wish you could see them comin' out of that hole all black and grimy. Their necks are ringed with dirt and their hands are cracked and bleedin'. It's sad, but it's a handsome thing to see, because some of them can still laugh and sing and even keep on hopin'."

Tears pricked her eyes. "How can you measure heart and drive and spirit? Shouldn't a man—even a poor man— be able to hold up his head without fear doggin' his every step? Is man no more than some beast of burden to be used up and broken down, then forgotten about when he can't produce any longer?

"Is man no more than this?"

She clasped the rail again. "You've been given a wonderful opportunity that few men get. This is your chance, here and now—the next hour, in fact—to change some of the bad things in this old world. The decision you make will change a whole town full of people's lives forever."

Through her tears she looked at the judge. "Judge Baker is waitin' for a truthful judgment. Seventeen hundred miners and their wives and children are waitin' for a truthful judgment. Justice herself is waitin' for a truthful judgment." She looked at the jury and paused, trying to control her voice. "I beg you . . . be stouthearted men today. Don't creep through life like a dog on sore feet always doin' what's safe 'cause you're scared to death. Rescue me . . . rescue the miners from despair's embrace. When you're in that little jury room in the back of this courthouse . . . search your heart and choose what's right. Choose truth. Choose justice."

Carrie glanced at Matt's vacant seat at the press table and loneliness surged through her. She wanted him to be here with her—to stand with her in victory or defeat. All at once the noise of shuffling feet echoed from the antechamber. Judge Baker straightened and called the court to order while the jury came back into the courtroom. The sound temporarily tugged Carrie's thoughts away from Matt.

She nervously eyed the wall clock, whose hands pointed at five-thirty. Had the jury really been out two hours? She remembered their stolid faces as the judge had read them their instructions and they had filed into an antechamber. What had taken them so long? Wasn't it a simple question about whether she had been telling lies about Worthington? Perhaps North's bravura summation had put her plain words to shame. Perhaps something had gone wrong.

The judge looked at the jury foreman. "Has the jury reached a verdict in this case?"

The foreman, a tall businessman with a full beard, stood and snapped out a sheet of paper. "It has, your Honor."

"Please read it, then."

Carrie's heart pounded.

"This jury," the foreman began, "finds Carrie O'Leary innocent of all charges brought against her by John Worthington."

Pandemonium erupted in the courtroom. Deep joy flooded through Carrie. She had done it. She had defended herself in a case no lawyer would touch—and she had won. She glanced at Worthington and North, who sat like statues, their mouths downturned. Suddenly Worthington leaned forward and put his head in his hands; North stood and started jamming papers in his portfolio.

Behind her, the students whistled and applauded while the delegation from Crested Butte broke out with shouts of celebration.

Henderson hugged Carrie, and in her excitement she hugged him back.

Judge Baker banged his gavel once again. "The business of this court is not finished," he intoned over the happy voices. The curious spectators settled down and waited. He stared at Worthington. "Sir, I'm ruling that you shall pay all legal fees. Furthermore, it is my belief that your management of the Silver Queen is endangering the lives of those miners in your employ. Therefore, I'm recommending to the powers-that-be that an inspector investigate the mine at a future date. You will in no way hinder this man's efforts."

Again the room rocked with shouts of triumph. Carrie

wiped away the tears streaming down her face and looked at Matt's empty chair. If only he had been there to share her happiness, her joy would have been complete. With him gone, an aching loneliness marred her perfect victory.

When the noise had simmered down, the judge looked at her and smiled. "Miss O'Leary, if there is any way this court can help you in the future, it will. Good luck and God bless you. This court stands adjourned."

Carrie stood while the judge entered his chambers and the noisy crowd disbursed. After the reporters had taken her statement, some of the smiling students got her autograph. The raucous miners, the last group to leave the courtroom, came by to congratulate her personally. Tears glistened in many of the grizzled laborers' eyes. Finally, Carrie and Henderson were left standing in the silent courtroom.

Henderson took her elbow, then gently guided her up the aisle. "What a day we've had, my dear! You were wonderful—magnificent, in fact."

She sighed as they exited into the vestibule. "All that matters is that we won, Mr. Henderson. We won, when everythin' was against us. And without your financial help we couldn't have done it."

"Think nothing of it, my dear. I was glad to help—and I'd like to help some more."

"No, you've done—"

"No, not really," he interrupted. He placed an arm around her shoulders and gazed at her earnestly. "Carrie, let's celebrate our victory! I'll take you to your hotel to change, then we'll dine at the finest restaurant in Denver and go to Tabor's Opera House. Before the evening is over, I have something I want to propose."

"Something you want to propose?"

"Yes, something very important!"

Chapter 20

Henderson escorted Carrie to their seats in Tabor's Opera House. "Well what do you think, my dear?" he asked.

Carrie glanced at the huge chandeliers that sparkled from the ceiling. "Oh, everythin' is lovely. I've never been in such a fancy place." Then she lowered her gaze and eyed Henderson's expensive evening clothes. Erect and dignified, the man was a pillar of society. All the women had stared at her with envy as she entered the plush opera house on the banker's arm. After her victory in court, this was a day to remember.

Then why was she so sad? Despite the glamour around her, tears welled in her eyes. With a tremulous sigh, she burrowed into her comfortable seat and tried to get a grip on her emotions. This should have been the happiest night of her life. Why did she have to keep thinking about Matt?

Trying to slip into a festive mood, she scanned the audience, who waited expectantly for the eight o'clock curtain. Garbed in bright silks, the ladies smelled of perfume and powder; the black-tuxedoed gentlemen, of shoe polish and mustache wax.

While the minutes melted away, her mind recalled Peony's admonition as the girl had helped her into a taffeta petticoat earlier that evening.

"Missy Carrie," she had chided, "you should forget about Mr. Henderson and try to talk to Mr. Matt."

Carrie had answered while she stepped into a new pink

silk gown. "I don't even know where he's stayin'. Besides, Mr. Henderson has done so much for me—I kind of owe him a victory celebration. After he changes he'll be back to pick me up for dinner and the opera."

Peony slipped the gown over Carrie's head and did up the back, saying softly, "Well, at least you'll get to hear Miss Dovie sing."

"Now you're doin' it, too, Peony!" Carrie whirled and snatched up a copy of *The Denver Star*. Her likeness dominated the first page, but a page-two article raved about Dovie's performance. She tapped her finger on the singer's picture. "It's hard to believe one woman could be so perfect. Maybe tonight she'll hit a sour note or somethin'." Pride prevented her from saying that Matt's sharp words were like a thorn in her soul. *You could learn something from Dovie yourself,* he had said. Well, Dovie could learn a thing or two herself.

Tension hung in the air while Peony added flowers to her mistress's upswept hair and a pearl choker to her neck. At last, Carrie slipped on her shiny evening shoes and stood, ready to go. The low-cut gown, which set off her glossy hair and creamy complexion, made her look like a gorgeous china doll. Near the door, the Chinese girl handed her a satin-lined evening cape and a pair of long white gloves. "Missy . . . I have a bad feeling about tonight. Please be careful," she ventured to say.

With a frown, Carrie had sashayed into the hall and glanced over her shoulder. "Would you quit worryin', Peony? Everythin' is goin' to be fine. I'll be back late; don't wait up for me."

The woman seated to Carrie's left suddenly touched her arm and brought her mind back to the present. "My dear, if you've never heard Dovie Benningfield sing before, you're in for a treat. She's simply divine."

Carrie replied, "Yeah, that's what someone else told me once."

The socialite batted her eyes. "Why, I hear Miss Benningfield leaves a string of broken hearts everywhere she goes.''

Carrie studied the woman's overrouged face. "I can believe that.''

With a gentle pat on her arm, Martin Henderson claimed her attention. "The curtain will be going up soon, my dear. I certainly hope you enjoy Miss Benningfield's performance.''

Carrie sighed. "Oh, I'm goin' to try.''

"Good. As hard as you worked at the trial, you deserve a treat.''

Gradually the houselights dimmed and the crowd's outline faded into darkness. A murmur swept through the audience as the silver-haired conductor took his place. When he was in position, the heavy curtain creaked upward to reveal a stage setting of white columns and flowery trees. A magical moment charged the air; then the musicians struck up a soulful melody. At last, looking like a gorgeous butterfly, Dovie floated onto the stage in a frothy orange creation. Carrie smoothed up her long gloves and sat forward. She tried to find fault with the singer's appearance, but she couldn't. Dovie was perfect.

The Englishwoman sang several popular melodies, which were received with thunderous applause. Then she performed a comic sketch with two outrageously dressed actors. Carrie noticed the men fought for stage space, which Dovie held like a field marshal. Finally the sketch ended and the singer dipped gracefully, ignoring the comedians. Afterward, a rose-twined swing dropped from the stage scaffolding, and Dovie pumped herself into the air and tossed flowers to the happy audience. Talent and energy oozed from the singer's pores. Her exotic eyes sparkled, her wide smile dazzled, and her magnificent voice reached notes that left the audience applauding for more. Four more wildly successful songs followed the number in the swing.

Dovie's performance left Carrie crushed and demoralized. The singer hadn't hit any sour notes, she hadn't made one mistake. No wonder Matt thought so much of the woman. She was gorgeous and talented, and dripped sensuality.

Next to such a gorgeous creature, Carrie felt small and insignificant—like a clumsy little scullery maid who had interrupted a fancy tea party given by her betters. She could almost feel herself shrinking in her seat as Dovie sang. She was only an uneducated miner's daughter; Dovie would be at home at Queen Victoria's dinner table. What chance did she have competing against a woman like that?

An inner voice warned Carrie that she might be sick if she sat through another hour of Dovie's brilliance. Thank God intermission had to be near. Perhaps she could feign tiredness and persuade Henderson to leave early. Silently, she rose from the red plush seat and hurried up the thickly carpeted aisle. Once in the gilded lobby, she retrieved her cape from the checkroom. As she shrugged it around her shoulders, Henderson caught up with her. His face was perplexed.

"What's wrong, my dear? You left your seat so swiftly— are you ill?"

She smoothed her hair. "No . . . not really ill . . . I'm just tired. You know . . . the trial and all."

Henderson nodded. "Of course—how thoughtless of me. You must be exhausted. Well, perhaps it's all for the best if we do leave early. It will give me more time to show you my surprise."

"Surprise?"

He smiled and accepted his top hat from the checkroom lady. "Yes," he replied as he ushered her toward the theater's entrance. "I'm hoping you'll like it."

Henderson clicked a key into the lock, then opened the huge oak door. He looked at Carrie's astonished face and chuckled. "Go on in, my dear. Take a look . . . walk around."

Her heels tapped across the huge marble-floored entry as she walked into the shadowy mansion. She sniffed the air, smelling damp paint, sawed wood, and fresh stucco. Why, the place was new, brand-new, she thought. "Whose house is this anyway?" she asked. "Why won't you tell me?"

Henderson entered and laid his top hat on a wall table supporting two Chinese vases. "I'm saving that for a surprise. I'll tell you soon."

She frowned.

He coughed nervously, then removed her cape and laid it aside. Moving past her, he disappeared into a doorway to the left. She heard him making quiet noises while he lit the lamps. Seconds later, soft light pooled from the parlor onto the slick marble floor. "Come into the parlor, my dear," he called. "It's just to your left."

Uneasiness assailed her. She sensed something was wrong, but hadn't the man been the soul of courtesy so far? With a shrug, she peeled off her gloves and left them with her cape. Perhaps he just wanted to discuss his future plans to help the miners. She entered the gigantic parlor and found him standing by a bright crystal lamp. More lamps dotted the room's fancy mahogany tables, and on the far wall, gas candelabra blazed beside the mammoth fireplace. Red roses on the side board scented the air and added to the room's aura of wealth.

She blinked and scanned the remainder of the room. A thick Oriental carpet stretched over the shiny parquet floor. Upholstered in the finest cut velvet, overstuffed settees and chairs clustered about a low marble table. Carrie sank down on a coral-colored settee and stared at Henderson. "Mother Mary, this place is gorgeous," she exclaimed, spreading out the skirt of her pink silk gown. "Who *does* it belong to? Is it yours?"

Henderson walked to the carved sideboard and selected a brandy decanter from the group of decorative bottles. He poured the amber liquid into a snifter and glanced at her. "An after-dinner brandy, my dear?"

When she shook her head, he sipped the liquor and

finally answered, "No, it doesn't belong to me. It belongs to *us.*"

Alarm surged through her. "Mr. Henderson, what are you talkin' about? I think you'd better explain yourself."

Brandy in hand, he moved to her side and sat down. "All right, I shall explain." Slowly, he stretched out his arm and fingered one of her ringlets. "Carrie, I'm sure you realize how deeply I care for you. It would be impossible for you *not* to realize, wouldn't it, my dear?"

She eased the long curl away from him. "Yes, Mr. Henderson, I realized you had some feelin's for me."

"Some feelings? Why, ever since that first night I saw you at Worthington's party I've loved you." He lowered his lips to her hand, then raised his eyes and said, "Carrie, this house is ours."

Warning bells clanged in her head. "Mr. Henderson, are you askin' me to marry you?"

He set his drink aside and laughed. "How I wish that were possible, my dear. Unfortunately, I still have a wife in St. Louis who is very much alive. And what a dreadful creature she is!"

Carried jerked her hand away and tried to stand, but he shoved her back down on the settee. "You'd better let me go!" she snapped. "I may not have a college education, but I know an indecent proposal when I hear one."

A superior smile split his lips. "You don't know anything at all until you hear what I have to say. This could affect your whole future and the future of your cause, my dear. Will you grant me five minutes?"

Her heart thumped. So this was his proposal, his great surprise! Shock and hurt knifed through her: she felt crushed. Why, the man had stood to applaud her summation, and now he was insulting her with this humiliating proposition! He was nothing but a crazed, rich fool who was used to getting his way. Faith, he might even be dangerous. Perhaps she should sit still for a few minutes. Maybe she could think of a way to escape while he talked.

She stared at him woodenly and wondered if anyone

would hear her if she screamed. "All right, you've got five minutes, but then I'm leavin'. Peony will be wonderin' what happened to me."

He gestured at the luxurious parlor. "I have the power to make a queen of you—to set you up in considerable luxury for the rest of your life." When she only scowled in response, he continued. "For certain considerations," he added, his voice thick with insinuation, "I would also use my political weight to help the miners."

"I thought you believed in the miners' cause already," she said.

He laughed cynically. "My dear, surely you don't think I *really* subscribe to your high-flown philosophy."

"You said you did!"

He chuckled. "That sort of thing is all well and good as after-dinner talk. But when it comes to real life—we must look out for ourselves, mustn't we?" Anger hardened his expression. "Don't you realize what I can do for you, you little baggage?"

"I realize you can make some kind of whore out of me!"

His eyes glittered with malevolence. "Now, don't start playing the innocent with me. I heard Jenny Parker's testimony. Everyone knows you're a plucked rose, and they know who did the plucking—Matt Worthington." With a soft chuckle, he caressed her cheek, then let his fingers slide down her neck. "How do you like that?" When she pulled away he asked, "Oh, what's wrong? Aren't my hands as skilled as the handsome editor's hands? I assure you there are a number of Denver women who will attest to my accomplishments as a lover."

A pulse pounded deep in Carrie's brain. Matt had been right about Henderson all along, but she blinded herself with her own desperate need for assistance. It seemed that Matt had been right about many things. Her gaze flitted about the room while she searched for a way to flee. Finding no exit except the way she had entered the room, she looked back at Henderson. "You mangy-haired skunk. You lied to me!"

He began to stroke her trembling arm, his eyes sparkling with a lascivious light. "My dear, you must allow me a few liberties. I've already invested so much money in you."

Fueled by white-hot rage, she shot to her feet and moved away from him, her underskirts rustling with every step. His face twitching convulsively, he stood and edged toward her. Before she knew it, he had her backed into a corner. He pressed her against the flocked wallpaper and fingered her breast. "I thought you might be grateful to a man who could help you," he said, leering at her. "I'm one of the richest men in the Rockies, you know."

She raised her hand to slap him, but he forced it to her side. With his other hand, he continued to paw and pinch her breast. Summoning a strength she didn't know she possessed, she wrenched away from him and inched toward the shadowy entry. "You great fool! Don't you know all the money in the world can't make a racehorse out of a jackass?" Her pulse fluttering, she swiftly backed away. When he followed her into the entry, she snatched up one of the Chinese vases and cracked it over his head.

"You little bitch!" he wailed. Stunned, he slapped a hand over his bloody brow. "You had your chance, my fine lady, and you foolishly threw it away. I'll see that you pay for this."

Abandoning her cape and gloves, she gathered up her skirt with one hand, and with the other, wrenched open the heavy door. Before Henderson could stop her, she had slipped out and slammed the door in his face.

The night air chilled her bare arms while she raced past a line of misty gaslights. Her shoes crunched over the dry leaves as she zigzagged betwen the tall, elegant houses. When a long hedge loomed in the darkness, she darted across the lawn and scurried behind it. Blood pounding in her ears, she gasped for breath. Finally, very cautiously, she peeked around the hedge and saw Henderson stumble from his house.

He cupped his hands and called, "Carrie . . . come back. We can talk things out."

She froze and listened, her heart stroking like a piston. Then she crouched in the mellow-scented leaves and waited. Minutes later, she peeked around the hedge once more and watched Henderson jog down the street and circle back to search his own property. At last, holding a white handkerchief to his brow, he reentered the mansion.

Misery seeped over Carrie like an achy fever. She leaned against a huge oak and picked dried leaves from her gown. She groaned as the autumn moon cast its silver beams among the tree's bare limbs and highlighted her stained skirt. She felt humiliated as if her honor were as stained as her ruined gown. She swallowed back her tears. How could she ever have compared Henderson to Matt; and how could she ever tell Matt how she felt?

Then she realized she wasn't really free of the man yet. Henderson's cut might keep him busy for a while—but then, as angry as he was, he would try to retaliate. Her heart told her what she should do. She and Peony needed to flee the hotel they were in and disappear into Denver before he could find them. And tomorrow she would search for Matt! Fresh hope lifting her spirits, she crunched over the brittle leaves and ran toward the sound of a horsecar.

Except for Matt and one other customer, the Windsor Hotel's velvet-draped lounge was empty. Matt tossed down his newspaper and scanned the vacant sixty-foot bar. At the other end, a natty barkeep met his gaze. "What'll it be, Mr. Worthington?"

Matt glanced at his pocket watch and noticed it was only five-thirty. "How about a beer?"

When the other customer picked up his drink and carried it into the patrons' lounge, the barkeep moved to a barrel of lager. With a glance over his shoulder, he eyed the newspaper. A likeness of Carrie plastered the front page. "How about that O'Leary woman?" he asked as he drew a yeasty-smelling beer and slid it toward Matt. "Ain't she a dandy? Guess she's got all of Colorado stirred up."

Matt frowned at him, then snapped open the newspaper again. "Yeah, I hear she's managed to stir up several things." He sipped his beer and read *The Denver Star*'s headlines. One headline screamed, "Angel of the Slopes Wins Libel Case." Another declared, "Miner's Daughter Secures Justice for Oppressed Workers." *Lord,* he thought, someone's going to nominate her for sainthood before the year's out. He pored over the paper for a while, then glanced through the barroom door and watched light dapple the hotel's red-carpeted lobby. Suddenly a familiar face caught his eye. Wasn't that Peony pressing her nose against the leaded glass window?

He immediately shoved the beer aside and paid the barkeep. Curious, he strode into the lobby. Yes, he had been right. There on the other side of the window stood Peony—and Carrie! He noticed she looked lost, frustrated, and worried. He also noticed Carrie clutched a carpetbag to her bosom and Peony toted an overstuffed suitcase. With a resigned sigh, he brushed past the green-uniformed porter and exited the hotel.

The noise of dozens of carriages and horsecars washed over him as he paced up the sidewalk. "Well," he called to Carrie, who stood gazing up at the five-story hotel, "are you going to come in or just stand there and watch those damn flags all day?"

She jumped, then straightened her green suit and raked back her messy hair. "Matt, you scared me!"

He studied her again. Deep creases wrinkled her clothes and weariness clouded her eyes.

She rushed up and grabbed his arm. "I was hopin' you'd be here. I've got to see you."

He narrowed his eyes. "You've got to see me?"

"Yes!" She pulled him into the hotel's outside entrance and motioned for Peony to follow. "I've been searchin' all over Denver for you, Matt," Carrie added in a horarse whisper.

Surprise flooded through him. "Why, for God's sake?"

"I'm runnin' from Henderson."

He frowned at her, knowing he wasn't going to like this story. "I want to hear about this! Both of you come in here this minute," he ordered, hoisting Peony's suitcase and ushering them into the exclusive hotel. Once inside, he summoned a bellboy. Several fashionably dressed matrons eyed Peony's exotic dress and Carrie's disheveled appearance. Matt pushed Peony toward the fresh-faced bellboy. "Take this young woman to the kitchen and feed her," he commanded. Then he looked at Carrie. "And see that both Miss O'Leary and her maid have a room on my floor. Put it on my bill."

"Yes, sir, Mr. Worthington!" the boy answered as he picked up the heavy suitcase and led Peony away.

After the lad's footsteps died away, Matt took Carrie's arm and eased her onto a soft love seat. "Lord, what have you got in this carpetbag?" he asked as he thumped it down.

Sighing, she ran a hand through her hair. "Oh, it's packed with clothes, and shoes, and lots of stuff. We just threw everythin' in. We had to hurry away from our hotel."

He raised his brows. Here it comes, he told himself. "And why, may I ask, did you have to hurry from your hotel? I have a feeling it has to do with Henderson."

"Yeah, I tried to bash in his skull last night."

He stared at her while a muscle worked convulsively in his jaw.

She lowered her eyes in chagrin. "Oh, I know, I know. You tried to tell me. Well, if it gives you any satisfaction, you were right. He's no gentleman. He's just a mangy-haired skunk out for what he can get—just like all men."

Matt was suddenly livid.

"Did he hurt you? Did he—?"

She looked up. "No, no. But I had a couple of tight

minutes before I could back out of that mansion he'd built to keep me in.'' When Matt clenched his fists, she widened her eyes. ''Oh, don't be gettin' nervous! I cracked him over the head with one of his expensive knickknacks before he could do anythin'.'' A satisfied grin spread over her lips. ''I'll bet he's still seein' stars.''

''Good Lord, where did you sleep last night?''

''Seein' how mad he was, I was afraid to stay in my old hotel. After me and Peony got into another one, it was two o'clock in the mornin'. I slept a little; then I've been lookin' for you all day.''

He sat down beside her and studied her face.

''Go ahead and say it.'' She gave a nervous sigh. ''I know you're just achin' to say it.''

He raised his brows.

''No—go ahead.''

Concern for her safety and well-being tumbled through him like a storm. At this moment all he wanted to do was hold her in his arms and make sure she was all right. ''Couldn't you tell what Henderson was leading up to?''

She sighed and hung her head. ''Why are you pickin' on me?''

''You said to say it!''

''I know, but I didn't come here to get a lecture from you! You were right—and I was wrong. What else do you want me to say?''

''It's not a matter of fixing blame, it's a matter of what could have happened.''

She glanced up. ''But it didn't. I'm here, I'm safe, and I'm with you.''

''Yes, and you're going to stay with me. If you think I'd let you go back to some hotel by yourself tonight, you're crazy.''

''Why are you bein' so bossy?''

He stood and lifted the carpetbag, then nodded at the long grand staircase. ''I'm not being' bossy—now get up those stairs!''

''Why?''

"We're going to my suite and order dinner. That's why. We have a lot to talk about."

Standing, she glared at him. "All right . . . as long as we ain't talkin' about Henderson. I don't want to be raked over the coals about him anymore."

He took her arm. "I'll accept that—for one night at least."

Inch by inch, dusk touched the corners of the luxurious hotel suite. Low flames crackled in the fireplace and the aroma of a finely cooked meal lingered in the air. Setting down the slender champagne bottle in his hand, Matt rose from the table and ignited the gaslights mounted on either side of the fireplace. On the way back to his chair, he discarded his jacket and picked up a corkscrew from the sideboard. Then, with a thoughtful sigh, he sat down again, loosened his tie, and began working on the champagne cork. A lock of black hair flopped over his forehead as he twisted the corkscrew.

Amused, Carrie sat across from him and watched. As he worked, she ate grapes from a fruit centerpiece and scanned the room. Newspapers littered the floor. Plates of leftovers from the Windsor's best roast beef dinner dotted the lace-draped table. Nestled in ice, another bottle of champagne waited in the wine stand. At last, her gaze rested on Matt.

Just being here with him made her feel warm and secure. His very presence gave her strength and blotted Henderson's memory from her troubled mind. Thank God Matt had kept his promise and hadn't brought up last night again. She burned to ask him some personal questions, such as how he knew that Worthington was his father, and more importantly, why he had jeopardized his whole future by testifying at the trial. But deep in her bones she realized the time wasn't right.

She popped another grape into her mouth and blinked as the cork finally exploded into the air. It bounced from the ceiling and spun across the top of a rosewood table.

"I think you're a better editor than you are a wine steward," she commented with a laugh.

With an injured look, he lit a cheroot. "Oh, you do? Well, I thought you'd show a little more enthusiasm for my efforts."

She paced across the bright Oriental carpet and pushed back a red velvet drape. "Enthusiasm . . . isn't that right next door to insanity?" she commented over her shoulder.

He caught her gaze and laughed. "Lord, that sounds like *me*—not you!"

Sighing, she looked out the rain-splattered window. A blue twilight was sliding over Denver. Rows of gas lamplights twinkled from Brown's Bluff, and on the graveled courtyard below, elegant carriages wheeled to the Windsor's private entrance and deposited gorgeously dressed ladies and gentlemen. A strange, quiet loneliness hung on the evening drizzle and tugged at her heart.

She pulled the curtains together, then walked back to the table. "One time you said my ideas had started to rub off on you. Maybe the same thing is happenin' in reverse."

He raked through his thick hair and grinned. "I'd think after your great victory you'd be even more an idealist."

With a quick wink, she smiled. "Think what you wish. I think if your hand is in a dog's mouth you should draw it out *very* gently."

The cheroot clenched between his teeth, he laughed and picked up a tall fluted glass. "How about some champagne to go with those grapes you've been devouring?" He poured her some wine. "Considering Judge Baker's ruling, I think a celebration is in order."

"All right, I'll take a glass," she agreed as she scooted her chair into place.

He took a long draw on his cheroot and peered at her. "You were wonderful at the trial, you know. By the time it was over, you had the judge eating out of your hand."

She arched a brow and sipped the bubbly champagne. "Did I, now? And how would you be knowin' that, when you left before my summation? Why did you do such a thing?''

A dark look crossed his face. "I didn't want to talk to John anymore—and I knew you'd win."

"What about your story for Hardin?"

"I talked to the other reporters after the trial. I got enough facts to write Hardin a good story." He grinned and shook his head. "A man from the *Star* said you were quoting *King Lear*, no less, and that you had the jury in tears."

"I *was* quotin' *King Lear* and I *did* have them in tears. But it wasn't a trick. I meant every word I said. And best of all, I got to use some of that dull stuff you used to make me read. It's really pretty great."

He chuckled, then splashed champagne into his glass.

Waltz music floated up from the ballroom and seeped into the suite. A warm, silent intimacy welled up between them while they discussed the trial. All the grapes had disappeared and the ice around the champagne had melted by the time they finished analyzing everyone's testimony.

Rising, Carrie crossed to the window and pushed back the drapes again. Rain peppered down outside, blurring the gaslights. Umbrellas popped open and carriage doors slammed. The first of the late-night revelers were just leaving the Windsor. Laughter wafted upward on the cool, fresh air and spurred her own need. Despite her best efforts, a dark, wet excitement started to well up from deep inside her. She stole a glance at Matt and wondered if she would have the strength to leave him if he asked her to stay the night.

He ground out his cheroot, then joined her at the window and stood close behind her. His warmth and the scent of his bay rum hovered about her like a reassuring aura. When he rested his large hands on her shoulders, tingly heat rushed down her arms. "Let's open that other bottle. This is a very special night," he whispered.

Carrie felt suddenly shy and vulnerable.

"I don't know. Peony's goin' to be—"

"Peony has a whole staff to take care of her," he said as he moved to the champagne and lifted it from the slushy ice. He shot her an amused look while he yanked at the cork. "Surely we can make one final toast to the Angel of the Slopes." He grinned as the cork shot into the air. "Hey, it worked! Did you hear that explosion? We're not drinking twenty-rod anymore."

She walked to a pink-striped sofa and sat down. "No, but we're the same people, ain't we?"

He poured champagne into the glasses and moved toward her. "Not exactly," he answered, handing her a glass. "I'd say we're both a lot wiser." His strong, deep voice pulled at her senses.

"That's for sure," she replied after taking a big sip.

The fire had burned low, and the wood spluttered and popped, making the room wonderfully peaceful and cozy. Another lush waltz drifted up from below. She scanned his relaxed face and thought perhaps this was the time to ask those questions. "Matt, there's somethin' I've been wantin' to ask you," she began. "How did you find out about John bein' your father?"

A cynical look tightened his features as he sat down. "He told me. He had a whole fantastic story."

"His story didn't mean anything to you? He *could* be your father?"

Matt shrugged, then drank some champagne. "I'm ready to take that gamble. His revelation just gave me more ammunition to shoot back at him."

"There's somethin' else I don't understand. Uncle or father—he's still your own blood. You put the miners' case up against that after some of them destroyed your office?"

"Like I told you before the tour, a few hotheads did that. What goes on in the Queen affects hundreds of people."

Shame stole through Carrie. How often had she doubted his motives? She now realized he had been sincere in his desire to help the miners all along. She had badly misjudged both Matt and Henderson. Henderson's concern had been false; Matt's concern, although concealed, had been real.

He took her glass and placed it by his on the end table. Then he brushed his finger across the tip of her nose. "Any more questions, Counselor, or are you in the mood for a recess?"

She studied Matt's full eyes and knew what would happen, knew he would kiss her and make love to her. And she welcomed it. She was tired of fighting her need, tired of her heart being dead as a clod of frozen sod. She needed his love to fire her blood and stir her spirit. As if by mutual consent, he moved forward and she slipped into his strong arms. She could smell the scent of his hair and body and his clean, starched shirt—all stirred by his body heat.

Joy radiated through her like the warm sun as his lips came down on hers. It had been so long, and she had wanted him so badly—all though the rail tour, all through the trial. When she tasted the tobacco-tinged flavor of his mouth and felt the silk of his tongue against hers, a great wave of tenderness crashed over her. And that sharp, sweet throb began pulsing between her legs again.

She felt his hand brush her breasts and anticipation washed over her. Soon her green jacket gaped open, and his hand was inside her shift. He found her nipple and teased it, making her gasp with pleasure. His fingers continued stroking as he eased his mouth away to kiss her ears. "God, how I've been waiting for this," he muttered. "It's been months."

He slipped off her suit top and tossed it aside. "You don't mind if we get rid of this, do you?" He gently tugged at her other nipple, then twirled his tongue over it for long minutes.

It felt so wonderful—but then, it always felt wonderful. Blood roared through her ears. The objects in the room blurred before her eyes. She also noted that the pleasure between her thighs had spread backward and now throbbed under her bottom. "I'm goin' out of control, Matt. It's . . . it's happenin' again."

He raised his head. "So let it happen."

His hand unbuttoned her skirtband, then he moved his fingers back to her breast and relentlessly flicked his thumb over her nipple.

Lord, she was already bursting with pleasure, moist, aching, just waiting for fulfillment. Her shaky hand instinctively groped for his thick maleness. He groaned at her touch and she felt him tremble and shudder. "Matt, I . . . I'm sorry . . . I . . ." she stuttered.

"Hush, love." Without another word, he scooped her up and carried her into the bedroom. The room was dark and smelled of leather and wool. Soft light spilled in from the parlor and gleamed over the bed's taffeta counterpane. A moist chill hung in the air from the rain. With one hand he jerked back the covers and laid her on the cool, silk sheets. Then he fanned her hair over the clean, fresh-smelling pillowcase, and caressed her white breasts, which gleamed in the shadows.

Quickly, he removed her shoes and tugged her skirt and petticoat over her feet. Finally, he eased her thin shift over her head and slid her bloomers to her ankles, then tossed them away. Now, childlike and defenseless, she lay nude except for her black silk stockings, which contrasted sharply with her milky thighs. He groaned in anticipation.

Aching with pleasure, she watched him undress in the faint light. He was silhouetted against the soft backlighting that gleamed over his thick hair and bulging muscles. An almost reverent awe touched her as she considered the perfection of his body. He was so heartbreakingly beautiful. Her spirit flowed out to him. This was *her* man and she loved him more than life itself.

Soon his weight creaked the bed. Very slowly, he rolled down both of her lacy garters and slid them from her legs. Then he peeled off her stockings and kissed the sensitive arch of her foot. Leisurely, languidly, he nibbled his way to her thighs. A flame of delight shot up the insides of her legs and nestled in her most secret places. "Matt, I think—"

"Hush, Carrie." She gasped when she felt his warm breath against her moist inner flesh. He paused, and she, too, held her breath, suspended between modesty and raw desire. Then he leaned forward and the heat and wetness of his tongue jolted a current of pure ecstasy to the tips of her toes. Repeatedly, he lavished her womanhood with attention, his warm breath and soft tongue caressing her until she could stand no more. She moaned his name, then shuddered and clenched the silk sheets. Outside, the rain beat against the windows; inside Carrie's heart, an overwhelming desire to please him, to give to him, blossomed like a soft flower. Somewhere deep within her, her spirit stirred with fresh vulnerability. When she finally sighed and stilled, he slipped the cool sheet over them and pulled her close to his large body, allowing her to relax and gather her strength.

His hard, matted chest rubbed against her bare breasts, exciting her afresh. With a little whimper, she twined her arms around him and feathered his hair. She traced his corded neck and broad back, then worked her hands down to his tight buttocks. When he took her mouth again, she felt his swollen hardness stir and press against her thigh. Again she instinctively caressed him.

Instantly, he wound his long fingers in her silky tangle, toying, teasing; then he relentlessly stimulated the seat of her burning need with his thumb. For long minutes he tantalized her by gently pulling and stroking her slick womanhood. Meanwhile, his mouth sought her nipple and tugged, sending sizzling tingles over her breast. He brought her to the very edge of release again and again, then eased off, only to begin once more.

She could feel his heart thudding, hear his ragged breath, smell the scent of his ready seed. When she felt warm moisture against her thigh, she pushed against his hard buttocks, urging him on top of her. He kissed her face and closed eyes, then thrust inside her moist warmth and filled her to bursting. Easing from her a bit to protect her from his heavy weight, he began a slow, erotic rhythm.

With each stroke her excitement grew, mindlessly answering an ancient call. With loving arms, she drew him to her. She felt warm, fulfilled, cherished. She tensed her inner muscles and tightened herself around him. He groaned with pleasure and increased the savage rhythm that was almost too much to bear. At last, they exploded together in a firestorm of love, becoming one body and one spirit.

Chapter 21

$\sim\!\!\!\sim\!\!\!\partial\!\sim\!\!\!\sim$

Matt opened his eyes and glanced at Carrie sleeping peacefully beside him. Her bare bosom rose and fell rhythmically; soft light flooded through the bedroom window and illuminated her face. In the rosy daylight she looked younger—even more vulnerable than usual. Tenderness engulfed him, prompting him to caress her cool arm.

As he drew the sheet over her shoulders, a faint rap at the door attracted his attention. Frowning, he glanced at Carrie to see if she had moved.

Still asleep, she moaned and rolled over.

Quickly, he rose, slipped on a robe, and padded through the bright sitting room. When he opened the door, a young bellboy pushed a silver tray at him. On the tray lay a folded note.

"Message for you, Mr. Worthington," the boy said.

Matt took the missive and watched the boy walk down the corridor, then he thoughtfully closed the door. With great curiosity, he opened the message and read: "Meet me at the Tabor Opera House this afternoon—Dovie." Resentment seethed inside him. How dare that baggage summon him like a servant! Hadn't she done enough to ruin his life already? Doubtless she wanted to harangue him about his fatherly duties again. Without giving it a second thought, he sailed the note across the carpet.

Then, as he walked into the bedroom, an idea popped into his mind. Perhaps he *should* go to the opera house—

303

and right now. His heart warm, he looked at Carrie and thought of the night they had shared. He knew he couldn't let anyone put those precious emotions in jeopardy. His jaw tightened as he thought of Jenny and the trouble she had stirred up. He owed it to Carrie to confront Dovie and have it out once and for all.

Carrie murmured in her sleep. His first impulse was to wake her and tell her the good news. Then he reconsidered, recalling their lovemaking. He chuckled. She hadn't had very much time to sleep, and he knew she was emotionally exhausted from the trial. Surely he could take care of things with Dovie and get back by noon, just as she was waking.

After dressing in a dark suit, he slipped from the room, then left the hotel and hailed a hackney. On the way to the Tabor Opera House he thought of his relationship with Dovie, which seemed to be all for her benefit. He knew he must cut any association between them forever—and do it today. Still one nagging thought rolled about in his head. What if Percy were actually his child? How could he deny his own seed?

Once at the opera house, he entered the empty lobby. The huge place was a bit chilly and smelled of cigar smoke and perfume. The dim theater itself seemed rather soulless without an audience. He took a seat in the back row just as the orchestra began rehearsing. There in front of him on a stage bare of scenery stood Dovie. Dressed in a gaudy red evening gown, she was singing her heart out. Halfway through an aria, she stopped.

"You stupid imbecile," she screamed at the silver-haired conductor while he urged his musicians through a difficult passage. "You should be playing this passage allegro!" She flounced to the orchestra pit. "Allegro! Do you understand?" Her beautiful face contorted into an ugly mask, she ripped her music in half and hurled the pages at him.

"God Almighty." Matt sighed as he sank into the plush seat. How could this horrid woman be the mother of his child? When the singer looked at the shadowy seats and smiled, he noticed the figure of a man sitting toward the front of the theater. Henderson! Lord, what was he doing here? Matt had no idea, but he'd bet his last dollar someone backstage could enlighten him.

Deciding to skip the rest of Dovie's tantrum, he rose and exited into a long, narrow hall. The smell of fresh paint told him he was headed in the right direction. He blinked as he entered the brightly lit backstage world of ropes and scaffolding.

In one corner two stagehands daubed white paint on a blue backdrop, trying to simulate puffy clouds. Nearby, other workers pounded nails and screeched saws through long planks. He noticed two gaudily dressed comedians smoking cigars as they talked to one of the stagehands.

A frazzled woman walked past the comedians carrying a fat squalling baby. With some embarrassment, Matt realized the infant was Percy. The baby, who had grown enormous, stiffened his arms and fought at the poor woman as she maneuvered her way around a stack of backdrops.

The comedians shook their heads as the nurse wrestled with the unruly child. Their strong cockney-flavored voices rang out over the backstage noise when she finally took him away.

"Lord, somebody ought to do somethin' to that screamin' brat Percy," one of them said.

"They can't. Dovie won't let 'em," the other replied.

"Et's jest like I told you, mate," complained the first. "Dovie thinks she's a bloody queen or somethin'." He took a long draw on his cigar, then mimicked the singer's regal voice. "I don't care if it is intermission, you can only take five minutes. And don't smoke that bloody cigar in here. You'll ruin my voice!" Both of the comedians laughed at his imitation.

"That's right," said the second as they neared Matt. "I'm damn tired of 'er airy ways, I am. Since she slapped that breach-of-promise suit on that poor Worthington bloke, we ain't 'ad a minute of peace, 'ave we?" He nudged his companion in the ribs. "Someone ought to tell the bloke she's rakin' 'im off."

The words rang through Matt's head like freedom bells.

"What 'ave we 'ere? A real gent, to be sure," the first comedian said. Clicking his oversized shoes together, he bowed before Matt, then raised his merry eyes. "At your service, sir. And 'ow can I 'elp you?"

Matt stroked his chin. "Excuse me, but I couldn't help hearing your conversation. What do you know about this Worthington fellow?"

"I only know what Dovie tells me 'bout 'im." He looked at his friend and rolled his eyes. "All day long she tells us 'ow she's goin' to make a ton o' money off this suit she's got 'cause of that brat Percy. Ain't she, Tim?"

"You say she's rakin' Worthington off?" Matt prompted.

The second comedian leaned closer. "O' course she is. Me wife travels with the troupe as a seamstress. And Dovie told 'er she was two months gone afore she ever met this Worthington gent back in London. She only thought o' this scheme when she found out 'is uncle was bloody rich!"

"Are you sure about this?"

"O' course we're sure," the other shot back. "Dovie don't know for sure who Percy's dad is—but she does know it ain't Worthington!"

An enormous feeling of relief flooded through Matt's heart. He couldn't wait to tell Carrie the good news.

The first comedian squinted at Matt. "Say—you never did tell us 'ow we could 'elp you, mate."

Matt smiled and pumped the man's hand. "You'll never know how much you've helped me already. I just have one more question. What is Martin Henderson doing here?"

Both of the men raised their brows and laughed. " 'E's watchin' Dovie rehearse like 'e does three times a week!" the second comedian said. "The blighter is stuck on 'er, and 'avin' a sharp eye for money, she's leadin' 'im on in case 'er deal with Worthington falls through."

Matt grinned and filed the juicy tidbit in his head for further use.

Bright light streamed through the window, waking Carrie at about ten in the morning. She felt safe and secure in Matt's love, and a warm afterglow hummed through her as she thought of their night of passion. Three times she had felt him harden and stir against her, and they had made love again and again. They had finally fallen asleep wonderfully tired and fulfilled. He had cradled her in front of him and cupped her breast in his warm hand as they slept.

She felt fresh, strong, whole—reborn. Life shimmered with a golden glow. Things would work this time, she knew they would. But right now she wanted to burrow next to his hard body and doze a few minutes longer. Closing her eyes, she rolled toward his side of the bed. Her eyelids flicked open when her fingers touched only the cool sheet. Confused, she sat up and looked at the spot where he had slept. Panic raced through her veins; then a still, inner voice told her he must be writing. She laughed at her own foolishness. Yes, that was it. He had left her sleeping while he went into the next room to write, and to smoke those damn cheroots.

She got out of bed and slipped into her clothes. Her heart dipped as she entered the next room. Newspapers still littered the floor and the gaslights still burned on either side of the fireplace; last night's dinner had dried out and caked the bowls; a water stain darkened the white tablecloth under the champagne bottle—and Matt was nowhere to be seen.

Her heart raced, but she gripped the back of a dining chair and tried to think. He must have just gone downstairs to take care of some business. Of course, that was it. He'd come walking through that door any minute now with a big grin on his handsome face and say something to make her laugh.

She scanned the messy room, deciding she needed to

clean up a bit before he came back. "And, Holy Mother, I need to find Peony. The poor girl's probably scared to death," she muttered under her breath. After she turned out the lights, she put on her discarded suit jacket and began gathering up the newspapers. A folded note card lying on the carpet caught her eye. Strange, she thought, she hadn't noticed it last night. Carelessly, she picked it up and moved toward the wastebasket. A gardenia scent wafted its way upward from the note. An alarm clanged through her head. With only a small pang of guilt, she opened the note and read it. Her heart, which had been so warmed by love, now chilled with fear and pain. Biting her lips, she crumpled the stiff note and hurled it across the room.

She ran to the window and jerked open the drapes. The bright sunlight made her blink back her tears. Everything looked clean and fresh-washed outside, but she felt dirty and used. Matt had betrayed her just like Henderson—but she had never really trusted Henderson. Last night she had given Matt her heart and soul, and her precious trust that she had always guarded so jealously. A profound sense of loss flooded over her. There was no need to wonder where Matt was any longer. He was with Dovie. The singer had summoned him, and he had gone running to her.

Tears streaming down her face, Carrie walked away from the window. Mary, Jesus, and Joseph, why hadn't he mentioned last night that he was still carrying on with Dovie? How could he pretend he loved her? Her throat tightened with tears as she reviewed all they had talked about. He'd never mentioned the word "love." In fact, he'd never made any promises at all. They had just drunk a lot of champagne and enjoyed each other's bodies. The night that had seemed so glorious, so fine, only a few minutes ago now seemed cheap and tawdry and shameful.

Then a new thought struck her. Maybe he had just made love to her because he had felt sorry for her. Lord, that hurt worst of all! Sobbing, she paced around the room. Faith, when would she ever learn? she wondered as she tugged a handkerchief from her pocket. Oh, yes, Dovie was the perfect lady, while she was little better than a shantytown whore. She had proved that last night when she had conducted herself so shamefully and let Matt take her into the bedroom without one word of protest.

"Well, I may not be a fancy lady like Dovie, but I finally know what's goin' on," she murmured. Hot tears rolled down her cheeks. Matt had taken her for a fool. And he was right—she *was* a fool. He had only been teasing her while he amused himself. "If he thought anythin' of me, he'd have told me about Jenny and Dovie when we first made love in the cabin. It's not a thing an honest man would keep hidden."

A wall clock softly chimed ten-thirty.

She glanced at the clock, trying to whip up her courage. There was no profit in feeling sorry for herself. She had made a great mistake, but she had to find the courage to go on, to keep moving.

She rammed the handkerchief into her skirt pocket and sniffed back the last of her tears. She had cried enough, and she wasn't going to cry anymore! She would find Peony and they would pack their things and leave the Windsor. Before Matt came back from his tryst with Dovie, they would be gone. On the way to the railroad station she would send a telegraph message to Jack and tell him she was coming home.

"I'll not waste one precious moment thinkin' about Matt," she muttered. "He ain't thinkin' about me." With as much dignity as she could muster, she pushed up her sleeves and swept into the hall. Maybe Matt didn't need her, but the miners *did*. She was going home!

Matt said good-bye to the comedians just as Dovie swaggered backstage. Seeing her stormy expression, the comedians frowned and hastily left.

Hands on hips, she moved forward aggressively. "Matt, you aren't supposed to be here until this afternoon. For the love of God, what are you doing poking around back here anyway?''

"Just talking to some of your friends."

She grimaced. ''That riffraff? I'd hardly say they're friends of mine.''

"And I'd say you're right.''

She stepped closer, so close Matt could smell her cloying gardenia scent. ''Dearest, I called you here to talk about Percy, not some cockney trash. I just thought I'd give you a second chance to admit that Percy is yours so we could settle this out of court and remain a happy little family.''

"Happy little family? Good Lord, that's something we'll never be.''

She clutched his arm. ''How can you be so cruel?''

"It's not too difficult, my dear, when I remember what you're trying to do to me.'' He glanced down at her hand and gently removed it from his arm. ''Dovie, I bought you a wardrobe and wrote your story—now you're trying to pass your bratty infant off on me. When you try to scalp a man more than once, you start running out of hair!''

"Matt, I want your love. The child and I need your love!''

"You *want* money. And you *need* a good paddling. Why don't you try your luck with some docile old fool you can manage? I'm sure you could sell your sad story to some arthritic lord or retired brigadier. Perhaps even Henderson would buy it.''

"How—how did you know about him?'' she stammered.

"I've found that arriving early often pays off, love.''

"But, Matt, he's gone now—I just sent him away. I don't care a fig for him. I love you . . . I just wish you could understand.''

He moved toward the exit. ''Oh, I understand everything very clearly.''

She ran after him. ''Percy is yours. You must believe it!''

He raised his brows. "That's great acting, Dovie, but I believe you were two months gone before we met."

Her face whitened under her heavy rouge.

"I now have several witnesses who will testify to that fact," he added.

"They're from the East End!"

"So are you!" He glanced at her shocked face and grinned. "One can't be on the stage all the time, can one? When you talk in your sleep, you sound just like them. And during the course of the trial I'm sure that dark secret would come out. Think how disastrous that would be to your career." He left the hall and headed to the front of the theater.

"Matt—come back!" she screamed desperately.

He glanced over his shoulder and grinned again. "Sorry, old girl, but you just plain lost." He shook his head. "Didn't you know you can't drive a range-raised horse over a rattlesnake?" From the corner of his eye he saw her clench her hands and kick an open bucket of paint. He laughed when it bounced backward and splashed over her skirt.

Whistling happily, he left the theater and hailed a hackney. As the carriage jostled toward the Windsor, he savored his victory and planned what he would say to Carrie. He raced into the hotel and took the soaring staircase two steps at a time. Chuckling, he walked through an upstairs lounge and strode down the hall. He unlocked his door, expecting to see Carrie sitting in a chair with a smile on her face, but when he peeked into the room, he found it to be immaculate—and vacant. His heart plummeted. Like a death notice, a white note on a dark polished table caught his eye. A muscle throbbing in his jaw, he picked up the note and read:

Matt,
    I've gone back to Crested Butte. I found the note from Dovie, and as far as I'm concerned—we're finished. I guess you two are more suited to each other

than we'll ever be. But I ain't a plaything for you to
tease, or some kind of light-skirts either! Don't try to
follow me to talk me out of my decision!

                                                    Carrie

Matt crumpled up the note and threw it across the room.
Damn! The little spitfire had done it again—stalked off
before he had a chance to explain things. And just when
he had everything all worked out.

He paced the room for a while, then flopped down on
the couch and lit a cheroot. Fine and dandy, then. If she
needed some time to cool off, he would give it to her.
Hardin had been begging him for weeks to come to New
York and negotiate some contracts. This would be the perfect time to make that trip back east. He could deliver the
last batch of his Angel of the Slopes stories personally. He
leaned back and propped his legs on the tea table, then
puffed smoke rings into the air. "Yes . . . yes . . . yes,"
he said with a chuckle. "I'll let her stew in her own juices.
By the time I see the little hellion she'll be desperate to
talk to me. Then I'll make her listen!"

Dressed in a simple blue dress and a knitted shawl,
Carrie relaxed as the train chugged toward the outskirts of
Crested Butte. In the seat next to her, Peony rested quietly.
Her coral satin pajamas were freshly pressed, ready for
her arrival back home. She had placed a flower in her hair,
and her face glowed with a warm, expectant look.

Carrie studied the girl. With her shiny hair brushed out
loose, she was quite lovely. Her facial bones were fine,
her mouth sweet, her complexion faultless. She wondered
if the girl would ever grace a man's home, or enjoy moth-
erhood. What a shame for her to be consigned to drab
servants' quarters for the rest of her life. With a sigh, she
pushed the thought away. She had enough troubles without
worrying about finding a husband for Peony!

She sank back into the plush seat and felt the rails sing
beneath her feet. Thank God the trial was over. Thank

God she was going home to Botsie—and even Jack. Jack Penrose was a good man. A good man who deserved someone who loved him. She pressed her lips together; she had almost thought—*the way I love Matt*.

Just the thought of Matt made tears swim in her eyes. Despite the pain, memories of their last night of love flooded over her. She blushed and eyed the packed car, realizing how shocked the passengers would be if they knew her thoughts. Just half an hour ago Matt had appeared to her in a dream as she slept on the train.

She closed her eyes and remembered. In her dream he came to her with a warm smile. His eyes dark with love, he took her in his arms and kissed her, sending a shaft of pleasure through her breasts. They were both nude, both unashamed, both gloriously happy. As their passion flared, he gently settled her on the soft grass of a moss-green meadow and caressed her body with his strong hands. He unleashed wondrous sensations that tightened her breasts and made her womanhood throb with ecstasy. After long, rapturous lovemaking, they climaxed together as one. As she relaxed against the seat, she could still feel her body pulse with pleasure.

The train rumbled over a switch crossing. The sound reminded her that harsh reality lay just a few miles away. But she struggled against the thought and submerged herself in the dream once again. Still aglow with erotic pleasure, she realized she was separated from Matt not only by miles but also by a barrier of her own making. Tears seeped from the corners of her closed eyes. She was so tired—so very tired. She felt the train slow and, with great effort, opened her eyes.

Her face glowing with happiness, Peony pointed out the window. "Missy, look—we're home!"

There on the railroad platform stood Botsie and Jack. Smiles plastered their faces. His tail wagging, Bandit stood by the Cornishman's side. Slowly, the steel crept back into Carrie's heart. No matter how tired she was, she had to fight for those she loved—and for her dreams. If she didn't, she would curl up and wither like a dry leaf. She sat up and waved at the welcoming committee.

Then something else caught her eye. Behind the men, a gaggle of tight-faced women hovered about Jenny Parker. The women all held homemade signs. Some read, "Save Our Homes From Immorality." Others read, "You Shall Not Tolerate a Harlot Among You." Jenny's sign blazed, "Crested Butte's Ladies' Society Demands Carrie O'Leary's Resignation as News Editor."

Carrie felt like strangling someone. How dared that whey-faced liar call for her to do anything! Hadn't the hypocrite already smeared her reputation all over Denver and defamed poor Shamus?

Before the train had grated to a complete stop, Carrie shot to her feet and, grabbing her carpetbag, headed for the door. Peony followed, dragging their heavy suitcase. The first one out the door, Carrie embraced the men, who then helped Peony with the bulky bag. Bandit went crazy, barking and jumping on Carrie's legs.

Botsie looked at her and grinned. "Dang, it's good to have you home!"

She narrowed her eyes at him and picked up her dog. "Have you and that printer been gettin' the paper out all right?"

"You bet. You had so much stuff written up, the feller just read it over and picked out what he wanted. He wrote up a few school suppers and the like hisself." He rubbed his nose and grinned again. "Why, we been doin' so good, I had to hire a boy just to help me sell papers."

She put Bandit down and smiled at Jack.

He held her at arm's length, his eyes smiling warmly at her. "Let me see you, girl. Coo . . . I'm so proud o' you I could bust!"

"You look awfully happy for some reason."

"Well, I am! You're 'ome and me brother is comin' in from Cornwall. I just got the news this week."

"That's fine, Jack. That's really fine. Maybe you won't be so lonesome."

Sudden insight flashed through her when Jack greeted Peony. The big brute of a man was blushing. She couldn't believe it. He was blushing at the tiny China doll standing by her side! Peony looked down modestly, then covered her mouth and giggled. Faith, how could she have missed what had happened under her own nose? The freshly pressed pajamas, the loosened hair with the flower, the radiant look. Peony loved Jack. And by the look on his face, he felt the same!

She smiled at the pair; then worry triggered another question. "Is Worthington here?"

"Aye, 'e's 'oled up like a bear in that big mansion of 'is," Jack replied.

"Yeah? Well, if I know him, he ain't hibernatin'," Carrie quipped. She shifted her gaze to Jenny and her pack of vigilantes.

Regret shadowed Jack's eyes. "Sorry about them," he apologized. "They asked me when you was comin', but I didn't know they was goin' to do *this!*"

Carrie patted his huge forearm. "That's all right, Jack. It's not your fault." She strode forward to meet them.

Like a timid litter of mice, the women looked to Jenny for direction. Dressed in a bright pink gown, the preacher's daughter glared at them, and tentatively they raised their signs as their leader blocked Carrie's way. "Carrie O'Leary, these righteous women and I are here to stop you from entering Crested Butte." She smoothed her blond hair and eyed her adversary angrily. "We feel a person of your reputation should not influence public morality by being an editor. But obviously, your illiterate speech proves you *aren't* an editor."

Carrie smiled and scanned the pink gown. "Obviously, your immodest dress proves you ain't a preacher's daughter."

The blonde narrowed her eyes. "How dare you say that, you little hussy!"

"I say it because I believe it's true." Carrie glanced at the nervous vigilantes, whose eyes registered shock. "Hold on a minute. I guess all you folks here in Crested Butte ain't had a chance to read the latest Denver papers. They just came in on the train with me today." She pulled a paper from her carpetbag and pointed at the bold headline, which read: "Angel of the Slopes Raises Questions About Minister's Daughter's Morality."

The church ladies gasped.

"It's true," Carrie went on. "Matt Worthington testified before a jury and a packed courthouse that he and Jenny did everythin' that he and I ever did." Jenny's mouth flew open, but Carrie cut her off before she could speak. "And say, how do you reckon she keeps herself dressed in these fancy duds? And how long has it been since your menfolk checked on that church-buildin' fund? Did you know Jenny's been braggin' about how much money she has to spend on diamond rings?"

The women looked at one another questioningly.

"There's somethin' else I've been wonderin' about for a long time," Carrie continued. "Did anyone ever check on the reverend's credentials when he arrived here, or did everybody just accept him at face value?"

"Shut up!" Jenny ordered.

"I'll shut up when I've had my say," Carrie countered. She faced the women. "Have any of you really looked at the reverend? If I were you folks, I'd be mighty suspicious of a Christian who was about as happy as a sick jackass." She eyed Jenny again. "And no real preacher's daughter would spend so much money on fancy clothes. I think *Reverend* Parker is just some down-at-the-heels drummer who passed himself off as a man of God because he thought it would be easy work." She narrowed her eyes. "God never told anyone to be stupid!"

Jenny cried, "You little devil!"

Carrie tossed her shawl onto the platform. "Get out of my way and let me down this ramp, woman," she demanded through clenched teeth.

Instead, Jenny charged her, and the pair rolled down the ramp, skirts flying.

Jack called, "Are you all right, girl?"

Carrie rose shakily. "I'm fine, Jack. This is somethin' I've been needin' to take care of for a long time." She looked at Bandit. "And keep that dog out of it."

Jenny suddenly lunged forward, but she lost her footing when Carrie twisted her arm. Again they fell to the ground and rolled down the crowded street in a cloud of dust.

By this time Botsie was leading a crowd of cheering miners after them. Many gave their mentor encouragement, shouting, "Pin her arms back!" and "Get your knee on the heifer's stomach!" Their eyes bewildered, the ladies' auxiliary trotted behind in high heels. Some started sobbing and dropped their signs.

Still swinging, Carrie and Jenny fought past the Elk Mountain House, and customers ran out with napkins tucked in their belts. At Finnigan's Saloon, Betty B'damn rushed onto the planked sidewalk and hollered, "That's it, honey—keep hangin' onto that stringy blond hair. Sling her down again!"

Carrie paused to get her breath. All the buttons were gone from her bodice, and her shift flashed through the open garment. Tangled hair hung in her sweaty face. Jenny looked worse. A ripped ruffle dangled from her dirty dress. Lank, damp hair stuck to her red face; long scratches streaked her skinny arms. One of her sleeves was missing altogether. With one of her shoe heels gone, she limped forward in an uneven gait. A snarl contorted her face.

With a sudden burst of energy, Carrie knocked her to the ground, then grabbed both of her outspread arms. While the miners shouted, she dragged the blonde to the water trough in front of Jacob Steiner's jewelry store. With a great heave she hoisted Jenny and splashed her into the dirty water. When Jenny tried to climb out of the trough, Carrie grabbed her hair and plunged her under again. "This is for sayin' those mean things about Da," she hollered.

The crowd roared.

The spluttering woman sat up again, water streaming

from her slick hair. Carrie ducked her once more. "And that's for pretendin' to be somethin' you ain't."

His arms moving faster than his thin legs, Jacob Steiner ran toward them. "Young ladies, young ladies! What's all this?"

"Aw, leave 'em alone," shouted a grizzled miner. "Jenny's got it comin'—and this is the best danged fight we've had in months."

Carrie dunked Jenny several more times, then half pulled her from the trough and draped her, arms down, over its side. Jack stepped forward and enfolded Carrie in a great bear hug. Peony ran up with Bandit in her arms. The excited dog yipped and licked his mistress's face.

"I didn't know if I could do it, Jack, but I thought I could," Carrie said between long gasps. "Her kind are usually all gurgle and no guts."

"Look—there's Reverend Parker!" shouted one of the beefy church ladies who had managed to catch up.

His face white, the reverend ran to the trough and knelt by his daughter, whose eyelids fluttered like butterfly wings. While he looked her over, the vigilantes surrounded him.

Their new leader glared at the reverend. "That O'Leary woman has been sayin' some things that are startin' to make real good sense. My Jim will be over this afternoon to get a report on that buildin' fund you're always pushin' so hard."

Carrie looked at Jack and winked. "Well, what do you know? It looks like the reverend may have to give the best sermon of his life—and real soon, too!"

Chapter 22

Peony put her small hand on Carrie's shoulder. "Don't be so sad, Miss. Mr. Matt will come back. I know he will."

"Holy Mother, what makes you think I want him to come back?" Guilt washed over Carrie when she noticed the girl's hurt eyes. "I'm sorry, Peony. I didn't mean to bite your head off. Go on with you, girl. It may be Sunday mornin', but we've still got papers to fold, ain't we? Why don't you get started—I'll be right over."

Carrie picked up her coffee cup and watched Peony walk out of the hotel's dining room. Her dark eyes lowered, the girl slipped her crossed arms into her loose satin sleeves and silently disappeared. Faith, why had she been so sharp with the child? What was wrong with her?

Trying to control her nerves, Carrie drew in a long breath of air, smelling ham and hot biscuits. She wasn't that hungry and she knew why—her emotions were in a turmoil. She needed to get a grip on herself. She hadn't been sleeping well, but that was no excuse. If she could just quit thinking of Matt, everything would be all right. She had asked him not to follow her—and he hadn't! Why was she so upset?

Every morning when she awoke from her warm, erotic dreams to face life's hard realities, she wondered if he would *ever* come back to Crested Butte. From all reports, his hired man was managing his ranch without difficulty. With a sigh, she eyed her simple blue skirt and white

319

blouse, than looked at the poorly dressed people eating breakfast in the Elk Mountain House.

Even in their clean Sunday clothes they looked downtrodden and pitiable. An air of defeat seemed to cling to them. What was there in Crested Butte for Matt, anyway? Nothing but desperate people, a burned-out newspaper office, and a sharp-tongued woman, too stingy to share her printing press.

With a loud bang, a door slammed, calling her attention to the hotel's entrance. His heavy boots scraping the planked floor, Jack wandered in and sat down by her.

She eyed him as he ordered coffee and breakfast. He looked like he had enjoyed a good night's sleep, and seemed to be in a decent mood. Perhaps this was the right time to bring up Peony. "Jack," she began, "did you notice how pretty Peony was when we came back from Denver?"

He plunked down his coffee cup and blushed. "I sure did. When she undoes those tight little pigtails, she looks like a different girl."

Carrie leaned forward slowly and searched his eyes. "Well, do you like her? What do you think about her?"

"I—I like 'er just fine," he stammered. "I got to know 'er pretty good when she was sittin' with Shamus afore 'e died." He toyed nervously with his food. "Are . . . are you tryin' to tell me somethin'?"

Sighing heavily, she widened her eyes. "I sure am, you thickheaded Cornishman. The girl loves you! Blessed Mother, can't you see it?"

He spread his work-hardened hands over his chest. "She . . . she has feelin's for me?"

"Of course she does, but she's so quiet and gentle like a little fawn, you're goin' to have to take the first step."

"Me?"

"Yes, you!"

He stared at her silently and blinked his eyes.

"Look, I'll always be your best friend, and I'll always remember that you offered to marry me. But we ain't got the right feelin's to be married. You and Peony do. Her face was glowin' when she saw you. And I noticed you looked pretty happy to see her, too."

As Jack thoughtfully rubbed his chin, Botsie rushed into the dining room. "They're gone! They're gone!" he yelled.

Carrie stared at his excited face. "Who's gone?"

The old prospector waved his hands in circles. "*Them*— they're gone!"

She pointed at a chair and motioned for him to take it. "Gone? Who the devil are you talkin' about, man?"

"I'm talking about *them*. I know for sure, 'cause I talked to somebody who was there, didn't I?"

"I don't know what you did! You ramble so much, talkin' to you is like tryin' to hem a herd of hogs in a ditch!"

The old man plopped into the chair. "Carrie, do you want to hear this or not?"

She glanced at Jack, then at Jacob Steiner, who sat at the next table reading the *Star*. "I have a feelin' you might want to hear this, too Jacob."

"I'm coming, I'm coming," he said as he moved to her table.

Finally she looked back at Botsie. "All right, you've got everybody's attention now. Go on and tell us what you're ramblin' about."

Botsie cleared his throat, then spoke in an irritated tone. "Well, just like I said, I met Mrs. McFalley comin' back from church this mornin'."

"And what did the good woman say?" Carrie asked.

He threw up his callused hands. "Mrs. McFalley said there just wasn't anyone there."

Jack scratched his ear and screwed up his face. "There weren't any people in church?"

Botsie shook his head and laughed. "No, no, no, there weren't any preacher. Reverent Parker just weren't there— Jenny either."

Jacob tossed the newspaper down and adjusted his sliding spectacles. *"Oy vey . . .* Where were they, then?"

The old man looked pleased with himself. "Nobody knew at first. But after everybody had been sittin' there thirty minutes like chickens in a henhouse, somebody decided they might be sick." He glanced around to see if he still had their attention. "Several of the families went over to the parsonage to see about them."

"And?" prodded Carrie.

"And they was gone! That place was stripped out cleaner than a salt-washed skillet. They'd lit out durin' the night and took everythin' they could carry with them on a wagon."

Carrie threw up her hands. "Mary, Jesus, and Joseph— what about that buildin' fund?"

Botsie tugged at his whiskery ear. "Well, that Deacon Brown done some good thinkin' on that. After your tussle with Jenny, his wife gave him an earful when he came home at noon. You remember, she was the big chunky one?"

Carrie nodded her head.

"The deacon is cosignatory on that fund, so he withdrew the money from the bank Friday afternoon. I guess when the reverend went to take it out hisself, he saw which way the wind was blowin'."

"Stealing from God?" murmured Jacob with a frown. "Smart, they aren't. What a *hoo-ha.* "

Carrie smiled. "Yeah, no tellin' how much Parker skimmed off the fund each week before he put it into the bank. That's the pity of it."

"Oh, those church folk was catchin' on to him, all right," Botsie continued. "Several of the menfolk had a meetin' set up with him this afternoon to go over things."

Carrie cocked her head and looked at the old prospector. "I reckon the reverend just decided to save himself some embarrassment." She glanced into a mirror on the wall and noted the scratches on her arms, then she chuckled. "Well, at least somethin' good came out of that fight."

Botsie laughed and slapped his cracked palm hand on the table. "Yeah, it sure did. We got rid of the reverend and Jenny!"

She thought of the old man's words as he talked to the others. Since Reverend Parker had stolen from the church, she wouldn't have to contend with Jenny's presence anymore—but that solved only part of her problems. She still had to worry about Dovie. With a stab of pain, she caught herself. She was still thinking about Matt as if he were part of her life, and he was hundreds of miles away.

Why couldn't she forget him and go on with her life? She had been worrying about herself too much lately. She needed to look outward, to think about others and their needs.

With a smile, she watched Jacob read the paper. Her disposition brighter, she got up, took a coffeepot from a warming tray, and caught his attention. "Want some coffee?"

He caressed his silky whiskers and sniffed the brew's pungent aroma. "Don't mind if I do. I think we should celebrate."

While she poured the coffee into a cup, he turned another page. His eyes lit up as he stared at a bold headline. "Have you seen this yet, my darling?"

She scowled and glanced at the paper. "Is it another of them stories about Dovie Benningfield? If it is, I ain't interested."

"No, no. Read it."

Carrie's eyes widened as she read. Gradually, a joyous glow spread through her body. She stared at the Cornishman. "Jack, take a look at this. We've got more than one thing to celebrate today. That government mine inspector is goin' to visit the Silver Queen—just two weeks from now!"

Fourteen days later, Jack stood in the entry of the Elk Mountain House and looked up at Carrie with a worried frown. "I just came by to see 'ow you were doin' afore I left. Are you really goin' to try to get into that mine, girl?''

She buttoned her blue shirtwaist's high, starched collar and eyed him sternly from the second-floor landing. "I certainly am."

He glanced up the stairs and shook his head. "Do you think ole Worthington will let you in with those fancy people?''

Marching down the stairs, she threw on a knitted shawl. "He'd better! The paper said two reporters from Denver are invited. As the only workin' editor in Crested Butte, I should be in there, too, don't you think?''

"Aye, I do, but I ain't 'im!" He slapped on a battered bowler and sighed. "Most of the miners are down there now, standin' at the gates. Everybody's waitin' to see what that inspector's goin' to say." Chuckling, he tilted his bowler back. "At least we've 'ad a good 'oliday. First time I can remember that 'ell 'ole 'as been closed for a whole week.''

He picked up a canvas grip and shuffled toward the hotel's front door. "What a day for me to be goin' to Denver. If me brother wasn't comin' in tomorrow, there's no way I'd leave and miss the fun." He looked back at her. "You comin', luv? I'll walk you to the mine afore I get on the train. Peony and Botsie are already standin' at the gates.''

Suddenly she remembered her misplaced notebook and pencil. "No, I've got to find my writin' stuff first. You go on to the train. I'll go to the mine as soon as I find my things.''

His eyes nervous, he paused at the door. "Carrie, I dun't know 'ow to use words like you, but I just wanted to say—you're special. You're really fine, girl.''

She moved to him and touched his muscled arm. "Thank you, Jack. Now you'd better go meet your brother." He ducked his head for a moment, then finally looked up and left. She stood at the window and watched him stride down the empty, puddled street.

Then, biting her lips, she ran up the stairs and found

her notebook and pencil. When Bandit whined to go with her, she said, "Well, come on, then. Maybe you've got some idea what I can say to Worthington if he won't let me in the mine—'cause I sure don't." Quickly straightening her back, she moved down the stairs and left the hotel. His tail wagging, the dog trailed her steps.

Once outside, she glanced up and noticed a tiny patch of blue pop through the clouds. Heavy thunderstorms had moved through the misty mountains the night before and left fresh, crisp air behind them. The snow will be comin' next, she thought, remembering the bitter day she had abducted Matt.

With a tug at her droopy shawl, she marched down the empty street, forcing the painful thought from her mind. As she walked over the sticky earth, she heard a buggy splash through the puddles behind her. Soon, its black canvas top up, the smart rig rolled ahead of her. A hundred feet beyond, it stopped, obviously waiting for her.

"Now, who could that be?" she muttered to Bandit, who trotted by her side. "Everybody but me is already down at the mine." Sunlight broke through the clouds and glinted from the puddles, forcing her to shield her eyes. On the buggy's side, a shiny gold name glistened under the beads of rain.

When she had almost reached the rig, a deep voice boomed out, "You need a ride, lady?"

Her heart lurched. That voice was unmistakable. It was Matt's!

Reins in one hand, there he sat, his Stetson tipped in greeting. A breeze ruffled his glossy hair and his white teeth clenched the familiar cheroot. An expensive suit encased his muscled frame and a fancy brocade vest flashed against his starched dress shirt. His eyes twinkled with good humor just as she remembered. And, damn it, his lips curved in that same mocking smile—just as she remembered.

For an agonizing moment neither of them spoke. At last he extended his warm hand and she grasped it and climbed up beside him. Without hesitation, Bandit bounded to the footrest, then leaped into the buggy and settled at her feet.

With a lopsided grin, Matt slapped on his Stetson and studied her. Her heart thudded like a circus drum. She wanted to say something wonderful, something witty. Instead, she said, "What the hell are *you* doin' here?"

He chuckled and flicked the reins against the team's rumps. "Still the same old Carrie, I see."

"You didn't answer my question. I asked you what you were doin' here."

His eyes amused, he smiled at her while they moved forward. "The same thing you are. I'm reporting the mine inspection."

"For who?"

"Do you mean for *whom* am I reporting the inspection, love?"

She ground her teeth. "Blood and thunder—you know what I mean!"

He maneuvered the team around a pothole and glanced at her again. "For H. H. Hardin. Who else?"

Pulling her shawl about her, she stared straight ahead. "Where the hell have you been?"

"Back east."

"Back east? How did you know about the inspection, then?"

He looked at her with a surprised air. "The telegraph wires are still up, you know. I've been keeping up on things out here."

"What in the world were you doin' in the East, anyway?"

"Signing contracts and finding out how much Hardin likes my writing. Remember that piece I did on your libel trial?"

She rolled her eyes. "*No*, I'd forgotten all about it."

He laughed softly and tugged down his hat. "That piece won me a prize. As you might say, Hardin said I busted new ground for that type of writing."

She squinted at him. "I'm surprised you ain't busted your hat off yet."

He snorted. "Lord, you sure can think of the words—you always could." Interest brightened his face. "How's your walkout going?"

She straightened her shoulders and perked up. "Fine. But I need to write a good long editorial for *The Miner's Press* right after this inspection. They'll need to be nudged a bit just before the walkout. You know how folks are—some of them need a midweek prayer meetin' to keep their religion goin' till the next Sunday."

He nodded, his eyes glinting with amusement. "You got everything else set up?"

"You bet! I've been writin' lots of letters. Union leaders from back east will be comin' right after the walkout. They'll help the miners organize. Who knows what good might come out of this!"

Bandit glared at Matt and growled.

"You know, Carrie, I don't think I've ever seen that dog when he was in a good mood," Matt commented.

"Oh, he's just like everybody else. He's happy when he's got somethin' to be happy about—when he ain't, he ain't." She eyed the dog. "Guess he just doesn't see anythin' to be happy about." She grinned and looked at Matt again as he slowed the team.

At the end of Elk Street, grim-faced miners lined the last graveled stretch of road to the Silver Queen's tall gates. There a noisy, expectant crowd milled about. All eyes focused on John Worthington and the inspector while they strolled to the ornate gates. Wearing press badges, two nattily outfitted reporters dogged their steps.

When Carrie spotted the well-dressed tycoon, she looked at Matt and asked, "Did you and old John ever work things out?"

"Nope. Have *you* talked to him?"

"No. As far as I know, he ain't talked to nobody but Clayright since he came back from Denver. He's been holed up in that mansion of his." She searched the crowd, finally spotting Peony and Botsie. The minute Clayright unlocked the gates, the crowd surged forward and her friends were lost in a sea of derbies.

Matt touched her arm; his face was serious. "I make a two-day stop in Denver before I came into town. I needed to catch up on the news and take care of some business for Hardin."

Her heart thudded. Denver meant Dovie.

"I talked to some friends at the *Star.*"

She clenched the side of the buggy. "I figure you talked to somebody else, too."

"If you're referring to Dovie, you're right. We need to talk about it."

The last pieces of Matt's puzzle clicked into place and Carrie didn't like what she saw. "Wait a minute. Why were you tellin' me all that stuff about how much Hardin likes your writin'?"

He took a long drag on his cheroot and narrowed his eyes. "Hardin wants me to move east permanently—to work for him. He wants me to edit one of his big papers."

Her heart plummeted. As long as he was here, she had a chance. But if he went back east for good, she was lost. Thousands of miners and their dreams tied her to Crested Butte. She raised her chin. "I suppose Dovie is happy the way things turned out?"

A perplexed look flickered through his eyes. "As a matter of fact, she is."

Carrie felt herself flush. Mother Mary, she couldn't believe what she was hearing. He was dusting her off like some light-skirt while she sat on a rig in front of seventeen hundred miners. Hadn't he humiliated her enough? Everything was plain as day without them talking anymore. He was taking the job with Hardin and he and Dovie were moving to New York, where she would be the toast of the city!

Matt eyed her as she stared rigidly ahead. "I *said*, I need to talk to you, Carrie."

Fear that she was too proud to acknowledge chilled her

heart. Without a word, she climbed from the buggy, tugged
her shawl about her, and crunched toward the mine gates.
Her dog followed at her heels.

"Carrie!"

She looked back over her shoulder. "I don't have time
to talk to you, Matt Worthington. Those Denver reporters
are goin' into the mine and I'm goin' with them." She
added, "Besides, we don't have anythin' else left to talk
about!"

An hour later the warmth of the mine prompted Carrie
to remove her shawl and drape it over her arm. She glanced
through the dim light at Matt, who walked the timbered
room with the Denver reporters. Then she turned away,
not wanting to meet his eyes. Wasn't it embarrassing
enough that he had pleaded her cause to the mine inspector
when the others had tried to bar her entrance? Using Hardin's famous name and phrases like "support of the small
press," he had wheedled her into the mine.

And the way he had talked the man into admitting Bandit ranked right up with the major miracles. Oh, the man
had a silvery tongue, all right, she thought bitterly. She
should know; hadn't he deceived her enough with his
smooth lies and half-truths?

She played at adjusting her kerosene lantern while John
Worthington and Clayright joined the reporters, and the
group passed her in silence. Nervous as cats, Worthington
and Clayright flashed lantern light on the dark, craggy
walls and led the way. With some interest, she noticed
how they seemed to be sending each other messages with
their eyes.

Earlier, when everyone had boarded the newly repaired
hoist, Worthington had ignored the inspector and reporters
and snubbed Matt. She shivered at the memory; could
John really be Matt's father, as he had attested? If so,
neither had physically verified the claim. Their eyes had
glittered with unspoken emotion far colder than the bar-
reled ice here at the thousand-foot level. She took out her

notebook and watched Worthington extend his hand and proudly address the gray-haired mine inspector.

"So as you can see, sir, I use only the finest timbers in the Silver Queen."

The conservatively dressed inspector ran his hand over the newly sawed timbers. "Yes, everything seems to be new."

Carrie's stomach knotted in anger. How dare old John try to deceive the man! She approached the quiet, thoughtful inspector and touched his arm. "Sir, you said those timbers were new. If you'll take a second look, you'll see how new they really are. They were put in last week."

Worthington edged away from the group and whispered to Clayright, who was dressed in a new suit. Soon the superintendent walked to the hoist and rang the bell. Now, where's *he* goin'? she wondered as the huge cage creaked upward with him inside. Puzzled, she looked back and watched the inspector stoop and pinch up a dab of sawdust from the rough floor.

His countenance tense, he nodded his head. "I believe you're right, miss."

Quickly, she pointed at the moving hoist. "If you want to see what this mine's really like, let's go to some other levels."

Worthington coughed and rubbed his chin, "Oh, I don't think that's necessary. It all looks the same. We would just be wasting the man's time."

Matt snapped his notebook together and looked at the inspector. "I think you have time, don't you, sir?"

The man stood and cleared his throat. "Yes, yes, absolutely. I didn't come all this way to look at just one level."

Worthington's eyes stormed up. "Very well, then. I'm not trying to hide anything. Let's go down to the two-thousand-foot level.

"Why don't you let us pick the level, John?" Matt shot out.

"Yeah," Carrie chimed in. "You would expect the man

to go to two-thousand feet 'cause it's hottest there. I'll bet you've got a ton of ice there today. Let's go up. Let's go to five-hundred."

"That's right," agreed one of the other reporters. "We could start at five-hundred and go down systematically."

For seconds all was quiet except for the sound of the great hoist engine returning the cage. For a moment Carrie thought she heard a deep groan from the bowels of the earth, but she dismissed her apprehension, and attributed the noise to the engine.

Worthington finally mopped his shiny brow with a silk handkerchief and blurted, "All right, all right, if you insist. We'll go up to the five-hundred-foot level. Clayright has already put some carbide lamps there."

The sound of their quick steps echoed against the walls while the others walked away. Matt hung back to talk to Carrie. "Are you thinking what I'm thinking?"

At that moment she wasn't in the mood to talk to him, but the problem at hand transcended their quarrel. Bitterness chilled her husky voice. "Probably. I'm seein' a patch job. The mine's been closed for a week. I'll bet old John forced Clayright and his crew to repair a few spots for the inspector. Bet he didn't think this inspection would really happen. I know he hasn't had time to overhaul the whole mine—there's a nightmare above and below if we can find it."

"Exactly," Matt agreed as he took her arm and ushered her toward the waiting hoist.

Once they stepped aboard the hoist, a bell rang and the dark shaft shot below them. Seconds later they burst into the light of the five-hundred-foot level. When they exited the noisy hoist, the sixty-foot room swallowed them up. Light from four carbide lamps flared over the expansive room's pitted walls. Carrie held out her lantern and stared at the bluish-gray ore, which shone with a metallic luster. Masses of copper pyrite and nests of clear quartz studded the room's timbered walls. The minerals reflected light from the bright carbide lamps and flashed like crystals.

As they walked farther into the room, she noticed a pack of frenzied rats scurry down some timbers. Squeaking, they hopped to the uneven floor and skittered about crazily. His ears raised, Bandit studied them with interest. With a weary sigh, Carrie looked over at Worthington, who was talking to the inspector across the room. "Now that's a pretty sight if I've ever seen it," she told Matt as he neared her side. "Old John's selling the man a bill of goods, if I know anythin'. He's probably tellin' him he replaces old timbers on a regular basis."

Matt scanned the partially retimbered room. "That's right. We need to keep moving until we find a room with all its old timbers. I think we should go lower again."

Carrie watched him stride to the group and speak with the inspector. From the heart of the mine, a deep rumble caught her attention. Overhead, the timbers creaked and groaned. A fetid, musty smell filled her nostrils. Apprehensively, she peered upward and saw dust sift from the high ceiling. The others gazed upward also while the crazed rats swarmed over the wooden braces.

Seconds later the inspector snapped his notebook together; then he, Worthington, and the reporters ran past her toward the hoist. Stunned, she waited for Matt, who trailed the group. The moment he reached her, he grabbed her hand and snatched up Bandit. "Come on, let's get out of here! I don't like the sound of things."

Almost immediately, two overhead timbers cracked and deep lines shot up the room's walls. Dust and debris gushed from the ceiling and a rumble like heavy thunder split the air. Clutching her lantern, she ran with Matt toward the hoist. Fear squeezed her heart when she heard the hoist bell ring. Not bothering to look back, Worthington slammed the cage door behind him. With a great whoosh, air swept into the room and almost sucked out her lantern. Its bell rang continuously while the hoist roared upward.

Matt jerked her back as she dropped her shawl and

reached for the moving hoist. "No, stop! It's too late!" he shouted, pulling her away from the open shaft.

A second later, raw earth pelted her head. Far above, great timbers split and popped from the ceiling, then crashed to the floor. Dirt and debris covered the jiggling carbide lamps, and one by one they flickered out. A darkness blacker than the devil's heart wrapped around her. Carrie cried out as timbers cracked from the shaft and plunged into the sump.

Then wails and screams split the air as the hoist roared past her and whizzed downward into the blackness. Nausea churned her stomach, and even in the heat her blood ran cold. Holy Mother of God, she thought. Those poor reporters and the inspector. They never had a chance. Another great rumble shook the earth and more timbers fell. Cracking, splintering noises pounded against her ears. Witless with fear, she clung to Matt and sobbed, feeling Bandit's trembling body pressed between them.

Great clods of ore rained down on them: then, with great force, something tore her from Matt's arms and knocked her to the rough floor.

Chapter 23

Bandit sprawled by Carrie's side and nudged her with his damp nose. When she didn't move, he whined and licked her face. At last she moaned and brushed his silky tongue from her cheek. Nightmarish memories shot through her mind while she stared at the inky blackness around her. Gradually, she remembered the sound of cracking wood and the musty, rotten odor of the timbers as they thundered from the high ceiling. She also remembered the sound of the whizzing hoist and the men's screams.

Finally, she thought of Matt's concerned face at the moment the carbide lamps flickered out. Her heart ached at the thought of him. How long had they been separated? Was he even alive now? And how long had they both been trapped in this hot, black hell?

Dazed, she pushed Bandit away and tried to sit up. Her sore body ached like it had been beaten by a legion of Satan's demons. When she propped herself up on one elbow, she noticed a great weight on her legs. Whimpering like a child, she managed to sit up and move her scratched hands downward. Dozens of ore chunks pinned her skirt to the floor. One by one, she tossed away the rough ore and listened to it thud into the blackness.

Water trickled from the room's walls, and moist steamy air closed in around her, making her feel even more trapped. Tears swam in her eyes as she hugged Bandit to her bosom. His warmth and the thump of his small heart gave her some measure of reassurance. "Sweet Mother of God," she whispered to the panting dog. "We're buried alive in this dark hell!" With a stab of loneliness, she realized she would never see another starry night, or smell ripe peaches, or hold a fuzzy baby chick.

Bandit snuggled closer and licked her face. She caressed his furry neck and tried to think. She knew Matt had to be nearby. But where? Her battered arms ached as she stretched her hands outward. After some desperate straining, her fingers touched a warm form in the darkness. Matt! Hope filled her heart while she inched toward him. Bandit whined and crawled along on his belly behind her.

Like a blind person, she ran her shaky hands over Matt's body until she located his torso. She prayed like she had never prayed in her life, then laid her ear to his chest. There she heard a strong, steady heartbeat. She repeated his name and gently shook him. When he didn't move, she realized he was unconscious. Unconscious—but alive. Yes, thank God, he was alive.

For a moment she sat by his side and prayed. Her heart pounded. The thick, almost tangible darkness threatened to suffocate her. To add to her worries, she heard rats chattering nearby. Despite the oppressive heat, a chill ran along her arms at the thought of the rats skittering over her body. Holy Mother, if I only had a light, she thought. If I only had a light.

Like a bright flame of hope, an idea whipped into her mind. Not wasting a second, she searched for the lost kerosene lantern. When her first clumsy efforts failed, she crawled forward a foot at a time and patted about her in half circles. "Stay with him," she yelled back at Bandit. At last her grimy fingers touched something hard and slick. With a whimper of joy, she loosened the lantern from some debris, then, guided by Bandit's whines, returned to the spot where he waited with his charge.

She located Matt's chest and slipped her fingers into his vest pocket. "Faith, this is the first time I've ever been glad he smoked those damn cheroots,'' she said to her dog. After some awkward groping, she found several matches and put them into her skirt pocket. Very carefully, she scraped a match against the side of the lantern. Her heart dipped as it fizzled and went out. When the second match flared into brightness she said a prayer of thanks and lit the lantern.

The small light flickered eerily over the room's walls and illuminated broken timers and piles of debris. The noisy rats chattered and scampered away when the light washed over them. She gasped as she turned her gaze toward Matt. A timber lay near his head. Now she realized why he had been torn from her arms so quickly. She scanned his unmarred face in the weak light, then listened to his steady heartbeat again to reassure herself he was alive. Carefully, she caressed his scalp and discovered a huge lump on the side of his head.

Confusion clouded her mind as she reseated herself. What could she do? A breaking timber had plunged the useless hoist into the sump. Doubtless, the remaining cable had snarled. And who knew what havoc the accident had done to the hoist engine? Foot by foot, she turned the light and saw that no exits existed in the chamber. Depression unfolded deep within her while she watched the rats' eyes glitter in the shadows. Unless the men on top rescued them, this room would become their tomb. She and Matt would die together.

She loosened Matt's tie and trailed her fingers over his hot, sweaty brow. Mother Mary, what she would give to have him safe, safe and out of this hell. Sharp realization stirred her heart, and at that moment she knew she loved him above all things. It didn't amount to a hill of beans that his last name was Worthington anymore. It didn't amount to a hill of beans that he planned to go back east with Dovie and forget she ever existed. Nothing in the world amounted to anything but his safety and well-being.

Sighing, she pulled Bandit's furry head onto her lap. ''Oh, Bandit, I've learned a lot today. More than I've ever known in my life. I found out someone's name don't mean anythin' if you really love them, and what their kin have done to your kin don't mean anythin'. It ain't even important if they love you. All that *is* important is them and their happiness.'' Her throat choked with tears. ''It's just too bad that I learned everythin' too late!'' She slumped against a pile of rubble and touched Matt again. ''At least I can be with him,'' she muttered. ''And at least he's not hurtin'.''

As she leaned against him, she felt his hard pocket watch. With shaky hands, she removed it and popped it open. The time was three o'clock. Two hours had passed since they had entered the mine. Two hours ago she had been healthy and hopeful; now she was buried in a living grave. Her eyelids drooping, she finally dropped the watch into her lap and dozed with one hand on Matt's warm chest. Dark, tumultuous dreams raced through her mind. In her nightmares she relived her fight with Jenny and saw Dovie's lovely, mocking face.

Sometime later, Bandit's barking stirred her awake. Blinking, she glanced at the watch. The hands pointed at four o'clock. Hotter than ever, the thick, moist air closed in and choked her with its fetid smell. Perspiration streamed from her torso and glued the shirtwaist to her skin. A frown tightened her brow as the dog continued barking. Weak and drowsy, she raked back her damp hair and peered through the darkness. She saw Bandit faintly in the murky light. His head cocked, he stood near the hoist shaft and barked crazily. ''Bandit, hush!'' she scolded.

Completely ignoring her, he continued with more urgency. Fear trickled through her insides as she stood and picked up the lantern. With a great effort, she forced her tired legs to walk to the dog. Along the way she heard the bit of fuel that was left slosh in the lamp—the flame had eaten up most of the kerosene. She inwardly cursed her foolishness. Why hadn't she blown out the light before she fell asleep and wasted precious fuel?

Her eyes widened when she neared the dog's side. There in the open shaft a small platform, secured inside a nest of ropes, inched downward. Another coiled rope rested on the contraption's floor. The men on top had used the hour to fashion this makeshift hoist. Thank God they had guessed someone might still be trapped inside. Since the small platform hung from a thin cable, she guessed the hoist engine was gone and weight was of the essence. Operated by muscle power, the device would probably be winched up by a windlass and a team of men.

Her heart soared with joy. Because of the miners' initiative, they would be saved. That is, if she could catch the contraption and get Matt on it. She picked up a long, stout piece of timber and frantically batted at the platform. After several tries she managed to catch it. By this time, slack loosened the cable, but she walked into the room and tugged it with all her might. All at once the cable stopped inching downward. Obviously the men on top realized they had found life.

Her hopes blossoming, she laid the contraption near the hoist shaft, then went back for Matt. She realized she couldn't lift him, so, ever so gently, she dragged his body toward the platform. Sweat streamed down her sides, her back ached, and her head hurt, but she moved ahead, telling herself she was closer to success with each step.

Finally, with great relief, she tugged his body onto the platform and eyed its meager space—there was only room for one person. She couldn't trust tying Matt into a sitting position; it just wasn't safe enough. Since he was unconscious, his long form needed to be strapped to the platform so it wouldn't slip into the steamy sump.

Her father's voice rang inside her head. Don't forget the lads, he had said. The date for the walkout loomed near and the miners needed her alive and well to lead them— but Matt needed her most. What was their fate compared to his safety? Besides, the men could lower the contraption for her next.

Resolved, she loosened the coiled rope that had been

attached to the platform and looped it around Matt until the rope was almost gone. Perspiration beaded her brow and aching hands. She glanced at the tiny light and wondered if it would gutter out before she finished. Her shaky fingers trembled with fatigue by the time she had tied the last knot to secure Matt's body to the narrow platform. Finally the moment of truth was at hand. Could she manage to push the contraption into the hoist shaft? And if she did, would it swing out and slam into the side of the shaft and injure Matt?

She mopped the sweat from her eyes and quietly prayed as she gathered her strength and courage. When she had calculated that the cable slack was correct, she gave the lifeline a great tug. Bit by bit, the cable inched upward and she pushed with all her might, putting her heart and soul into her efforts. At last, aided by the cable's upward pull, the platform scraped over the room's edge and swung into the open shaft. Her heart thudded like a trip-hammer as the platform swung out and missed smashing into the shaft wall by a few inches. Gradually, the swinging movement stopped and the platform eased upward.

Little by little, her heartbeat slowed and her spirits rose. If the men on top kept up this steady movement, the platform would make it. Matt would be saved. While the lantern flame struggled, she stood at the edge of the chamber and watched the device inch upward into the shadows until it disappeared. Now the room grew darker. Relief and loneliness surged through her at the same time. Her legs trembling, she moved back to her spot and sat down again. She popped open Matt's watch and checked the time. Just as she snapped the case closed, the lantern flickered out and left her in blackness. Tears welled in her eyes, but she counted herself lucky. She had been given a chance to save Matt's life.

She clasped his watch, and waited for what seemed like an eternity. Finally she opened the watchcase and struck a match. Almost thirty minutes had gone by. He had to be at the top now. He was safe. Now it would be her turn.

She put her arms around Bandit and listened to the mine rumble and groan. From above, she heard new timbers shoot into the shaft and lodge across it, making it useless. A huge roar bellowed from the shaft, then the earth gave way. Ore poured down on top of her and buried her in the darkness.

Matt lay near the big shaft entrance on the hard wooden floor. His head aching, he opened his bleary eyes and groaned. Their faces concerned, a group of grimy miners clustered about him. As his eyes cleared he peered at the faces of Doc Pritchard and Tim Delaney.

"Here he comes, lads," the stocky Irishman said, studying Matt's face. "Stand back. Give him some air now!" The miners eased back while Dr. Pritchard examined Matt's eyes.

For a moment consciousness brought relief but when Matt remembered the sound of the falling hoist, uneasiness flooded over him. "Where's John?" he muttered in a thick voice.

The bearded doctor clasped his shoulder. "Your uncle is gone, sir. I'm afraid he and the reporters and that inspector were lost. Some falling beams snapped the hoist from the cable." He studied Matt's eyes. "Don't you remember?"

When the doctor's words finally registered, emptiness washed though Matt. True, John had become an enemy, but he was his only link to the past, his family. An instant later, anger pushed the emptiness aside. After all, John had caused the accident with his bungled efforts to deceive everyone.

Doc Pritchard bent over him. "You've been out for a long time. You got quite a whack on the head."

Still groggy, Matt propped himself up on one elbow. "Yeah," he remarked in a raspy voice. "It's a good thing I've got a hard skull."

Delaney laughed and caught his eye. "Aye, you're a lucky man. I've never seen such a shift in the mine. All this rain swelled the ground—it's full of clay, you know. Someone's been monkeyin' with the timbers, too. The mine's as unstable as a Christmas puddin'. The pressure of that swellin' clay just finished things off.''

Matt rubbed his sore head, then stuck out his hand. Haven't I met you before?''

Delaney grinned and pumped his hand. '' 'Deed, you have. I got a real good look at you while you were out. I took you through the Queen several months ago. Remember? You told me you were a greenhorn named Tom Johnson, but I knew you were somethin' special even then.'' His eyes twinkled. ''You asked too many questions.''

Matt smiled and glanced around the crowded room. He noticed Botsie holding Peony in his arms while she cried. Nearby, Father Newly comforted several of the miners and their wives. Suddenly, like a hand of steel, a cold, heavy feeling closed about his heart. ''Where's Carrie?'' he blurted.

Some of the miners cleared their throats, while others backed away. After glancing at the doctor, Delaney put his hand on Matt's shoulder. ''She's still in the mine, mate. She's the one who strapped you to the platform and sent you up.''

Fire flickered through Matt's spirit. ''Still in the mine? God Almighty, why hasn't someone got her out?'' He tried to rise.

''Take it easy. Not so fast,'' the doctor ordered.

Delaney eyed Matt and sighed. ''After she sent you up, the mine shifted again.''

''I don't care if the mine did shift again, we've got to get her out!''

The Irishman clenched his fist. ''Holy Mother, we just can't! Do you think we'd be sittin' here if we could? After the second shift, some timbers popped off the side o' the shaft and lodged across it. The whole thing's blocked. We couldn't get a piece of twine down there without twistin' it up. We'll have to get some kind o' fancy engineer from Denver to figure out how to clear that shaft.''

Matt stood on shaky legs. Horror flashed through his

mind. He knew by the time the man arrived, Carrie would be gone. He had to get her out now! He *had* to talk to her. After all they'd gone through, things couldn't end like this between them.

"Wait a minute," he mumbled, rubbing his temple. "I used to play around here when I was a kid. I think there's an old shaft on the hill that runs parallel to that room. It was one of the first diggings here." He glanced about. "Where's Clayright, anyway? He might know."

"We ain't seen him," Delaney said with a shrug. "Me and some of the lads drug in a windlass and rigged up that contraption we sent down.

Anger shot through Matt again. Because of Clayright's absence, Carrie's rescue would be delayed. He looked at Delaney. "Damn it, man! We've got to get her out. We need to find someone who's worked here from the very start. And we need some old maps and charts. Do you think you can help me?"

The Irishman grinned and winked at him, "You bet, mate. Carrie O'Leary is the best friend the miners ever had." He glanced toward the huge entrance. "The best place to be lookin' for those maps would be the mine office near the gates. I heard Worthington has a passel of old stuff stored there in the safe. I'll talk to the lads and find out who's been here the longest—then I'll meet you at the office directly!"

When Matt arrived at the mine office he squinted in surprise. Light from a green-shaded banker's lamp glowed through the small building's dirty window. Now, who the devil was in that office—and what were they doing? he wondered. Carefully, he eased open the door. The scent of burning paper assaulted his nostrils as he gazed about the room.

Crouched by the open safe, Clayright pawed through a ream of documents. Engrossed in his work, he hastily tossed some aside, unaware of Matt's presence. Nearby, other papers smoldered in a tin wastebasket.

"Find everything you were looking for?" Matt asked.

Clayright started and turned, his eyes brilliant with fear. "Worthington? What . . . what are you doing here?"

Matt clicked the door shut behind him, then sat on the edge of his uncle's desk. "I might ask you the same question."

With a guilty look, Clayright picked up a water pitcher from the desk and doused the small fire. "I was just cleanin' out this safe a little. Just helpin' Mr. Worthington get caught up."

Matt laughed. "During a mine cave-in? As superintendent, you should have been on the site, directing rescue operations."

Clayright glanced nervously at the office clock.

Matt raised his brows and followed the man's lead. Oh, that's right . . . you did leave the party early, didn't you? Don't understand how you could have missed all the excitement, though. A cave-in causes quite a stir, you know."

Clayright stood, clutching some papers. "Cave-in?"

Matt blew out his breath and eyed him again. "Yes, that's what I said. Don't tell me you didn't know?"

Clayright's face paled under his tan.

Matt picked up one of the half-burned documents and scanned it. "Damn, I can see why you wanted to tidy things up a bit. The miners might get upset if they saw this. And that high-minded mine inspector? Well, it just wouldn't do, would it?" He smiled tightly and shook his head. "What amazes me is that you and John didn't take care of these papers last week. You two were so sure you could pull things off, you just didn't bother, did you?"

The burly man's eyes glittered with cold anger. "Now look here, Mr. Worthington, I don't know what you're talkin' about!"

Matt stood and slowly approached him. "Oh, I think you do, Clayright. John sent you up here to get rid of any incriminating evidence when the inspection started to fail. After the cave-in you found out he had been killed, so you decided to search for valuables.'' He tugged a wad of money from the man's hip pocket and pitched it on the desk. "I see you got to the money first. I imagine you thought everyone was so busy you had plenty of time to burn anything that would implicate you before you left Crested Butte.''

His face livid, Clayright threw down the papers and lunged forward. Matt countered his attack and shoved him against the wall. The man's tight shirt ripped open, shooting buttons across the room.

For an instant Matt stood transfixed and stared at a pinkish scar across the man's hairy chest. Then he grabbed the superintendent by the throat and slammed his head against the wall. "I see that we've done this before. We met in a rainy alley this summer while you were on John's business. And earlier, you tampered with Shamus O'Leary's brake lever, didn't you?''

Stony-faced with anger, the big man only glared at him. In response, Matt slammed his head against the wall again and increased the pressure on his throat

"Right . . . right!'' Clayright finally spluttered as his face purpled. "I *had* to. He was spoutin' off too much.''

Matt smashed the man's head against the wall yet again. "And I suppose you also threw that brick through my window and set the fire that burned my office?''

"Mr. Worthington told me to! You and that O'Leary woman were fixin' to publish a lot of stuff about the Queen. He said everyone would think the miners did it if I scratched those words on the press.''

The man's confirmation chilled Matt's blood.

"Mr. Worthington, I . . . I can't breathe!''

Anger ripped through Matt, but he finally dropped his hand and turned away. Then the gold-sealed document the superintendent had tossed down caught his eye. Holding Clayright's arm in an iron grip with one hand, he picked up the yellowed paper with the other. The words "birth certificate" reverberated in his mind. He scanned the document.

With great joy, he found Tom Worthington's signature written in the space designating "Father." John had lied about the birth certificate just as he suspected. It did exist. Worthington had tried to hide it because Tom was his father. All at once, weeks of worry and regret tumbled from his shoulders.

The superintendent moved, forcing Matt to drop the paper and grab his other arm. "It wasn't my fault. Mr. Worthington made me do those things," Clayright pleaded. "He said the law would catch on if we didn't hush things up."

Matt heard Delaney and a gang of excited miners approach the office. "I don't have time to listen to your excuses, Clayright. However, I believe some of the healthy gentlemen who will be bursting into this office at any moment will be keenly interested in anything you have to tell them. In fact, I'm sure they will entertain you until the wee hours—before they turn you over to the law." He threw the superintendent a grin. "Unfortunately, their judgement may be clouded by a certain amount of bitterness. You do understand, don't you?"

Chapter 24

A cool breeze, carrying the scent of crushed grass and wet earth, ruffled Matt's hair. Kneeling on one leg, he anxiously studied an old mine chart spread out on the weedy ground. After the miners had burst into the office and started cross-examining Clayright, Matt and Delaney discovered some yellowed maps and hurried away. Accompanied by another gang of miners, they had paced to a grassy spot not far from the main mine building, whose windows now flashed gold in the sunset.

Matt glanced up from the cracked paper and peered at Delaney, who held a battered shovel. "Are you *sure* this is the shaft?"

Delaney stepped out of the ring of men clustered about the small, grassy knoll. "It has to be, sir. Old Jess worked in these parts before anyone stuck a shovel in the ground. He says the shaft has been sealed up for twenty-five years and the grass has taken over the top." He pointed at a rough spot with his shovel. "But you can bet there's a shaft under that sod—and it runs right by that room."

"How close?"

"Maybe fifty feet." Receiving no response, Delaney rushed on, his Irish brogue thick as a payday stew. "Sir, all we'd have to do is open the shaft, get two men down to the five-hundred-level, and drill straight across."

Ready for work, the grimy miners mumbled their approval and picked up shovels and pickaxes. His mind racing, Matt carefully folded up the old chart, which threatened to fall apart in his hands. He realized that even double-jacking, the best team of drillers in Colorado couldn't break through before Carrie died from starvation or thirst. And who knew how badly she was hurt? But they still had to make an attempt to save her. He couldn't bear to think of what would happen if they failed. With a great sigh, he stared through the dim light at Delaney again. "Isn't there some way we could get to her quicker? She'll be gone by the time we drill through fifty feet of ore."

Delaney blew out his breath and scratched his head. "Well, we could drill three holes into the side o' the shaft and get our dynamite man to set some small charges. Then we could blast part o' the way cross, a bit at a time."

"Sounds dangerous."

"Bejabbers, it would be, sir. But if we blew a hole from the side o' that shaft, 'twould help the drillers."

"Oh?"

"Aye, they'd have a ledge to stand on, instead o' tee-terin' about on that contraption we made to save you." He searched the miners' faces as if he were already se-lecting men. After we'd blasted out enough to hit a soft spot, we could get teams o' double-jackers in there and work around the clock."

Matt's heart held fast to the idea. "How far could we blast in?"

"Maybe halfway, sir. We couldn't risk blowin' right into the room." Delaney shook his head thoughtfully. "Aye, the blastin' 'twould save a heap o' time. We might just reach her that way."

Absently, Matt hurled a rock from the weeds, then stood and stared at the cocky Irishman. "With the mine so un-stable, wouldn't blasting bring everything down?"

"Aye, it might, sir. The timbers in that old shaft have to be as rotten as dirt.It would be a real risk. You goin' to make the decision, sir? Somebody's got to."

Dark thoughts darted through Matt's mind. His better judgment told him any kind of blasting in an old shaft would be foolhardy. But what other chance did they have? Suddenly he remembered Carrie's statement about all of life being an uphill battle and people taking risks. At that point he knew what they should do. Carrie would keep fighting—and they should, too. "Let's get started," he ordered in a firm tone.

Delaney grinned and rubbed his stubbled chin. "It ain't that easy, sir. Somebody's got to set off the rattails on that dynamite." He stabbed his shovel into the moist sod and whistled. "Even with Bickford safety fuses it won't be easy."

Matt's jaw tightened. "Well, go on. Tell me more. How bad can it be?"

"Wicked bad, sir. The man would have to light the fuses, then signal us to winch him up."

"What about the debris?"

Delaney tugged his ear and looked thoughtful. "We could stagger the charges to blow the debris downward into the shaft. I seen it done once."

"I see," Matt muttered, suddenly realizing the debris would kill the man if they blew upward.

"I don't know, though," mumbled Delaney as he scraped a thumbnail across his chin. "Only God knows if we could get the man out before the dynamite blew. The beggar would be danglin' on a string with lit dynamite sparklin' beside him. Besides that, he'd be dependin' on somebody else to yank him straight up before the charge exploded. And he'd have to do it several times." He scanned the solemn miners, then looked back at Matt. "Holy Mother, where are we goin' to get a volunteer for somethin' like that?" Matt stared at him without blinking. The Irishman groaned and shook his head. "Sir, you can't be thinkin' what I think you're thinkin'. You're a haylofter, not a miner."

"I can't believe it would take a lot of skill to touch off those rattails."

"No, it wouldn't. But it would take a lot of nerve—

damn dumb nerve, too. Why, the bloke would have to be near daft to do it. He's be needin' a miraculous medal, that's for sure.''

"Like I said earlier, Delaney, I've got a thick skull. Let's get after it. The sooner we get started, the sooner we'll get Carrie out.''

A slow grin broke over Delaney's face as he stuck out his work-hardened hand. "Right you are, sir, and every man jack o' us will be helpin' you any way we can.''

Twenty minutes later, the men had cracked off the old shaft seal and pulled up a windlass with a wagon and mules. A red sun streaked the western sky and silhouetted the men's forms as they worked. A scant forty minutes later, an expert blaster went down into the shaft with a lamp and drill and set the dynamite charges.

After Matt had situated himself on the platform with a glowing carbide lamp, Delaney looked at him. A twilight chill touched the air. "Remember to give that cable a good yank as soon as you've touched off those rattails, sir. Me and the lads will be watchin' and waitin'.'' Delaney crossed himself, then looked at Matt again. "Well, I guess there ain't much more to be said, is there? You ready, sir?''

Matt studied the Irishman's face through the cool dusk. Behind the miner he saw the twinkling lights of Crested Butte, but in his mind he saw Carrie O'Leary's shimmering green eyes and impish grin. "You bet. There's a hard-headed little mick down there that needs saving.'' Delaney chuckled as he gave the signal, and the platform inched into the shaft. Over the groan of the windlass, Matt heard him shouting directions; but finally, dark silence swallowed up all sounds from above. His heart thudded as the platform slipped lower yet. The heat choked him and plastered his shirt to his back. He brushed away strands of thick cobwebs, which netted the shaft. Dusty, fetid air burned his nostrils and cracked his lips as the platform sank into the blackness. Their eyes shiny in the murky carbide light, sleek rats skittered over the rotten, upward-moving timbers.

A strange relief surged through him while the platform creaked downward. The commitment had been made; it was too late to turn back now. If Carrie was going to die, he was going to die trying to save her. He smiled as he remembered her fiery eyes and sharp words. All the frustration he had ever felt for her melted away like morning fog. He didn't care that she hated his last name; he didn't care that she didn't trust him with Dovie; and he didn't care that she drove him absolutely crazy with her temper. Damn it all. Damn everything to hell. He loved the woman—and that was all he cared about!

He visualized her face and thought of their stormy months together. She had lifted his spirits and touched his heart. More importantly, she had taught him what one dedicated person could accomplish. And she had stirred his sense of justice and made him believe in the strength of the human spirit again. Yes, ornery or not, that infamous O'Leary woman was *his* woman and worth a dozen others.

When the men on top calculated he was at the five-hundred-foot level, they stopped the windlass. The heavy platform supporting Matt jiggled, then bumped against the side of the mine shaft. Matt flashed the light over the shaft wall and finally spotted the three charges spaced in a triangle. Bickford safety fuses dangled from each charge. This was it, he thought. His life and Carrie's life depended on a makeshift windlass, a few matches, and the grace of God. Sweat stinging his eyes, he lit a long match with shaky hands, then touched off the first fuse. It sizzled into life and disappeared as the fire devoured it. When he held the match to the second fuse—it fizzled out.

Sweat sheened his fingers and made them slippery while he fumbled with the matches. His pulse scampering, he scraped another match across the platform, then lit the remaining fuses. At the same time he watched the first fuse streak toward the charge. Finished at last, he gave the taut cable a mighty yank and gazed upward. The fuses crackled by his side, shooting toward the dynamite. "All right, you feisty Irishman, get going!" he mumbled.

Now it was all up to God—and Tim Delaney.

Chapter 25

When she heard a knock at the door, Carrie rolled over on the soft feather bed and groaned. Another visitor, another annoyance. Every inch of her flesh was sore; every bone in her body ached. She looked at her bedroom ceiling and sighed. She wasn't sure if she would ever walk again. If she did, it would probably be as a hunchbacked cripple, she though dramatically. Matt had brought her out of the mine two days ago, and a heavy, tired feeling still surged through her when she tried to sit up. With another groan, she stared at the door. "All right, all right, come on in," she muttered in a dispirited tone.

Clad in her familiar satin pajamas, Peony eased open the door and smiled. She carried a tray of food covered with a starched napkin. Carrie noticed how radiant the slender girl looked. Obviously things were going well with her and Jack.

"You eat now, Missy," Peony ordered in a warm, melodic voice. To back up her command, she whisked the linen napkin from the tray. The wonderful aroma of roast beef permeated the air, but Carrie had no appetite. Then she glanced at her friend's expectant face. How could she refuse?

"Thank you, it looks delicious," she said with a smile. Slowly, she picked at the food, but soon put down her fork.

Irritation marred Peony's smooth countenance. "When

Mr. Matt brought you here, he told me to feed you good. Now you don't eat.''

Carrie pushed the tray away. Matt, Matt, Matt, she thought. When would her visitors stop talking about him? She had heard his name a hundred times the past two days. In her own limited vocabulary, Peony had described in detail how he had lit the fuses that enabled the miners to drill through the ore in record time.

With great effort, Carrie tried to remember the event, but couldn't. She only remembered waking up clean and fresh, thinking she had gone to heaven and sprawled on a soft cloud. Guilt washed over her as she thought about Matt. She should have been happy: his life had been spared, just as she had wanted, and she *was* deeply grateful for that. But she had hoped he might love her—just a little. His absence confirmed her worst fears. Each hour he stayed away, her spirits sank lower. "I keep hearin' about Matt Worthington, but I ain't seen hide nor hair of him," she finally said in a dull tone. "Can you tell me why that should be?"

The slight girl shifted her eyes toward the door. "Mr. Matt is a very busy man, Missy."

Carrie pounded her pillow. "He's busy, all right. He's probably in Denver cavortin' with Dovie Benningfield this very minute."

A blush rode Peony's high cheeks. "I can't tell you where he is . . . he made me promise."

"I'll bet he did. Why, the nerve of the rascal, burdenin' you with such a vow."

Her hands gentle, the girl smoothed back Carrie's loose hair and arranged her moss-green bed jacket. "Now, Missy . . . he *did* rescue you, and bring you here in his own arms."

"Well, I guess even *he's* got enough decency left in him to save a person's life." Frustration roughened her voice. "But I see he's stayin' away so I don't get any wrong ideas about him havin' any feelin's for me." As soon as the words left her lips, she regretted them. During the cave-in Matt's safety was all that mattered; now she selfishly wanted his love, too.

When Peony edged toward the door, she called after her. "How about a newspaper or somethin' to read? It gets kind of borin' just talkin' to Bandit, you know."

Peony opened the door and the dog darted in and curled up on the bedside rug. "Maybe later, Missy," she offered as she closed the door behind her.

Carrie crossed her arms tightly and stared at Bandit. "Now I *know* somethin' is goin' on around here. That girl is actin' real peculiar." She blew at a curl dangling in her eyes. "Why, she won't even give me a newspaper!"

With a long-drawn-out sigh, she piled up her pillows so she could see across the street. She glanced out the window and watched the wind shake the red-leafed trees next to Finnigan's Saloon. Her eyes welled with tears as she thought of her da's words: "Don't let the lads down." She had done that very thing.

The walkout had slipped past while she recovered, and she hadn't been able to write anything for *The Miner's Press.* When she mentioned the topic to Peony, the girl looked nervous and quickly changed the subject. Obviously the walkout had failed and she was trying to keep the news from her, trying to protect her so she would recover faster. Carrie snatched up a handkerchief and blew her nose. Mother Mary, what else would happen to depress her before she left this room?

At last, autumn sunlight teased Carrie's teary gaze down the street. When her eyes locked on a figure walking across the street, she tossed the handkerchief away. Her heart began to beat harder. For there, bigger than the devil himself, Matt Worthington strode confidently toward the hotel with several newspapers under his arm. Supple suede pants outlined his long legs. As he neared the hotel, the sun streamed through the trees and dappled his handsome face and shearling jacket. Memories of his masculine scent and the warmth of his body assailed her.

Holy Mother, he'll be in this room any second now, she

thought frantically. Undoubtedly, he had come to formally tell her good-bye before he left to go back east with Dovie. Her stomach flip-flopped while she arranged her loose hair, pinched her cheeks, and checked her sheer bed jacket. Even if the man had no feelings for her, she couldn't let him see her for the last time looking like some washed-out drab, could she? Thank God she had enough strength to put up a good front.

Just as she settled into the downy pillows, Peony knocked and opened the door. "There's someone here to see you, Missy." she announced with a warm smile.

"Well, show him—I mean show them in," Carrie stammered.

The sound of a familiar stride rang from the hall. Seconds later Matt entered, filling the open door. Still as a huge lump of black coal, Bandit raised his wary eyes and growled. Matt glanced at him and grinned. "I knew I should have left that dog in the Silver Queen. I've regretted the mistake ever since I got softhearted and made it."

Peony laughed nervously at the comment. After her voice faded away, silence frosted the air, but Matt finally tossed his Stetson at a table and stripped off his jacket. "Well, are you all right?" he asked as he studied Carrie. His face was genial and he spoke in a warm easy way.

Peony's eyes twinkled as she closed the door behind her.

Ignoring Bandit, Matt claimed the bedside chair and picked up Carrie's cold hand.

At his touch, a radiant warmth rushed up her arm and turned her bones to honey. All the powerful feelings she had ever felt for him swept over her like a huge wave. She felt hot and tremulous, but she steeled herself and pulled her hand away. No, she decided, she couldn't let him play havoc with her emotions ever again.

He looked at her and smiled warmly, "I thought you'd want to see yesterday's edition of *The Miner's Press.*"

She glanced at him with parted lips. "There was no *Miner's Press* yesterday."

He placed the paper on her lap. "What's this, then?"

She saw the bold headline: "Rally and Walkout!" Tears flooded her eyes. "Who wrote this?" she asked.

"I did," he said, rolling up the sleeves of his blue wool shirt. "I went to work as soon as I left you here. The minute the papers came off the press, Botsie and I put them on the Denver and Rio Grande. Your key men distributed them all over the Western Slope." He winked at her. "I couldn't manage your colorful style, but I got the message across."

"You mean . . ."

A wide grin creased his tanned face. "Yes, indeed. They walked out all over the Slope. Of course, the Queen was closed for repairs, but the miners halted clean-up operations in a unification gesture. And those union leaders you wrote are speaking with the men today." He glanced at the door. "I swore Peony to secrecy about this. I wanted to break the news myself."

Carrie picked up the handkerchief and dabbed at her eyes. "Why did you do it, Matt?"

Surprise sparked in his dark eyes. "Well, I couldn't let everything you worked for go to waste, could I? Besides, I think some of your preaching must have rubbed off on me. You have an irritating way of being right about things, you know. You were right about John—and Clayright, too."

Her heart pounding, she blinked at him. "What are you tryin' to tell me?"

"Clayright damaged Shamus's brake lever," he explained in a gentle voice. "He confessed everything to the local sheriff today." As tears rolled down her face, he caressed her hand and went on softly. "Of course, John was behind the assault in the alley and the fire—all of it. He lied about Maggie, too. The whole story was only a desperate ruse to gain my loyalty at the trail."

"I see." Her brain struggled with the startling revelations. The good news about the walkout filled a hollow spot deep within her. At the same time, the news about the brake lever stirred painful memories. And deep down in her soul, another bruise still ached. "I suppose you'll be seein' Dovie soon."

Matt laughed with gusto. "I really doubt that, love." Then he looked at her seriously. "Before we talk about Dovie, let's talk about Martin Henderson."

She braced herself on one elbow and sat forward. *"Henderson?* Why should we talk about him? He's in Denver, ain't he?"

"Not anymore. After I came back I talked to the editor of the *Star* about carrying more of Hardin's columns."

"And . . . ?"

"In the course of the conversation I found out Henderson skipped the country. It's the talk of Denver. He went to South America."

"What!"

"Seems he *was* involved in those shady financial affairs everyone was gossiping about, and things were starting to catch up with him."

"How does Dovie come into all this?"

He caressed her shoulder and grinned. "This is the good part. When I heard the news I made a special trip to see her."

"Why, for heaven's sake?"

"Henderson was infatuated with her."

She crossed her arms. "You mean the scoundrel was chasin' me and Dovie at the same time?"

"I'm afraid so. I'd hoped to persuade her to join him— but things worked out even better."

"This is gettin' interestin'."

"You bet it is. Henderson had sent her a ticket to South America, but she couldn't make up her mind about joining him. I told her reliable sources were saying he took a ton of money with him."

"Did he? Did the rascal really do it?"

"Hell, I don't know, but it worked!"

She sucked in her breath and blinked at him. "Dovie believed your story? She's on her way to South America?"

A huge smile spread over his lips, then he nodded. "Yes. At first she doubted me—but a chance at that much money was just too tempting for her. She took Percy, too, thank God. Great, isn't it? We get rid of Henderson, Dovie, and Percy in one neat package. I hope they all drive each other crazy."

She chuckled. "Dovie and Henderson together—can you imagine it? Well, I guess that just proves one cockroach always knows another."

He laughed, then, sure and gentle, his warm fingers caressed her shoulder under the bed jacket. "I told you we needed to talk. You never had a thing to worry about. Dovie always thought my right hand was the most interesting part of my anatomy."

"Your right hand?"

"Yeah, the hand that doled out money."

She widened her eyes. "What about the breach-of-promise case?"

"Dovie withdrew it. A reporter friend told me two comedians she fired from her troupe were telling everyone in Denver about her colorful background. She was two months gone before we met in London."

Relief poured over Carrie in great waves—she no longer had to worry about Matt being Percy's father. How could she have let her imagination run wild about the situation? Had her trust been that low? Then her high spirits crashed with a dull thud. Dovie and Percy might be out of the way, but what about that editing job back east? "Are . . . are you goin' to take that job with Hardin?" she blurted out.

"Lord, you *do* have an active imagination." He chuckled and raked a hand through his hair. "I said he had offered me a job back east. I didn't say I was going. I wouldn't trade my little piece of Colorado for the whole eastern seaboard."

"But you said you signed contracts!"

"I did. I'm going to write a series of columns for Hardin about the West. A Westerner's view of the West, so to speak—pieces to let the folks back east know what we're thinking.''

For once she was speechless. Still as a china doll, she stared at him.

He cupped her face in his warm hand. "I'm going to stay right here and challenge John's will. He cut me out, but after Clayright's testimony I think every court in Colorado will be sympathetic to my cause. When I'm the owner of the Silver Queen, I'll make sure it's the safest mine in the state. And I know a feisty little Irishman named Delaney who'll make a great superintendent." Affectionately, he brushed his finger down her cheek. "I also thought we might combine the *Courier* and the *Press*. That is, if you could put up with my stuffy style."

Joy darted through her heart. Were her ears deceiving her? Was she hearing him correctly? Could the man she had loved and battled for nearly a year actually be telling her these things?

He laughed at her expression, then ruffled her hair. "Seems like we've talked about everything but Cousin Jack. How's the lad doing?"

Blinking away tears of happiness, she smiled. "Oh, he's doin' fine. His brother is here now, so he ain't so homesick . . . and best of all, he and Peony have found each other."

Matt's face lit up. "Good. I won't have to challenge him to a duel, then."

She giggled and covered her mouth. *A duel?''*

"Of course. The presence of a leftover suitor could prove a bit embarrassing after a while, you know."

She squeezed his big hand. "I . . . I never thought of him that way." Curiosity softened her voice. "Are . . . are you tryin' to tell me somethin'?''

He opened up the second newspaper and spread it out on her lap. "I certainly am. Read today's issue of the *Courier*. I thought I'd put it in print so I'd have the whole state of Colorado on my side. Judging from the past, I could use the help."

Happiness bubbling inside her, Carrie scanned a front-page "personal." The huge headline read: "Will You Marry Me, Miss O'Leary?" The article pointed out a dozen reasons why she should. "Matt . . . I thought . . ." she whispered as she dabbed at her eyes again.

He took the handkerchief, then lifted her chin and wiped her face. "I know what you thought," he said. "That's why I went back east to let you cool off. As ornery and infuriating as you can be—I found out I can't live without you." Grinning, he tossed the handkerchief aside and took her into his arms. *"Carrie O'Leary* . . . so wide in soul and bold of tongue," he murmured.

When he claimed her mouth, a joyous fire shot through her veins. The kiss seemed to warm her very soul. Her body responded passionately as he explored her mouth, and soon her whole being throbbed with ecstasy. He slipped his warm hand under the bed jacket and caressed her breasts, lingering long and lovingly at each nipple. She eased her mouth away. "Ohh . . . that feels good." She sighed. "And *that* feels even better!"

"Lord, I've waited a long time for this," he breathed.

"I know . . . but you may have to wait a little longer."

He held her against his thudding heart and stroked her hair. "I suppose we shouldn't start a fire we won't be able to put out for a few days." he remarked in a husky tone. "But I want you to know I've reserved a suite at the Windsor for next week, and you'll be damn lucky if you see the light of day while we're there."

"Matt, I'm sorry," she suddenly sobbed. "I didn't mean all those wicked things I said. I was so foolish . . . I didn't know . . . I didn't understand. I . . . ."

He tightened his hands around her arms. "I've said some things I regret, too." Gently, he brushed away her tears with his thumb. "Let everything that ever caused us pain die right now . . . every cross word, every careless act."

She sniffed back her tears and nodded her head.

His eyes warm with happiness, he studied her face.

"Well, what do you say to my proposal, girl! It seems the way is clear to me. John is dead and Clayright will soon be in prison. Dovie and Henderson are basking their hides in South America, and the miners told me you ran the Parkers out of the country like the rabble they were. Even likable Cousin Jack and Peony will soon be setting up housekeeping." He glanced at Bandit, who immediately growled at him. "Of course, that dog still hates me. But I suppose every man needs some type of opposition to keep him in check."

For a moment she stared at the red leaves flying past the bedroom window. Then a curious observation hit her with great force: instead of being on the outside, she was now on the *inside* looking *out*—warm and secure, wrapped in Matt's love, which had always been hers for the taking. She finally had it all. A huge smile tugged her lips upward as she threw him a sidelong glance. Her husky voice blazed with mischief. "Will I marry you? Why, you flamin' fool—you'd have to put a bullet in my heart to stop me!"

Author's Note

Spitfire is pure fiction, but the conditions described in the Silver Queen were based on fact. In the late 1800s, Cornishmen in Central City, Colorado, walked out of a mine when their wages were cut to $2.70 a day. Joined by other "Cousin Jacks," they set out organizing a union. From this small impetus grew the Colorado unionization movement. With tongue in cheek, one newspaper editor dubbed the group the "Cornwall Secession Movement."